SCOUNDRELS AND DREAMERS

DEANNA R. ADAMS

To Rothy

I hope you enjoy Charlee's story!

SOUL MATE PUBLISHING
New York

Thanks for keeping Peace + Love alive! :)

Deanna R Adams

BY DEANNA R. ADAMS

FICTION

Peggy Sue Got Pregnant

NON-FICTION

Rock 'n' Roll and the Cleveland Connection

Confessions of a Not-So-Good Catholic Girl

Cleveland's Rock and Roll Roots

Praise for Deanna R. Adams

Peggy Sue Got Pregnant

Deanna Adams picks us up in a cool yellow Cadillac, transports us to another era and later drops us off at home again with a better understanding of how music can interpret our lives and, if we're lucky, how it unites us and sets us free. This chronicle of the times follows the music, with a lyrical story enriched by the author's encyclopedic knowledge of rock 'n' roll. — ***Gail Ghetia Bellamy,*** author of *Cleveland's Christmas Memories*

Like the early days of rock 'n' roll, *Peggy Sue Got Pregnant* is a story about an innocent time juxtaposed with not-so-innocent actions. This is a novel for anyone who remembers an era of 45-RPM records—and for those who don't, but want to take a trip back in time with Adams, who knows her subject so well. — **Scott Lax**, author of *The Year That Trembled*

Adams' first foray into the world of fiction takes a doe-eyed Peggy Sue from bobby socks and saddle shoes to Bob Dylan and faded Levi's. Along the way, readers of a certain age are treated to details that will make them grin with fond memories. You will not be able to put this book down until the pages run out, because this Peggy Sue is that kind of friend. — **Erin O'Brien**, author of the *Irish Hungarian's Guide to the Domestic Arts*

The music history here is first-rate. Deanna Adams's nonfiction tome, *Rock 'n' Roll and the Cleveland Connection* published by Kent State University Press, was a finalist for an ARSC Award for excellence in research. And while *Peggy Sue Got Pregnant* is a work of fiction, Adams's vast knowledge of the music of this era lends authenticity to this believable and entertaining story. — **Carole Calladine,** author of *Second Story Woman.*

Deanna Adams transports you back to the '50s in vivid detail. You'll ride every twist and turn of Peggy Sue's life; you'll feel you're right there with her. You'll not be able to set this page-turner down, and it will leave you wanting to read more about Peggy Sue. And now we can—with the sequel, ***Scoundrels & Dreamers***—**Trudy Brandenburg**, author of Emma Haines Kayak Mystery Series

Praise for Deanna R. Adams

Scoundrels and Dreamers

Scoundrels & Dreamers is a trip-down memory lane for music loving children of the 1980s. But the music is just a soundtrack to a darker tale about family, children, the power of love and the power of art. Great Read." **Laura DeMarco, *Plain Dealer* Arts & Entertainment Reporter**

A rollicking ride through the early years of MTV and the struggles to balance fame, family, and friendships. A great sequel to ***Peggy Sue Got Pregnant*** and stand-alone novel in its own right. **- Nicole Eva Fraser, novelist**

SCOUNDRELS AND DREAMERS

Copyright©2014

DEANNA R.. ADAMS

Cover Design by Rae Monet, Inc.

Published in the United States of America by
Soul Mate Publishing
P.O. Box 24
Macedon, New York, 14502

ISBN: 978-1-61935-598-9
eBook ISBN: 978-1-61935-590-3

www.SoulMatePublishing.com

As always, to Jeff,

for traveling with me

through this long and winding road.

And to those who have touched my heart

with the music they play.

Acknowledgements

I love writing this part of the book because it gives me a chance to publicly thank those who are true godsends to me as a writer.

First, I thank Debby Gilbert at Soul Mate Publishing, whose keen editing eye always makes my work better, and for being so great to work with. And to Rae Monet for the great cover.

Special thanks to my advanced readers, Laura DeMarco and Nicole Eva Fraser. To Deanna Rowe at Homestead House B & B, in Willoughby, Ohio, and Gina Holk at the Red Maple Inn, in Burton, Ohio, for granting me needed sanctuary to work on this book in peace and beautiful surroundings with no interruptions! To Brian Reeves, for answers to my queries on investigations. And my BFF, Nina M. Cetner, who always makes me laugh.

Then there are those terrific writers I meet with once a month—who tell me when something's good and when something's off. And they are always right. I'm so lucky to have them, not just as writing colleagues, but also cherished friends: Anne Bruner, Geri Bryan, Carole Calladine, Karen Fergus, Aileen Gilmour, Cheryl Laufer, Barbara McDowell, Anne McFarland, Karen Peterson, Nancy Piazza, and Diane Taylor. You all rock!

And, of course, the amazing people who are my family. Everlasting love and gratitude to my husband, Jeff, daughters, Danielle and Tiffany, and our little Zoey, who is her grandmother's brightest star. Thank you for being my foundation in life, and surrounding me with so much love and joy.

Side 1 — Stand By Me

Prologue

Charlee McLean-Campbell awoke that morning knowing her life would never be the same. She was a twenty-three-year-old woman who didn't know the first thing about mothering. She'd never once babysat, or even changed a diaper. All she knew about was being a rock 'n' roll singer, having spent most of her youth writing and recording songs and traveling the world. But after becoming pregnant, she vowed to stay off the road for a couple of years to make a good home for her husband, Dusty, and this child. Holding her newborn son in her arms for the first time, she couldn't wait to get started.

Sandra Jacobs awoke that morning also knowing her life was about to change. She would soon be a mother, too. Without labor pains, without giving birth, without paying a doctor bill. All she had to do was dress in her brand-new nurse's uniform, complete with cap and shoes, sneak into the room where her baby lay, and tell the mother the little one needed his vitals taken. If she got out the entrance door without anyone stopping her, well, then, it was God's will.

Charlee named her baby boy Dylan, after two creative artists, Dylan Thomas and Bob Dylan.

Sandra named her gift from God Benjamin, after learning it meant "son of my right hand." The bonus came when she read in the Book of Genesis that the biblical Benjamin's mother had died during his delivery. Perfect. Yes, it had to be Benjamin.

1. Don't Cry Out Loud: March 1980

The emotional high Charlee had been enjoying the past two days was waning fast. She sat upright against her pillow nursing her baby son thinking how quickly it all had gone, like a movie on fast-forward. Her pains had started at the top of the nightly newscast and by the time the music to the *Tonight Show with Johnny Carson* began, she was in active labor. Like a runaway train, it had built up speed faster than she and her frantic husband could've anticipated, fueling them with adrenalin as they threw things into the car and sped to the hospital. They made it there in record time. Charlee was whisked off to the delivery room while Dusty was forced to stay behind to sign paperwork. Thankfully, he made it back just in time to see little Dylan's head pop out at 3:15 a.m. When Charlee called her mother a few hours later to announce his birth, Peggy Sue laughed.

"Ah, yes, a little night owl, just like his mama," Peggy Sue said, adding that Dylan had a good zodiac sign. "Pisces men are creative, caring, and idealistic." Good traits for a man, she'd told her and promised to be there as soon as morning rush hour would let her.

There were some perks to being a star, Charlee thought. Her private room was large and comfortable and there were no stringent visiting hours, so her family and friends came streaming in all day long sharing the joy. The downside was the baby couldn't be in the room while everyone was there, for sanitary reasons, of course. While the first day had been full of excitement, Charlee's son had spent much of that day confined to the nursery, where Charlee and company gazed at him through the glass debating who he looked like.

During lunch, she'd gotten to cuddle Dylan while a kind LPN helped her get him to nurse and answer her many 'new mom' questions. Then he was whisked back to the nursery. They all came that day: Peggy Sue and her husband, Billy; Uncle Patrick and Aunt Nina; Aunt Libby and Uncle Dave. And her best friend, Ruby, along with select others from their little town of Sherman Falls . . .

Both Charlee and Dusty were disappointed his family couldn't be there. His dad and younger sister, Diana, were the only ones left now, and they lived in Anaheim, California. And who wanted to fly into Cleveland in the dead of March? Though they hoped to make the trip come summer. In the five years she and Dusty had been together, Charlee had only met them once, in L.A., during her final Echo & the MissFits tour, before she went solo.

She also wished a few others were here as well, but they were a lot farther away. The couple who'd raised her, Ray and Jo McLean, had been dead now over eleven years, and her grandmother, Peggy Sue and Patrick's mom, had died just the month before. How she wished her son could know them. But she and Dusty had not voiced those thoughts out loud. They were too happy to dwell on things they couldn't control. All that mattered was this special time in their lives. A time they knew they'd always remember. Ignoring the cot the hospital aides set up for him, Dusty had crawled into her bed and they'd spent hours recounting every moment leading up to their new status as parents. Today had been much the same as the first day. More friends had stopped by, and though fun, the near constant revolving of visitors had taken its toll.

"Why don't you go home and get some real sleep?" Charlee said, referring to the short round of winks they'd gotten since Dylan's birth the night before. "You kind of look like a homeless person," she added with a grin.

Dusty still wore the Aerosmith T-shirt he'd arrived in, his blue jeans wrinkled from not bothering to take them off the night before, and his shoulder-length chestnut curls were tangled and, well, a bit on the greasy side.

He didn't argue. "I think you're right," he said, as if glad she'd brought it up first. He leaned over and gave her a lingering kiss on her lips, then grabbed her hands and kissed each one, a wonderful habit of his. "I'll see you first thing tomorrow, Sunshine."

Charlee grinned, feeling the familiar thrill she always got when he called her that. The John Denver song "Sunshine on My Shoulders" had come out soon after she'd met him in 1973, and he had taken to singing it to her. A lot. Sunshine became his name for her.

"I love you," she called out as he disappeared behind the door.

She immediately rang for the nurse. She had to admit she'd been longing for this moment. Finally she'd have Dylan all to herself.

Now he lay in her arms fast asleep and for the first time, she thought about how she would raise him. She wanted him to have a normal life, despite his parents being in the music business. She hoped they could keep him out of the limelight enough that he could enjoy just being a kid. She wanted him to grow up happy. And to be kind. A good person. Patting down the defiant black strand sticking up like Alfalfa from the Little Rascals, Charlee began singing softly to her son.

Dylan's eyes opened just then and she swore he smiled at her, even though everyone had been telling her that babies don't smile until they're at least a few months old. But of course he recognized this song. She'd been singing Lynyrd Skynyrd's "Simple Man" to him for months in utero—even though she hadn't been sure he was a *he* yet. If the baby was a girl, the song's message still held true. Follow your heart. Be something you love and understand. And, don't forget that there is someone up above.

Charlee wanted to be sure her child knew all of this from the get-go. She'd grown up with those values, and the traits had come in handy at fifteen—when she learned her "parents" were actually her birth mother's aunt and uncle. And that her real father was none other than Frankie London, the beloved rock 'n' roll hero who had died in a plane crash. The shock of that news had sent her into an emotional tailspin. Everything she'd known about her life had been a lie—or at least that's how she thought at the time. She later came to understand that it wasn't her biological mother's fault. Peggy Sue had been forced to give up her baby because back in 1957, society dictated that a pregnant seventeen-year-old was no better than a whore. And because of that, Peggy Sue had to relinquish her God-given role and hand her baby over to Ray and Joann McLean. But Charlee had been lucky. They had given her everything a little girl could want or need, including a good home and tons of love. And despite the deception that had surrounded her early years, love was a constant in her life.

Thank God that was all in the past now. And while Charlee wished with all her heart that Jo and Ray could be here today, she knew that, despite their sudden deaths in 1968, they were here, in a sense. They would always be a part of her.

"You, my little Dylan, will always be surrounded with love," she promised him, nearly nodding off as she spoke. It was only eight o'clock, but she was so exhausted she feared he might slip out of her arms, so she kissed his forehead and holding tight to her bundle she rose out of bed and placed him gently in the safety of his bassinet. She was asleep as soon as her head hit the pillow.

Sometime in the night, she opened her heavy eyes to see a blurred image of a nurse holding Dylan in her arms. Startled, she jumped.

"Oh, sorry, I didn't mean to disturb you," the blond nurse whispered, lightly touching Charlee's hand. "I'm just here to take the little one to check his vitals. You go back to sleep now. I'll be right back."

In her daze, Charlee wondered why they had to do that in the middle of the night, but fell back asleep before giving it any more thought.

When she woke again, a middle-aged, dark-haired nurse entered her room. "Why good morning, Mrs. Campbell, sleep well?"

Charlee smiled. Rarely was she addressed by her married name. She was still Charlee McLean to her family and friends. To her fans, she was known by one name, "Echo." She liked "Mrs. Campbell." It made her feel all grown up. And now as a mom, she certainly was that.

"Would you like me to get you some breakfast before I leave my shift?"

Charlee glanced up at the wall clock. 6:25 a.m. "Your shift? Wow, that's some service I get. Two night nurses when all I did was sleep."

The woman looked confused. "Excuse me?"

"You know, the other one, who came in last night."

The woman shook her head. "You must be mistaken. I'm the only night nurse assigned to you, though I had no time to check in on you last night. It was a madhouse around here. We had *three* laboring women come in almost at the same time. You're just lucky you're down at the end of this hall or you wouldn't have gotten a wink of sleep." She leaned over and whispered, "Two of them women were real screamers, let me tell you. Yelling and swearing like banshees." She picked up the pitcher beside Charlee's bed and poured water into the plastic cup. "We're still waiting on baby number three to make his way out, but I'll be in my own bed by then. So, you hungry?"

Charlee rubbed her eyes. Wow, she must have dreamt that. "Not yet, but I'll take a good strong cup of coffee." She got up and walked to the bassinet. "Hey, where's my baby?"

Charlee frowned. Maybe she hadn't dreamt it after all. "There *was* a nurse in here last night and she said she was taking him to get his vitals checked. *And* she said she'd bring him right back."

The woman leaned into the crib as if to be sure Charlee wasn't seeing things. She shook her head. "Maybe they called in another nurse 'cause we were so busy. He must still be in the nursery."

"But his bassinet's *here*."

"I'll go check what's going on," the nurse said, trying to sound calm, but failing.

Charlee grabbed her robe at the foot of the bed and slid into the paper slippers. "I'm going with you." She glared at the woman as if daring her to argue.

Charlee ignored the pain of her stitches as she rushed to keep up with the nurse's brisk pace. When she threw open the glass nursery doors, Charlee was right behind her and headed straight to the woman rocking one of the babies. She wasn't the nurse Charlee remembered from last night and one quick glance at the tow-headed infant told her this wasn't little Dylan.

"Where's my baby?" Her question startled everyone, including the other babies who started wailing.

"You're not supposed to be here," the nurse said gently.

The expression on the woman's face caused an icy rush of fear to shoot up Charlee's spine.

"Where is my baby?" Charlee demanded.

Without another word, they both ran to the nurses' station. While the staff searched every room, the head nurse ordered a shutdown of the floor and allowed Charlee to call her husband. She could hardly believe the words coming out of her mouth.

"Dylan's missing. I don't know! Someone was in my room last night. She was in a nurse's uniform but no one knows who she was!" She could hear someone calling the police on the other phone. "Oh God, Dust, get here soon as you can. Dylan's got to be here!" Even as she said the words, she knew they weren't true. She'd only been a mother for a few days, but her instincts were as sharp as one who'd spent a lifetime mothering.

Those instincts told her with certainty that her baby was gone.

Sandra Jacobs stood staring out the window at the people outside her fifth floor room at the Holiday Inn, conveniently located across from Holy Cross Hospital. Everyone down there seemed to have somewhere to be, and she'd been itching to join them. To get on with her new life. Every morning for the past week, she'd scanned the baby announcements in the Cleveland newspapers searching for the right one. She had always wanted a boy. Boys loved their mamas. And she would be the best mama ever.

Finally on Wednesday, she read that there were two boys born at Holy Cross. One to a couple from the east side of Cleveland. No. She didn't want a city boy. The other to a "Dustin and Char Campbell of Sherman Falls." Bingo! You had to have money to live in that ever-so-quainty town, and she wanted a boy from high-class parents with good genes. Yes! Her baby was finally here.

Sandra couldn't wait to get him, but she knew she should wait a day or two so he'd be all checked out first. She sure wasn't going to go through all this and have a sickly kid on her hands, or worse, have him die on her. So she forced herself to be patient and concentrated on the magical time when she'd bring him home, where he belonged. She had his baby room all made up in the Zanesburg, P.A., apartment she'd rented that winter. Everything new and blue. A comfy crib with sky-blue bedding, where he'd dream his little dreams. She'd even made matching curtains with the fluffy lambs by hand. After all, she had nothing but time. She particularly liked the wallpaper she'd picked out, with all the cute baby animals. She couldn't wait till her little Benjamin spotted the baby mobile with the jungle creatures all hovering above him!

Lucky for her, Nicky, the college boy next door, had been home the day before she'd left for Cleveland. Frustrated by her useless attempts at putting the damn toy together, she'd thrown on her maternity clothes—complete with stuffing— and knocked on his door to ask for help. She'd given him a few beers for his trouble.

Now it was time to get her new baby. She dressed in her crisp white uniform and headed out the door.

She waited in the parking lot a full fifteen minutes until she summoned up her nerve. Adrenalin pumping, she grabbed her Ralph Lauren Polo bag and walked briskly through the automatic doors. As she passed the reception area, she flashed a guilty frown to the old lady at the desk, as if she was a nurse running late to work. Stepping out of the elevator on the third floor, she saw the empty hall and could hear activity in several of the rooms. Perfect. She snuck into the storage room, dropped her bag on the floor, and walked out leaving the sack behind. Casually, she slipped into the restroom to bide her time.

She could hear a woman's agonizing shrieks and told herself that, despite her heartache over the miscarriages, God had been kind to her, saving her from such horrific pain. The sound of nurses zipping in and out of rooms trying to keep order in the midst of chaos, gave Sandra the go-ahead. She made her way down the hall.

Sandra knew where he was. She had called the front desk that morning. "Hello? I'm an old friend of Char Campbell on the maternity floor? I'd like to surprise her and need to know what room she's in."

"I'm sorry, ma'am, we cannot give out that information. Do you want me to ring her room?"

"But that'll ruin my surprise."

"I'm sorry, but that's our policy for those who aren't family."

Damn, she should've thought of that. Having had a mother who once worked at a hospital, Sandra knew this well-to-do couple must have a private room.

"Okay, fine, please ring her."

When the mother answered, Sandra took a wild guess, hoping the woman would correct her. "Yes, is this Room 310?"

"No, sorry, you have to the wrong room."

"But my sister's in a private room. Isn't that 310?"

The mother didn't have to answer, but once again, God was on her side. "No, this is 320. The front desk must've made a mistake. I'm not sure what the other room numbers are. Try them again."

"Okay. Thanks." And she hung up.

So there it was. Room 320.

Leaving the hospital had been just as easy. After getting Benjamin in her arms—and what a close call when the mother woke up for a second—she rushed into the storage room directly across the hall and gently placed her baby into the leather bag. At three in the morning there was no one in the elevator and the lady at the reception desk had her head down, either playing solitaire or perhaps nodding off. Sandra managed to walk right out of there. No problem.

She casually got into her car and drove off, back to Zanesburg. She had pulled it off! It had been easier than she imagined. With all that commotion going on from those laboring women, the hospital had unknowingly served as her accomplice. Sandra giggled to herself as she hit the freeway.

That night, she enjoyed a celebratory Budweiser as she rocked the fussy baby in her living room and watched *The Love Boat* and *Fantasy Island.* Benjamin had just fallen asleep when it was time for what she'd been waiting for all night. She was bound to make the eleven o'clock news! She got a little thrill when she heard the broadcaster begin with the "breaking news" about a woman who, dressed as a nurse, had snatched a baby from Cleveland's Holy Cross Hospital.

But not just any baby.

"The child is the infant son of rock star, Echo, the former singer of the all-girl rock band, Echo & the MissFits. This is her first child. If anyone has any information, please call the Cleveland police immediately."

Sandra shot out of the chair so suddenly the infant damn near spilled out of her arms, and the brisk movement shook him awake. She ignored his cries. And the knocked-over bottle of beer.

"Ah shit! Oh my God!" she shouted at the TV.

Sandra hadn't recognized Echo at all when she was in that room. The lighting had been dim and the rock star obviously had no makeup on.

"I'll be a son-of-a-bitch!" She laid the screaming infant on the couch. "Now what'll I do?" She started pacing the floor, her hands covering her lips. "Shit, Shit, SHIT!"

This wasn't at all what she expected. Not in her wildest dreams. Sandra had always been a big fan of Echo & the MissFits. Even after the band's breakup, she'd purchased all of Echo's solo records. Sandra's skin prickled and her mind raced with shock at whose kid she had stolen. *Damn.* Leave it to her to fuck up this bad. And this was bad. It meant the media and cops would be all over this until they found her. And *him.*

The baby's howling forced her to pick him back up. She bounced her new son up and down as she paced the room.

"It's okay, it's okay." She petted his soft head. "There, there, little Benji. Don't you worry. We'll be just fine. I won't let them take you away."

Part of her was horrified that she had nabbed Echo's first-born kid. But there wasn't a damn thing she could do about it now. She was stuck.

Sandra pursed her lips, fighting off pangs of guilt. She willed herself to concentrate on the positive side of things. She finally had her baby. And discovering who he was only made him that much more special.

"Yes, darlin', we're gonna be just fine, my little sweetheart." She kissed his forehead and headed to the kitchen. Balancing the baby in one arm, she opened the fridge and pulled out two bottles. One for him. And one for her. She stuck his in warm water to get the chill off, while taking a big swig of her cold Bud. She smiled down at her bundle of mixed emotions. "You, my lil' boy, are an exceptional child, did you know that?"

And now this exceptional, famous, child was all hers.

2. Bad Moon Rising

1 day earlier

Peggy Sue snuggled up to Billy in the car on the way home from the hospital, glad his new Buick Riviera still had bench seats, unlike many of the cars today. She always liked sitting close to him where she could smell his Old Spice, feel his leg against hers. After sixteen years together—excluding their two breakups that neither of them thought about anymore— she was still smitten with Billy Dalton. He was no longer the '60s deejay known as Rockin' Billy Mercury. Now he was a highly respected owner of two Cleveland radio stations, spending much of his time looking for young, hip deejays, like he once was, to keep listeners dialed in.

She placed her hand on his leg, and to her delight, he grabbed it and squeezed. Now in their forties, they were responsible, law-abiding citizens so he usually kept both hands on the wheel. But this glorious night brought back that old, wonderful, habit.

This was only her second day of being a grandmother and Peggy Sue couldn't get over how exciting and thrilling it all was. Like falling in love. A feeling she knew well. She'd been lucky to have been in love, deeply, twice in her life. First, with her new grandson's grandfather, Frankie London. Then with the man next to her, whose body warmth was as comforting to her as a home fire in winter. Both men had changed her life in immeasurable ways.

And now another man had entered her life, and he, too,

would surely bring her the same enchanting happiness. In fact, he already had.

"Oh, Billy, isn't baby Dylan just the cutest newborn you've ever seen?"

"How could he not be with the genes that little guy's inherited?" Billy grinned at her at the stoplight. "Betcha top dollar that kid'll be a rock star someday, too. Like his mama and grandpa." Billy's eyes reverted back to the road, but kept the smile on his face.

Peggy nodded. "I wouldn't doubt that. He's already a rock star, considering all the people who came by just to get a peek at him." Her excited tone turned to a sigh. "I know they're all dear friends, but I wish they'd given poor Charlee and Dusty a space break. They both looked exhausted."

"And that's just the beginning." Billy squeezed her hand again, and threw her a wink. "I'm actually looking forward to when we get to babysit. But not till he's a little bigger than a peanut."

"Yeah, I couldn't believe how nervous I was holding him. He's just so *tiny.*" Her mind flashed back to when she'd given birth to Charlee. She didn't recall her daughter being so small and fragile, but then Peggy Sue hadn't gotten to hold her much in the hospital. And she'd had a lot on her mind back then. Like how she'd have to hand over her baby to her aunt and uncle—and vow to forever deny that she was the girl's real mother. It had all turned out for the best, she supposed. Yet, more than two decades later, Peggy Sue could still recall that ache in her heart whenever she recalled that sad, painful time. So she rarely let her mind go there. And she wouldn't now, either.

"Mario's is always so crowded on Friday night," she said, feeling guilty they were running late, having had a hard time breaking away from that baby boy. "I hope Al and Angela will get there in time to save us a table."

"Oh, most likely." Billy glanced at his watch. "Al said they were leaving by four this afternoon and you know how he drives. Three hours turns into, like, two and a half. Especially when he knows a dinner at Mario's Steakhouse is waiting for him."

Peggy Sue laughed. "True, true . . . I sure hope Ange gets a good crowd at her book signing tomorrow. She said she'll stop at the hospital first, though. Wait till she sees little Dylan, she'll go nuts!" She dug in her purse for some lipstick. "Oh, did I tell you she's coming with me Sunday to help Charlee get settled after she's released?"

Billy turned into the parking lot. "No, but that's okay. Maybe I'll round up Al and some of the guys to watch the Cavs game at the house."

"Oh look, they're here." Peggy Sue pointed to the black couple walking toward the restaurant's front door. She recognized Al's big frame and Angela's signature Afro, which was now several inches shorter than she wore it in the '70s.

After excited hugs and hellos, they were, thankfully, seated right away and immediately ordered a bottle of champagne. Time to celebrate. Not only for the Dalton's new status as grandparents, but also for the success of Angela's book, *Tracks of My Tears*. The memoir had been well received from the start. It opened with Angela's early years as a child growing up in Tulsa, Oklahoma, then of her years working at Hitsville U.S.A.—the original home of Motown Records. The most poignant section, however, was when she wrote about finding the son she'd been forced to give up at sixteen, only to lose him again, permanently, when CJ died of a drug overdose in 1974.

The book climbed to the *New York Times* bestseller list and six months after its release, Angela Johnson was still in demand for signings and personal appearances. Peggy Sue was thrilled that her longtime Detroit friend could finally schedule a signing in Peggy Sue's hometown.

When the Johnson's came to Cleveland, they always met at Mario's. Owner Mario Cirino was another longtime friend. Now their son, Mario Jr., an aspiring singer/guitarist, had just been signed to Peggy Sue Records after she'd heard him play at The Sahara, a popular local club. Peggy's mission in starting the record label was to protect musicians from getting ripped off. She didn't want young, talented hopefuls being taken advantage of, like what had happened to Charlee and her band, Echo & the MissFits. A devious record exec had taken undeserved songwriting credit, as well as skimmed money from their accounts.

Al had been the girls' manager at the time and he'd been blindsided, too, by the scoundrel. Peggy would never forget how devastated Al was. He'd been overworked and didn't catch the sly maneuverings. He felt responsible and assumed all the blame. That's when he convinced Peggy to take over the MissFit's career and start her own company. Now she had all the clients she could handle. But there was always room for more. Like Mario, Jr.

Dining on Mario's famous steaks, the foursome chatted about the good fortune they were all enjoying now. Peggy was especially thrilled about her dear friend's success.

"I always knew you'd be a famous writer," Peggy Sue said, clicking Angela's glass in a toast. "I'm so proud of you! Do you know I still have all those wonderful letters you wrote me back in the day?"

Angela let out one of her signature cackles. "Girl, I've no doubt. You save everything."

Yes, she did. In fact, Peggy Sue still had that pink diary, and the photograph of her with Frankie, the father of her "illegitimate" child—items that had once been the source of much trouble. Funny how she hardly thought of Jimmy Tanner anymore, or the years of misery he'd caused her. Such a blessing that good times, like these, can throw shade on the bad.

Billy piped in. "You should see the boxes *and boxes*, of magazines, books and records dating back to the '50s. Peggy's gonna need to open up a museum soon."

"Hey, that's not a bad thing," Peggy said, giving her husband a playful slap on the arm. "Mark my words, those items will be worth something someday, and I'll be having the last laugh."

"You tell him, Peg." Angela nodded and smiled. "I, for one, believe you're right. I always get people at my book signings telling me nostalgic tales of their youth. Talkin' like it was all so idyllic." She rolled her big brown eyes. "Yeah, sure. How soon they forget all the bull we had to go through."

Peggy knew exactly what Angela meant. Not that long ago, "colored" people had to sit in the back of buses, use bathrooms separate from whites, and couldn't drink from the same public water fountain. And the discrimination didn't end there. Women as a whole were considered second-class citizens. And Lord help a young girl who got pregnant outside marriage, as Peggy had in 1957.

How is it that people reflect on the past with rose-colored glasses? Peggy Sue wondered. But then, it was probably a good thing, to reflect only on sweet memories, while appreciating today's modern changes. Things had indeed improved for both blacks and women. Who would have thought in the 1960s that a forty-year-old woman could own and operate her own record label? Or that a black woman from the gritty city of Detroit could be universally accepted as an intelligent woman of words—a successful published author.

After Billy insisted on paying the bill, they walked out together, with plans on meeting again at Billy and Peggy's Sherman Falls home, where their friends would stay the weekend.

As snow began to fall outside the window, they all relaxed over cocktails in front of the fireplace in the den. The men stood leaning against the mantel while Peggy and Angela shared the leather settee. Still reeling from the joy of her first grandchild, Peggy felt a profound sense of gratitude as she basked in the warmth of hearth and home amid those she loved.

Angela held a special place in Peggy's heart, ever since meeting her on that miserable bus ride from Texas to Ohio a lifetime ago. Her parents had plopped her on that Greyhound, bound for Cleveland, so that her growing "condition" wouldn't embarrass the family. As they traveled through the Midwest, Peggy had learned of the older girl's own unwed mother story, which prompted a bond between them that had lasted to this day.

Could that possibly have been twenty-three years ago? Peggy wondered. They had certainly shared a lot through the years.

"You ever hear from the Hitsville gang anymore?" Peggy asked as Al and Billy talked sports. They'd all been so busy in their lives, it was a perfect night for catching up.

"No, not really. Not since the big change," Angela said, referring to Motown's 1972 move to Los Angeles.

"I just thought you might after the book came out." Peggy tucked her legs up beside her.

Angela grabbed her pack of cigarettes from the suitcase-sized bag she called a purse. "Oh, I did get a congratulatory call from Berry. I was so relieved about that. Wasn't sure how he'd take my lettin' a few wild cats out of the bag."

Peggy nodded. "Well, I think you were very respectful, didn't tell all you know."

"Oooh, you kiddin'? I knew better than that!" Angela laughed. "Besides, I didn't want to be a gossip monger. I wanted it to be *my* personal story, not theirs."

"And it's wonderful. It really is."

"Thanks, Peg, that means a lot. I really enjoyed writing it. Even the tough parts were kind of therapeutic. Say, how's Libby and Dave doin'? That little Jack must be getting big."

"That's for sure. He started first grade last fall."

"Really? Wow, that's such a milestone. Libby, and now Charlee, have so many of those to enjoy . . ." Her voice drifted off.

Peggy noticed Angela's eyes lower, her smile fade. The pain of losing her son, CJ, would never leave, Peggy knew. No amount of time can erase that kind of heartbreak.

"In fact," Peggy added quickly, "Libby was supposed to call tonight. She and Dave can't make it to the signing 'cause Ian Hunter will be at the record shop promoting his new album." She glanced at the wall clock. "They're probably still there getting ready for it. But tomorrow night, we'll all meet up at Ruby's Place. That's her new bar & grille restaurant."

"Oh good! I'm glad she found another path." They both recalled Ruby's failed solo career after the MissFit's breakup.

"And it's a great place. She has local musicians and bands come in several nights a week, so it's great exposure for them. Of course, rock 'n' roll's the theme. The walls are filled with posters and old records, and the party room honors Echo & The MissFits' career. Billy and I went with Charlee and Dusty to the grand opening in December. Ruby and Charlee are still the best of friends." Peggy sat up a bit to fight her growing fatigue. It had been a long day.

Angela nodded, taking her cigarette and tapping it on the coffee table before lighting up. Peggy could never figure how her friend could smoke those non-filter Chesterfields. "I'm glad there's no bitterness between them."

"Yeah, me, too. It was hard at first, with Charlee's last album doing so well and Ruby's never really taking off. I know Ruby's a great R&B singer and bass player, but going solo is tough. I heard her label didn't have a clue how to market black artists."

Angela nodded. "Yeah, why'd she go with that other label anyway 'stead of yours?"

Peggy gazed at the fire. "I don't think she wanted to compete with Charlee. But in the end, it didn't matter. She seems really happy now."

"Is she married yet?"

"No, but she's living with Rob, her business partner. Nice guy. And white," Peggy said with a grin.

Angela let out a hoot. "Well, good for her! Sure a different world now, ain't it? People—most, anyways—don't make a deal out of the interracial thing anymore, thank God. Now if Reagan doesn't become president, I think I'm gonna like the '80s."

They both laughed. Angela and Al were staunch Democrats.

It was past midnight when they finished their nightcaps and turned in for the evening.

The ringing of the phone startled Peggy as she rolled over in bed and glanced at the clock radio on the nightstand. Six-forty? "Who's calling now, on a Saturday morning, for heaven sakes?" she asked aloud, though she noticed the phone hadn't rattled Billy.

"Hello?" she said a little irritably. She was hoping to be able to sleep in at least until eight.

"Mom! Mom! Someone took Dylan! A woman came in my room last night and just took him. He's gone, Mom. *Someone stole my baby*!"

"Wait, slow down, honey, there must be some mistake. No one could get away with that." Peggy's brain couldn't process what she was hearing.

"*She* did! Last night this woman dressed like a nurse took him from my room, and no one knows who she *was*. The hospital doesn't have a fuckin' clue!"

"How can that be? Is Dusty with you?

"He's on his way, and I don't know what to do." Charlee's sobs made it hard to understand her.

"We'll be right there."

Billy was fully awake now. Setting the receiver back in its cradle, Peggy started shaking. She spoke in gasps, trying to explain to her husband that their precious grandchild had been kidnapped.

She threw on some clothes, then ran down the hall to wake her guests. Amid jumbled conversations, the four ran downstairs. Questions as to how and why and who mixed with the rush of fear pumping through their veins. Billy was first out the door as Peggy grabbed her coat, telling the Johnsons she'd call them later, and joined him in the car.

Throughout the hectic flurry, Peggy felt detached, like she was suspended above, watching their actions play out like a movie. Surely, she must be dreaming. It was all too terrifying to be true.

But something in her brain registered it as real as she sat next to Billy in the car, just like she'd done yesterday. Overnight, their world had spun them into a dark, evil galaxy. "Oh, can't you go any faster?"

Billy tapped her leg. "I'm already going past the speed limit," he said softly. "We're almost there."

"It has to be for ransom," Peggy reasoned out loud. Her daughter was famous now. It had to be blackmail.

"We'll do whatever it takes," Billy said, bringing her hand to his lips.

"Oh, Billy, how could someone do this? And a woman? How could any woman steal someone else's baby?"

Peggy couldn't fathom such a thing as she struggled with the questions filling her head. How could anyone get away with stealing a baby? In a hospital of all places? Where was her little grandson, and what kind of monster had him?

"My God, how could this *happen*?" she asked aloud to the universe.

By the time they pulled into the parking lot, Peggy's

head and heart were throbbing. She remembered a woman in the news not long ago who talked about her child who had been missing for years. She recalled the mother saying that the not-knowing was the worst.

Now Peggy Sue could fully understand the truth of that statement.

3. We've Got Tonight

Charlee didn't wait for the hospital to release her. As soon as the police did their interviews with her and the staff—and assured her they would do all they could—she tossed her things into her suitcase and told Dusty to get her the hell out of there. She knew he and her mother wished she'd stay one more day as the doctor ordered, but both knew better than to argue the point.

Charlee needed to be home when the kidnapper called with the demand that she was so sure would come. But the wait turned endless. Day after day, she and Dusty waited for the call that never came. Day after day, she phoned the detective in charge and asked for updates. On day six, the man had told her in a curt tone that he'd be sure to call her as soon as they had any "information of note."

That appeasement did nothing to ease the paralyzing fear drumming through her insides. "Those son of a bitches. They aren't doing a damn thing to find him!" she screamed at Dusty. They were sitting in the living room with *Saturday Night Live* blaring through the television that neither was watching.

Her husband's face showed his frustration through tight lips, saying nothing. Charlee knew his annoyance wasn't all due to the police's lack of progress in finding their son. She owned up to the fact that she'd been unbearable the past few weeks. But wasn't she justified? After giving birth, her homecoming resulted in her walking through the door of a barren room, empty-handed. She'd stood in the foyer gazing at all her expensive furnishings, the gilded-framed paintings on the wall, the taffeta floor-length drapes, the cathedral ceiling boasting skylights . . . and suddenly these beautiful things she'd worked so hard for, been so proud of acquiring, meant zilch. She couldn't help think that if she wasn't a celebrity this nightmare would never have happened.

That first week Dusty had taken care of everything. She knew she should've at least acknowledged her husband's efforts. Before she came home, he had locked up the baby's room so Charlee wouldn't be tempted to go in. No sense injecting poison into the wound. He also went out and shopped for all her personal needs—even those items most men would cringe at, such as sanitary napkins and hemorrhoid cream. He reminded her to take her Sitz baths, and he even blended her daily milkshakes (she had no appetite, but she always loved a good banana shake), and held her tight as she cried through the night.

Somewhere in her psyche she knew she should comfort him. After all, he, too, had been stripped of parenthood. He, too, was in pain. She recalled how excited he'd been at the prospect of being a father, and that proud look on his face when the doctor pronounced it a boy!

In their seven years together, she had seen his sensitive side emerge through that tough-guy image many times, but she had never seen Dustin Campbell cry. Until their son was born. Seeing his son for the first time, Dusty had let the tears run, unashamed.

Charlee had never loved him more than she had that day.

She knew he needed her now, as much as she did him. But she simply couldn't muster the energy to give him anything but another request. "Honey, will you get me another blanket?" "Can you make me some more tea?" "Hold me tighter, please . . ."

At least she did say "please" and "honey" a lot.

She couldn't help herself. Sure, her stitches still hurt and her breasts still lactated, yet her physical ailments were not what kept her up nights or held her captive through the day.

It was the images. A strange woman holding her baby. *Using* her baby, for whatever fanatical reason. God knows where they were, or if her little boy was being properly cared for. Or at all. That last thought was the one she fought constantly to push out of her mind.

Yes, it had to be because she was well known in the music business. There'd be no other reason. Her damn face was always being plastered in music magazines; *Creem, Melody Maker, American Rocker,* even *Rolling Stone.* Charlee hated herself for not being more aware of the risks of being famous. There were always people who wanted something from her. An autograph. A photo, a hug . . . *her baby.*

How could she have let that woman just take him like that? She'd tried telling herself a million times that since the thief wore a nurse's uniform, it was a natural assumption, but where was that motherly instinct she was supposed to have? Misguided as she'd been, she had allowed it to happen, trusted a total stranger. She should've known to be more wary, because of who she was. But, no. She just went right back to sleep, like the naïve little ass that she was.

Dusty's snoring interrupted her self-rant, and she rose to turned off the set. Then she fell back on the opposite couch, curled up into a fetal position, wishing she was dead.

The tabloids, of course, had a field day through the next few months. But it was through those steams of stories that Charlee found a trace of comfort. Thousands of letters in huge sacks began arriving at Peggy Sue Records. Some were simple letters of condolences, filled with love and compassion, while others gave suggestions as to how to handle such devastation. Charlee became pen-pals with the mothers who had also lost a child through various means. Between the FBI "Tipline" and Billy's radio station setting up a special line for the general public to call with leads, she and Dusty felt a minute sense of hope. Yet, even with all that support, Charlee couldn't squelch the deep despair in her heart.

One afternoon that summer, her mother came over with yet another attempt to boost her. "I have a surprise for you," she said, pulling her up off the couch, where she could be found most days. "Come on, honey," she urged, noticing her daughter's mussed hair. Charlee didn't have to tell her she hadn't showered in two days.

"But before we go, let's give you a little makeover," Peggy said with a wide smile, trying to avoid any chance for offense.

Charlee knew everyone was careful around her these days.

Especially Dusty, who began finding all kinds of excuses not to be home. Peggy, who called Charlee every day, had long stopped asking if Dusty was there.

When they entered Ruby's Place, Charlee looked halfway decent with clean hair, a new pantsuit Peggy had bought for her, and a strained smile. Ruby greeted them at the entrance. She still looked like the fifteen-year-old in Charlee's eighth-grade class. Short stature, skinny, shoulder-length black hair, ironed straight. Only difference now was her bangs, and her happy smile. Charlee's best friend hadn't known much happiness in her life, not even when their band's single hit *Billboard* charts.

"Hey! My two favorite people in all the world," Ruby yelled, causing heads at the bar to turn. She hugged Peggy first, then Charlee, holding her much longer. "I've missed you," she whispered in her ear. When she pulled away, she kept Charlee's hand in hers. "Come on, I got us a table in the corner."

The trio began with idle chitchat as the waitress brought over Ruby's famous Chick 'n Spice pizza, before telling Charlee why they were all there.

"Honey, I think you need to get back to your music," Peggy began. "I know it's hard. It's been hard on all of us. But the best thing you can do right now is work, keep your mind busy."

"And keep the faith, girl," Ruby interjected. "We're praying every day, I hope you know that. But in the meantime, you gotta do your thing."

Charlee slouched on the chair across from them, her eyes tearing up. "That's just it, I don't think I can. I have no energy, no creativity, I have nothing left."

Peggy leaned forward. "Now that's where you're wrong, Charlee. You have family and friends and all those great fans who are supporting you, love you," she said, grabbing her hands across the table. "*And* you also you have a husband who loves you very much, and I know you love him." She stopped for a moment as if questioning whether she should say any more. "And you're pushing him away."

The words hung in the air, before she added, "Maybe you can take all those emotions you're feeling right now and put them into song. You know, pain often brings out the best writing, and creating lyrics might help you through this dark time. This, this sitting around isn't doing anyone, least of all you, any good. You can't just opt out of life like this because if . . . *when* . . . they find Dylan, he's going to need his momma to be whole. You have to prepare yourself to be ready for when they find him, when we get him back."

"But the bastards aren't doing anything, Mother. It's like that crazy bitch stole my baby and everyone's just accepting it."

Peggy sighed. "Well, *we're* not going to accept it." She leaned further in, still gripping her daughter's hands. "As of today, we're going to take matters into our own hands. See, someone at 'MMS told Billy he knows a private detective who's got an amazing track record. That's my surprise. We hired him."

Charlee sat up, releasing her mother's hands. "Really?" She welcomed the renewed sense of hope. "Ya know, I just mentioned to Dust the other day that maybe we should hire a

PI, but he said we should let the police do their job," she said with a scowl. "Apparently he has more faith in them than I do. But hey, you and Billy shouldn't have to pay for him."

"We want to, honey," Peggy said. "But we do want something in return. I need you to get writing again. We'll get you back in the studio to make a new album, then organize a big '81 promotional tour."

Peggy threw a hopeful look toward Ruby, who had been munching on the pizza, politely listening. "I was telling Ruby the timing should be perfect. There's something big coming up, a whole new concept in music promotion. Billy can explain it to you better, but it has to do with a new TV channel that's supposed to launch next year. Something about showing short music clips to pump up new records. We can get in at the inception. This can be a great new outlet for your music and career."

Charlee managed a smile, wanting to cooperate. She rose from her seat and gave her mother a hug. The idea sounded fascinating and her career needed to be on board with anything that was new in the industry. She was scared at the thought of trying to produce music again, yet couldn't stifle a refreshed craving to get productive again. And though she had her doubts that she could come up with anything worthwhile, she was willing to try. Best of all, the thought of having a professional investigator work on Dylan's case gave her an added shot of adrenalin.

By the time her mother dropped her off at her house that night, Charlee felt revived. She now had something to look forward to. Especially when she saw Dusty's car in the drive. She vowed to show him how much she appreciated him, loved him. If she could put her trust in someone who found missing persons for a living, it could lighten her anxiety, allowing herself to concentrate on other matters. Like her music, her husband. She couldn't go on existing like she had been. Living every moment with crushing fear of what might be happening to her baby. The constant wondering where he was. The self-hatred, the helplessness she felt over it all. It was making her crazy. She realized she had to get a grip or her entire life would fall apart. She'd already seen what it was doing to her marriage, and she couldn't let that happen. She loved Dusty with all her being. She could not risk losing him.

She walked inside and found Dusty in the kitchen. He was standing over the counter flipping through the mail in his stocking feet. She always loved the sight of him. She loved how he was just tall enough that she had to raise up on her tiptoes to kiss him. And how his tight blue jeans outlined those long legs that often wrapped around her when they'd lie together on the couch watching television. Or used to. She loved that his sandy-colored hair had gotten longer, with loose curls that seemed to dance on his shoulders when he played his guitar. She often teased him that he could be a *Playgirl* model, and it was true. He was a beautiful man. She snickered whenever she recalled how mesmerized she'd gotten when she first met him—when his country band opened for the MissFits at the Agora. How proud she always was when they'd walk into a room together, her arm folded into his, at the many functions they attended.

How she missed that.

Her mother was right. She'd been ignoring him for far too long.

She walked straight into the kitchen, took his hands, and placed them on her breasts. "Let's go to bed," she said, mincing no words.

He looked surprised. "But it's not even seven o'clock." Then he grinned.

She kicked off her Prism heels and pulled him by his belt buckle toward the stairway.

As they undressed each other, she reacquainted herself with the man who had been her first love. Her true love. She marveled at how he could always make her weak with just one stroke of his hand, one bad-boy look in his eyes. And how he'd draw her toward him, press her against his body, envelope her. Make the world disappear.

How could she have forgotten all that?

But tonight she remembered.

Tonight, she'd be his wife again.

"Welcome back, Sunshine," Dusty whispered in her ear as he gently laid her on their bed.

"I've missed you, Cowboy." How long had it been that she'd called him her favorite nickname?

Too long, of course. Everything good between them had been missing too long.

Especially their baby. No. *No.* She would not let his tiny face enter her mind tonight. She ached for a reprieve from all thought. And her handsome guy was there in her arms, loving her again. For the next few hours, that had to be enough.

4. Don't Look Back

Sandra never imagined it would be so hard. Day after day, it was the same routine. The abrupt waking each morning by insistent cries. The feedings, the diaper changes, the rocking, the lack of sleep when Benji would scream, for no apparent reason, in the middle of the night. The kid was awfully demanding for being so little, looking so innocent and helpless. It was as if he was determined to make her life miserable. Punish her for what she'd done.

Still, the little guy *was* the prettiest baby she'd ever seen, even for a boy. She'd gotten lucky, that was for damn sure, having had to choose a kid sight unseen and have him look like this. She loved all the attention they got when she ventured out with him to the grocery store. Strangers came up to coo him, comment on his perfect little face, his dark curly cues on his head. She basked in taking all the credit. Funny, after a while, she started believing she'd actually given birth to him herself. She'd even concocted an elaborate story about her labor to another mother in the baby section of Giant Tiger's department store.

Those were her favorite times. Going to that store. How surprising that a little hick place like that would have so many nice baby things. At first she missed the bigger, better stores at the mall in her former city of Cleveland Heights. But after a while, she found herself getting comfortable. Of course, it helped that her daddy had left her enough money to be comfortable pretty much anywhere.

She began enjoying living in this rural area, far from anyone she knew. Here, she'd developed a whole new persona. Back in Cleveland, she'd been the plain-looking, chubby girl everyone ignored. Nothing about her stood out there. In Zanesburg, being somewhat different, awkward, dull as dirt, were perfect traits to blend in here, like shades of gray in plaid. No one knew anything about her, nor much cared. Here, she was not Sandy Jameson, but Sandra Jacobs. Here, she was not the girl no one had asked to the prom— let alone take to bed—but a woman whose poor husband died soon after she'd become pregnant, victim of a terrible construction accident. She'd gotten that idea out of a book she'd read. She had really wanted her fantasy husband to have died serving his country, but wasn't it just her luck, the Vietnam War was long over by now.

In this quaint little town just outside Erie, Sandra could walk around in a homemade pregnancy suit and tell those she made small talk with at the stores and library, that she was due "soon," never giving an exact date, of course. Now with baby in tow, she could show off her newborn miracle and be a mom like everyone else.

Only problem was, she couldn't quite get the knack of motherhood. And why would she? She'd had no role model when it came to that particular trait. Her own slut of a mother skipped town with the surgeon next door when Sandra was three. Didn't even stick around to give her a little brother or sister. Her whole life, it had been just her and Daddy. Which was fine with both of them.

But now he was dead. Two years now. Sure, he'd left her with all that money stuffed in his mattress, but he also left her totally alone in that old house she'd grown up in. At thirty years old, she'd never been on her own. Never needed to. She liked staying put and taking care of her papa, who she knew was getting old. Still, the heart attack came out of nowhere. And so had her loneliness. That was when she'd decided to start a whole new life. Having money now, she quit her job at Amy Joy's Donuts—though she did miss those

Eclairs—and moved to a downtown loft, where she'd get all gussied-up on Saturday nights with her new glittery clothes and head to the Nite Moves disco, Cleveland's answer to Studio 54. My, did she have fun there. Dancing, snortin' coke, and one time, she even had sex with the hot bartender after hours on the leather couch in the back room.

Yes, she'd had her share of one-night stands. So once she made the decision, it took no time at all getting knocked up. That part was easy. But then she began bleeding two months later and that was that. It happened again a year later, same time the disco closed in late '79. So nothing was happening around there anymore. She sold the old house, cheap, and skipped out of town, just like her mama had done. Escapism could be good for the soul, she reasoned. She picked Zanesburg out of a gas station map, and rented the nicest apartment she could find. Renting allowed her to up and move anytime she might need to.

And, boy, did she ever want to move now. Away from this screaming baby.

"Damn it, kid, what the hell do ya *waaant*?" She was standing in front of the TV rocking him back and forth, back and forth, but all he did was scream.

So she screamed back. She knew she shouldn't, but she couldn't help herself. That shrill noise was driving her up a frickin' wall. It was two in the morning and she'd never been so exhausted in her life. And rightly pissed. This wasn't working. But now she was stuck. Or was she? By four a.m. she was envisioning wrapping him up and leaving him on someone's door step. She would even be kind enough to leave a note, explain who this child was. The kidnapped son of that rock star, Echo.

But then what? She'd be all alone, again. And she surely couldn't pull off something like this twice. She'd read all about how they were going to make stricter rules in hospitals "to prevent any chance of something happening like what had occurred at Cleveland's Holy Cross Hospital."

By dawn, he'd finally fallen asleep. She laid him in his crib, sank into her own bed, and they both slept until noon. After giving him his bottle, he burped loud and strong, then gave her the biggest smile, along with an even bigger pile in his diaper.

There, that's all it was! Okay, maybe she'd give him more juice instead of formula. And feed him more. He was almost five months now, and the books all said he could be introduced to cereals and such by six. Well he must be ready now. Ahead of his time. Of course. He was the product of two smart, musically talented people. She had to remember he wasn't like most kids. This boy had pedigree.

And she had hope. Maybe she *was* getting the hang of it. Maybe they'd get through this phase together and she could for once enjoy this motherhood thing. Despite nights like the last one, she'd taken a real liking to this little boy. She really didn't want to abandon him. She knew what that was like, and it sucked. "Don't worry, lil' Benji, I won't do that to you. I promise. No, I *wooon't*," she said, snuggling him up to her face, then laid him on the carpet with his blankey so she could go wipe the sweat off her forehead.

If it only wasn't so damn hot! That was part of why they were both cranky. Early August was already breaking records for sweltering heat, and her apartment had just one window air-conditioner in the living room, which threw out cool, never cold, air. But because "it works" the landlord wouldn't fix, or god forbid, replace it. All summer long, she'd lived in her shorts and halter-tops; Ben, in nothing but diapers. All those cute outfits she'd bought him in the spring now sat in a drawer, some still with tags. That was another disappointment. She'd bought all those fancy little boy clothes so when she took him for walks in the stroller or to the store, people would stop and say things like, "Oh, what a cute baby, and that outfit's just adorable!"

But no, they spent most of the time cooped up in this apartment. Even when she ventured out to the corner grocery store, she'd just throw one of his little T-shirts on because it was so dang hot, the humidity smacked you right in the face the minute you walked out the door. She hadn't even seen that nice neighbor boy, Nicky, for two months.

Which gave her an idea. Maybe she should go over there and ask him, *beg*, him to do her a favor and watch Benji for a bit sometime. Give her a break a night or two a week. She could afford to make it worth his while.

That was what she needed. A babysitter. Or, better yet, a husband. And she sure wasn't going to find him stuck in this shit hole.

She was tired of being hot. Tired of being tired. She had to get out. Have some fun. "Get it while you can," as Janis Joplin would say. Sandra knew she wasn't getting any younger, that was for sure. She needed to get it together, set things in motion for her future. No way could she raise this kid by herself.

5. Mind Games

Through that summer of 1980, Charlee had kept her promise to her mother and made it her mission to stay glued inside her home studio writing songs. The first one she wrote came to her easier than she'd expected. One day she heard a MissFits record on the radio and got all nostalgic, pining for her younger days. She almost started crying remembering when the group first formed and all the good press they'd gotten as an all-girl rock band whose members played their own instruments, a unique status back in 1973. That led her to think about their first hit record, their European tour, and how, during that same time, she'd fallen crazy in love with Dusty Campbell.

It was as if she was reliving those moments through her pen, giving her a glorious break from her present reality. When she completed "Waxing Nostalgic," both Dusty and Peggy Sue agreed it should be her first released single off her new album.

She'd also needed some songs that were more pop, fun to listen to, with a danceable beat. Disco was dying out—thank God—but people still liked to dance, and they always appreciated good, relevant lyrics. So the album, completed in late-September, boasted a good mix of songs. Some about life's tortures, some touting life's joys. Moments everyone could relate to. In that sense, *Echo* had delivered.

Now if only Charlee could be so complete. Her mother had suggested they title the album, *Up From the Ashes,* because titles often convey an album's theme, and Peggy felt that premise might help Charlee believe it. But she wasn't there yet, and talked her mother/producer to settle on *Genie for Sale*, the title of the last song on the LP. "Now that's a relatable topic," Charlee had said. "Who doesn't wish they had their own genie—a magical entity that could make all their dreams come true?"

Charlee sure did. Since that horrible day in March, she prayed for some such spirit to make two, *just two*, of her most fervent dreams become reality.

One dream, of course, was getting her son back. The other was getting her marriage back. Her music career was important, too. But nothing meant more to her than Dylan and Dusty. Her family. An errant ball of yarn that was unraveling more each day.

Tom Reeves, the private investigator her mother had hired, kept telling her to be patient, that he was following every lead. But it was December now, and her baby was still missing. And Dusty seemed more distant than ever.

Funny, with all her money and success, she couldn't buy the two things she wanted most in the world.

She was, however, getting satisfaction in the music department, she reminded herself as the song came on her car stereo. She cranked up the dial and belted out the tune. She didn't turn her head to see if anyone was looking, or maybe recognize her. She didn't care. This was her second single from the new album to play on the radio. "Stripped Away" was getting heavy rotation, even more than "Waxing Nostalgic." It felt good to be relevant again.

Just a few years ago, she'd been part of the first female rock band to make it big. Then, as a solo singer, she'd remained one platform above Cher and Linda Ronstadt. They were more pop than rock, and Echo had been the Rock Princess of the '70s. How things had changed. There were a slew of women dominating the charts in this new decade. Charlee was particularly concerned about rising artists, Blondie, and the Pretenders' singer, Chrissie

Hynde. And that new chick, Pat Benatar, had suddenly become rock's new darling. To Charlee's dismay, all three had surpassed her in overall record sales. That alone gave her the motivation she'd needed to get back in the studio and produce new material.

She flicked on the windshield wipers, hoping this first sprinkle of snow wouldn't amount to anything. She gunned the gas pedal heading up the freeway ramp, hitting the high notes of the song's chorus. Hearing your own song on the radio never got old. And this one, especially, meant a lot to her. Although she did have mixed feelings about it. The lyrics to "Stripped Away" made her feel as naked as the title suggested. Now everyone would know her innermost thoughts and feelings. And yet, isn't that what good songs did? Besides, what else could she possibly write about these days? Surely not about teenage angst, like her MissFits songs. Since the kidnapping, she was practically expected to write about it.

So for the sake of art, Charlee relived the horrific event, jotting down all the words that described her shock, fear, heartbreak, and anxiety she lived with every day. And as a result, "Stripped Away" debuted on *Billboard* charts at Number 18, and was sure to go higher with the airplay it was getting. Charlee had to be pleased about that. It had been nearly three years since she'd had a hit, and that was a long time in the music business. People may love you when you have a hit record, but there was always someone new to take your place on the charts, your place in fans' fickle hearts. That was a legitimate concern. So yes, a song "with a bullet" was good indeed.

Yet Charlee couldn't help wonder if people would listen solely out of curiosity, rather than pure enjoyment. A way to pry into Echo's head, invade her shattered soul. But then, good songwriting demanded invasions of the soul. Tormented stories of love and loss are what people want to hear, to feel. Charlee reminded herself it had to be done if she were to reclaim her status as America's rock princess—a tag one journalist had given her when the media found out she was the daughter of rock king Frankie London.

Still, deep inside her core, it felt sacrilegious. To use her devastating pain to sell a record. Yet that was the bottom line in this industry. Whatever it took to get that gold, or better yet, platinum, record.

Her heart quickened as she pulled next to the curb at the airport lot under the 'Arrivals' sign. She was glad that Dusty had gone to Nashville to audition for that band. She knew he'd missed being a part of a group. After six years of playing backup for her and working as her mother's A&R man at Peggy Sue Records, he yearned for that kind of close-knit camaraderie among male musicians.

And while that meant a change for both of them, Charlee wanted her husband to be happy. No telling how long it would take *her* to feel happiness again, but if Dusty got there first, she was sure it would help her, if only by proxy.

She hadn't waited long when she saw him emerge through the sliding doors. Oh how she'd missed that strut! And that lean, chiseled physique, apparent even with his buckskin jacket on. The past nine months he'd been working out more than ever, had even become a member of a health club. A way to cope, she supposed. And the result was right there in front of her. She'd always admired, appreciated, his handsomeness, but when was the last time she'd told him that?

He spotted her cherry-red Ferrari, shifted his duffle bag, and walked in brisk strides toward her.

"Hey," he said, opening the car door and throwing the bag in the back. As soon as he plopped down in the passenger seat, she leaned over, anxious to kiss him. His lips were cool from the brisk wind, but their familiar suppleness warmed her like a welcoming blanket. He pulled away all too soon.

She spoke quickly to fight the threat of silence. "I got a surprise for you. I booked us the Presidential Suite tonight. At the Ritz-Carlton."

Pulling out of airport traffic, she couldn't see his reaction, but hoped it was good. She merged onto the freeway.

"Wow, you didn't have to do that. I mean, what's the occasion?"

"The occasion, baby, is you've been gone for over two damn weeks." She threw him a sly grin. "And I'm horny as hell." She laughed at her own bawdiness, hoping to get a snicker out of him. It had been a long time since they'd laughed together, or been anywhere special together, just the two of them. Not even last month for their second anniversary. They'd gone out to dinner with her mom and Billy, drank too much, made requisite love, and the next day, gone back to doing their separate things. She wanted to act like the young people they really were. Even if they both felt old.

No snicker.

"Besides," she went on, "I can't believe we've never been there, the best hotel in our own hometown. Ruby's even stayed there once. So I called up and got lucky. A Saturday night, and it was available!"

"Wow, cool. I could use a little luxury after that flight. Bumpy all the way."

"Oh really? Well, glad you're here, safe and sound." She smiled and turned up the radio to elevate the mood. But WMMS was playing a Blondie record, *again*, so Charlee pushed another button. Billy Joel. Better.

They listened to half of it before she finally had to ask. She turned the knob back down. "Well, so, how'd it go?"

"Good, but I can tell you about it later." Dusty took her right hand off the steering wheel and placed it in his lap. Oh thank God. He'd missed her, too.

At a stoplight, he said, "Like your skirt."

Her smile traveled all the way to her heart. "Glad to hear it." She was also glad she'd left her coat in the back so he could appreciate the effort. And with the outside temp at 32 degrees, she was doubly glad that her car had a good heater.

She'd bought the little skirt for this very reaction. Her husband was a leg man, and luckily she'd been blessed with kickass legs. (According to Dusty.) The miniskirt was black leather, tight, and short. When sitting, it crept up to the top of her thighs. She'd matched it with black high-heeled leather boots, and a white stretchy polyester top over her new Fredrick's-of-Hollywood bra that made her barely B breasts look two sizes larger. That part was for her. She'd always wanted ample breasts.

Dusty squeezed her hand, then pulled it higher on his lap to prove the skirt was working.

Her insides tingled. His mood was shifting nicely.

"Like your hat." She winked at him, not daring to move her hand away.

"Oh, yeah. I got it at this store on Music Row." He let her go, sat forward, and took off the posh sandy-colored hat that matched the shade of his hair. Running his fingers across the inside band, he added, "It's a Stetson."

She laughed. "No doubt."

"Got you something, too."

There it was, the can't-resist-me grin. She almost ran the car off the road.

Since the day she'd set eyes on him, that grin had always made her weak. A Clark Gable kind of smirk known to veer many a good woman astray. Charlee felt a surge of something akin to joy. And hope. Maybe being apart for a time had been the answer all along.

To her delight, their room did not disappoint. Expansive living area, kitchen with refrigerator, Jacuzzi. Lured by the big picture window, Charlee walked toward it. The panoramic view of downtown included glimpses of the Cuyahoga River as well as Lake Erie. With the scatter of snow glistening down, the scene was postcard perfect.

Dusty shook off his coat and tossed his bag on the king-sized bed, the hat remaining on his head. Gazing out at the city, Charlee's mind went to where she hated it to go—wondering where in this world her son could be. Was he sitting in a high chair right now eating his baby food? Was he crawling yet? Was that woman *taking care of him*?

So caught up in thought, she jumped when Dusty came up from behind her and wrapped his arms around her waist. He immediately retreated.

She twisted around and shook her head apologetically. "Sorry, you just startled me." She replaced his arms and turned back to the window. "Do you think we'll ever get him back, Dust?" She didn't want to do this, speak that language, risk the vibe, but she couldn't help herself. It had been ages since they spoke of it. "It'll be Christmas soon, his first one . . ." The tears came fast, flowing freely, like the river below. *Damn it.*

Dusty leaned his head into her neck, his hat falling to the floor. He kissed her shoulder, softly, as one would a fragile kitten. "I know. It all scares me, too," he whispered. "I wonder and I worry . . . same as you." He turned her around to meet his eyes. "But we can't keep torturing ourselves. We can't. It'll kill us. It's already killing us. We can't let it ruin our lives . . . our—" he hesitated, though they both knew the word coming next "—marriage."

She nodded. "I know, I know. But how do we *do* that?"

He lifted her chin, wiped her tears with his thumbs, and kissed her lips. Then he whispered in her ear, "I guess we just keep living." He kissed her again. Not gentle this time, but firm. As if he was trying to inject his own strength, his steel resolve, into her soul through his lips.

When he released her, he walked over to the table and lifted the champagne bottle out of the ice bucket, and his tone changed. "My, oh my, Sunshine, you thought of everything, didn't you, girl?" That grin made everything else go away.

He unwrapped the foil, rolled up his sleeves in a mocking way. "Stand back, Sunshine, I'm poppin' my cork."

The laughter streamed out of her like air in a balloon.

The burst of bubbles seemed to spray away all threats of gloom. Like a shower of renewed optimism. She grabbed the pretty flutes.

Two sips, and she pushed him onto the bed. She wanted him now. Before happy hour, before dinner, before either had a chance to think anymore. There had been times since the kidnapping they'd had problems in bed. She planned to do everything she could to rectify that.

She stripped off her clothes, and his. She fondled and stroked and kissed every inch of that hard body of his. With fervor, and playfulness, and urgency, Charlee made love to her husband like it was her last mission on Earth.

The next morning she awoke to see a small box on the end of the long pillow.

"I forgot to give this to you last night," Dusty said, snuggling up to her, one hand holding up his head, wearing nothing but his Gable grin.

She wiped her sleepy eyes and cupped the box in her hand. "From Nashville?"

He nodded.

She sat up and lifted the velvet cover. She saw the shiny gold chain first. When she pulled it gently from its box, her eyes caught sight of the small platinum record pendant outlined by tiny diamonds. She'd never seen anything like it before. "Oh, Dusty, it's so beautiful. And so unique."

"Like you," he said, kissed her cheek, then moved behind her to clasp the necklace around her. "This is to your first platinum record."

"My, aren't you are the optimist." She grinned, sitting

up on her knees to look into the mirrored headboard. "Wow, even the length is perfect."

"Well—" he grinned, staring at her reflection. "I've learned a few things about what you like through the years. And I just wanted to let you know how proud I am of you." He turned her around to face him. "That album's really good, Charlee. I played it to the guys the whole time I was there."

She wrapped her arms around his neck. "Thank you. You've done good, Cowboy." She stared into his hazel eyes that were more blue than green today. Always a good sign. She'd always found it fascinating that his eyes shifted color depending on his mood—greenish when angry, bluish when happy, or in a romantic mood. In fact, she'd bought him a mood ring one Christmas as a joke. Not long ago, she saw he still had it in his sock drawer. "I love you so very much."

Neither had pressing obligations the following week, so after the desk clerk told them no one had booked the room, they decided to stay a couple extra nights. It was their mini-vacation from the world. For the first time in months, there were no clipped words between them, no uncomfortable silences. They romped on the spacious bed, flirted playfully in the Jacuzzi, called in for room service . . . enjoyed having fun again.

Maybe their healing had finally begun.

Charlee was so happy she didn't even mind watching *Monday Night Football* with him their last night there. Nestled in Dusty's arms on that big bed, she felt safe and comfortable and even the sport she usually found so boring seemed exhilarating.

"Do you know," she said during the commercial, "we've hardly even smoked much since we've been here?"

"Yeah, well, that's kinda hard to do with our hands being

so busy." Dusty leaned over to the nightstand to retrieve his hat. "So, little lady, would ya like another go-round?"

She giggled and stole his hat, placing it on her head. "Only if I get to wear it this time."

They had just begun another lovemaking session when she heard Howard Cosell's voice drop to a low, ominous tone.

"*An unspeakable tragedy—*" They both sat up. "*—confirmed to us by ABC News in New York City. John Lennon, outside of his apartment building on the West Side of New York City, the most famous, perhaps of all of the Beatles, shot twice in the back, rushed to Roosevelt Hospital, dead on arrival.*"

Charlee and Dusty flopped back against their pillows, too stunned to speak. They were both ardent fans of Lennon. Charlee had even met him once. She'd never forget that time the MissFits were in New York, recording at the famed Record Plant Studio. Lennon had appeared during their session like an apparition, popping in to check them out. She could still hear that legendary voice with the English accent say to her. "I think you've got a future there, my girl." Then he'd flashed a peace sign and disappeared out the door.

The memory slapped her in the face as Cosell tried to shift his shocked audience back to the game.

Like that first night without their child, she and Dusty cried in each other's arms, shaking their heads with disbelief. How could this be?

John Lennon. A Beatle. Dead? He had been part of their existence, their adolescence, their musical journey, since they were babies.

What kind of world was this?

Charlee recalled asking that question many times in her life. Like when she watched the TV images of the Kent State Shootings. She'd been only twelve, but she had already suffered the huge loss of Ray and Jo, who she had loved and considered her parents.

She'd asked the question when learning about her real father, who had died tragically, senselessly, in a plane crash at twenty-one years old. Asked it again three years ago when members of the Lynyrd Skynyrd band met the same fate. That had touched her personally, too, because she had met them on tour not long before that.

She'd asked that question again, and again, when Dylan got snatched from the hospital.

Now this. Another great man, like President Kennedy, his brother Bobby, and Martin Luther King—all who had done the world some good—had been murdered.

Through her shock and pain, Charlee was grateful for at least one thing. The madman who'd killed Lennon had been caught and sent to jail.

If only that were true in her case. If only they could find that mysterious woman, that awful, heartless woman, and get her and Dusty's son back in their arms again.

If only something good could come out of evil.

6. You're Only Lonely

Sandra had wanted to have a party. Her little Benji was turning one, and didn't every mother have a party for that occasion? And didn't *she* deserve a party after all she'd been through?

It sure had been a wacked-out year. But she'd made it. Through the nighttime cries, the bouts of colds, diarrhea, constipation. All those diaper changes.

And that crazy ordeal when he'd had the flu and his temperature shot up to 103. Man, that had scared the wits out of her. She'd rushed him to the emergency clinic that night (why do kids always get sick at the most ungodly hours?). Luckily, she'd had cash in lieu of an insurance card, and the thought occurred to her, for the first time, what she would do when the boy reached school age. All that paperwork they asked for. Well, she'd figure something out. As the doctor examined him, darker thoughts intruded. What if the little guy was diagnosed with some fatal disease and dying? Then what would she do? He was her world.

That was evident when she realized she hardly had anyone to invite to his birthday party. Well, there were the few people she'd managed to meet this past year at the Snake Pit Tavern. There was Rita, the barmaid. And Yukon Sam, the old man who drank Snake Bites (in keeping with the bar theme), and Cecily, the old widow who came in around three and stayed till closing, every night. She was a little weird, but nice enough to talk to on a slow night. There was also the nighttime barkeep, Georgeanne. But no way would she invite her. The bitch.

Of course, there was Nicky. But would he even come? She hadn't seen him the past few weeks, what with his schooling and playing guitar on weekends at the local Ground Round (seemed everyone wanted to be a rock star these days). This really bummed her out because Nicky was her favorite person. Young, smart, sweet . . . Oh, if only she were twenty again.

That totaled four people she could invite. *Four.*

So in the end, she didn't have that party. Why bother? Benji wouldn't know the difference. Still, it would've been nice. And it would've helped her out of the god-forsaken winter doldrums. Sometimes she got so lonely. Even with the kid.

Sandra leaned over the coffee table to squash out her smoke, and headed to the kitchen to get another beer. When she opened the refrigerator, she saw the empty crisper drawer. Damn. How could that be? She could have sworn she'd bought enough yesterday. But then she remembered she'd stayed up late last night watching *Bonnie & Clyde*, a movie she never got tired of seeing.

She glanced up at the wall clock. Only 8:30? Ah, hell. How could she survive a Saturday night with no more beer? She *had* to have some when she watched *The Love Boat* and *Fantasy Island*. And especially *Saturday Night Live*. That one always made her laugh, no matter how bad things were.

Those shows got her through nights like these when she was forced to stay home with no one to watch Benji. At first, she'd been thrilled when he started going to sleep around eight, but soon she realized it only made the nights that much longer.

She sighed and shut the fridge door, thinking. Well, the store was just a few blocks away. She went into the small bedroom and peeked in on her boy. Good. Sound asleep in his crib. Then she grabbed her pea coat, purse, and keys, and slipped out the apartment door.

At Lawson's, she stood in the checkout line with her cans of Schlitz when a man called out from behind her.

"Hey, Sandra. How's it goin'?"

She swung around to see Herb, a guy from the bar. "Oh. Same ol', same ol'. What'cha up to?"

"Headed to the Snake. They got that band tonight. The one that played on New Year's Eve, 'member?"

She did indeed. She had paid Rita's twelve-year-old daughter, who didn't seem to have a brain in her head, big money to babysit. She had been that desperate. But it'd been worth it. She'd danced and drank and even got that halfway good-lookin' man, whatever his name was, to take her home. Only disappointing part, he'd gotten what he wanted, then disappeared into the night.

"Jerry and the Mindbenders? Aw, you're kidding me? I love those guys."

Herb pulled out a ten-dollar bill and paid for her six-pack. "You should stop up. They'll be startin' in 'bout an hour. Fact, I'll grab ya for the first dance."

"Ya know, I just may take you up on that."

He followed her out to the car, opened the door for her, then swung around the passenger side to set the brown bag of comfort next to her. She leaned across the seat. "And thanks for the beer, Herbie. See ya soon!"

When she got inside her door, she threw the cans in the crisper, then rushed into her bedroom to decide on what to wear. She chose the stretchy neon pink top that made the most of her C-cups, with the short, pleaded, black skirt that swirled when she danced. She rifled through her jewelry box and pulled out hoop earrings, then the silver chain that hung over her boobs like Christmas tree tinsel. She put on all her fancy rings, then teased her hair, hoping she had enough Aqua Net in the cabinet.

Ready to go in a record twenty minutes, she went into Benji's room and was relieved to see him lying there like a little doll. Most of the time now, he slept through the night. She hoped this would be one of those kinds of nights. She started to give him a little pat on the head, but drew back, afraid to stir him. She opted for blowing him a kiss as she closed the door halfway, slipped on her dancing flats, and tiptoed out.

She hadn't planned on staying long. Just for a couple of dances. But then, the place was packed with folks all wanting a good time. She boogied to "Hang on Sloopy," "Honky Tonk Woman," and slow-danced with Herb to "Rain Drops Keep Fallin' on My Head."

When the band took its second break, someone hit the jukebox and played two songs by Echo and the MissFits: "Shine it On" and "Not Your Daisy May." Normally, any songs by Echo launched adrenalin rushes of guilt and remorse right up her spine at what she'd done to the girl. But by now, she'd had enough Sloe Gin Fizzes to mask any of those gnawing emotions.

Until the next morning. When she opened her eyes and, slowly, lifted her head off the pillow, wondering for a second where she was. Her hand shot up to her throbbing forehead as she looked around and saw that she was in her own bed. *Well, that's a comfort*, she thought to herself. She was glad to see that somehow she'd made it home okay. Last thing she remembered was Georgeanne's irritating voice yelling, "Last Call, People!" In fact, the shrieks still resonated in her ears.

Or was that something else?

She tilted her head for a better listen and realized the screaming she remembered wasn't what she was hearing now. This sounded like a baby.

"A*H HELL*!"

She bolted off the bed and raced to his room. She opened the door that was still ajar from last night and there was Benji, standing up in his crib, tears streaking his face. "Oh, baby! Mama's sorry." She lifted him up and the smell of urine attacked her so violently she almost hurled right there. She threw her head back and sucked in some clear air. He was soaking wet, not only from tears, but a saturated diaper.

She surprised herself by keeping her nausea at bay while she changed him, and put him in the highchair. She made herself some dry toast, snapped opened a jar of Gerber's oatmeal with bananas, and together they sat in the kitchen alternating bites of nourishment.

The rest of the day, they spent in the living room—Benji in the playpen with a bottle and a bunch of toys, she on the couch, nursing her hangover and vowing to herself never to do that again.

And she wouldn't have to if she had a man around. She wouldn't need to go out trying to have some fun, though she had to admit from what she recalled of last night, she'd had a grand ol' time. If she could just find a good man, her life would be perfect. She already had her baby. And he needed a male role model. In a couple years, he'd begin to know he didn't have a daddy. And Sandra sure hadn't come across any decent candidates the past year. The few prospects she had only came around to get laid. Like she was just this factory for lonely hearts.

She decided maybe it was time to move again. To a bigger city. Back to Cleveland, perhaps? After all, the fuss over the kidnapping had died down, practically forgotten. She was sure of it because she went to the library on a regular basis to check for any stories on Echo's missing baby. In the past six months, Sandra hadn't seen a thing in *People* magazine, *Rolling Stone, American Rocker,* or even *Cleveland* magazine.

Of course, there was bound to be something in the news because of his first birthday. And sure enough, that

Thursday, she picked up the *Pittsburgh Press* at the local grocery store to see if there was any mention. And there it was, page two.

Today marks the one-year anniversary of the disappearance of the baby of rock star, Echo. In a press release, Echo and her husband, Dusty Campbell, states that they are refusing all interviews. "Our son's first birthday is an especially difficult time for our family, and we ask for privacy at this sad time."

The two-day old infant was taken from Holy Cross Hospital in the early morning hours on March 22. The FBI has confirmed that they have followed up on every lead. However, so far, there are no suspects in the child's disappearance. Both the FBI and Cleveland Police continue to investigate the case.

The article gave Sandra huge relief. They may say they're still investigating, but what's there to investigate? The kid's one years old now. He looks nothing like the infant he was back then. For one thing, his hair is lighter, not black as Echo's anymore. More of a caramel color, like her hubby, Dusty's. Which was closer to Sandra's. That certainly worked in her favor.

Yes, it would be safe to go back. Back to her old stomping grounds of Cleveland Heights. Even though her daddy was long gone now, and her childhood home occupied by strangers, it would be good to go back. She had to admit she missed the excitement of a bustling city. She missed her home.

When her head stopped pounding, she would give that idea more serious thought.

7. With a Little Luck

Charlee had to get out of the house. In one week, her baby would turn one and the nightmares had been increasing. With Dusty away, she'd never felt so alone. She awoke abruptly that morning from a horrific dream about her baby falling into a man hole and her screams had made her whole body jerk upward. No way could she stay home after that.

Aunt Libby lived in a cool-looking chalet-style home in a suburban town called Willowgrove. It was perfect— far enough in the country to enjoy all the rural amenities— wide-open prairies, farm animals, country stores—yet just a half hour's drive to downtown Cleveland, where she and husband Dave ran Rockin' Robin's Record Shop.

Today was Sunday so Charlee knew the Fosters would be there. She also knew she didn't need to knock. While not blood related, her mother and Libby had been best friends since high school, so they were extended family. Besides, in the country, few felt the necessity of locked doors.

As soon as her heels reached the porch, Charlee peeked in the picture window and saw her aunt on the floor. She opened the door to the voice of Jane Fonda.

"Now get those legs up, ladies. One, two . . ."

Libby's head turned toward Charlee at the sound of entry, but she continued doing the lifts. "Hey, sweetie, I'll be right with you. Get yourself some coffee, and one of Dave's famous cinnamon buns. You must have smelled them all the way here!"

"Don't mind if I do," she said, blowing her a kiss. She took off her rabbit fur jacket and walked into the kitchen to see

Dave icing the rolls. She grabbed his shoulders from behind and kissed him on the cheek. "Mmm, smells scrumptious," she said, as Dave turned around and gave her a hug.

"How's our girl doing? Been a while," he said, reaching in the cupboard for coffee cups.

She knew. The last time she'd seen them had been over the Christmas holiday. Three months ago.

"So how's it goin'?" Dave's repeated question didn't escape her notice.

"Keeping busy, you know—"

They all knew.

"Whew, that Jane can really work ya." Libby came in stretching her back. She wore a black leotard, with black tights and hot-pink leg warmers. Her dark hair was wrapped up in a ponytail scrunchie, though some strands had let loose. Charlee always admired how pretty Aunt Lib was. Even at forty, she could almost pass for Charlee's age. Maybe thanks to those Jane Fonda workouts.

Libby threw her arms around her. "Oh, it's so good to see you. Come, sit."

Dave served them at the breakfast bar. She remembered when Dusty used to make Sunday breakfasts, but since January, he'd been on the road with a new band he'd met in Nashville—something he'd told her about *after* their Ritz stay. She tried being happy for him, but after the glorious December when things had seemed so promising between them, she missed him more than ever. Especially today.

Charlee looked around. "Where's little Jack?"

Libby pushed the pastry dish away. "Dave, you know I'm not going to eat that. Vegas, remember?" She gave him a smirk, then turned her eyes back to Charlee. "He's taking me there for our anniversary next month. Cannot wait! Oh, and Jack's over his buddy's house down the road. They're into these new video games and the Powell's have one in their basement. Wait'll you see him, gettin' tall like his daddy."

Charlee felt the familiar tinge of envy. "Sorry I haven't been over for a while. I wanted to spend as much time with Dusty before he left. Plus, I'm starting to write songs for the next album."

Dave pulled out a chair and joined them. "Another one so soon? That's great, Char. And Billy tells me you're going to be making some kind of music video for a new TV channel or something?"

Charlee nodded, her mouth too full to answer. Unlike her aunt, she wasn't watching her figure. In fact, she'd gained twenty pounds since last summer. Which equaled out, sort of, since she'd lost fifteen the first few months Dylan went missing. She knew she had to start getting them off, though. She had to look good for that video.

Tomorrow was Monday. She'd start tomorrow.

She downed her last chew with her coffee. "Yeah, they're calling it Music Television. An awesome concept. Great for artists pumping new records. Like me." She smiled, glad to be able to say that again. "Mom and I decided to hold off doing the American tour we talked about. Wait for the video to come out and keep the interest in the last album, and amp up excitement for when the next one comes out."

Libby stood up and gave her a tight squeeze. "Sound like you're back on track. That's the first time I've heard you be excited about anything for too long." She pulled way to gaze at Charlee. "You're moving on, hon. I'm so proud of you."

They spent the next hour talking about the record store, industry gossip, and the March weather. When Dave left the room to shower, Libby scooted closer to her. "So tell me, how are things with Dusty?"

Charlee sighed. Part of her wanted to talk about it; part of her did not. She usually confided in Ruby, who had stayed with her a couple times after Dusty left, but things had changed between them. Ruby was immersed in her restaurant/bar business, often there ten to twelve hours a day. Charlee felt her best friend had no time for her troubles. And while Charlee was close to her mother, she didn't want her worrying too much. As a grandmother, Peggy Sue was hurting too.

So maybe Libby was the perfect person to confide in. Charlee grabbed one of Libby's Pall Malls from across the table and lit up.

"Well they *were* going good. Wonderful, in fact. But since he left, well, maybe I expect too much. But after the first week he was gone, he stopped calling every day. I always looked forward to that. So when he finally does call lately, I've got an attitude and the conversation is kinda tense, you know? I want to sound cheery, make him miss me, but I can't. I just want him home. I thought it'd be good for him to get in a band again, but first off, it's a *cover* band, so no originality. Dusty plays the same songs over and over. Don't know how he stands it. He used to love working on new songs. He says he still writes some during the day, but I don't know.

"*And* all those other guys are single and you know what that means. All they wanna do is play and *play,*" she said, emphasizing the point. "They're down in Florida now and have gigs every night. So, too busy to call wives and girlfriends while they bask in the warm weather and play all those bars along the beach strip."

The words poured out of her. "Yeah, he's havin' a good old time. Been to Atlanta, Charleston, Hilton Head, and now Ft. Lauderdale. *Gotta* hit the party towns. And here I am, the little wifey waiting for her man's gallant return."

Even she hated the tone of her voice. Her watery eyes blurred her vision as she talked into her coffee cup. "Even when we say I love you, it's more habit than anything else. I feel like I'm being whipped around a fuckin' vicious circle."

She leaned back in her chair in frustration. "Oh, Aunt Lib, I'm so afraid I'm losing him. He won't talk to me about anything he's really feeling. If he's feeling anything at all. He acts like life just goes on—"

Libby placed her hand on hers. "Because for him, life *must* go on. Because it's up to him to make sure it does. Don't you see, men deal with things differently. It doesn't mean he's not hurting, too. But he's the man, thinks he's gotta hold up the world. You know he loves you like crazy."

"Sometimes I'm not so sure." Charlee stood up. "I gotta go to the bathroom." This was true, but she also wanted to blow her runny nose and get her own pack of cigarettes out of her coat pocket. She hated Pall Malls. When she returned, her nose was still drippy.

Charlee lit the Salem. "He's coming home tomorrow night. Least I didn't have to argue that point."

That point was that he needed to be with her on the one anniversary no one would want. That Saturday would be a full year since their baby's been gone. Disappeared, like some crazy magic trick.

"So, you're goin' to Vegas, huh? Cool."

Charlee stayed with the Fosters all day, and when Jack returned, they talked her into staying the night. An invitation she was grateful for. When the phone rang the next morning, Charlee was standing in the kitchen helping Libby with the dishes.

"It's for you," Dave said, holding the receiver out toward her.

"Me? Oh, Dusty?"

Dave shrugged. "Don't sound like him."

"Hello? Tom! You have news?"

"Hi, Charlee. Your mother told me I'd catch you there. Now don't get too worked up. I just wanted to give you an update. I found out over the weekend there's a couple in

Dayton, just arrested for kidnapping a boy Dylan's age. I'm going down there today."

"I'll go with you!" She was already mentally in his car.

"No, stay put. I'll call you when I find out more. You told me to keep you posted on everything, no matter how small, and I want to honor that. But like I've said, these kinds of things happen all the time, leads that ultimately go nowhere. So please, just hang in there. Don't get your hopes up."

She couldn't help it. Her hopes had already launched.

8. Slip Slidin' Away

The first thing Charlee did was call Dusty. Or rather, she tried. He was due to take the nine o'clock flight home that evening, which meant he wouldn't leave his hotel for the Ft. Lauderdale airport until at least seven. It was ten in the morning when she first called, but the phone rang and rang. Surely the incessant tone would wake him, she thought. And if he wasn't sleeping, then where was he that early? Dusty was a typical musician, a night owl who often slept till noon. She called the front desk.

"I'm sorry, ma'am, Mr. Campbell checked out yesterday."

Charlee slammed the receiver down, her blood hot. "Son-of-a-bitch! He's not there. Where is he?" She turned to her aunt, who was near the breakfast bar, sweeping the kitchen floor. "Why wouldn't he call me before he left there? Now I have no way to reach him. Damn him! Probably did it on fuckin' purpose."

Seeing little Jack sitting at the end of the dining table, she cringed and mouthed, "sorry" to Libby.

Jack, who'd been only playing with his eggs anyway, made a beeline out of there, toward anywhere the air was less volatile. Allowing Charlee to continue her rant. "That's what I'm talking about, Aunt Lib. He just comes and goes as he damn well pleases with his damn ass life. I swear he's forgotten he's married."

Libby leaned the broom against the wall and came over and hugged her. Which only provoked her emerging tears. "Honey, your mind's jumpin' to conclusions. Maybe he didn't like the room and moved to a different hotel. Maybe one closer to the airport."

"But this may be it, Aunt Libby! They may have found Dylan! And I can't even get hold of my husband to tell him!"

"Come on, you know he'll call soon as he gets up. Maybe the guys met up with friends and all crashed at a buddy's house."

"You sound like you're making excuses for him."

"No, I'm just being practical. It could be a number of things. You don't know."

"Precisely." Charlee released herself from Libby's embrace. "I. Don't. Know."

She walked over to the table and snatched up her purse. She caught sight of Dave through the kitchen window, tinkering with the old Chevy he was restoring. She sighed, wishing her husband could be like that. A man always close by. "I gotta go. I told Tom to call me later at home."

Once there, she busied herself around the house doing mundane chores. Normal routines in automatic fashion, working in a daze. She hadn't even turned on the stereo. She wanted nothing to distract from the waiting. Waiting for her life to miraculously turn into what she'd been dreaming about since she learned she was pregnant. After achieving her rock and roll dreams, her heart had been set on experiencing another part of the good life, a family life: Picturesque home in the suburbs. Loving husband. A child, maybe two. Big Dog. Furry Cat, maybe two.

She already had the home, the husband. And while they'd never gotten around to getting a pet, that could come later. After her baby was found.

All it took was getting Dylan back to make the rest of her dreams come true.

By noon, she threw down her polishing rag and started to panic. She still hadn't heard from Dusty and her emotions kept flipping back and forth, from anger to fear. But mostly anger. While a part of her was terrified that something bad may have happened, she wouldn't allow herself to go there. She'd rather be pissed off.

She fumed at his thoughtlessness, despite Libby's reminder that "men don't always think." But Dusty always had. Yet they'd both had changed the past year. While she tried staying sane by writing songs to channel her pain over their baby's disappearance, Dusty chose to withdraw. Even during that romantic time at the Ritz last winter, she'd felt it. That elusive pocket of dead air between them. After the holidays she thought of suggesting counseling, but she knew Dusty would poo-poo it. He was too proud.

And being a proud man, he wasn't immune to compliments from fawning females. She had to wonder, in his vulnerable state, could he resist all those women praising him every night? Offering themselves, free of charge? She knew how it went in the music world. She'd seen, and experienced it, far too many times.

She went into the first-floor bathroom, closest to the phone, and began scrubbing the floor. Her heart revved up recalling a night, not long after she and Dusty had gotten engaged, when he was playing some college club. The band had taken a break and she had gone to the ladies' room. When she came out, Charlee noticed a girl talking to Dusty by the speakers. Actually she was no girl, Charlee soon realized. That always amazed her, the age range of groupies. No biggie, Charlee told herself. Someone probably just requesting a song.

It was the woman's outfit that began to set off warning bells. Even at that distance, and in the dark lighting, Charlee could see more skin then fabric. As she got closer, she stared at the off-the-shoulder gauzy top, tight mini-skirt, and flirty manner. When the woman turned her head toward Charlee as she approached, the heavy, sparkly makeup was practically blinding and Charlee wondered what in fool's name she was doing at the Viking Saloon. This one belonged further downtown at Night Moves, the disco club.

Dusty, one-woman man that he was, had spotted Charlee and immediately brushed past the groupie to give her a big kiss on the lips, then pulled her in and whispered, "Thanks for rescuing me." They both had chuckled as the spurned chick disappeared into the crowd.

But now Charlee wasn't in Florida to do any rescuing, flick away the swarming barflies. In fact, she couldn't recall the last time she'd been present at one of Dusty's gigs. It wasn't her fault they each had separate commitments. Yet her absence allowed those kind of visions to gnaw at her. Taking her anxiety out on that tile floor, Charlee pictured her handsome husband lying in a strange bed last night, next to one of those eager pleasers he'd met at some Lauderdale club. With sleek blond hair, large robust breasts, and a heart-shaped mouth kissing him in all the places only Charlee had permission to . . .

"*Stop that!*" she yelled aloud, swiping at errant strands of hair from her eyes. No. Dusty was loyal, trustworthy. She *knew* he was. So no. No way.

What was happening to her? To them? That despicable thief had robbed them of much more than their baby. She had stolen their peace of mind. Embezzled their very souls.

Could it be possible she really was losing her husband? She had to admit, that exciting passion they'd known, that closeness they'd shared, was burning away. That scorching hot spark they'd shared had died down, like a flicker on a candle's wick. Despite their efforts to keep that fire aflame.

She pulled herself from the floor to gaze down at her one shiny accomplishment of the day. She looked at the phone. Dusty still hadn't called from wherever he was. What if he *had* been in an accident, and here she was, suspecting, accusing, him? What if he'd been mugged and lying in some alleyway gasping for breath? Hadn't she just read about drug-crazed kids mugging Florida tourists for money? He could be in a hospital right now, calling her name.

She ran to the kitchen and looked up at the clock. Weren't you supposed to call the police after not hearing from someone you expected to after twenty-four hours? In fact, she hadn't heard from her husband since that Friday before his gig.

Just as she reached for the phone, the receiver jingled, startling her so much it slipped out of her hand when she picked it up. She grabbed the winding cord just before it hit the floor and yanked it up to her ear.

"Hello?" Her voice shook with anticipation.

It was a local reporter wanting to do an interview about the first anniversary of the kidnapping—despite the recent press release stating she would not do interviews. First, it had been the national magazines wanting an "in-depth story" for their March issue. Now the Cleveland papers. Oh God. No more!

"Leave me the fuck alone," she screamed, not caring if it pierced the guy's ears, then slammed the phone down.

Man, she would pay for that one. Reactions like that only gave them permission to write what they wanted. Peggy Sue had taught her from the beginning to be polite to those interested in her career, be it photographers, fans, or journalists. But being polite was the last of her worries right now.

The phone rang again. She grabbed it, ready to lash out at another reporter. "Yeah?"

"Charlee, any news?" Her mother. "I had a meeting all morning with these guys about to rip each other's heads off. You know, same ego thing. If I didn't believe so much in their record, I'd have kicked them out hours ago. I've had it with *creative differences*. So anything?"

Charlee had almost forgotten she'd called her mother right after Tom's call. "No. Just playing the waiting game." She paused. "And Dusty is MIA."

"Whad'dya mean?"

"He checked out of his room yesterday and I haven't heard from him . . . since Friday." She began to shake. Saying it out loud jammed the needle of anger and fear in deeper.

"Oh jeez, Charlee, did you call the police, hospitals? That's not like him."

"I know, I know." She started crying, looking again at the clock. "I thought I'd wait 'cause he usually sleeps till noon on the road. But it's almost two. Oh, Mom, you think I really should call the cops or the hospitals down there?"

"Yes, you can try, though I'd think you'd have heard something if anything bad had happened. I'm coming over now."

Her mother's reasoning, and the promise that she was on her way, gave Charlee a faint sense of comfort. She hung up, grateful that there was at least one person in her life she could depend on.

Finding out that Dusty was neither in a hospital nor locked up in a jail cell, did nothing to ease Charlee's mind. She smoked one cigarette after another until Peggy arrived. Just having her mother there calmed her nerves. Somewhat.

Finally, just past two-thirty, Dusty called.

"Where the hell are you?"

"I'm sorry, babe, I stayed at this guy's house and just woke up. It was an unreal night."

Now she had permission to be pissed off. "Yeah, well, it's been an unreal morning, starting with a call from Tom, and then come to find out you weren't where I thought you were." She didn't care if her voice accused him before hearing him out.

"Tom? What he say?"

She decided to let him languish a bit. "*Excuse me?* I think I deserve more of an explanation then *it was an unreal night*!" She could feel her whole body blushing with rage. Peggy placed a gentle hand on her shoulder trying to calm her down. This time it didn't work. "Why haven't you called me since Friday?"

His audible sigh made her want to squeeze through the phone lines and shake him senseless.

"God, Charlee, that can wait. What did Tom say?"

She knew she was being cruel, but then, he'd been cruel first. She was about to explode from the burst of scattered emotions pumping through her. One of them was hope, and that scared her the most. Hope had deceived her far too many times.

She choked back tears. "He said Dylan may have been found. But that it might not be him. So I don't know what to think. And where the hell are you? Not here!" Her voice shook and the tears came. "Just get your ass home." She banged the receiver down, and immediately regretted it. Who was this horrible person emerging from inside her?

"Why'd you do that?" Peggy said, underscoring Charlee's instant regret. "I realize you're angry, but that was cruel."

"I can't help it, Mom, he just makes me crazy sometimes."

By eight that night, Charlee told Peggy she'd be fine and sent her home since Tom still hadn't called. Dusty was due home sometime around midnight and she needed time to herself, prepare for what would not be much of a welcome home. Her emotions were so scrambled, she didn't know how she should react when he walked in that door. Still angry? Happy to have him home? Which, despite everything, she would be?

Half a dozen times she'd flinched with regret at her earlier behavior, dying to call Dusty back and talk to him, share with him the excitement of "maybe this is it!" But in her fury, she'd failed to get the number where he was. *Damn.*

As time ticked away, her nerves began to fray. Her eagerness over Tom's hopeful call began to plummet into a quaking mound of doubt and anguish. What if the baby wasn't Dylan after all? Or any baby they may find after this? How many times would she have to go through this? The rest of her life?

The question that remained in her thoughts every day was the most haunting. What if they never found her son?

Ever?

9. Watching the Wheels

That night, Charlee stood in her bedroom and flicked on the stereo by her bed, just in time to hear "Bette Davis Eyes," her new favorite song. She was grateful for Kim's soulful voice echoing through the room. The catchy tune lightened her spirits as she opened the door to her walk-in closet for just the right thing to wear.

Despite telling herself she shouldn't bother dressing up for Dusty's return, she wanted to look good when he walked in the door. If only to make him drool. She had no intention of letting him near her.

So the outfit had to be pretty and sexy, but not too obvious. If there had been a groupie that had tempted her husband—and she prayed he'd resisted—she wanted to remind him what he had at home, while at the same time, not appearing like she'd forgotten his negligence.

When Dusty finally walked in the door, he looked like someone had beaten him and left him on the curb. She, however, was shower fresh in tight black leggings and sheer ruffled blouse the color of the pink roses he'd sent her on Valentine's Day. She had swept her dark hair up in a sterling barrette because she knew he loved it that way. She wanted him eating out of her hand. *So to speak.*

He didn't look at her as he set his bags down in the foyer, took off his jean jacket, tossed it on the velvet chair. She could tell he was as unsure how to act as she was. She decided to take the high road after seeing how awful he looked.

"Hey." She smacked his cheek. "You hungry? I have shrimp cocktail in the fridge." She tried to sound casual.

He shook his disheveled hair. "Naw, I just need sleep." He kissed her back, half-heartedly, on the lips.

She followed him up the stairs, finally telling him all the details of Tom's call.

"I know."

"What do you mean you know?"

"Well, when you wouldn't tell me, when you *hung up* on me, I called him myself."

She cringed, but stood her ground. "I was *upset*. You can't blame me because you neglected to call me, for *days*."

"Don't start, please. I feel like crap. I told you I was sorry. There were circumstances out of my control. You wanna hear about it or not?"

She hated it when he turned things around like that. Made her feel like *she* was the unreasonable one. She sat on the bed, crossed her legs. "Okay, go."

He pulled his obviously new Parrot Lounge T-shirt over his head, then sat next to her on the bed. Gave her an apologetic look. "I'm sorry. Really. I didn't mean to put you through unnecessary bullshit." Those puppy dog eyes succeeded in erasing any leftover anger. Even tired and scruffy, his presence softened her heart.

She leaned back against the pillows, feeling as exhausted as he looked. Her defenses down, she let him kiss her, this time softly on the mouth. He then sat back next to her, cupping her hand in his.

"Okay, here's what happened."

He told her about his "lost" weekend. How the Friday and Saturday night gigs went smoothly at the Parrot. "Then came Sunday. We met this dude at the beach who acted like our biggest fan, and when he learned we were leaving Monday, he offered to give us a going-away party at his place a few miles away. We were dying to let loose by then, before we all went back. We checked out of our rooms and

I was going to call you then, I swear. But then we had a few shots at the hotel bar, chatting it up with the barkeep, then proceeded to the guy's house . . ."

He rubbed her hand lightly with his fingertips. "Later that night, Ryan reminded us what pricks the cops are 'round there—we saw several pull-overs that weekend—so we decided to just crash there. Oh, and this dude? Called himself Caesar. That right there should've raised a flag." He gave a cockeyed grin. "He was a bit weird, and I think gay. I avoided him much as I could, but somewhere along the line I felt queasy and sank down on this lounge chair by the pool. I remember him talking some kind of shit to me, but I was too wasted. I think he slipped me a Mickey, to tell you the truth. I woke up in the same place, on that lounge chair. Still wearing my shorts, thank god . . . so that gave me some relief." He winked and laughed, shaking her hand to get her to join in.

To her, none of it was funny. The image of her teenaged best friend and writing partner, CJ, came back to mind. He had died from someone giving him a bad drug. "God, Dusty, you didn't even know the guy. He could've given you anything. You gotta be more careful."

"Yeah, I know. Stupid. Believe me, soon as I used his phone to call you, I gathered up the boys and we hightailed it outta there." He gazed into her eyes with that grin that always made her weak. "Can you forgive your idiot husband? Who loves you deeply?"

She sighed. What else could she do but love this man? She tilted her head on his shoulder. "I missed you so much, Dust. You idiot." She looked up at him and grinned.

He loosened the clip from her hair, then ran his fingers through the curled strands. When he leaned down to her lips, there was no doubt where this kiss would lead. He stopped just long enough to say, "I can't tell you, Sunshine, how good it is to be home. With you."

Funny, she thought, how just a few words can make the world right side up again.

Tom called the following day, St. Patrick's Day, asking them to hang in there a little longer. "There's some loopholes involved," he'd said. "It's complicated, but I should find out something in the next day or two."

On Thursday morning, Charlee slipped out of bed, not wanting to disturb Dusty, hugging his pillow like a child with a stuffed toy. She longed to fall back asleep, but she knew that was impossible. The minute she opened her eyes, her stomach cramped into one big knot.

She had no idea how she was going to get through this day.

Her little boy's first birthday. Somewhere in the universe.

She stood by the window for God knows how long, gazing out at their sprawling backyard that was perfect for an active child. She watched the sun rise ever so slowly between the huge Elm trees that held a large hammock in the summer.

Sunrise. Sunset. Spring, summer, fall, winter . . . life went on, regardless. She clenched her chest with crossed arms, as if to keep the pulsating pain from bursting out of her like a volcanic explosion. Her heart hurt so bad she thought it was bound to stop beating. She leaned against the windowsill, letting herself cry, while trying to keep the whimpering sound from waking her husband. Finally, she headed toward the bathroom. She quietly shut the door behind her and walked to the cabinet on her side of the his-and-her sinks. Pulling out the bottom drawer, she reached toward the back, her fingers rolling the bottle forward. She slid it out, opened up the childproof cap, and shook out one, then two, of the pills. She only took them on days like this. When no amount of alcohol, or *Billboard* hits, or even Dusty's best lovemaking, could make it all better.

When Dusty awoke an hour later, neither discussed the calendar date. After all, what was point? At breakfast, he asked, "Wanna go into the studio with me today? I'm working the sound for Mario's EP."

She nodded. Of course she would go. No way did she want to be alone. "Mom finally found some music for him, huh?" She recalled that Mario Cirino was no songwriter, Peggy had learned that through trial and error, but an EP highlighting his playing, with cover songs, would help get him more work. They all agreed Mario was a good guitarist.

It was dusk when they returned, and Charlee and Dusty began making dinner together. It was one of their rituals when both were home. Tonight they'd opted for tacos, simple. Plus, the chopping of vegetables and frying of meat, kept their minds busy.

After pouring them each some Merlot, Charlee touched Dusty's arm. "We need music." Glass in hand, she walked to the stereo and picked out the mix tape they'd made together last summer. An eclectic collection of songs that reminded them how much they'd shared in their years together. Rolling Stones, The Eagles, Three Dog Night, Bob Seger, Billy Joel, with some Raspberries and Beach Boys mixed in. And although it made her nervous that so many female artists were making it into the Top Ten, she couldn't deny that most were deserving. So yes, they'd included on that mix tape, Blondie, Chrissie Hynde, Linda Ronstadt, Ann and Nancy Wilson, Joan Jett, Pat Benatar, and Charlee's personal hero, Tina Turner. As her competition edged their way past her, up the charts, she sometimes regretted pushing back her concert tour. But no way could she go out there, pretending all was fine. Far better to postpone than to go on stage and not give it your all. Fans don't forget bad performances.

The phone rang just as she slid the tape into the player. She jumped, her heart accelerating. Four days now she'd reacted the same way. Every chime of the phone brought expectation. Hope against hope.

Dusty got it on the first ring. "Hello? Oh, hey, what's the word?" He immediately pushed on the speaker button.

"Sorry it took so long for me to get back," Tom began. "I had to wait to hear from the detective assigned to the case. Like I told you before, they don't much like PI's hanging around the precincts. There was the typical red tape, lot of rigmarole. But in the end . . . I'm sorry. It's not Dylan. The couple bought this baby through the black market, even had what looked to be a legit birth certificate, but was fake. For a year, the real parents thought a stranger had stolen the baby, but turns out, it was the dad's uncle who had a gambling problem. Took the kid one night and sold him. I just got the confirmation call now and—

"Son of a BITCH!" Charlee hurled her wine glass hard as she could.

Dusty whipped around at the piercing shattering of glass. "Tom, lemme call you back."

Streams of crimson liquid splattered against the cream-colored kitchen wall, spilling down like bloody rain. Before Dusty could reach her, Charlee picked up a kitchen chair and threw it against the refrigerator, making a huge dent in the door.

Her son wasn't coming home.

Charlee fell to the floor howling. Dusty's knees buckled, too, and his warm wet tears merged with hers as they clung to each other on the cold marble floor. Her head against his chest, he stroked her hair, and spoke softly. "We just can't catch a break, can we, Sunshine?"

This new blow had slapped the wind out of them both. But for Charlee, it marked the need for change.

Once they were all cried out, she pulled away slightly, combed her fingers through his thick blond hair and gazed into those blue-gray eyes. "I can't do this anymore." She nearly gagged on the words, but she had to get them out. "I just can't keep up this roller coaster of emotions that always end up with our hearts broken. Can't you see it's destroying us? We're young, successful. We used to be so happy."

Dusty leaned back, tilted his head with squinted eyes, as if not sure what her words meant.

She wiped her cheeks with the back of her hand, then his with her thumb. "I was so sure this was it, Dust." She let out a sarcastic sigh. "Yeah, so much for my mother's intuition." She shook her head, angry at her own inability to see things clearly. "I can't live like this. All this waiting, hoping, praying, wondering. It's been a year, and there's been nothing. *Nothing*! And today's his birthday, for God's sakes. We get this on his *birthday*? I can't take anymore, Dust, I can't!"

She stood up, wet a dishrag and began wiping the streaked wall, wiping away the past. "Ya know, a long time ago I read that when you concentrate on something too hard, it keeps it away. Like you're not letting the energy flow through the universe the way it should. I think that's true with us. Or at least, me." She stopped to look over at him as he lifted himself off the floor, walked over to her. "My other mom, you know, Jo, who raised me, used to have a saying. 'Whatever happens is meant to be. If something you want doesn't happen, then God has other plans.'

"Dusty, I think God has other plans. Much as it hurts." She resumed her scrubbing, kept her gaze locked on the stain. "I think Jo's been trying to tell me that all along. I wake up in the middle of the night sometimes, sweating. Then I feel this cool, almost cold, wave of air brush across me, like she's there. A few nights ago, I actually heard her words come from somewhere. It was her voice, no mistake. She said, 'Time to let go. Let God.' But I forced myself not to listen. Didn't want to."

Dusty took her free hand and led her away. "Come on, sit down. I'll paint the wall tomorrow."

She stopped. She had not one ounce of energy left.

Dusty grabbed the rag, threw it in the sink, led her into the living room. Side One of the cassette tape long over, the silence made Charlee nervous. She saw something in Dusty's face she didn't like. They sat on the couch.

"So you're tellin' me you're giving up?" Dusty looked into her eyes, searching her soul.

She took in a gulp of air, then exhaled. "No. 'Course not. Not really. But let's be realistic. What are the odds they'll find Dylan and that woman now? Or worse yet, what if she sold him, like that man had done with that other baby? Oh my God, I can't take the very thought!"

"But they *found* that baby," Dusty leaned in to her. "So there's always hope."

"I know. But it's exactly that burden of hope that makes it worse. Every damn day I wonder where he is, what he's doing, who's he with. Is he *okay*? And does all that do me any good? No. Just makes me more crazy."

She folded her hands, like in prayer, an effort to stay calm. "It feels like we're just spinning our wheels. Like a roulette wheel and the odds are against us . . . We can worry, and wonder, and *hope*, but we can't *do* anything about any of it! I want to get back to how we were, Dust. The only way we're gonna stay sane is to move past this." She took another big breath. "Starting with letting Tom go. The detective seems capable and the FBI is on the case. I don't think Tom's gonna find anything that they wouldn't. I can't go through this every time he calls with a lead."

Dusty sat forward. "But you're the one who wanted him to call about any little news."

Charlee nodded. "I know, it was a mistake." She stood up. "I can't allow this to run my life anymore. I don't want to think about it anymore. I just want to live a normal life."

Dusty couldn't believe his ears. The only thing he heard was how *she* felt. He wanted to scream, *You* want, *You* want!

This had always been about her, he realized, not *them*. Since that awful day, she'd been convinced Dylan was kidnapped because of *her* celebrity. He couldn't convince her that it might have been a random act, not necessarily because she was famous. Could've been just some crazy person who didn't even know it was Echo's baby.

No. She had to make it her own personal tragedy. He'd been merely her crutch. Dusty shook his head as he watched her go up the stairs after saying she needed to go to bed. Once again, never asking him how *he* felt about anything. He wanted to shout at her, I hurt too!

He recalled around Christmastime when things between them had gotten good again. He had brought up the topic of having another baby. That had been her decision too. "There'll be no baby to replace Dylan," she'd said. "I don't want to risk having another boy. I had my boy. Maybe, *maybe*, down the road, we can adopt a girl. But no way am I going through another pregnancy and risk having *that* baby stripped from me, too." And that was that.

Me. Not us. It was *she* who was the famous one. Who cared what *he* thought, felt?

The next day, Dusty did call Tom. Told him how his wife felt. Then he made a call to Ryan. Yes, he'd take that offer to play with the opening band for Rick Springfield's summer tour. And any other offers out there. He was open.

10. Video Killed the Radio Star

The stewardess on the flight to New York recognized Charlee the minute she and Peggy Sue boarded the plane.

"Let me know if there's anything at all I can do for you, Miss Echo," she said with a broad smile as they settled in their seats.

"How 'bout a tranquilizer?" Charlee replied with a half grin. She'd been flying since she was sixteen, yet it still made her nervous." She looked over at her mother, already starting to read *No One Here Gets Out Alive,* the new book about Jim Morrison's life.

"We'll be on the ground in just a little over an hour," said the smiling stewardess. "Can I get you a cocktail?"

"Not now, thank you," Charlee answered, expecting her to move on. There were others in first class that the woman could be attending to, but she stayed locked in position next to them. Charlee knew she'd be signing at least one autograph within the hour or so it took to La Guardia airport. She leaned her head back and closed her eyes, hoping the woman would get the hint.

Charlee replayed her new video in her mind, as she'd done countless times in the past week. She couldn't wait for it to air on MTV. It irked her no end that Pat Benatar's record, "You Better Run" had been the second music clip to air on the cable channel's debut night that August. And even the Michael Stanley Band, the biggest hitmakers in Cleveland, had trumped her, airing their video "He Can't Love You," just last week.

By now—October—Charlee's, or rather Echo's, video

would be no big deal. The channel was in its third month of twenty-four hour airing, so thousands of videos had already been played. Charlee still felt the weight of competition among female rockers, which had increased a hundred fold since the 1970s when Echo and the MissFits held center court as the quintessential all-girl rock band.

Charlee felt guilty about letting the two videos she'd made in the spring languish for months. She kept finding things wrong with them. She re-shot scenes, had three different people edit them. She'd been exposed enough in the past year and worried about every perceived perception.

Thank goodness for her mother. Peggy kept her wits about it all, and told Charlee that it didn't matter about all the videos that had already aired on the station. "A lot of people didn't even have cable a month ago," she reminded her. "Now that MTV's the hottest thing, music fans are suddenly subscribing in record numbers. Yours will be reaching a much wider audience now than those who came earlier."

Record numbers. That was what they were both hoping after the lackluster sales of *Genie for Sale*, despite what had looked like a strong start a year ago. Peggy had never said so, but Charlee suspected the decline in sales were most likely due to her personal problems. While the writing and recording of the songs had helped her deal, somewhat, with the kidnapping, she still lacked the energy for proper promotion. It'd all seemed like too much work. Such as going on tour to support the album.

Now Charlee wished she had forced herself to do it. Especially after Dusty had gone ahead and taken that job with Rick Springfield's tour, leaving her alone all summer. Although she did fly out to see him once, in Long Beach for the Fourth of July, the sparks were limited to the ones in the sky, rather than between her and her husband. They wouldn't admit it to each other, but they were growing further apart. And mileage had little to do with it.

She'd been livid that Dusty had left her high and dry. Not just marriage-wise, but band-wise. He'd been her session guitarist ever since she'd gone solo. Thank goodness once again for her mother. Peggy had gotten Mario to step in, and he'd pulled together a great backing band for her, one willing to go on the road. Whenever that time came, that is. Mario was even willing to give up his regular gig at Ruby's Place to do it, too.

Charlee was grateful for that, of course, regardless of the fact that Mario made her nervous. Mario and his damn dark good looks, and willingness to "help in any way I can."

Charlee exhaled a sigh of relief. Despite her fear of flying, it felt good to be on this plane. She had needed to get away. Though New York was hardly far enough.

The stewardess was back, after informing passengers of the flight and emergency rules—things Charlee purposely ignored, not wanting to think about the "*what ifs*."

"Ready for that cocktail yet, Miss Echo?"

Charlee sat up straight. "Yes, please. A gin and tonic, with lime." She got tired of drinking the same old thing and that mix, which her Aunt Libby always drank, sounded refreshing to her. When her new fan walked away, she nudged her mother. "Once we get to the hotel, I'll see if Nina wants to meet up somewhere to eat. I have a real hankering for Chinese."

As soon as she'd said it, Charlee flinched. She thought about Chung Wa's, the Chinese restaurant where she'd gone with Dusty the night she met him. Why did her mind always have to go *there?* To the past. When things were . . . normal.

Peggy flipped her book over, marking the page with her finger. "Sounds good," she said as the stewardess, smiling still, returned with their drinks and set them on the open tray.

When she left, Charlee said, "And don't you dare pick up the tab this time. It's the least I can do for Nina after she got the video moved up in the time placement."

Peggy nodded. "Yeah, that was awfully nice of her. Friday at midnight is much better than when everyone's watching *Saturday Night Live*." She winked. "Nice to have contacts."

How true that is, Charlee thought, lighting a cigarette as Peggy leaned back, reopened her book. Not only was Charlee lucky to have Peggy Sue Records as her label, but to have known Nina Blackwood long before she'd gotten the MTV job. The two hadn't been close friends, more like acquaintances, yet they had a hometown bond. Charlee and Dusty had been regulars at the Velvet Room in the mid-'70s when Nina would perform her classical harp on Saturday nights. They'd stay till closing time, conversing with Nina and her boyfriend/manager, Danny. When the couple moved to L.A., they'd lost contact. In June, Charlee read in *Radio & Records* that Nina had been chosen as one of the MTV "Veejays." She got her number through industry channels and called to congratulate her.

That was when Nina had asked her if she had any music videos for her new songs. Charlee had only been too happy to say yes. Even though she didn't think they were ready. That had prompted her to get her act together, make those clips the best they could be.

The idea to fly to New York was Peggy's. She'd said it could help public relations. Meeting the MTV staff in person would help establish important associations, thus, secure future airplay of Echo's videos. The competition was getting fiercer by the day. Practically every rock band, every singer with a record in America and the UK, was making mini-films in hopes of it airing on MTV. It was the new road to musical success.

That evening, they dined with Nina Blackwood, who then took Charlee and Peggy back to the MTV studio. Charlee got to meet all the Veejays: J.J. Jackson, Martha Quinn, Alan Hunter, and Mark Goodman, who was taping his segment. She'd been surprised to learn that everyone often stayed there most of the day and night. So she had plenty of company to watch the debut of her first video, and was thrilled to see their buoyant reactions.

"Stripped Away," had been her best-selling record off the album, so it made sense to air that one first. They'd shot the entire film on the beach, a lovely spot on the shores of Lake Erie called Huntington Beach, that was not only clean and wide with sand, but showed a great view of the Cleveland skyline. It opened with Charlee singing the song as she walked on the beach wearing layers of clothes. As the song builds, there was a dramatic stripping of her clothes down to her bikini as she hit the water. *After all, sex sells.* The video had little to do with Charlee's original meaning of the song. She wanted people to forget that very personal, public, horrific, time in her life. She wanted them to feel the emotional theme of the song and attach it to their own lives, not hers. She knew everyone feels it at some point.

The feeling of no control.

After the airing, they all shared high-fives and before leaving, Peggy handed the producer a copy of Charlee's second video, with assurances there'd be more to come. Charlee knew her mother would make sure of that.

She returned home Monday evening to an empty house. Dusty had been back from the tour for weeks, but he always seemed to have somewhere else he had to be. She set her suitcase and overnight bag in the foyer and headed for the kitchen, knowing there'd be a note. Dusty always left a note.

Tom had tickets to the Monday Night game. Browns vs. Bengals. 10-cent beer night!

Hope to be home before midnight, unless it goes into overtime.

Love, Dust

She stared at Tom's name. At first, she hadn't been sure it was a good idea for Dusty to stay connected with their former PI. But he'd become a trusted confidante and she knew Dusty needed that right now. Tom felt nearly as haunted as they were over the unsolved case and vowed to keep on it, when time allowed, pro bono. The silent agreement was that the subject would not come up if there wasn't anything to report. Fair enough.

Charlee grabbed a bottle of Southern Comfort from the bar. The clink of the ice as she dropped the cubes into the glass echoed through the room. She decided the big house didn't have enough life in it. Times like these she missed having a pet. Maybe tomorrow she'd go to the shelter and buy a dog. No, maybe a cat. Lower maintenance.

For now, she needed to talk to her best friend. She called Ruby's Place and asked to speak to her. "Hey, Rube, glad to catch you there. I just got back from New York and—"

"Hey, MTV star! We all saw it here last night. A kick-ass video, and you looked amazing. It's sure to spike album sales."

"Your words to God's ears." Charlee took a sip of the cold liquid that warmed her so. "I was thinking about coming up to see you." She stopped. "Maybe catch Mario playing." While Mario performed on Saturdays, he was also a regular at Ruby's "Open Mic Monday," a weekly opportunity for musicians to hang out and play together. The casual sessions had become popular, attracting customers who normally stayed home on dreaded Mondays.

"Actually we've been dead all night 'cause of the Browns game so I'm shutting down early. There are a few stragglers left, but I can leave my barkeep to close up. How 'bout I come over there? It's been too long since I've seen you."

Charlee felt a twinge of disappointment. She really wanted to go there. And see . . . She shook her head slightly holding the receiver. No. Best not go tonight. She needed alone time with her best friend more. Plus, Ruby would be here whenever Dusty came home. Good insurance. She and Dusty never argued in front of company.

Her husband hadn't done a thing wrong since he'd been off tour, yet Charlee always felt angry toward him, and she knew that was why he stayed away so much. It was getting to the point that neither were trying too hard anymore. The few times they'd made love the past month, they'd just gone through the motions.

Twenty minutes later, Ruby entered the foyer, cradling a bottle of champagne. "To celebrate the airing of your video!" she said, raising the heavy bottle and smiling that bright smile of hers.

Ruby. Always a refreshing sight.

"I've already started on Southern Comfort." Charlee said, grabbing the bottle. That was when she saw the label—the most expensive brand on Ruby's menu. Charlee returned the smile with a shrug. "Aw, hell, why not. That *is* an awesome video, isn't it?"

"Damn straight," Ruby said, giving her a hug.

After Charlee popped the cork—a skill she'd learned at the MissFit's first album release party—and poured her and Ruby a glass, they settled in on the living room sofa. They watched a Steely Dan video of "Hey Nineteen" on MTV as Charlee filled her friend in on her weekend in New York.

Then Ruby asked, "Have you figured out when you'll be doing that tour? I'll need to get another musician for our Saturday nights."

"Oh, right. I'm sorry about that. I know you need advanced notice. Well, it looks like you can have Mario till probably April. Mom's still working out the dates and cities."

"Okay, cool."

They caught up on people they knew, places they'd been to since they'd last been together. But mostly the conversation centered on Charlee, as often happened. Charlee thought their chats were unbalanced, too much emphasis on her career, and erratic life. Charlee envied Ruby's stable, normal, undramatic existence. She'd even told her once—after too many glasses of wine, which always made her sentimental—how lucky she was that her career hadn't taken off. "You avoided so much bullshit, Rube. It's so much simpler to have a nice, predictable life." She'd meant it as a compliment, but then saw the look on her friend's face and immediately wanted to retract the statement. How could she forget Ruby's disappointment when her record label dropped her? Ruby had had aspirations of being the next Aretha Franklin, and Charlee knew she envied "Echo's" success. Her and her big mouth.

"So how's things with Rob?" Charlee asked, changing the subject.

"Things are *great*," Ruby said with excited eyes. "Longest relationship I ever had, 'cept with the MissFits." She laughed.

"Yeah, really," Charlee grinned. "I'm so happy for you. You deserve it. Rob seems like a great—"

Just then the front door opened. Dusty.

Charlee looked up at the clock. Twelve-forty-five. She had left the game on in the other room to see when it ended. No overtime, Browns won. Way over an hour ago.

"'Bout time," Charlee greeted him.

Ruby shot her a look that told her it wasn't the best way to welcome your husband home, then, taking the last swig from her glass, she stood. "Well, I best be going. Gotta get up early for work, ya know."

"No." Charlee grabbed her friend's arm, almost like a crutch. "Stay here." The desperation in her voice startled even her. But she really didn't want to get into it with Dusty this late at night and Ruby provided the perfect deflection. "You shouldn't drive home now. It's the end of the month and you know how Sherman Falls cops are at night."

Ruby sighed. She glanced over at Dusty, taking off his

Browns jacket and throwing it on the chair near the door. Before she answered, he walked over to Ruby. "Yes, by all means, stay. I'm turning in anyway," Dusty said, giving Ruby a peck on the cheek. None for Charlee.

"I, uh, yeah, okay, guess you got a point." It wasn't an excited acceptance, more like an acquiescence.

"Great!" Charlee said, grabbing the empty glasses and heading to the kitchen. "You know where the guest room is. Make yourself at home." Then to Dusty. "You can have the couch." She set the glasses in the sink and proceeded up the stairs. No response.

Slamming the bedroom door, she threw off her clothes and yanked into her "no sex tonight" flannel nightshirt. She went into the bathroom, pulled out her goodwill drawer, and shook out two pills.

No. She'd already been drinking too much tonight. One Valium should do it. She gulped it down with water, then slid under the down quilt, swearing under her breath. How dare he not be here when she'd returned from New York? Was a damn football game more important than her? *What the hell?* She'd been gone a whole week. She'd anticipated a welcome, if not passionate, homecoming. But she had gotten no homecoming at all.

So now she lay in bed, alone, just as she had the past week. She punched her pillow. How she hated what was happening to them. But whose fault was that? *He's* the one who chose to go to the game rather than anxiously await her arrival. *He* was the only who chose not to rush home right after it was over. *He* was the one who was withdrawing, further and further away.

"Damn it!" she yelled out loud, wiping her wet face and flipping the pillow over to the dry side. Half of her ached for Dusty to come in and apologize, make it all better. And half of her didn't give a shit. Then she could stay mad.

She felt deserted, with no control over any of this. Like Alice in Wonderland, falling farther and farther down that hole. Getting smaller. Shrinking inside herself.

Charlee woke to a pounding headache, and blamed Dusty for that, too. The hangover fueled her anger over his tardiness last night, and for blowing her off soon after entering the house. The unwelcomed reality of morning, coupled with her intense anger, fueled her insides like a raging furnace. She sat up in her bed, her hands in a fist, heart racing. This feeling was so different from the nightmares about baby Dylan, when she'd jump awake sweating.

Charlee couldn't understand it, but this revved up feeling of intense fury felt good, almost orgasmic. She threw off the covers and planted her feet on the carpet, prepared to battle it out with her husband. But then she noticed how silent the house was. She looked at the clock. Nearly eleven. She rarely slept that late. Was Dusty even here?

She rubbed her temples, then stopped, remembering the dream. Now it made sense. Those stimulating feelings she'd woken to had nothing to do with anger. She played the visions over in her mind, every detail, like a video. An erotic video. So passionate, sexual, intense. She felt her face blush when she recalled the heated finale of the scene. The leading man had made her feel so wanted, desired, needed.

Yet, the hands and body that had caressed her all that night in her sleep had not been Dusty's.

11. The Best of Times

The knock on her office door startled Peggy so, she nearly jumped out of her chair. Her company was in a building that housed other businesses, but only she came in on Saturdays. To avoid the usual distractions. Like sudden poundings on the door.

She had just begun sorting through the piles of letters, contracts, and envelopes stuffed with demos from musician hopefuls. She slapped down the packet she'd just opened and gave an audible sigh before calling out, "Just a minute!"

Had to be one of her clients, she thought. Most likely a member of the Cheshire Band. There always seemed to be a problem, or *situation*, with those guys. She circled around the desk, walked to the door, and swung it open.

"Ange! Wow. What a surprise. How come you didn't let me know you were coming?"

She asked this while thinking of the hundreds of things calling to her from her workspace. As much as she always loved seeing Angela, this was not a good time.

"Oh, it was a spur-of-the-moment thing," she said, but her face told Peggy otherwise. "Al's in L.A. finalizing a deal, so I woke up this morning and said to myself, '*Think I'll take a drive and see my old Cleveland friend.*' So I hopped in the car, and here I am!" The voice sounded cheery, defying the expression in her eyes. "Got time to go out somewhere?"

Actually, no, Peggy wanted to say. She'd already gotten there late, having spent the early part of the day with Charlee, discussing her spring tour, now just four months away. But something about Angela's demeanor kept the words in her throat. She realized they were still standing in the doorway. "Uh, sure. If you can wait a bit. Come in, take off your coat."

Angela's bright lavender skirt suit brought color to Peggy's drab office of dark wood furnishings and gray file cabinets. Angela's fashion flair never disappointed. Peggy motioned to the chair in front of her cluttered desk. She ran over and scooped up the stack of CDs and cassettes from the chair. "Sorry, I didn't expect anyone."

"No, I'm the one should be sorry. You look frazzled, girl. And here, I was only thinkin' about surprising you. Shoulda remembered what a crazy business you got yourself into," she said with a raised eyebrow and slight grin.

Peggy grinned back. "Yeah, don't I know it?" She put an index finger to her cheek. "And who was the one who talked me into this world of crazy?"

Angela let out a hearty laugh. "Guilty." She plopped herself into the offered seat. "But I seem to recall you get bored easy. Bet'cha can't say that now," she said, a bit impishly.

"Got that right." Peggy nodded, swinging back around the desk. "I keep telling myself how grateful I should be for MTV. It's made a huge difference, as you know, for all of us in the industry. But it's put so much pressure on everyone to get a record out at the same time as a video that's well-produced and ready to air. And you gotta do it. Who knows how long it'll last?"

She remained standing, shuffling papers into various piles, fighting the pull toward getting this work done. At the same time, she reminded herself that she hadn't seen Angela since she and Al came down last summer, and phone calls just weren't the same. Her eyes flashed to the scheduling book lying open on her desk. Nothing written in on Sunday. That was because she always reserved that day for Billy, and family. But wasn't Angela family in her heart? Peggy would just switch it. Today, time with family. Tomorrow, work. Billy could have a Sunday to himself. He wouldn't mind that.

"How's that handsome husband of yours?" Angela asked, as if reading Peggy's mind. Angela was looking over at the silver picture frame on Peggy's desk, showing her and Billy arm-in-arm on the beaches of Manele Bay, Hawaii, where they'd celebrated their fifth anniversary three years before.

"Oh, you know Billy. Trying to keep up with all the changes in radio. Right now he's wavering between both stations keeping an all-rock playlist, or changing one to mostly pop, which seems to be dominating the charts these days. You know, Neil Diamond, Dan Fogelberg, Barry Manilow, Captain & Tennille? Sheesh." She turned to the shelf behind her. "Look at this. REO Speedwagon, ABBA, Air Supply, Hall & Oates. Sure, they're all good, but like Billy says, where's the rebel in the rock these days?"

"I hear ya," Angela agreed, flashing her long, blazing-red fingernails. "And don'cha miss those good Motown years? Their sound is changing, too. What they're pumpin' out now seems more white than black. I love what Michael Jackson's doing, but sometimes you can't tell who's a Motown artist anymore. Know what I'm sayin'?"

Peggy didn't, because she was only half-listening, focused on which papers should go into which manila files.

The room grew silent when Angela stopped talking, and the abrupt stillness brought Peggy's attention back to her friend. Feeling guilty, she shoved all the stuff to the side, next to the Hawaii snapshot and glanced at her watch. Four-thirty-five.

Early for dinner. She never ate before six, but if she didn't leave now, she'd find an excuse to choose work over friendship. "Okay. Think I'm done here. Let's go eat. I'll drive, you can leave your car here. Mario's?"

It was where they always went, so Peggy was surprised when Angela shook her head. "Nah, let's go somewhere different. How 'bout the Brown Derby up the street?"

Peggy shrugged. "Sure, why not? Let me call Billy first, let him know I won't be home anytime soon, and to get the guest room ready. He'll be thrilled you're in town."

At the restaurant, they ordered Pink Squirrels at Angela's suggestion. Peggy laughed as the waiter set the cherry martinis down in front of them. She hadn't had one of the sweet pink concoctions since the '60s. She took a sip. "Wow, I forgot how good these tasted. Sweet and luscious."

"Mmm. Sure is." Angela drank half of it before setting the glass down. She picked back up on their conversation on the state of the music industry, and the "good ol' days." She went on about the danceable tunes, the fun times, and all the great people they'd worked with way back when, and how sad they'd lost touch with most of them through the maze of living.

Angela seemed in a rare nostalgic mood. Peggy felt a chill rush up her spine. Angela was an Aquarian, not the type to look back. Wasn't *she* the one who often reminded Peggy of that, especially when they were younger with lots more problems?

By the time their dinner arrived, Angela asked, "So what's goin' on with Charlee and Dusty these days? Hope things are better."

Perhaps because of Angela's reflections on their earlier days, the question took Peggy back to another time the two of them dined out, the summer of 1970. Peggy had moved Charlee to Detroit the year before, an effort to start fresh after Aunt Jo and Uncle Ray's death. When Peggy had told Angela she worried that, with school out, the thirteen-year-old could find trouble while Peggy was at work, Angela saved the day, offering to have Charlee help her out at Hitsville U.S.A. That was the same summer Charlee began playing guitar, and the rest, as they say . . .

Peggy leaned in toward her friend. "To tell you the truth, Ange, I'm not sure they're gonna make it. It breaks my heart. But they can't seem to get past the horror of the kidnapping. And who can blame them? It's affected us all. I wonder every day where that little boy is. And yet, there's nothing any of us can do." Her eyes started tearing up. "We all feel so helpless."

Angela reached for Peggy's hands and cupped them inside hers. "I know. I know." Her eyes welled up, too. "It's so devastating. I think the not-knowing *is* the worst."

She caught Peggy's frown and added, "But, Peg, I *do* believe he is still out there somewhere. You gotta keep that thought."

She didn't add "because it's too horrifying to think otherwise," but Peggy heard it anyway.

After enjoying juicy prime ribs and stuffed baked potatoes, the waiter returned with the check and asked if they needed anything else. "As a matter of fact, young man, bring us over two Old-Fashioneds," Angela said, winking at Peggy. "Mi'ze well do it up right." She laughed her hearty laugh. "Let's pretend it's the '60s again. When life and people weren't so crazy."

"Not crazy? Has someone been playing with your head?" Peggy squinted her eyes in disbelief. "Remember social unrest, the Vietnam War . . . the days before Roe versus Wade?"

She reminded her that when they met on that Greyhound twenty-three years ago, they were troubled young women. Now they each had good marriages, successful careers. Peggy had Billy, and Peggy Sue Records. Angela had Al, and her renowned author status. Looking across the table at her longtime friend, Peggy noticed her hair, now worn in what was called a Jheri Curl, was still coal black, even in her late-forties. If she did have any gray hair, Angela, who prided herself in how she looked, would do what it took to hide it.

Angela shrugged. "Guess I'm just feeling nostalgic. The '60s really weren't all that great." She forced a laugh and polished off her drink.

Peggy caught a glimpse of the same obscure expression she'd seen on Angela's face earlier in her office. Something Peggy couldn't quite put her finger on. She wondered if it were thoughts of CJ that prompted Angela's odd frame of mind. December marked the seventh anniversary of his death. And since he died the day before New Year's Eve, Angela's holidays were always blanketed with a dark shroud. Christmas was two weeks away. Yes, that had to be it.

She knew her friend well enough to know she'd have to be patient and wait until this woman, who always kept her own troubles private, was ready to confide in her.

They walked out, agreeing to stop at Ruby's Place. With all the talk over the past and present, they were ready to see little Ruby, who had turned her own negatives—her disappointing music career—into a positive, as a successful business woman. With great live music and a menu fit for almost every palate, Ruby's Place had become the go-to bistro in Sherman Falls.

"Ruby always has two live acts on Saturday," Peggy told Angela as she pulled out of the Brown Derby parking lot. Glancing at her watch, she added, "It's not quite seven. We might still catch Mario, Jr.'s acoustic set he does during dinner hour. Then we can stay and check out the rock band!"

They entered just as Mario was announcing his last song. Heading straight for the bar, Peggy and Angela hopped onto the stools with comfortable leather padding—something the older crowd appreciated—and asked to see Ruby. "Oh, sorry, you just missed her," said the barmaid with beautiful long red hair. She was young, pretty, and stacked, all required features to attract a loyal male clientele. Angela attempted to order Old-Fashioneds, but the girl's blank stare reminded them of the obvious age gap.

Angela threw Peggy a knowing look. "We'll take a glass of rosé," she told the girl who said her name was Kat "with a K." "Probably shouldn't mix, but wine'll help me sleep. Been lacking in that department lately."

"Rosé's fine," Peggy said, wondering why Angela would be having trouble sleeping. Time for her friend to come clean. But just as she opened her mouth to ask what was up, Mario appeared.

"Hey, Mrs. D, how's it goin'?" he asked, one hand on the back of her chair, the other combing his dark hair off his face.

Peggy gestured to Angela. "Hi, Mario, you remember my friend, Angela Johnson?"

He held out his hand. "Sure do. Nice to see you again. How's things in Detroit?"

Angela swirled her chair toward him. "Pretty much the same. Sorry we missed your set."

"Well, if you're still in town Monday night, I'll be here for Open Mic." He waved Kat over. "Get me a Pabst and another glass of vino for these lovely ladies." Then turning back to them, he added, "And on New Year's Eve, I'll be part of a duo, ala Loggins & Messina. We're pretty good." He gave them a confident grin. "But I'm really looking forward to April, when I'll be going on my first tour." He patted Peggy's back. "With this lady's daughter."

Peggy tried to smile, look casual. The last she heard, Dusty was going. What had changed? Both Dusty and Mario played lead guitar. Charlee didn't need two lead guitarists. This was not good news.

Mario noticed her surprise. And ignored it. "Isn't that cool?" He smiled and grabbed for the beer bottle Kat set in front of him. Then answered the silent question. "Dusty's new band got a gig opening for REO Speedwagon around the same time, so Charlee asked me to step in. And I'm glad to do it. It'll be nice to get away. I just wish I could go now. I hate winter."

Peggy's forced smile stayed planted on her face. "Well, you wouldn't want to miss out on your family's holiday celebrations. Your parents really do it up."

He winked at her. "Yeah, well, we *are* Italian." He gave them each a quick one-arm hug and left to pack up for the night.

Despite not seeing Ruby, Peggy and Angela stayed for several hours, chatting and laughing, just like in their younger days. When the evening's band took a break, Peggy glanced at her watch. "Wow, it's after eleven. In my world these days, that's late."

Angela let out a chuckle. "I know what you mean, girlfriend. Let's hit it."

Peggy was digging in her purse for the house key when Billy swung open the door. "Hey, my lovelies, I was just going to send out the troops."

Peggy smiled and put her hand on his cheek. He was still every bit as handsome as when she'd met him at Rockin' Robin's a lifetime ago. His hair was still dark blond, but now his temples were outlined in gray. That made him even more handsome. "Do you know how sexy you are?" she said with a slight slur as she ambled into the foyer. "*Damn* sexy."

He grinned at her, enjoying the compliment. Then his face tightened. "Looks like you two should have taken a cab home."

"Yeeeaah, I think you're right." Peggy turned to her friend with a guilty look. "But Ruby's isn't far. And it was *so* great hanging out together, wasn't it, Ange?"

"You bet'chur ass." Angela threw an arm around Peggy, giving her a tight squeeze back. Then they giggled.

Once they settled on the plush couch by her fireplace, Billy went to make them coffee. When he returned, Angela caught Billy up on the Johnson's current events. After she finished, he stood up and stretched. "I'd love to stay up with you ladies, but I'm beat."

Peggy knew he, too, had been in his office today, rescheduling the afternoon deejay crew.

Angela's cheery mood dimmed as soon as he disappeared up the stairs and Peggy knew her friend was finally going to bring up what she'd been dodging since her arrival.

Angela sat forward on the sofa. Crossed her heavy legs. Pursed her face. Straightened her posture. "Okay, here's the thing."

It may have been the large mug of coffee Billy had urged her to drink, but when Peggy noticed Angela's hands shaking slightly as she brushed away a Jheri-curl from her forehead, she suddenly felt completely sober.

"What's going on, Ange? I've felt it all day." Was it Al? Peggy wondered. After all, Angela's husband *was* overweight and smoked those awful cigars. "Whatever it is, I'm here for you."

"I appreciate that, hon." Angela scooted closer to Peggy on the sofa. "But other than being here, there's not a whole lot you, or anyone, can do."

"Oh, Ange, what is it?" Peggy squeezed her friend's hands.

Angela blinked away tears. "Well, honey, you see, I got cancer."

12. I Love Rock and Roll

Charlee had asked Peggy to arrange her *Genie for Sale* tour so that she'd be somewhere else on Dylan's second birthday. Somewhere fun. And warm. So far, 1982 had brought nothing along those lines. The holidays, as they always were now, was something she just got through. But then came the Grammy nomination, her first, for "Stripped Away." She had allowed herself to get all excited, only to lose to Pat Benatar, which depressed her for weeks.

Added to that was the news of Angela's breast cancer. It didn't seem possible there was even a remote chance that the vibrant, robust, *tough* woman could actually have . . . Charlee couldn't even think the word. They all prayed that the recent mastectomy had removed all threats. But there was no guarantee, not even with the horrific treatments Angela had to endure the next few months.

Once again, Charlee felt helpless against the cruelty of life. She couldn't even control her own career. Her MTV videos no longer played as often because competition for airtime was stiffer than ever now that's the music channel was well established. As a result, Echo's two biggest records off her album had slipped further down *Billboard*. She was glad now that Peggy had encouraged her to get out on the road, become visible again.

How she needed to get the hell away. The first leg of the twenty-six-city tour would kick off the third Friday in March, in San Francisco. The day before Dylan's birthday. Perfect.

With one week to go, Charlee decided to get a head start and organize her wardrobe, get it all packed up. She put Joan Jett's new album on her stereo. She finally had time to listen to it, and with the house all to herself, she could sing along to her favorite rival, thanks to an in-house system allowing the music to be heard through every room. She wanted to get in the mood, feel like the rock star she once was, and hopefully, still was.

Singing "I Love Rock and Roll" loud and strong in the middle of her bedroom, Charlee pulled out her planned outfits from the walk-in closet. Blazers, leggings, leather skirt, crop tops, pairs of spiked heels and boots, and the awesome red leather pantsuit with the shoulder pads and wide silver belt that somehow made her look, and feel, taller. She laid some out on the bed, others across the back of the Vincent Bergere chair. Then she yanked out two suitcases for her casual wear, hair products, cosmetics, and anything else she could squeeze into the bags.

"There," she said out loud. All set for the tour bus.

This would be her first tour since the MissFits' final one, in the fall of '75, seven years ago. She had planned another one in '79, after the release of her first solo album, but then she'd learned she was pregnant. No way would she go on tour with a big belly and swollen ankles. Plus, she knew the rigorous schedule would not be healthy for a mother-to-be. She'd been disappointed because that album had received rave reviews, but had felt there'd be another time soon after. Sooner became later.

Charlee was surprised hearing Joan's rendition of "Bits and Pieces," an old '60's tune from the Dave Clark Five, on the same side as another cover, Tommy James's "Crimson and Clover." Both were excellent. Charlee wondered now why she hadn't thought of doing a few oldies-but-goodies on her album. It sure would've given her less pressure to come up with so many original songs.

Side One was over by the time Charlee finished packing. She sat on her suitcase to get it closed, and it reminded her of that long ago time when she was in a room full of MissFits that last day of their U.S. tour, bouncing up and down on her suitcase for the same reason as now. She recalled how, despite all the other excitement happening to her and her bandmates, Charlee's mind had been mainly on the boy in the room down the hall of the Sheraton. His band, Scarecrow, had been the girl's opening band for the last few cities and by the time they'd arrived in Philadelphia, she and Dusty had made plans to marry.

Now sitting on a much newer suitcase, Charlee closed her eyes, wishing they could go back to that time. She and Dusty had been so in love. Had never even had an argument through the whole four months they'd bounced from city to city. Not through the stress of getting every show right, not even through both having to fend off backstage groupies. Charlee wondered if her husband would fight them off this time while he was gone on tour. One that wasn't hers.

He'd told her about his decision to join the REO tour without even *asking*. Not even after she reminded him that she had put off extending her own tour through the U.K. because she didn't want them apart for that long. When she pried as to his reasoning, he'd simply stated that he "had to do it."

"I just don't think touring together would be good for us right now," he'd said. "I think we should be apart for a bit. They only need me for a few months. You'll be back soon after that, and then we can regroup. Maybe take off together somewhere exotic. Like a second honeymoon." He'd added that sweet smile that always made her loins ache.

That smile gave her images of the two of them lying on a secluded beach, making intense love like they used to. The thought of a romantic getaway after being apart so long had pacified her, erased all the other feelings burrowing beneath her skin. Still, she'd asked him, "You believe absence really makes the heart grow fonder?"

Gazing at her with those hazel eyes, he'd replied, "Yes, actually I do."

So what could she say to that? If he felt the need to break away for a while, instead of suggesting a divorce—which had been her fear of late—then what choice did she have? Besides, part of her had to agree. Being home together lately was only tearing them more apart.

Despite her uneasiness about their separation, Charlee couldn't help feeling excited about being out on stage again. That was the best part of being a singer. She loved songwriting, too, but that was a lot of work. Of course, so was performing, but she loved the art of it, working the crowd, getting them emotionally involved, whether it was through a balls-to-the-wall tune, or a slow tender love song. It was the artist's job to play them like a marionette. To take them on a musical ride. She couldn't wait to get out there, be a part of rock and roll again. Make people scream. Be a star again.

Charlee lugged the heavy Samsonites into the hallway and set them in the corner. Whatever else she needed down the road, she could buy. It would give her a chance to shop in different cities and towns, which should be fun. She didn't enjoy shopping by herself, but as the only female on that bus, she'd have to make do. She didn't know a single man, certainly not her crew, who enjoyed the fine art, and plain fun, of shopping.

Standing in the hall, hands on hips, she decided to get Dusty to haul the luggage down the long stairway when he returned from his practice session. Though she knew she'd hear about how he'd wanted to install an elevator when they'd first bought the house. She had scowled at the notion, saying that home elevators were for old people. Now she could see his reasoning—just like his reasoning to go on the road. Maybe he was right. They both needed to get away. She began to wonder if her husband was more right than wrong about their issues and that she was letting her stubbornness get the best of her. Of them.

Maybe she could change her attitude, lighten up a bit.

She turned and started down the stairs. Just as she hit the last step, the front doorbell chimed. She peered through the peephole and had to blink twice at the image of the young girl standing on the porch, the yellow cab behind her pulling out of the drive. Oh, jeez, not *now*? Dusty's sister had been talking about coming out ever since Dylan was born, and though Charlee looked forward to getting to know her better, the girl couldn't have picked a worse time.

Charlee inhaled a breath and opened the door.

"Surprise!" Diana greeted, arms extending. She stopped mid-flight, noticing Charlee's face. "Oh, I hope I didn't come at a bad time. I wanted to surprise Dusty . . . and you." Her arms fell back down to her sides, one hand resting on her big straw shoulder bag that looked like something from a Philippine's flea market. "I tried calling when I got in the airport, but no one answered. You see, I wanted to find out what you guys were up to first, and was going to say that I was calling from home, that way I could time my arrival just so and make it a big surprise for you guys, but when you didn't pick up, I figured, well, wherever you were, you'd be back, so I just got me a cab and . . . well, here I am!"

My, she talked fast.

Taking a break, Diana raised her eyebrows in an effort at a sorrowful apology, then grinned. "Guess I should've given more warning, huh? I forget not everyone likes surprises like I do."

"No, no, it's fine." Charlee gave her a hug, feeling bad at her initial reaction. "Come on in."

That was when she noticed the suitcases behind her. Two large ones, the other a sizable makeup case. Was the girl planning on staying the whole summer? Did she not remember she and Dusty would be gone most of that time?

Well, she *had* told Diana she was welcome "anytime." Charlee forced a smile and tried to sound delighted to see her. When Diana took another breath, Charlee said, "I'm sorry I didn't hear the phone. I was packing for my tour and I had the music on." She took her arm. "Really, it's great to see you."

Diana talked on as they brought the bags inside. "I just thought it'd be fun, you know, and I wanted to see Dusty before he went on the road, and with me starting college and . . . *Oh*, this is lovely," she said, gazing around the expansive foyer. "I knew you guys had a beautiful house, but wow!" Then she whipped around to Charlee and squeezed her tight. "Oh, I'm so glad to see you again. Do you realize we haven't seen each other since before you guys were married?"

Charlee winced a bit. She and Dusty had escaped to an island off the coast of Maine, and at the last minute decided to marry there, depriving both families of a proper wedding. That was how much in love they were. They wanted to keep even that special day to themselves.

As Diana rambled on, Charlee found herself smiling. Now that she had gotten over the "surprise," she couldn't help feeling happy to see the bubbly girl. Diana, who resembled Carly Simon, with her long, tousled golden hair and big bright eyes was a breath of fresh air.

Charlee waited for an opening to talk, then quickly interjected, "Just leave your things here. Let's go catch up. Last time I talked to your dad, he said you're planning to enroll in Cal State?"

"Yep, though not sure of my major yet," Diana said, following Charlee into the kitchen.

She hopped up on the one of the bar stools at the island counter as Charlee opened the fridge. "I was just going to make myself a Margarita. And now that you're twenty-one"—she threw her a wink—"you can join me. We'll celebrate your arrival!"

She might as well enjoy Diana now, Charlee thought, since she'd be gone most of the time the girl is here.

"Great, I love those!" Diana leaned forward, hands folded, elbows on the marble countertop. "You said you were packing? I didn't think you were leaving yet."

"I'm not. Not till Thursday, but I needed to get it all done ahead of time. I had to get another guitarist 'cause Dusty took that other gig, you know, so we'll be spending all next week practicing with Mario, his replacement." She stayed busy mixing the drinks, hoping she appeared nonchalant. No sense in having Diana know she was still disappointed, and a tad mad, that Dusty wasn't joining her.

"Oh, I do hope we can get *some* time together before you leave," Diana said, with a frown. "You're my only sister-in-law, you know."

Charlee smiled. How nice that sounded.

They talked easily for the next hour while Charlee refilled their glasses and fried up chicken for the Fajitas she decided to make. Charlee was putting the food on a platter, buffet-style, when she heard Dusty come through the door.

"We're in here!" she called out.

He entered the kitchen and his mouth gaped open. "Di? Oh my God." He rushed over and gave her a big bear hug.

Charlee had to stand and wait for her own, but how could she mind? The siblings hadn't seen each other in more than six years. And the wait was worth it. Dusty's glee over seeing his baby sister extended to his wife now, and he grabbed her with gusto. She squeezed back just as hard, not wanting to let this moment go. How she'd missed that kind of enthusiasm from him. Right there, she wanted to beg him not to leave her. Beg him to go upstairs and pack for *her* tour, not REO's. But Diana blew the thought away.

"I told Dad I'd be staying till after Memorial Day when you leave for your tour."

Charlee piped in, handed Dusty a drink. "I'm glad you were surprised. Thought for sure you'd see her suitcases in the living room." *And wait till you see how many.*

"Naw, my mind was on food." He sniffed the pan on the stove. "I haven't eaten all day. But, man, the band sounds tight. Hope we don't outshine REO." He grinned at them, adding, "Well, actually I do."

How Charlee loved this side of him. Later, as they sat chatting in the living room, Dusty finally caught sight of his sister's bags and Diana admitted her lengthier stay. "I know you all will be away this summer, but I was kinda hoping I could stay on a bit. Dad's driving me crazy. Getting to be a crotchety old man."

So there it was. Charlee wasn't sure how she felt about someone living in their house while they were away. Her first instinct was no. She barely knew the girl, and this was her home, her sanctuary. She and Dusty would have to discuss it, maybe think of some excuse, but then she heard him say, "I don't see why not," without even looking at her. "It'll be nice for us, too, someone holding down the fort."

Another strike against her. Didn't her feelings count at all anymore?

Yet as the evening wore on, Charlee's ambivalence began to dissipate. She found herself softening toward her sister-in-law, whose cheery personality was infectious. For the next few hours, Diana had them both laughing—when was the last time they laughed together?—as she talked about her youthful escapades and humorous dating failures. "I'm hoping the guys are more mature here," she said at one point, to which Dusty and Charlee looked at each other and said in unison, "Don't count on it," sharing another chuckle.

Charlee could tell Diana didn't have a clue there was trouble between her and Dusty. And how could she? All night they sat snuggling on the couch, smiling at each other, enjoying their unexpected company.

By the time they got Diana settled in the guest room, Charlee and Dusty fell into bed tired, but also anxious. They wrapped their arms around each other, and as Journey's "Open Arms" played softly in the background, began making love, erasing all the wrong notes they'd hit in the past weeks. It had been that long since they'd even touched each other and now they embraced with gentle kisses that grew more powerful, their movements in synch. Best of all, their union was intense again—as if they'd truly *needed* each other.

If sex was like this after just a few weeks of barely touching each other, how amazing it might be after being apart for months. As much as she hated to admit it, Charlee thought, as they lay spooning in bed after, that Dusty might be right this time, too.

13. Hungry Heart

After a great start in San Francisco, then Sacramento, Oakland, and Bakersfield, the U. S. tour hit Los Angeles at the end of May. Charlee was thrilled for a chance to see her Uncle Patrick, now a photographer for *American Rocker* and living outside Hollywood. However, the visit was relegated to quick hugs backstage before they each had to get to their respective jobs. She had wanted more time with his wife, Nina, too, but the tour bus was leaving right after the concert, heading for San Diego, then Houston, then on to whatever the next city would be. After all, that was rock and roll.

Charlee surprised herself with how easily it all came back to her. Her nerves had been shaky at first, but when she realized the enthusiastic crowd was ready for anything she had to give, she gave them her all. By the second concert, she was entrenched in Echo mode and couldn't wait for each show to begin. During those months of psyching herself up for this, she had hoped it would be as fun as she'd remembered, but it was so much more than that. She'd forgotten about the goose bumps that tingle through your body before going out on stage. And the adrenalin rush that surges through your veins through the entire concert. And the encore! That was always the best. To stand there on that big stage looking out at the mass of people, your *fans,* all cheering and honoring you by lighting up their Bics . . .

The whole experience was exhilarating. Just what she'd needed. The pain of the past two years had settled somewhere deep in the recesses of her soul, where it remained quiet, undisturbed.

When Fourth of July hit, however, so did a sudden longing for home. But wasn't that normal? Holidays often produce homesickness when you're away. Charlee tried sounding upbeat that morning on the phone with her mother and Billy, but then, Peggy told her about the party they were having and all who'd be there. Then she talked to Aunt Libby, who told her how Jack was getting his first pack of sparklers. And Ruby, who was headed to the Sherman Falls Summer Festival. Ever since she was little, Charlee always loved that small town event.

By the time Dusty called her that afternoon from Miami, she was crying. She felt lonely, she told him, despite all the people around her. Although he said all the right words, they didn't feel that sincere. He sounded like he was enjoying himself an awful lot without her. He talked about the rock stars he was meeting, and that their next stop was Boulder, Colorado, a place Charlee had longed to add to her own tour, but hadn't worked out. Then came the clincher.

"I'm off to Hal Levin's party now. He's the hottest music producer in Florida," Dusty said. "I'll try calling you again later." She didn't like the word *try,* and Dusty seemed to sense it. Maybe due to the dead silence. "Ah, I'm sorry, Sunshine. You know yourself this is all part of it and you gotta make the best of it. Before we know it, it'll all be just a memory and we'll be old and gray, with all these great road stories, thinking back on all the awesome opportunities we had."

Oh, yeah, he was definitely having more fun than her. And part of her hated him for it. Despite the fact that he said such luscious words to her before hanging up. "I can't wait to hold you again. To rip off your clothes and make mad passionate love to you. To stay in bed for a whole weekend with you . . . I really do miss you." Then he sang the Styx song, "Babe," to her, which made her cry, though in a good way. After the last note, he added, "Remember, I only have another few weeks and I'll be home. And soon after that, you will be, too. Then we can lock ourselves up in the house and live on rice cakes and love."

That got her laughing. She'd tried going on a "Rice Cake" diet before her tour and it was like eating Styrofoam. "Let's stick to Cracker Jacks." She hung up thinking of simple pleasures like that. Home, watching TV, sharing snacks with her husband.

As much as she had enjoyed those first few months, being on the road this time was a whole different experience than when she was a starry-eyed teen. She was a married woman now, with a different mindset. Yet, that was normal, too. She needed to remind herself how lucky she was. Dusty was right. (Again.)Best enjoy this time. It wasn't going to last forever. She was lucky it was happening at all.

By the next concert, Charlee forgot her bout with homesickness. She reveled in her rocker status, basking in the love she felt at every concert. For the first time in years she was totally independent, and that was liberating. She pushed away all dark thoughts. She was free. Confident. Strong. With no immediate problems or worries.

God, it made her want to be on the road forever.

They were halfway through the Midwest—Milwaukee— when it first happened. Charlee's crew had a day off and gone separate ways. John, the bass player, and Mikey, the drummer, took off to unleash some energy at a bar called the Rock Dog, while she and Mario spent the afternoon shopping for various needs. Charlee envied the guys because as her tour backup band, they were hardly recognized when they were out and about. "Echo," on the other hand, had to dress in disguise—auburn wig, fake freckles dotted with brown eyeliner, and the big-rimmed glasses everyone was wearing nowadays, which helped her blend in any crowd. She also refrained from wearing her trademark hoop earrings. She didn't want people coming up to her in a mall, or a park, or especially not in a bar where alcohol fueled folks' confidence, giving them bogus permission to interrupt a pool game, asking for an autograph, wanting to become best friends.

Walking around the Northridge Mall with Mario, she'd been glad for his company, though times like these, she missed having girl time. Normally, she liked being "one of the guys," but shopping with a man wasn't much fun. When she stopped in front of Fredrick's of Hollywood, she had to shoo Mario away. She wanted to buy new lingerie, something sexy to wear for when she got home to Dusty, amp up their reunion.

Pointing out a record store across the way, she said, "Why don't you go there while I go in here?"

"Ah, come on, Charlee, I've seen women's underwear before," Mario had said with a grin and a wink.

She laughed and shoved him away. "Go on, you. And while you're there, get me that new Huey Lewis album." She let out a sigh. "And okay, might as well pick up the Stevie Nicks one, too." She'd held up a hand to silence what might come out of his mouth. He knew she had not been happy that *Rolling Stone* had just named Stevie "The Reigning Queen of Rock and Roll." Still, she loved the songs on her new album.

At Fredrick's, Charlee found a number of items she knew would thrill her husband. Not just outfits, but sprays, lotions and even an interesting sex game "designed for lovers."

The day had been fun. No one had recognized her and the shopping spree had given her a feeling of normalcy.

Then Mario kissed her.

Looking back, she should've seen it coming. And maybe she did, but ignored the signs. True, she and Mario had been spending a lot of time together, shopping, eating, sight-seeing when they could. And although Charlee knew she was attracted to him, she also knew they had bonded solely as friends. He was easy to be with, and he often confided in her. Like when he told her about his last relationship and how he'd lost Linda, who had found out that he'd been seeing Ruby's bartender, Kat, on the side.

"I know it was really wrong, and *really* stupid," he'd told Charlee over burgers and beers. "But Kat kept coming on to me, and one night, well, I was angry at Linda for something I can't even recall, and threw caution to the wind." He shook his head. "Lesson learned. I don't want to be a cheater. It's not a good feeling."

But apparently, he didn't much care about someone else being a cheater.

That evening, she, Mario, John, Mikey and their road manager, Ken, had all joined in for some poker. She'd stayed up later than she'd wanted to. The guys were doing cocaine, something she'd wanted no part of. She prided herself in her resistance of the drug that everyone seemed to be doing these days. But that night, numerous shots of "Hawaiian Shooters" had weakened her stance. It was just too easy with that white pile there on the table, and she wanted to have fun, too.

Before she knew it, someone said it was after four in the morning.

She jumped up, sending coins flying. "Holy shit, I'm going to bed. We got a concert tomorrow night! You guys better hit it, too."

"Hey, we've got all day to sleep," Mikey said, retrieving his winnings from the floor.

She shook her head. "Not all day! We have to be at the coliseum for sound check by three, remember?"

That last statement was ignored as Ken slapped down a full house and everyone yelled out in protest as he scooped up the tall pile of coins. Charlee turned and stomped toward the back of the bus to her room. Was this why the last few concerts hadn't sold out? Had partying begun to take precedence over the shows? She made a mental note to have a meeting the next day.

She was just ready to slam her door when she turned to see Mario standing right behind her. She gasped in surprise. "Mario? What?"

He just stood there, shining that charismatic grin of his, white teeth against a bronzed face. She'd started asking him why he'd followed her there when he casually took hold of her shoulders and kissed her.

It wasn't a long, lingering kiss. It wasn't particularly passionate. "Just wanted to say good night," he said, his dark eyes boring into hers.

But then he kissed her again. Just a quick, friendly peck on the lips. "Night, Charlee, sleep tight." Then he turned and left.

Of course she couldn't sleep after that. The rest of the night, she lay there, half shamefully thrilled, half put off at Mario's nerve. What was his purpose in kissing her, *on the lips*? Or did it mean anything? It probably had been just a friendly goodnight kiss. Well, technically, two.

Why read too much into it? They *were* friends. How could they not be, after spending every day together for months? He probably just didn't want her going to bed upset like that. Maybe she was making something out of nothing. She sometimes did that.

She remembered that night she'd dreamt of him, and still felt guilty about it, despite dismissing it as "just a silly dream." Yet she couldn't erase the growing suspicion that something more heated was developing on his end, too. Even minus the kisses, she could tell by the way Mario looked at her that he saw more than a friend.

This was her fault. She had needed someone to share the excitement, the ups, and downs of being on the road. There weren't any other females around, and Mario was ever present. So she had encouraged this deeper friendship between them.

Until now, she hadn't known Mario that well. She'd met him at his parents' restaurant. And a few times, she and Dusty had gone with Peggy and Billy to the Cirino's famous house get-togethers. Then they started going to see him play at Ruby's, and it was always very casual. So when Mario offered to be available for the tour, Charlee was confident enough in his talent to hire him.

Tossing around wide awake in her bed—thanks to those lines of coke she'd succumbed to—Charlee revisited the day when she'd gone to Mario's place, before they'd left for the tour. He'd been excited about buying his first house and anxious to show it off to her.

"After all, you're helping me make the payments," he'd quipped over the phone that afternoon. So she stopped over on her way to say goodbye to Ruby. He'd given her a tour of the spacious ranch home. Including the bedroom. He opened the door with flair, saying, "And this is where the magic happens." His wide grin and wink made her giggle like some schoolgirl, and she'd tried even then to will away the warm body blush making its way to her breasts, and other parts. The room was surprising spotless, but clearly male. A lot of male. Black and . . . plush. With a life-sized velvet portrait of Elvis above his dresser.

That made her really laugh. "You're kidding, right?"

He chuckled, pulled out a Camel. "Hey, it's cool," he said, lighting up. "Got it last year when me and my buddies took a trip to southern California and spent a day in Tijuana. Everyone needs a velvet Elvis, don'cha think?"

She didn't answer because her eyes had shifted to the other wall. Above his king-sized waterbed, covered with a zebra-print satin quilt, hung another velvet portrait, one of a nude woman. The beautiful girl with long dark hair draping across her shoulders, sat erect with legs tucked under a perfectly formed rump, her perky breasts, uplifted and proud.

Charlee felt her cheeks blaze with heat and she quickly turned toward the door. "You keep your room very neat," was all she'd managed to say as she walked straight out hoping he couldn't see her telling face.

She knew that Mario was a ladies' man, a natural-born flirt. But she also knew, or had always thought, that he was safe territory. Because he came from a good family and had morals. That was before she'd learn of his tryst with Kat. She remembered, too, one night at Ruby's when a woman everyone knew was married, had come on to him after his set and he'd brushed her away. Charlee had been impressed by that. Later he explained, "Why get myself into that kind of trouble when there're all these lovely *single* ladies out there?" he'd said, sweeping his arm across the room.

She'd actually felt slighted by the statement knowing she was attracted to him and wondered if he was at all toward her. Appalling, she knew, but was just a little mental game she played. A mere fantasy. *Safe territory.*

Now she was baffled. Were his flirtatious ways just in fun, in friendship, or was he trying to convey something else to her? And if so, then she, *the married one*, would have to be the one to nip it in the bud, as they say.

Still, she could be wrong. What if it *was* all innocent? How embarrassing it would be if she confronted him, only to find out he wasn't at all interested in her that way. She didn't want Mario rolling his eyes at her imaginings, and blame it on a puffed-up rock star ego, thus putting a dent in their friendship.

The next day, she tried acting like nothing had happened. And in turn, he did, too. She decided then it had been nothing. How silly of her. Being away for so long, she'd started fantasizing about all kinds of things. And that wasn't always a bad thing. She'd written two new songs on the road because of it, that she planned to include on the next album.

Inspired, she thought she might write another song, one that dealt with feeling alone in a crowd of people. Although they hadn't talked about it, Charlee suspected Mario felt the same way. In the beginning, he'd had a few fun flings with backstage groupies, and would hit the town afterward for a few drinks at some local pub. But lately, he gave the impression he was bored with it all. He seemed to want to spend his free time with his band mates, his close pals. And Charlee had simply become one of them. No big thing.

But then it happened again.

This time, after the concert in Kansas City. They'd all been overjoyed because it had been the first complete sell-out in the last four cities. She'd been so happy about the resurgence that she gladly signed autographs for fans before making her way to the upstairs VIP lounge. After several glasses of champagne, she'd flung a finger at her disciplined self, and once again joined the others in partaking of the white powder, making several trips to the mirror on the large coffee table.

As a result, they'd stayed up all night knowing they had the next day off, and the luxury of a hotel room. Charlee slipped away while everyone was engaged in mindless conversations and took the elevator up to her suite. Once in her room, she kicked off her stilettos, washed off her makeup, and wiggled out of her tight black sequined tank top. She couldn't wait to fall into a bed that wasn't mobile. She was brushing out the gelled spikes in her hair when there was a knock at the door.

She whipped around, then threw down the brush. *Who wanted what now?* She squinted into the peephole. *Aw, shit.* The tank still in her hand, she wiggled back into it, straightened her twisted skirt, patted down her messy hair, and swung the door open before she lost her nerve.

"Hi."

Mario stood there grinning, and, despite his blood-shot eyes from having been up for nearly twenty-four hours, just as she'd been, his five o'clock shadow made him more handsome than she ever recalled.

The familiar warm body blush began thrusting through her like an air pump. She hated her response to that attractive grin, that toned body. How many times did she have to tell herself they were just *friends?*

"What are you doing here?" She tried sounding indignant, but a hint of excitement leaked out. Her voice was deep, hoarse—a result of singing, then partying all night, which also made her sound much too seductive.

"Can I come in for a minute?"

No! "Uh, yeah, sure."

She shut the door behind him, her eyes focused on his smooth dark shiny hair, longer now because he hadn't cut it since the start of the tour. She could tell he'd just finished carefully slicking it back like . . . like . . . she giggled inwardly . . . well, like Elvis.

"I can't sleep."

"Whad'dya mean? You've hardly had a chance to try. Didn't you just leave after me?"

He nodded a bit sheepishly. "Well, yeah, I didn't think you noticed." That grin again. *Shiiiitttt.* He then grabbed her shoulders and kissed her so hard, so passionately she nearly lost her breath. Now there was no mistaking, misreading his intentions.

"I want you. So bad," he whispered, pushing her against the door and pressing himself against her. She nearly blacked out for a minute from lack of oxygen as he held her captive against the wall, his lips exploring hers. Cupping her neck with one hand, he slid the other along the side of her body. Her own body responded because it had been so long since she'd been touched.

"I *want* you. I know you're feeling it, too. Please, Charlee, please."

His passionate pleading weakened her resolve as he began to caress her body. The soft, heated words against her ear made her legs tremble like a filly's.

The scenario seemed familiar. She'd been nineteen, and had just returned from the American summer tour with the MissFits. She and Dusty had snuck out of a hotel ballroom party and ran into an elevator, kissing and grabbing, the whole way to the 22nd floor where he had booked a room. They'd been so anxious for each other. So in love.

So in lust.

"Oh my God! What the hell are we doing?" She pushed Mario away liked he'd struck her. Her force was so strong, it threw him off balance and he tumbled backward onto the leather couch. "Get out," she said in a shaky voice. "Now!"

She knew she had shaken him up as he sprung from the cushion, combed his hair with his hands, and looked away like a reprimanded puppy. When he reached the door knob, he murmured, "I'm sorry, Charlee. Really I am." Then he shut the door behind him.

Charlee woke up to the proverbial hangover, but the throbbing headache was nothing compared to the throbbing stream of guilt slithering through her veins. She felt so ashamed. Drinking, doing coke, and then . . . How could she have even let Mario touch her like that? What the hell was wrong with her?

She sequestered herself in her room most of the day, lying naked under the sheets, thinking. Maybe it wasn't either of their faults. Mario was used to having any woman of his choice, and he *had* been high. And so had she. Mix alcohol and drugs with loneliness and you have yourself a recipe for . . . weakness. She knew, had witnessed, many of those kinds of incidents. She was all too aware of the decadent behavior on the road, the one-night stands, the bed-hopping with whomever happened to be available at the time, and she'd always been glad she and Dusty were married and had avoided all that.

But that was back when nothing stood between them. Now it seemed everything did.

Still, she'd never thought she'd ever be tempted to so much as kiss another man when she was so committed to Dusty. What was she becoming? *Who* was she becoming? Surely not the same girl she had been when they'd met. Not the girl he had married, or that happy mother-to-be, so anxious to bear his child.

But then, that horrible person took Dylan away. *That's* when she'd turned into *this*. A rock star who partied into the night, drinking, doing drugs, surrendering to sexual temptation.

Well, okay. She sighed with relief. At least they hadn't gone too far. But the Charlee she had once been would've slapped him away at his first touch. Yes, she had changed. And that fact frightened her more than anything. She recalled Dusty saying once in a heated argument that while he still loved her, he didn't always like her at times. Now she knew just how he felt.

Charlee crawled out of bed when she saw the nightstand clock. Half-past one. She took a couple of aspirins, glad she had nothing pressing to do today, other than get herself back on the tour bus by four to head out toward Indiana.

Well, there was one more thing. She had a phone call to make. Not to Dusty. To his sister.

The Echo tour had four more cities to go until the end— Indianapolis, Chicago, New York, and Cleveland—and no way was she going to leave herself vulnerable again. Diana was still staying at their house, and now would be there indefinitely. She'd decided to stay in Cleveland and attend a veterinarian school. Charlee thanked her lucky stars that Diana's career indecisiveness had led to her enrolling late, allowing her free time until October.

Charlee picked up the phone and dialed. "Diana. How's it going? Yeah, I know. It's lonely here, too. So hey, I got an idea. Since you've got some time on your hands, how'd you like to keep me company on the last few legs of my tour? Yes, really. No, don't worry. I'll cover it. I'll have a ticket for you at the airport and will meet you in Indianapolis. Oh, you're welcome. Really, the pleasure's all mine. Okay, talk to you then."

Charlee clicked the button and redialed. Dusty was staying in an Oklahoma City Holiday Inn. He answered on the second ring.

"Hi, it's me."

"Hey, Sunshine."

Visualizing that grin of his made her miss him that much more.

"Listen, Dust, I have two things to tell you. First, I invited your sister to come and finish up the tour with me. Second, I love you madly and counting the days till we're both home. Together." Then she asked him to hold on. She turned up the boombox she'd requested for her room and played the first song of the new mix tape she had made for him. "Faithfully," by Journey. "This is our new song, Cowboy. I want you to know you will always be my one and only."

He listened a bit before responding. She hoped he wasn't reading too much into it. Like her guilt. "Aw, yes, that's a beauty. And so are you, Sunshine." His tone reassured any self-doubt. "I'm so ready for home. And you." His words made her heart pound with happiness.

They talked some more and when they finally hung up, she did a little dance, with not a stitch on.

Things were going to be just fine! In just a short time, she and Dusty would be reunited, and it would be just like starting over, like the John Lennon song. She shimmied toward the bathroom, hopped into the shower, and scrubbed away the layers of guilt, pain, and loneliness, watching them all swirl down the drain.

14. Shake it Up

Charlee hadn't called Diana so much to keep Mario at bay, but more to keep her own weak temptations away. The relief and resolve she'd felt the day she called Diana, then Dusty, gave her a needed shot of steel. As the bus wound through the next few cities, Charlee was too busy with Diana to let that Italian seep into her skin.

By the time they reached New York City, around three in the morning, Charlee and her sister-in-law had become close friends. Now they stood together, leaning over the dashboard looking out at the glittering city though the large window. "I have to call my mom after we get some shut-eye, see if we sold out," Charlee said as the bus pulled in front of the Hotel Chelsea.

"You kiddin'?" Diana shook her blonde head. "This is New York! You know they love you here. And you're playin' Madison Square Garden! Only the very best play there." She pushed Charlee's shoulder away. "Crazy girl." Then she pointed to the majestic hotel and cast-iron balconies. "And look! We're at the Chelsea. How cool is that?"

Charlee let out a laugh. Diana had a bit of groupieness in her that Charlee found refreshing. She remembered when she'd been like that. She had been just as starry-eyed during that first MissFits tour. She even remembered how her hands shook when she was introduced to Bruce Springsteen backstage when she was eighteen. And how thrilling it was to play to her hometown crowd at one of the "World Series of Rock" concerts at the Cleveland Stadium. All that now seemed a lifetime ago.

Maybe Diana can bring back the old Charlee.

They'd purposely arrived late at night to avoid a slew of onlookers. Charlee knew whenever a big tour bus parked in front of the infamous Chelsea, there'd be spectators, and cameras. She sure didn't want anyone seeing her now. After tossing and turning all night on that bus, she resembled Steven Tyler. Not a good look for her.

As the boys unloaded the suitcases and gear, she recalled how adamant she'd been about staying at this particular hotel. For years, she had read about all the "characters" who had resided there through its 100-year history. The address was renowned for famous artists, writers, actors, and musicians. Notables like Mark Twain, Arthur Miller, Janis Joplin, Patti Smith, and Bob Dylan, whose son, Jesse, was born during the singer's stay there.

There were also two famous people who never left there alive. Charlee's favorite poet, Dylan Thomas, had contacted pneumonia and died in one of the rooms in 1953. And there was that hideous stabbing of Sex Pistol bass player Sid Vicious's girlfriend, Nancy Spungen, in 1978.

Despite the horror stories, Charlee's curiosity, and yes, ego, demanded she be one of the stars on that historic roster. But now, as she and Diana said goodnight to the guys and headed to their room, she wondered if her status was even worthy.

Referring back to her and Diana's earlier conversation, Charlee said as they entered, "I hope you're right about the sellout. You gotta remember, Van Halen just played the Garden a few days ago. There's probably still a lot of metal fans here."

Diana frowned at her, dumping her luggage where she stood. "Man, Charlee, you worry too much."

That she did. Charlee smiled at her new friend. "Yeah, well, I get that from my mother."

Charlee felt a bit better when she noticed the advertisement of her and her band in one of the magazines on the table in their room. She recalled the phone interview a few months back for the October *New York Rocker* magazine. She made a mental note to pick up a copy while she was here. Diana was right. She shouldn't get herself worked up. Instead, she pulled out the bag of cheese and crackers she'd taken from the bus fridge and held it up. "Want some? I'm famished, and I can't sleep on an empty stomach."

"Sure. I'm not the least bit tired." Diana grabbed a cracker and plopped onto one of the beds. "I call this one."

"Have at it." Charlee gave her a wicked smile. "Though I do believe that's the very bed where one of the famous Chelsea ghosts has been known to appear."

Diana sprang up. "Hey now, don't start that!" She gave the bed a questioning glance, then sat back down. "I'm trying to forget those gruesome stories you told me about this place."

"Well, there *are* some ghost tales circulating. I find it rather fascinating."

"You would. You and your *spirits*." Diana threw the Ritz at her. Missed.

Charlee grinned. She recalled the other night in Chicago when they'd both had too much to drink and Charlee started talking about baby Dylan, and said that she was thinking about going to a psychic for help. Diana's comment now made her embarrassed she even believed in such things as paranormal activity.

"Well, you should read up on it," Charlee said, defending her stance. "There's a lot that can't be denied."

Diana rolled her eyes, jumped off the bed, and snapped opened her suitcase. She pulled out a nightgown, her crimping iron, a bag of makeup, then yelled out, "Oh! I almost forgot." She shook out two wigs. One light blonde, the other, a bright shade of red. "I got these the other day to surprise you. I figure we can walk around the city here without being bothered by all your fanatical fans." She put on the platinum hairpiece, styled in a wild-looking shag, and checked her image on the wall mirror above the dresser. "So whad'dya think. Do I look like Blondie?" she said, referring to the singer's bushy hair on her new album, *The Hunter*.

"Yeah, sure." Charlee humored her by lifting the curly red wig out of the plastic bag. She tucked her dark shoulder-length hair underneath the cap and joined Diana in front of the mirror. "And I look like Danny Bonaduce."

Diana let out a roar. "Yeah! Actually you do!"

"Whaaat?" She shot her a feigned look of horror. "That's it, I'm kicking you off the tour," she said, shoving her onto the bed.

"Aaahh, I know you don't mean it, you love my company."

Charlee fell back onto the bed beside her sister-in-law and smiled. What could she say? They both knew it was true.

To Charlee's great relief, the concert had indeed sold out and the crowd's energy sparked her band's best performance since their debut in 'Frisco. As the tour wound down, Charlee felt invigorated, knowing she was getting closer to her home.

The day after that successful show, her band and road crew sat at a long table at the Tick Tock Diner for brunch. Charlee couldn't bring herself to wear the wig Diana had bought, but the big-rimmed glasses, no makeup, and floppy hat seemed to work just fine at keeping fans from recognizing her. She had an interview that afternoon with MTV Veejay, Mark Goodman, but after that, she was free. Before arriving in New York, they'd all agreed to give themselves three extra days in the city before returning to Cleveland, where they'd give their last 1982 performance. But now Charlee wanted to rescind on those plans. Dusty was home from his own tour, and all she wanted was him.

"Let's head home tomorrow, guys, so we can enjoy time with our families before the Cleveland show," Charlee said, with crossed fingers under the table. She was hoping they were as homesick as she was.

"I'm not ready." Mario sat across from her, his dark eyes looking at her with what appeared to be regret. She knew it wasn't because they weren't going sightseeing.

Charlee quickly looked down at her coffee cup. She had successfully kept Mario at arms-length since Diana came on board, but last night on stage, he kept angling next to her, rubbing his back against her as she sang. Playing it up for the audience, sure, but she knew it was also playing it up for her. She could still feel his hot breath against her face from when they'd shared the mic for the vocals on a couple of the songs.

Before she could respond to his comment, he sat upright in his seat and added, "I told Diana I'd take her to the zoo tomorrow." He pointed his fork at Diana sitting beside her, took a sip from his Pepsi, then added, "Buddy of mine told me they're less crowded on Tuesdays, and with her wanting to be a vet and all, she's gotta see the famous Bronx Zoo."

Charlee's head spun toward Diana, who smiled guiltily, and shrugged. "Well, I've always wanted to go there, so I thought, while we're here—"

Traitor! Charlee screamed in her head. But then she had to remind herself Diana didn't know anything about Mario and her, and hadn't a clue that she was supposed to be Charlee's blockade against temptation. Yet why hadn't Diana mentioned this little side trip? Oh God, did she have a crush on Mario?

"Yeah, and I'm going to CBGB's tonight," Drummer Mike piped in. "The Dead Boys are playin', so me and Stiv are gettin' together afterward and that'll take me into at least another day," he said, raising his eyebrows and grinning.

She knew what that meant. Stiv Bators and the other band members, former Cleveland boys, were notorious for partying all night, into the next day, and then some.

Clearly she was outnumbered. She grabbed the napkin in her lap and threw it down on the table. "Fine. Just fine." Then she got up and left. In the corner of her eye, she could see the stunned waitress standing there holding her Eggs Benedict. She nodded in Mario's direction. "He'll eat it." She told her, then smirked. "He'll take the check, too."

Pushing the glass door open, Charlee practically ran down the street, hoping the tears wouldn't let loose till she got to the hotel room. Despite the great concert the night before, she felt like a little girl whose Barbie was yanked from her and no one even noticed. Everyone had their own busy lives, and she was alone. She needed to go home. She needed her husband.

The manager greeted her as she stepped into the Chelsea, but she brushed past him without a word, focused on the elevator ahead. She stood hitting the Up button, heaving from frustration. She just wanted to get to her room. What was taking so long? She pressed the button again, and looked over at the stairway door. Maybe the workout would release some of the gnawing angst plunging through her. Could she really sprint all the way to the twelfth floor?

"Excuse me, lovely lady." The voice behind her gave her a jolt.

Oh great, a groupie. Just what she needed. She didn't want to turn around, but could she just ignore the guy? Hardly. She spun around to tell him, sorry, but she was having a bad day and preferred not to be bothered.

The elevator door opened just as she saw his face.

"Hi, gorgeous."

"Oh my God!" Her scream echoed through the foyer. Dusty's grin matched her joy. Her heart pounded as she stared at this handsome man, her hands clasping her mouth in happy amazement. What a beautiful sight for her sore, tired eyes. His soft hazel eyes, now blue as a river against a tan face, his chestnut hair, golden blond from the summer sun, loose curls brushing his neck. He was more buff, too, thanks to his morning gym workouts, now part of any tour. She grabbed him by his Steely Dan shirt and pulled him into the empty elevator.

As she began kissing his mouth, cheeks, ears, neck, Dusty responded by pushing the stop button. But not for long. A few minutes later, Charlee hit the elevator button again to the 12th floor. They were both anxious to get into her hotel suite.

Dusty's surprise visit had been heaven-sent. While the others spent the next day seeing the sights, she and her husband made love through the next two days. Charlee thought it odd, but it almost felt like they were strangers having wild sex, getting to know each other in the most intimate of ways. But then, they hadn't seen each other in months. And one of those months, Charlee had nearly risked it all for some egotistical ladies' man. So stupid. But the important thing was she *hadn't* succumbed to Mario's charm. And now she knew she never would. Every time Dusty touched her with those strong sculptured hands, caressed her entire body with his long fingers, kissed her with his supple, sumptuous mouth, Charlee knew there was no one in the world she wanted. And through some great stroke of luck, Dusty Campbell was already hers.

While the others returned to Ohio by bus, Charlee rode in Dusty's black Mustang, barely letting go of his hand to let him shift. As planned, the Echo crew met up at Ruby's Place Friday night for a welcome home get-together with family and friends. Ruby closed her restaurant early for the invite-only party. By the time Charlee and Dusty got there, the guests had all arrived, including her crew, and the jukebox was playing "Hurts So Good" by John Cougar. The first ones she saw were Peggy and Billy, who'd been waiting at the door to greet her. Right behind them were Aunt Libby, Uncle Dave, Al and Angela, whose once-robust figure had been drastically reduced.

After giving "it's so good to be home" hugs, and chatting with everyone along the way to the bar, Charlee's mouth was as dry as those rice cakes she used to eat. She had just started ordering a drink when Diana grabbed her arm. "Hey, I was looking for you! Come on, let's do a shot."

"Sounds good. That and a big ol' Margarita!" Charlee hugged her, dissolving her previous, selfish, annoyance at her sister-in-law. She was glad now that Diana had a chance to check out the zoo. And also, had treated herself to a new spiral perm before leaving the Big Apple.

"We'll take two shots of Kamikazes, and one good strong Margarita," Diane told Kat, who looked annoyed as she slammed down the shot glasses, then ran off to get the liquor bottles.

"What's her problem?" Charlee asked.

"Hell if I know," Diana said, fluffing her freshly curled hair. "Maybe it's just 'cause she's so busy. Look, even Ruby's helping behind the bar."

Kat returned and poured alternate shots of tequila, triple sec, and lime juice into the short glasses. Charlee wanted to say, "Don't forget the lemon slice and salt," but considering Kat's demeanor, thought better of it. She turned back to Diana. "I didn't get a chance to ask, how was the zoo?"

"Ah, man, it was great. We were there all day, so much to see." Diana pulled the shot closer and smiled. "I didn't tell you about the zoo ahead of time 'cause I knew Dusty was coming to see you. I made sure everyone had plans so you guys could have alone time."

"Aw, really?" Boy, did she feel like an idiot for her actions that day.

"Shot time!" Diana raised her glass in the air. "To a successful Echo tour! *And* some needed down time for you and your hubby to have lots more sex!"

Charlee blushed, feeling weird hearing her husband's sister speak of their sex life out loud. The girl always said whatever came into her head. But then, thinking of that very subject, she couldn't wait to get back under the sheets with her husband. In their own bed. She grabbed her shot now, too. "And to a totally rad future veterinarian!"

They threw the liquid back, then slammed down their glasses. Just then, Kat returned with Charlee's Margarita. "Here you go."

Charlee noticed Kat's tears, as well as her discolored cheekbone, shining bright under the bar light. She touched her arm. "You okay?"

Kat shook her head. "No." She scanned the crowded bar, then leaned forward. "I kicked my old man out today and it got really nasty. Wouldn't be surprised if he showed up here."

"But it's a private party," Charlee said, stupidly. She didn't know much about Vince, the guy Kat had been living with, but she recalled Ruby telling her about his mean streak, and that she'd barred him back in August. His showing up uninvited wouldn't be a shock.

Kat gave her the dim-witted look she deserved. "Yeah, like *that* would deter him. Hey, can you do me a favor and tell Mario over there to keep his eye out for him? He'll know why."

"I'll go," Diana offered.

Just then Charlee felt two strong arms wrap around her waist. She didn't have to turn around to see who they belonged to. "Hey, stud." She spun around and kissed Dusty's cheek. "I love you. Let's go to bed."

"Sounds good to me," he said, then kissed her hard on the lips. "I don't think anyone would notice at all if we just slid out the—"

A loud slam sucked in his last words like a vacuum. Everyone's heads whipped around in unison. The front door banged against the wall so hard it sounded like it came off the hinges.

Vince, the size of Arnold Schwarzenegger, had just arrived.

Charlee couldn't see anything from her spot at the bar until she stepped up on her stool for a better view over all the heads. Kat's boyfriend had already succeeded in getting behind the bar, and was grabbing her flame hair. Vince swiped at a guy trying to pull him away, then just as quick, let go of them both, and with one swift turn, snatched the pool stick on the table next to the bar and started swinging.

Dusty pulled Charlee off the stool. "Let's get out of here. You know Ruby's got backup." He squeezed her hand, grabbed Diana's too on the way, and towed them out the back door.

Outside, the parking lot had filled quickly with those who'd done likewise. Peggy ran up to Charlee. "You and Dusty should leave. You don't need to make the late-night news."

Charlee nodded. "Spoken like a true mother." She gave her mom a quick peck on the cheek. "And so should you."

Just then, Kat ran out the door. "Cops are on their way, but Mario's already got Vince in a head lock. Boy, when he grabbed that pool stick, I thought he was gonna kill someone."

"Where's Ruby?" Charlee asked.

"Standin' by, making sure he doesn't worm away. He's bigger than Mario, ya know." Kat stood in front of them trembling like a Chihuahua.

Charlee touched her arm. "Maybe so, but Mario's been workin' out all summer. He's strong as an ox, and knows all the tricks."

When the police cars began swarming the bar, the lingering crowd scattered out, save for two bikers, friends of Ruby's, who didn't budge, serving as vigilantes.

Charlee knew it wouldn't be right to leave Kat by herself. She ran toward Peggy before she and Billy got in their car.

"Hey, Mom, would you mind taking Kat with you? She's really upset. I don't think she should go home alone, and I'd offer, but—"

"You don't have to explain." Peggy was already walking back. "You need time with Dusty. Hey, Kat, get over here."

"I love you." Charlee gave her mother a smack on the cheek, then grabbed for her husband.

"We're outta here."

15. Games People Play

Sandra couldn't believe she'd forgotten Benji's third birthday. But then, she had been awfully busy getting everything ready for her big move back to Cleveland. That winter had been dreadful. Cold, snowy, lonely. She'd been tempted to get an actual job when she spotted a 'Help Wanted' sign at the corner store, but who would watch Benji eight hours a day, five days a week? That was why she'd stayed in town another two years. Nicky was the only one she trusted. And now he had a full load of classes so he could finish up that nursing school by May. She recalled her surprise when he admitted to her that he was going to college for *nursing*. Given his smarts, she just assumed he was taking business courses. He was halfway through his studies when he finally mentioned it, and her reaction told them both why he'd waited to tell her. At first, she did wonder if he was gay. How many manly men actually became *nurses* instead of *doctors*? He explained his reasoning one night they were having beers at her apartment.

"I think nurses contribute more." He leaned against the chair gripping his Pabst. "Doctors care for the illness itself while nurses care for the patient's needs, and that's every bit as important. Maybe more so. I remember my mom telling me how this one nurse stayed overtime when she was in labor with me—I was a bitch to get out she always said— and the doc got there just to catch me, so to speak."

Sandra shifted in her seat. Talk of women and labor made her jittery.

"Mom barely saw the doc before, or after. I want to be the person who's there for that woman in labor." He looked over at Benji asleep on the couch. "Just think, if you'd had waited to have Ben a year from now, I might've been your nurse!"

The familiar rush of heat burned her face. That damn guilt trip for what she'd done still snaked through her insides no matter how she mentally fought against it. She had to remind herself she wasn't a bad person. Not really. She often willed away the self-loathing monster by thinking of her good fortune, how lucky she was to be little Benji's mama. Other times, it took a good night out to ignore the haunting memory of how she got him.

Her mind always went back and forth like that. From guilt to pride, back to guilt, back to pride for the present she'd bestowed on herself. Why not be proud? She had pulled off an amazing stunt! Not many women, or men, in fact, could've accomplished what she did. And by now, it was a done deal. They'd never find her out after all this time. She was free to go anywhere she wanted with her son. Free to finally move back home.

She'd be a changed person, too, when she returned. She already was. For one thing, she'd learned to shake away her old man's prejudiced ways. Daddy hated anyone who was different. So much so that people, including her, often referred to him as Archie, as in Archie Bunker from *All in the Family.* So after hearing how Nicky wanted to be a nurse because he felt that was the best way to help people, why, she pushed those fag thoughts right out of her head. She remembered then how he often talk about girls he'd dated, and how between school and playing those open mic nights, he had little time to get involved. Nicky was no more gay than she was Benji's real mother.

Besides, she benefited much from Nick's career choice. He knew what to do when she didn't. Like bananas were good for diarrhea, and pears were better than apples for constipation. And all that juice she gave Benji thinking it was good for him? Well, that was why the kid wouldn't sleep sometimes, 'cause of the sugar in it, according to Nick.

She couldn't believe how much she didn't know until she'd made herself a mother. So no way would she hire anyone other than Nicky—*especially* not some other woman—to feed, cuddle and play peek-a-boo with her little boy. She sure didn't want Benji getting all attached to someone else, or to have to make excuses on why the boy wasn't going to preschool the following year. God knew what she'd do when she'd have to enroll him into elementary school. They'd want a damn birth certificate. Well, she'd cross the bridge when she came to it.

Right now, it was Sunday afternoon, a week after his birthday, and she'd just realized her blunder. She had just gotten Benji down for his nap after a frustrating morning of potty training, and was sitting at the kitchen table going through utility bills, keeping track of all expenses in her notebook, when she glanced up at the drugstore calendar and saw the date. *Ah, shit*!

Of course, Benji wouldn't know the difference. But still.

She ripped out a sheet from her pad and jotted down a list of things she could get for her birthday boy. She'd go to Kmart and get that Hungry Hungry Hippos game he always pointed to whenever the commercial came on, and maybe a few of those Hot Wheels cars and trucks. Then she'd go to Kroger's, where they had ready-made cakes and get the bakery girl to write his name on one, and hey, they could throw a couple of those plastic little GI Joe's on top.

She picked up the phone and dialed Nick's number. She knew he'd be home, after all week of schooling and his late-night gig at the Ground Round.

"Hey, Nick, how's it goin'? Yeah, I know, snowin' like a son-of-a-bitch. Now I'm sure you're all into relaxin' on Sundays, but I'm out of a few things and gotta run to the store for a bit. Can you come down and watch the little guy? He's napping so . . . No. No. That's nice of ya, but I, well, I need to go myself." She cringed a bit, too embarrassed to admit she'd forgotten her own kid's birthday.

When she got back, she deliberately left the cake and gifts in the car. She opened the door with her brown bag of milk, eggs, and beer and saw Nicky and a wide-awake Ben on the floor playing 52-Pick-Up. She tossed her winter jacket on the couch, watching her son run around the living room giggling with delight as he went after every card with gusto, slamming them, one by one, into Nicky's hand. It was the kid's favorite game to play.

As she laughed at the sight, she thought to herself, h*ere is the only person in the world who shares my love for this boy.* She decided right then that they should celebrate his big day together. Her face brightened as a great idea wormed its way into her head. Not only did Benji not know his own birthday, neither did anyone else! She could change the date, and that could prove quite beneficial in the future. It was so simple she couldn't believe she'd never thought of it before. If ever someone might suspect Ben to be the kidnapped baby Dylan, Nicky would "verify" that no, Ben's birthday is March 27th. He'd been there on his third birthday! Wow, she really was brilliant sometimes.

She set the bag on the kitchen counter, and headed back toward the door. "I gotta get a few more things from the car," she said, throwing Nick a wide smile. "I have a couple of gifts and a cake for the birthday boy!"

"Birthday? Really?" Nick crawled over to grab Ben. "It's the rascal's birthday? Hey, man, Happy Birthday to you, lil' Rascal!" He started tickling him. "Gettin' to be a big guy, aren't ya?"

Seeing the two together always made her feel all mushy inside. Nicky had been calling Ben "Lil' Rascal" since before he took his first steps. He was such a great help, a godsend, to her, and served as a big brother to little Ben. They were both lucky to have this young man in their lives. For the umpteenth time, Sandra wondered if moving back to Cleveland was the right thing to do. And yet, she ached to go back.

Nick stood up now. "Man, Sandra, you should've told me it was his birthday, I'd have gotten him something." He seemed genuinely hurt by the omission.

She pretended not to notice as she grabbed for the doorknob. "Oh, I wouldn't wan'cha doing that with all you got goin' on. Besides, I haven't seen ya all week." An added bonus. She could make him feel guilty about not always being around. Maybe he'd come around more now.

"I know, I have been busy. But come to think of it, I don't think you ever told me when his birthday was."

Sandra shrugged. "Well, guess I never saw you when that time came around." She knew it sounded feeble because Nicky *had* been around at least every month since Ben was born. She threw open the door. "Be right back."

Later, over yellow cake with cream frosting, she and Nicky chatted about their futures as Benji sat at the table scooping off icing with his fingers, then putting it into his mouth. "Only thing I'll miss once I get a real job is not playing the Ground Round anymore," Nicky was saying. "It'll be just too hard with working fulltime. Speaking of which, I just saw in the paper that Hamot Medical Center is looking for LPNs, and you know what a great hospital that is."

As he talked, Sandra snapped opened her second can of beer, and the sound seemed to click on another flash of brilliant inspiration. "Hey, Nick! I gotta fabulous idea! There's nothing going on around this town, that's why I'm leaving. And the economy around here sucks. And just the other day, you said how you'll miss us when we're gone. Sooooo, why don't you come to Cleveland after you graduate? I just bet you could get a job at the Cleveland Clinic! I'm sure they're always lookin' for good nurses. And you can stay with me for however long you want, and of course, I'll still pay you for when you watch Benji." She stopped and drew in a breath full of hope. "You know how much lil' Benji loves you, and, well"—she surprised herself when her eyes brewed with tears— "I'm kinda attached to you, too." She practically batted her eyebrows. "Come on, whad'dya say?"

Just then, Benji hopped off his booster seat and bolted toward Nick, jumping on his lap. "Play with me!" That was when Sandra realized the bag with his presents were still on the couch. She had planned on taking them to her bedroom to wrap them, but had gotten sidetracked, as usual. No matter, she thought, the kid wouldn't care about fancy wrappings and bows.

"Hey, Benji." She stood up and walked over to the big Kmart bag. "Mama's got something for you on your big day!" Her voice took on that high lilt that let her son know this was a good day.

After a lively game of Hungry Hungry Hippos, she and Nick put Ben into his Star Trek pajamas, announced "bedtime for bonzos," and tucked him into bed. Sandra closed the door halfway and Nick followed her into the kitchen where he helped her clean the cake plates. She was drying off her hands when he smiled at her and said the magic words she'd been waiting for. "You know, your idea's pretty good. I'll send my resume to both hospitals and see what comes of it. And either way, I'll come visit you and Ben in June, okay?"

Sandra threw her arms around the sturdy boy. "Oh, I'm so happy! You can stay with us long as you want!"

Nick gently pried her off his chest. "Well, if I get a job in Cleveland, I might have to take you up on that, temporarily of course, till I get on my feet."

"Sure, sure, but I just know they'll hire a smart guy like you! And remember, the Clinic is the best anywhere!"

By May, Sandra was on her way back to her hometown when she had to make an unexpected pit stop in Geneva. In the midst of a downpour, her old maroon monstrosity started sputtering, forcing her to pull off the freeway as the car staggered into the nearest gas station.

"Engine's goin'," the man in overalls told her five minutes later. "I'm afraid this baby's days are numbered."

"Son of a bitch," Sandra said, fighting tears. The old Impala had been her daddy's pride and joy. She remembered when he brought it home that day in '69, all shiny and new. And how he'd wax it up faithfully every three months. She told folks at the bar who eyed it that she'd run it to the ground before ever giving it up. She just hadn't expected it to happen this soon, despite the thirteen years, the 156,000 miles, the rust, the oil leak . . . *Damn it to hell*!

"Tell you the truth, ma'am, I don't think it's worth putting in a new engine," the mechanic said, wiping grease from his hands. "There's a guy here in town, Glenn's Auto's, couple miles down this road. He sells some nice cars." His eyes shifted to the back seat where Benji was curled up asleep. "Tell him Bob sent ya and he'll give you a decent price."

"Ah, man. I can't believe this." Sandra stomped her foot. Her and her big ideas. She should've stayed put in Zanesburg. She brushed back her bleached hair, now frizzy from the rain, as her eyes threw darts at the broken-down piece of shit. That was really what it was.

"I gotta think about this. Gotta smoke?"

The man pulled out a pack of Kools from his top shirt pocket, handed her one and lit it. Real gentleman-like. "Take your time. I have to get this other car over here done 'fore the owner comes to pick it up at five." He glanced at the round Sunoco clock on the wall. "If ya want, I can drive you over to Glenn's afterwards." Then he bent over to the side and saw her license plate. "Or maybe you need a ride back home? How far in P.A. you live?"

While she smoked and Bob wrenched, she told him she wasn't going back, but forward. "I'm moving to Cleveland. Kinda startin' over." He didn't ask what she meant, and that was okay.

As they chatted, Sandra glanced up at the small TV on the dusty shelf above, just as the *Price is Right* was coming on. She looked back at the man and noticed that he kind of resembled Bob Barker. *Not bad-looking for a mechanic.* And his name was Bob, too, so now she'd never forget it. She sauntered over to the side of the car, angling her head to see if he wore a wedding band. Sandra smiled. Nope.

"So Bob, you think that Glenn guy can really give me a good trade?" She squinted and blinked her eyes to work up some tears. "I'm just sick about this. I need a good car, a decent one with a child n'all." She tried getting her voice to sound sad. "But I sure don't know how I'll be able to pay for another one."

She wanted to appear a damsel-in-distress, see what she could get out of the deal. After all, she wasn't made of money. Three years ago, she thought she'd be all set, at least till she found a good man. But she had a bad habit of figuring her bills at night when alcohol convinced her she was some math whiz. So a few times she got sloppy with her figures and made a few, big, errors. She hadn't noticed the goofs until she looked at her savings account statement one day—she had a bad habit of not opening them—and saw her latest balance. Instead of the $32,000 she thought she had, the paper showed $19,159. And sixty-three cents.

That kind of money, if she wasn't real careful, might not last much more than two years. Tops. *Damn.* How could all that money her daddy left her go so fast? She thought for days about it and concluded that it was mostly because of the kid. Food and toys and whatnot didn't come cheap. She was lucky Nicky babysat a lot for free, just 'cause he liked Benji so much. And well, she did love to shop. When she started packing for this trip, she found all kinds of stuff she'd never used—fancy shoes and clothes she'd been saving for when she met Prince Charming. And all that jewelry she'd treated herself with! Well, if only that bastard landlord hadn't raised the rent *twice* since she'd been there, it wouldn't be so bad.

Most times, Sandra tried not thinking about what she'd do when the money ran out. But now the truth was staring her right in the face.

And that face had just emerged from the hood.

And he was smiling at her. A good sign.

"Tell you what," he said, still smiling as he wiped his greasy hands. "Lemme finish up here, and I'll take you and the little one down the street and bargain with Glenn. And how 'bout I take your ol' Chevy off your hands. I could use most of the parts. Say 'round four hundred? That be acceptable?"

Acceptable? Hell, it was downright generous. *Why, I think I just fell in love.*

She smashed out her butt in the dirty ashtray that was screwed onto the wall and flashed her new handsome prospect a shy, grateful grin. "Oh that would help me out so much, Bob! You're a doll."

The damsel-in-distress thing sure worked wonders sometimes.

16. Time

Charlee rose that morning at eight, threw on her bikini, poured a cup of coffee, and made it to her pool before Diana woke up. Charlee didn't mind that the girl still lived with them more than a year later—the house was certainly big enough—but Diana, being the talker she was, gave little chance to be alone with one's thoughts. And since Peggy's call yesterday, Charlee needed time to herself, to think about Angela, the woman who had been like another mother to her.

When Peggy first told her about the breast cancer back in January, Charlee denied it was possible. No way. Angela was the toughest person Charlee knew. Angela had been there during Charlee's angry teen years when she and Peggy weren't on the best of terms. She had been there to guide her through the MissFits, and all that girl drama. She had even been there for her when her best friend, CJ, died. And that was something, because despite experiencing a mother's grief, Angela took time to comfort Charlee, who'd kept vigil in her room for days after.

Charlee couldn't imagine a time when Angela wouldn't be there. No one could. That's why they all believed she would kick the disease in the butt. After the mastectomy and those god-awful treatments, they thought she had succeeded, too. Now it was late August, nine months after Angela had been diagnosed, and doctors had discovered the cancer had wormed its way into her lymph nodes. That was not good. That was scary.

So Charlee just wanted to lounge on her patio deck, gaze at the pool water shimmering from the morning rays, and say a few prayers. *Please, God. Angela is only forty-nine*. It made her think of her own life, too. Where would she be at forty-nine? Where did she want to be?

As thrilling as the tour had been, the months of non-stop activity had left her exhausted. She began to question if music was what she wanted to do the rest of her life. She felt she wanted something different. But for the life of her, she didn't know what.

How she envied Dusty, who had recently switched from being a musician to being a soundman. Last summer, he'd become fascinated by the audio equipment boards and decided that career choice offered more gigs, more money, and more security, than bouncing from band to band. Charlee had been hoping he'd return as her backup guitarist, but once Dusty made up his mind, it was pointless to argue. They both shared that same trait, stubbornness, which didn't help their quarrels any—because someone always had to win. Still, she couldn't help be glad he had found a career he was happy with. The drawback was that he was gone every day, including weekends, doing recording sessions with the bands signed to Peggy Sue Records.

The future scared her. Angela was dying, Dusty was busy, and her own life was at a standstill. She still dreamed of having a family, but the horror, the constant wondering where her first baby was, kept her from wanting another. And despite Peggy urging her to start another album, Charlee just didn't feel like it. Before the tour, she'd been making MTV videos, and before that, writing and recording songs. She'd hardly had time to relax in the last three years—since the kidnapping, when her mother had pushed her to get back to what she "loved doing."

Thing was, she wasn't sure what she loved anymore. Missing her boy and wondering what happened to him was like Angela's cancer. Eating away at her, day by day. And no matter how much she pushed it back, it was always there.

She wasn't even sure those songs she'd written on the road would see the light of day. They were decent ones too. One about being lonely, one about phony personas, and one about being attracted to someone you shouldn't be. But since then, she hadn't written a single thing.

"Hey, you're up early!" Diana emerged, already in her bikini, banana clip in hair, carrying a towel.

"And so are you."

"Dusty leave yet?"

"Yeah. There's coffee over there on the table."

As disappointed as she was that Diana had interrupted her thoughts, Charlee reminded herself to be grateful she was here. With Dusty gone so much, Diana's presence kept Charlee from thinking *too* much.

Before Diana, Charlee had missed having girlfriends. Ruby had been her only close friend for years, but in the last two, she'd been immersed in her own passion, her restaurant. Spunky Diana had gotten Charlee to go out more, enjoy a regular "girls' night." Best of all, Diana always made her laugh. Just the other night they'd gone to see her good friend, Carlos Jones, who played in a reggae band called I-Tal, at The Coach House. Towards the end of the night, a guy who looked eerily like Boy George tried to pick Diana up. When he asked for her number, she gave it to him. "867-5309." He'd actually written it down. The number in the "Jenny" song by Tommy Tutone. That had them laughing the whole way home.

Diana reminded Charlee that she shouldn't be so serious all the time. Having fun and lying around getting a tan had become Charlee's latest endeavor. She loved the freedom that came with having no pressure to do anything, *except* have fun.

And why not enjoy her self-appointed hiatus? She had just turned twenty-six, for God's sakes. She'd been working at her career since she was fifteen. Didn't she deserve to do whatever the hell she wanted? She was young; she was rich. She had a kick-ass swimming pool in the shape of a guitar in her backyard.

After they chatted a bit, Diana took a swim, while Charlee went in to do chores. Diana often helped around the house, but today Charlee told her not to bother. She needed the sense of spiritual cleansing she always got from scrubbing and polishing. Between that and grocery shopping, it was late-afternoon when she and Diana were reunited at her backyard pool.

Like many weekends, they hung out in the cabana, sitting on lounge chairs, drinking margaritas and talking about whatever came to mind. Charlee had finally managed to put aside those ominous thoughts of Angela when Diana, out of the blue, brought up a forbidden topic.

"Charlee, do you still think of Dylan much anymore?" Diana asked, flipping through the Saturday *Plain Dealer.* The question came out so casually, you would've thought she'd asked if it was going to rain today.

If it were anyone else, Charlee would've wondered about the person's sanity, and most likely, screamed, *"Are you kiddin me? What a stupid, insidious thing to ask!"* But this was Diana, who had become more of a sister than an in-law. Charlee often confided in her about various topics— with two exceptions. Charlee had to be selective when it came to Dusty and their relationship because Diana *was* his sister. Then there was the underlying rule that hadn't needed to be enforced: The subject of their kidnapped son was off-limits. In fact, it had only come up once, that time in Chicago, and Charlee had stopped her inquiries abruptly. Diana never brought it up again.

Until now. When something about the day's approaching sundown, and the steady sips of alcohol streamed doses of bravado into Diana Campbell's veins. Charlee knew this question had been burrowing deep under Diana's skin for some time. So if Diana could summon up the nerve to bring it up, Charlee felt a need to respond. And maybe she *should* talk about it. Rip that bloody, painful wound wide open.

Charlee was glad for the sunglasses that hid the tears rising like a river at the mention of her son's name. She leaned over, took a sip of calm from her near-empty glass, and sucked in a breath of courage.

"Of course I think about him, Di," she said, almost in a whisper. "Though I really try not to." She downed the last drop of her drink, then set it on the table next to her.

How could she even try to explain her unyielding torment? Diana had never been pregnant. Never been a mother. And it *had* been more than three years now. Everyone thinks that "in time" you forget about people who leave your life—forever.

Can those who'd never been there understand that you could go about your days seemingly fine, doing normal things, then all of a sudden, something pricks you. And there it is, the unrelenting thread of black pain, snaking through your insides, like being injected with a poisonous needle.

No. No one else could know how it felt. Except those who suffer from the affliction. Charlee often wondered how Dusty dealt with it. He never really told her. Never talked about his feelings about Dylan. It was always about hers. But then, had she ever really asked? Funny, she'd never thought about that before. As if she, being the mother, was the only real important victim.

"No one's gonna find him now, it's way too late," Charlee continued. "Babies change practically every day, and he's . . ." She lifted her glasses, brushed away a tear. "He's already three—and-a-half years old."

She recalled how she'd spent his last birthday. Like the others, in bed numbing herself with whatever anesthetic available. The first couple of years, Dusty would try and act normal, make busy plans for the day, but this year she wailed on him to just let her be. So he did.

Charlee struggled every day not to think of her son, but she couldn't control the dreams. Some were nightmares, where she'd relive that fuzzy night all over again. When that woman was in her room and had scooped up her baby and *she* had allowed her to leave.

In the dreams that weren't shattering nightmares, Dylan looked just as he did the last time she'd seen him, small, soft, precious. Other times, he came to her as a toddler, with dark wavy hair, running around her living room. But just last month, Dylan appeared to her as a teenager—looking a lot like the pictures she had of her father, Frankie London. That was the most disturbing dream of all. It had seemed so real. Her boy was a good-looking young man, maybe fourteen or so, with a gold Stratocaster strapped around his shoulder. She remembered having an actual conversation with him. Though she would never know what was said because her body had jerked her awake in the middle of it. She found herself sitting up in bed, drenched in sweat.

"You know, Diana, I wouldn't even recognize him now if I saw him somewhere. In a playground, on the street, in a grocery store . . . That's what's so haunting." She sat up in her lounger and pointed to herself. "Me. His own mother. Not being able to recognize her own damn child." She looked over at the still water in front of them, but her tears made the vision blurry. "Pathetic, isn't it?"

Charlee suddenly wanted to tell Diana everything. She told her about hiring, then firing, Tom, the private investigator. How there were still times she wondered if she should see a psychic. Or a shrink . . . About numbing herself every birthday.

When Charlee stopped talking, Diana placed the newspaper on the ground and came over to her, grabbing her so tight she nearly lost her breath. Yet the embrace felt good.

Like a heavy protective blanket. "Oh, Charlee. I'm so sorry that happened to you guys. It's so horrible, so cruel. So not fair! I hate that woman!"

Charlee knew Diana was crying, too, because her bare shoulder was getting wet.

"Diana, hate doesn't even begin to describe how I—"

"Oh my God."

"What?"

Diana withdrew their embrace, bent down, and picked the newspaper back up. "This headline. Now what kind of stupid woman would do such a thing?"

"What are you talking about?" Charlee gazed over at the paper Diana was holding up. The headline read, "Shopper Leaves Toddler in Hot Car."

"Some woman left her kid sleeping in the back seat while she went shopping in Kmart!" Diana read the article out loud. "'*I didn't want to wake him, the Cleveland Heights woman told the officer. I just ran into the store real quick, wasn't gone more than ten minutes.*'"

Diana flashed the paper to Charlee. "*And* because the baby was *unharmed*, they didn't arrest her 'cause she seemed . . . what's the phrase?" She glanced back at the paper. '*Genuinely sorry*? *And promised never to do it again.*' Well, isn't that special? And here you guys, who would be great parents . . ."

Charlee held the paper against the sun's glare and scanned the article, feeling a rush of anger. Some women didn't deserve to be mothers. Her fear heightened once again thinking of what kind of person had her son.

Diana caught the look on Charlee's face and realized her thoughtlessness. She snatched the paper back. "Ah, shit. I'm sorry. I'm an idiot. I just get so appalled when I read stuff like this. But people who do stuff like that to kids, animals, well, I just go off when I should keep my mouth shut. Sorr—"

"There're my bathing beauties!"

Dusty's voice rang through the patio as he approached them, looking happy. He always looked happy these days. It made Charlee achingly jealous. Nothing, not even fun, made her *happy*. Charlee quickly swiped her tears, but not quickly enough for Dusty not to notice. But he pretended he didn't.

He glanced at his watch. "You two hungry?" Charlee could tell Dusty wanted to break whatever mood he had walked in on. "How 'bout I take my best girls out to Ruby's, if you're game?"

"I am!" Kat came around the side bushes, bouncing toward the pool, her long red hair swirling in the wind with her cheery movements. She, too, was happy. That night when Vince had crashed Charlee's welcome-home party, he'd ended up in jail, and Kat ended up on Peggy Sue's couch, where she'd stayed most of that winter. Once Kat learned Vince had left town, she purchased a condo just down the street from Charlee and Dusty, where she became a frequent visitor to the Campbell home. Charlee didn't mind. Like Diana, Kat had become a close friend, too. Which came in handy when Charlee felt the need to discuss topics she couldn't with her sister-in-law either because the girl was too naïve in certain aspects of life, or because she didn't need to know Charlee and Dusty's problems.

"Do I count as one of your best girls, too?" Kat asked as she threw her arms around Charlee. "Hey, girl."

Dusty laughed and lit a cigarette. "Sure, why not?"

Charlee hugged her friend back, then asked, "Where you been lately?"

Kat pulled out a pack of Winstons from the back pocket of her white short shorts. "Now that's a question that needs to be answered on one of our girls' nights." She winked, then leaned toward Dusty standing between them. "Can I have a light, Dust?"

Charlee cringed a bit seeing Kat's shiny pink tube top slipping a little as she bent forward for Dusty to light her cigarette.

"I'll go change," Diana said, picking up her towel and going into the house.

Dusty began telling them about the session that day and before long, Diana reappeared, wearing tight blue Vanderbilt jeans and Charlee's old "Daffy Dan" T-shirt that read, "Cleveland: You've Got To Be Tough." Charlee had forgotten she'd given it to her.

"I'm ready!" Diana called out. "Come on, you guys, I'm starving."

17. One Thing Leads To Another

Ruby's Place was always crowded on Friday nights, so for a long time, Charlee had avoided it. After the tour, and especially after playing the Cleveland Stadium last autumn, people would come up to her at Ruby's, asking for autographs and wanting to chat. She didn't mind at other places, but not at Ruby's. That was, or should be, her safe haven. She went to Ruby's to see friends, listen to good bands, and enjoy herself. Not have to constantly be "on," with people watching her every move. But then after she'd mentioned—purposely—in the June issue of *Cleveland Magazine* that she'd wanted some privacy in her own hometown, people seemed to get it, and for the most part, let her be.

"Hey, my favorite people are here!" Ruby, small as she was, attempted to wrap her arms around the four of them when they walked through the door. She let go and waved her arms to the right. "Your table awaits!"

Charlee grinned. Ruby still had a little drama in her.

As the four of them settled at their usual round table in the corner, Mario snuck up behind the server, pointed to the group, and leaned into her ear. "Their money's not good here."

Charlee smiled, and didn't argue. Why not let him pay since she had kept Mario's finances flowing the past year with that lucrative tour. And he had been appreciative. You have to give him that, Charlee thought. Best of all, after her lusty after-tour reunion with her husband, her fiery little crush on Mario had been sufficiently—and thankfully—doused.

They ordered a round of appetizers and drinks, then

Mario playfully punched Dusty's arm. "Hey, Dust, I'll beat your ass at pool."

Dusty grinned and stood up. "You're a glutton for punishment, aren't ya, boy?"

"Wow. I didn't know Love Affair was playing tonight. Great!" Charlee said in a near shout to be heard over the band.

Charlee had first met the group at Billy's radio station when the band was there to promote their new record, "Mama Sez." She liked them enough to try and keep up with their appearances, but last she'd heard, they were playing gigs in Florida.

The place was packed and Charlee enjoyed chatting with friends and every once in a while, checking out the pool game. By now, Mario had succeeded, on the second round, in beating Dusty at billiards. When the two returned, Kat got up. "Okay, my turn," she announced, putting her arm around Mario. "I'll turn this Italian into a meatball." She winked as they all laughed, then stalked toward her mission.

The band took their break and Charlee introduced the members to Diana. When she got to Rich, the lead singer, Charlee swallowed a chuckle, seeing Diana's eyes light up. All the girls loved Rich, with his shoulder-length dark hair, kind eyes, and easygoing smile. Tonight he was wearing a Led Zeppelin T-shirt with cut-off sleeves and tight black leather pants. Charlee could tell Diana already had a crush.

When the band headed back for their last set, Diana followed, planting herself on the end barstool, next to the stage. With Kat and Mario over by the pool tables, Charlee and Dusty had time to snuggle.

But not for long. "Hey, hey, break it up, you love birds! Who wants to get in on the next game?" Kat had returned, a triumphant look on her face.

"You beat him already?" Even Dusty was surprised.

Kat nodded. "When you work in a bar, you get some good practice during slow times."

Charlee looked over at Dusty. She knew this was a challenge he couldn't pass up. "Oh, go on," Charlee said with a laugh and kissed his cheek.

When Love Affair wrapped up for the night, Charlee walked over to the jukebox. She punched in her current favorites: Elton John's "I'm Still Standing," Prince's "Little Red Corvette," and Stevie Nicks' "Stand Back." Charlee loved the Fleetwood Mac singer's new solo album, *The Wild Heart*, despite her personal jealousy over her great success. It was the same with Joan Jett. Charlee dismissed the guilty thought that Echo should be giving them more competition.

She stood there punching numbers and singing along to the songs, like she'd done as a teenager. She loved that she could do this now at Ruby's without anyone bothering her.

"Can I pick one?"

She jumped and spun around to see who had snuck up behind her. "Mario! Jeez, you scared the shit outta me."

"Sorry." But his grin said otherwise. "Can I be your jukebox hero?"

She gave him a smirk. He was always coming up with corny ditties, like working in random song titles in conversations. "There're a few more selections left. Have at it." She'd been glad that they'd remained friends, but right now he was high. And standing a little too close. She pushed him back, gently.

She grabbed her drink off the abandoned table, and hopped up onto the bar stool across from the pool table to watch her husband win the game. Kat didn't seem to care that Dusty had two balls left, compared to her six.

Mario came over just as another record began. She'd been so focused on the game she hadn't paid attention to the song until Mario leaned in and started singing in her ear. "Jesse's Girl." But he changed the lyrics, crooning "Dusty's Girl" instead.

Charlee had always liked Rick Springfield. She and Diana had even started watching *General Hospital* lately, when time allowed. But now his most famous song was coming out of Mario's mouth, and his message darted up her spine like a shooting firework.

She swung her stool around.

"Mario. Stop it."

What?"

"Stop singing."

"What, you don't like my voice?"

She squinted her eyes. "I don't like that song." *Not anymore.*

"Well, I do." He continued singing, a bit louder than before.

She tried ignoring him. Things had been fine with them since their close encounter last year. Mario had kept a respectful distance. But now, when alcohol mixed with the midnight hour, he had forgotten his place.

She didn't want to make a scene, so she was forced to sit glued to her seat as Dusty squinted at the 8 ball. Mario kept it up until the song's end, then looked at her like an innocent child. "Can't help it. I can relate," he said, adding a shrug.

She wanted to smack him with her purse, if only she had one. Instead, she gave him the evil eye, just as Dusty came over and placed his hand on her thigh. "Told ya I'd beat her," he said, smiling at her. His expression changed when he looked over at Mario. Charlee was sure Dusty hadn't heard a word of their conversation, but he didn't have to. He had male instincts.

"Where's Diana?" Dusty asked, looking around the now near-empty room.

"She left with Rich. They were going to a party."

Normally, Diana leaving with a musician could be worrisome, but they knew Rich well enough to know Dusty's sister would be in safe company. "He said he'd take her home later," Charlee added. And they knew he would.

Mario slapped Dusty's back. "Hey, man, how 'bout one more game before they kick us out? This time for a beer," Mario said, grabbing the stick nearby.

Dusty looked at Charlee, as if to ask permission to whip his ass. She nodded. Permission granted. "Rack 'em up," Dusty said, and the two disappeared.

Kat bounced up on the empty seat next to her. "Well, I *almost* beat him," she said with a little laugh. "Hey, Mark, I'll take another beer. And a margarita for Charlee, right?"

Charlee pushed her empty glass toward the bartender. "Yeah, okay. But just one more." Though she knew she didn't need another one.

Mark grabbed empties off the bartop. "One more is right . . . Last call, people," he shouted as he walked away.

"Charlee, I wanna tell you something," Kat said, scooting her stool closer. "I know I've never mentioned it, but I'm really glad we've become friends. I want you to know how I appreciate you and your mom being so kind to me . . . you know, after *the asshole*." She grimaced at her drink and rolled her black-lined eyes. "Plus, I've learned a lot just watching you and Dusty." She stopped to swig the last of her Miller Lite. "I mean, I know you guys have had your problems, but he always treats you with so much, well, he's just so sweet to you. I've made up my mind that's what I deserve, too. From now on, that's what I'm looking for in a relationship. Someone who treats me like Dusty treats you."

Charlee smiled. Yes, she really was lucky.

"I'm glad we're friends, too, Kat. I've been needing another friend. Someone to talk to. I love Diana, but some things I certainly can't discuss with her. Like, well, men." She glanced around to make sure no one was in hearing distance. Then she leaned in and whispered, "Like what do you do when another man's in love with you, and though you love your husband, you, well, one night you kinda goof, and can't stop feeling guilty about—"

She stopped now, seeing Kat's shocked face. "Oh, my. *Who*? Who is it?"

She pressed her lips tight as Mark set down their order. "Here you go, ladies, drink fast."

Charlee took a sip before continuing. She'd been aching to tell someone for so long, yet she felt almost guilty saying it out loud. She waved her hand. "Well, it's over now, but, over there." She shifted her eyes in Mario's direction.

"Oh my God, really?" Kat's hushed voice came out in a hiss.

Charlee giggled. Now she knew she shouldn't be having this other drink. "Yep, him. And though I'm *totally* over his charms, I can't get him to stop coming on to me. And I sure don't want *that* cat outta the bag."

Kat nodded, talking to her beer. "Yeah, really. But I know what you mean. He and I only dated a bit, but, boy, when that hot Italian latches on to you, he can be quite, uh, persuasive."

Charlee leaned back. She'd forgotten the two had once been an item. "Oh right. Guess you would know."

"So tell me, just how *persuasive*, was he?" Kat stared over at Mario, who was smacking a ball into a corner pocket. "Was it when you guys were on tour? I'll say this for him. That man sure can *kiss*."

Charlee giggled again. "Oh, yes. He *can* kiss." They laughed together like bonding girlfriends, enjoying the secret. Then Charlee straightened her posture. "He was persuasive for about five, well, okay, ten minutes, but then I got my wits about me and ended it before anything really, you know, happened."

Kat nodded and lit a cigarette. "Oh, good. I sure wouldn't want you destroying my perfect image of you and Dusty," she said with a wink.

"Okay, people!" Mark called out. "You don't have to go home, but you can't stay here." Then he cranked up the last song on the volume knob behind him, just as Dusty and Mario returned to the bar. Dusty had won. *Good.*

"Beat It" was playing, much to Charlee's chagrin. She must have heard that song every day this summer. She hopped off her stool. "Okay, I think it's time for us to *beat it* out of here," she said, enjoying the others laugh at her little joke. She rubbed her hand up and down Dusty's strong muscular arm, making sure Mario saw it. He had to be reminded that she *was* Dusty's girl. And always would be. "Ready, Cowboy?"

Dusty grabbed the back of her waist and pulled her in. "You bet'cha." He gave her a quick kiss, then waved to the others. His hand in hers, they headed out the door.

Waking with a headache that morning, Charlee wondered if maybe she shouldn't have mentioned that little rendezvous with Mario to Kat. She felt queasy about it now, but it had felt good to talk to another girl about it. And Kat was the only person she *could* tell. Ruby was too busy, Diana, too young—and a Campbell—and Aunt Libby, well, you just didn't tell things like that to your mother's best friend.

Besides, Kat had been through her own man troubles, so Charlee knew she'd understand. Yet, in the light of day, Charlee remembered something that had always kind of bothered her about Kat. And last night, she had noticed it again. How Kat never looked at you straight in the eyes when she talked. She looked at people when *they* talked, but when she did, she always looked elsewhere. At her drink, at the floor, at the wall . . .

Until now, Charlee had chalked it up to shyness. She recalled one timid girl in her sixth-grade class who used to do the same thing.

But Kat was an adult, and in no way timid.

As she slipped slowly out of bed, her throbbing, remorse-filled head took over and she told herself she was probably just looking for things to feel guilty about. It was her nature lately.

Still, as the afternoon wore on, Charlee couldn't stifle an overbearing, oppressive feeling of uneasiness. Where it came from, she had no clue. So she blamed it on the hangover.

18. Thank You for Being a Friend

In late October, Peggy and Billy went on a two-week vacation to Toronto. They strolled along hand-in-hand down Yonge Street, shopped and dined at the best restaurants, and stopped in at the local radio station, 1050 CHUM, where Billy met a deejay he'd often heard about. They returned home late Saturday afternoon, happy, but tired.

While Peggy unpacked, throwing clothes into the laundry room, Billy checked the messages on their machine. There were three. One from Stu at Billy's Akron station, one from a band member on Peggy Sue's label. And one from Al Johnson. Angela's husband.

"Hey, Peg, Billy. Uh, call me when you get this, okay?"

Peggy had just entered the kitchen when Al's voice came on, and she knew from his tone the news could not be good. "Oh, Billy."

Billy rubbed her arm. "I'll call him now." He dialed and put Al on the speakerphone.

Al picked up on the second ring. "Oh, Billy, glad you called. Is Peggy there?"

"She's right next to me. I have you on speaker."

"Oh, okay, good. I wanted to make sure . . ." Al stopped for a moment. Peggy could hear him trying hard to keep his voice calm and clear. "Oh, jeez, guys, I'm sorry, this is hard to say, but Ange, she's in the hospital, and, well, she ain't good."

Peggy and Billy clasped hands as they stood against the kitchen counter waiting for him to continue.

"Remember when Ange told them to just give her the chemo and radiation so she could whip its ass again and get on with her business?" He paused again. Peggy heard his voice catch. "Well, it's too late."

"What do you *mean* it's too late?" Peggy said louder than she meant to.

"More tests showed it's already in her lungs and liver."

"Oh God! No!" Peggy looked over at Billy, who grabbed her and held her against him. *Please, God, let me be dreaming.* How could this be? Angela had bravely let the doctors take her breasts to avoid chemotherapy. They all thought that would be the end of it.

"Peg, we actually found this out just before you two left, but Ange made me promise not to tell you. She knew you'd cancel your travel plans. When things got worse, well, I wasn't about to call you'all at your hotel room and ruin your much-deserved vacation. I mean, there's not much anyone can do."

Not much anyone can do. Peggy recalled Angela saying those very words when she'd first told her about the cancer. Her heart hurt thinking about it. Besides Libby, Angela had been her closest friend. Someone she'd shared hard times with, giggled with, and exchanged confidences with. Someone Peggy could go to for anything. From the moment her parents had put Peggy on a bus out of town, Angela had been part of her life. She forced back tears thinking of those years together.

"When you can," Al was saying, "I think you guys better come out. The doctor said it could be a matter of a couple weeks."

Peggy wanted to leave the moment she heard that, but she and Billy had been gone from work for so long, they had to first take care of pressing obligations before they could fly to Detroit.

Through the next week, Peggy called her friend every day. It broke her heart to hear the once hearty voice reduced to a weak tone that Peggy barely recognized. It had taken six days to clear their schedules, but finally by Friday, she and Billy were packed and ready to catch the early morning flight.

They were a day too late. When the phone rang at three in the morning, Peggy knew, before Al spoke the words. Their dear Angela was gone.

Peggy spent the two-hour plane ride staring out the window and crying. She hated herself for not getting there in time. After picking up the rental car, she and Billy drove the half hour to the Johnson home in silence. They were almost there when she turned to her husband. "Why didn't I just tell everyone they'd have to wait? That I had a sick friend and needed to go *now*? Why didn't we just get on the first plane after Al told us last Saturday?" She blew her nose. "I'll never forgive myself for not being with her."

Billy pulled the car over to the curb. He grabbed her and placed her head into his chest. "There's nothing to forgive. No one knew it would happen so soon. We all thought she'd make liars out those doctors." He took her chin, forcing her to look into the blue eyes that still made her heart melt. "I will not let you beat yourself up. It was just her time, you know. And you did get to say goodbye. Probably in the manner Angela would've preferred."

Peggy held onto his hand that caressed her face. He was right. Angela had told her that spring, "If worse comes to worse, I don't want no one visiting me, gawking at me lookin' all frail and shit. Don't want no one having that image in their minds when I'm gone."

She also recalled last night's conversation. Angela had sounded surprisingly upbeat. She'd told Peggy that she was at peace with it all, and actually looking forward to being reunited with her CJ in heaven. "I've lived a great life," she'd said, naming off her blessings. "I got to work for Motown, for God's sakes. And I found my son. You know yourself what a coincidence that was after all those years searching for him. *And* I wrote a damn book! A frickin' bestselling book!" She'd started to laugh, but it turned into a hoarse cough. When she recovered, Angela continued. "*And* been blessed with a wonderful, loving husband, and dear friends. Like you, hon. Meetin' you on that bus, back in the stone age? Why, that was God's plan, and you well know it. And this is God's plan, too, Peg. Ain't up to us."

"You are such a trouper, Ange. I admire you so much," Peggy had told her, choking back tears. "But I must say, I don't think God's ready for *you* yet." She tried to chuckle, failed. "I'll see you in just one more day. Love you."

Those were her last words to her. Billy was right. What else was there?

Even before entering the Johnson home that cold November day, Peggy knew she would never be back. Al opened the door without his usual buoyant smile, yet still with his vigorous hugs. "So glad to see you two."

The house was filled with people, many Peggy and Billy had known for years. Some from the music business, others from when Peggy had lived in Detroit. After the round of greetings, Peggy stepped out onto the outside patio, closed the door behind her, and sat in Angela's wicker chair, ignoring the seasonal chill. She wanted to feel her friend's effervescence presence. She wanted to be alone with her spirit.

What would she do without her? Her loyal friendship. That bawdy sense of humor. Her sense of fun, and eccentric fashion style that Peggy enjoyed so much. Angela Hanson Johnson had been so full of life. How could she possibly be dead? At just forty-nine years old?

Through three decades of life, Peggy had come to rely on Angela's resilience. During her teenaged pregnancy. Those years of Jimmy Tanner's threats to expose her family secret. Angela had been there for her daughter, too. When a broken-hearted Charlee discovered she'd been robbed of songwriting credits on the MissFits album. Angela even showed strength of steel during her own tragedies—when CJ died of an overdose. Rather than cower in a corner, she stayed busy keeping everyone else from breaking down that sad New Year's Eve. And when baby Dylan was kidnapped, Angela was there for them once again. With her steadfast strength.

Angela had been there, through all of their life's changes.

Sitting in Angela's chair, looking out at the beautiful landscaped back yard, Peggy recalled the good times, too. The day Angela showed up in her driveway—in a pink Cadillac, no less—that summer of '64, for the Beatles concert. And when she and Al danced the night away at her and Billy's wedding. And then, that day, almost a year ago now, when she'd stopped by Peggy's office. How thankful she was now that she'd put her work aside and made time for her friend. They'd had such a fun time that night. That is, until Angela had broken the news about her cancer. They both may have had too many drinks, yet it failed to numb the horrible reality.

"Hey there, you okay?"

Libby's voice shocked Peggy back to the present.

Libby stood inside the open door, as if waiting for permission to come out.

Peggy rose and gave her best friend a squeeze. "Oh, Libby, I'm so glad you're here!"

After a few moments, they pulled away, still clutching each other's arms. "Promise me you'll never die, Lib."

Libby tilted her head, and they both smiled at the absurdity of Peggy's statement. Libby held out her pinky finger. "I promise." Peggy's little finger wrapped around her friend's, and they whispered together, "Pinky swear." They hadn't done this since they'd been teens, and for a precious second, the action gave them back their youth.

Peggy nodded. "Okay, then. That's settled, let's go back in."

The funeral home was filled with a diverse crowd of people from all walks of life, representative of Angela's character. The room displayed dozens of collages with photos documenting a well-lived life. Angela with her famous Motown colleagues. Angela with Peggy and Billy in Cleveland. Angela with her cherished CJ, after they both discovered she was his mother. And, of course, Angela, with her loving husband. At center stage, stood a large framed picture of a buoyant Angela at her book launching party for her best-selling book, *Tracks of My Tears.*

Despite the attendance of celebrity singers from her days at Hitsville U.S.A., Angela's husband, Al, was the one who sang one of her favorite songs at the gravesite. As he crooned the lyrics to Bette Midler's, "The Rose," his deep tenor voice resonated through the cold crisp air on the hillside like waves of angels. The group of more than a hundred people stood around him clasping hands. Some mouthed the words along with him; others were silent in thought.

Peggy stood between everyone she loved. Billy, Libby, with Dave and seven-year-old Jack, and Dusty, holding a bereft Charlee. For the first time in years, she wished her mother were there with her. They'd never been close, but Peggy found herself thinking more about her in the five years since her death. After Peggy and Patrick had moved their mother to Cleveland, the women had made peace with one another. That, too, was due in part to Angela, who'd encouraged the mending of their relationship.

When the last song was sung, the final prayer recited, friends and family proceeded down the grassy mound. Except for Peggy Sue. Even Al knew to give her this personal moment with her longtime, cherished comrade in life.

She bent toward Angela's blue coffin covered with pink and red roses, and added two yellow roses, to represent their deep friendship, on top of the rest.

"Thank you, Ange, for sitting next to me on that bus. Thank you for being my pen pal when life seemed too awful to live. Thank you for being there for Charlee, too. Thank you for enriching my life, and saving it, more than once." She managed a grin. "And thanks for playing that song for me. I know it was you."

Peggy had been getting ready that morning in Angela's "powder room," as her friend always called it, applying the last touches of her makeup, when "Thank You for Being a Friend" came through the little turquoise radio mounted on the wall. She began singing along to it, feeling a chill rise up her spine. An oddly comforting chill.

Then she heard, *she heard*, Angela's voice singing along with her. No one would ever be able to tell her different.

Peggy wiped the tears from her cheeks. "Every time I hear that song, Ange, for as long as I live, I'll think of you. Oh yes, thank you for being a friend. We sure did travel that road, and always came back again." She grinned. "We came back stronger, and with more stories, huh? And with you riding shotgun, it was a road sure worth traveling. I will miss you terribly. But I also know you'll still be with me, as always."

Peggy wiped her dripping nose, blew her friend a kiss, then turned around. And there, in the distance, she saw her family. Billy. Charlee. Libby . . . and she let out a grateful laugh. How lucky she was.

Peggy kicked off her heels, picked up the shoes, and ran down the hill. Toward her loved ones, and the rest of her life.

19. Against the Wind

Sandra spent most of the summer of '84 setting up a makeshift "school" in her rented townhouse for her active four-year-old. Benji had befriended the kid next door, and after hearing, nonstop, about the preschool Tyler attended, Sandra knew it was time to somehow make her boy understand that he wouldn't be going to a regular school, at least not for a while. Schools asked too many questions, and she hadn't yet found someone she could trust enough to produce a fake birth certificate. Bob had proved too goody-goody. And she knew she didn't have the means to do it herself. She hoped to figure it out before the kid started first grade.

She had gotten real nervous the week of his fourth birthday when the *Plain Dealer's Sunday Magazine* published an article titled, "Whatever Happened to Echo's Baby?" with a cover photo of Echo holding her infant son the day after his birth. Sandra gasped reading that Echo and her husband had joked that their kid looked like Elvis, with the pitch-black hair and even a little snarl when he smiled. Sandra had said that same kind of thing to Nicky once. How her son had a little Elvis snarl. Damn. She'd balled up the magazine, pitched it into the trash, and hid the few snapshots she had of Benji as an infant.

Nick had seen Benji a few days after Sandra had taken him, when she'd first asked him to babysit. She was terrified he'd see that magazine photo and his mental flags would start waving. But then she got a grip on herself. All babies look alike. And Benji no longer had that dark hair.

And Nick had never once mentioned the article. Silly of her to get all worked up.

Still, she had to be especially careful now, not take a chance of ever drawing suspicion again. Last summer had almost done her in. When she'd made that stupid-ass mistake by running into Kmart for a few things while Benji slept in the backseat. He'd been so wound up that day playing with his friend that he fell asleep in the car and no way was she going to wake him just to go into the store for a bit.

She'd never forget walking out those doors with her bag and seeing that cop leaning into her car window with that old bitty next to him waving her arms like an enraged chimpanzee. Sandra thought for sure the jig was up. That they'd caught her red-handed with Echo's baby, and she'd spend the rest of her days in the slammer. *Oh dear God, what to do?*

Her first instinct had been to run. She'd even started walking briskly the other way, but in her heightened daze, she bumped into a family headed into the store, all five of them, so now she'd be the person they'd clearly remember when news broke that cops were looking for a stupid woman who left her kid in the car. *Yes, Officer? There was this lady in a white halter top and purple shorts who slammed straight into us with this guilty deer-in-the-headlights look*, they'd say in a phone call to the station. They'd probably add that her short stature was "on the heavy side," and recount her bleached white hair with black roots. That dye job had been another bad decision. She'd decided to dye her hair one lonely night after several beers, and after applying it, nodded off on the couch. The golden-blond shade she'd been aiming for turned out more like the platinum shade of a bad Dolly Parton wig. She'd then gone to Hot Clips for one of those cute pixie cuts, and well, now she looked like a silver-haired Liza Minnelli. And ever since Bob had left her that winter, she'd gained twenty pounds. Asshole.

She knew if she ran, they'd take Benji for sure, and she'd lose him by default. At least if she went over there and feigned innocence, she had a chance of pulling it off. She straightened up her posture, ignored her beating heart thrashing her chest, and turned on her best worried-mother look. "Oh, Officer! What's wrong?"

"Is this your car, Ma'am?"

"Why, yes. I just ran in the store for some baby aspirin. My child's sick."

She saw the cop's eyes fall to the package that was too large for a pack of baby aspirin. She gave him one of those *Oh, I'm so embarrassed* expressions and added, "I'm sorry, I did get a pair of tennies, and an Etch A Sketch for the poor lil' guy." She leaned in and said in her sweetest proud-mother voice, "My son's very artistic." Then she lightly touched the officer's arm. "I swear it only took an extra minute." She glanced at her watch real quick, for emphasis. "I was in there, jeez, no more than ten minutes."

Meanwhile, the bitch grandma was standing there all huffy, arms on hips, indignant. She'd started to say something to Sandra, pointing her wrinkled fingers in her face, but the cop, who looked like a rookie—a young, handsome rookie—turned to Grandma and told her that she could leave now, that he would take care of it. Sandra fought off a smirk. This bitch's over-the-top dramatics made Sandra seem like the normal one. That was when she knew she had the upper hand. The boy-cop had had enough of this "good citizen."

To Sandra's amazement, she'd convinced him that this was indeed an unusual circumstance, and added that would never take "such a chance again, let me tell you." All the while Benji had kept quiet, sleeping like the angel he was in his little booster seat.

Of course, the copper had to report it, damn it, so the incident landed in the newspaper. The article said that Grandma had flagged down the police car, which, her luck, happened to be pulling into the lot. It went on to say that although Sandra Jacobs wasn't arrested, child services would be duly notified. But that cop must have felt sorry for her. She never did hear from the agency.

Once again, God, her friend, was on her side. But she took His warning seriously. *Keep your shit together. Pay Attention.*

Now she was cooking over a hot stove in the middle of August worrying about finances. She hated the mere thought of getting a job. But all that cash her daddy had left her was slipping through her fingers like sand. It wasn't supposed to happen like this. It had been more than six years since he passed and she'd been sure that by now, she'd have found the man of her dreams. One that would keep her in the lifestyle she wanted to become accustomed to.

But no. The only one who came close was Bob, but he was just a mechanic. Still, she had really liked him, and he'd been generous with his earnings, buying things for her, and for Benji. She often reflected on that lucky rainy day when she'd met what she thought was a sure thing, at the Geneva gas station. She loved that he looked like Bob Barker, older and distinguished. She'd been so relieved when he persuaded that Glenn guy to let her have the '75 Ford Fairlane for practically a steal. Afterward, he'd taken her and Benji to a diner in Geneva-on-the-Lake called Eddie's Grill, then set them up in a hotel right on the strip, 'cause by then it was getting late. They stayed at the summer resort a full week. Bob paid for everything, so she knew he was sweet on her. They talked and talked while Benji rode those little amusement rides.

But then he up and left one day. Told her she made him "uncomfortable" sometimes. And that she drank too much. Well, how dare he get on his high horse? "You ain't nothin' but a grease monkey," she'd shouted. That comment—she knew as soon as she'd said it—would surely boomerang. And she'd been right. He never came back after that.

She could kick herself in the rear for shooting off her big mouth. She couldn't even watch *The Price is Right* any more. It made her cry.

So now what? The little bit of money she got from watching Tyler the two days he wasn't in school barely paid for groceries and her beer. The time was edging closer when she'd have to do something for money, and at thirty-four, it sure wouldn't be stripping, though she liked the fantasy. Plus, getting a job meant hiring a sitter. She'd been so happy when Nicky got that Cleveland Clinic job, but as an official LPN now, he was working fulltime, had his own place. So he only came around to see Benji a couple times a month, like a divorced father who'd up and made another life for himself.

She missed Nick's presence, of course, but she missed Bob's more, much as she hated to admit it. It didn't help none that she still had a daily reminder of the guy. That last day at Geneva they'd come across a pet store, and Bob told Benji he could have any animal he wanted. Of all those cute kitties and doggies in the place, *her* kid picks a skunk for his pet. Sandra had been so keyed up in the fact that she'd caught a live one herself, she gave her okay. Turned out to be yet another decision she'd come to regret.

"Get that damn thing off the kitchen table," she screamed at the boy as she popped bread into the toaster.

"What're are we havin' for supper, Mommy?" Ben asked, scooping up Pepe' Le Pew.

Sandra wanted to say "shit on a shingle," which *was* what it was called, but she had promised herself not to swear in front of the kid. "Chipped Beef on toast."

Ben put Pepe into his cage in the corner of the living room, and ran back to the table as she was dishing it out. He was always running, always doing things a mile a minute. That scared her a lot because if he ever got hurt and she had to take him to emergency, they might think she beat him. *That's* all she needed.

He even ate fast.

"Slow down. Remember what I told you? Chew like you're a turtle."

"Don't wanna be a turtle. I wanna be a lion. Roooarr!!" He made his wild animal face.

When the doorbell rang, she ran to the door, hoping for some, any, adult company.

"Oh! Hi, Nicky." She threw the door open. "Look who's here, Benji!"

Her eyes shot to the petite auburn-haired girl standing next to him. He had a girlfriend? Well, no matter what his new ventures included, Nicky loved her boy and would always find time to see him. Though, now it would surely be less.

"Sandra, this is my girlfriend, Ashley." He gestured to the girl as they entered the apartment.

Ashley extended her hand. "Nice to meet you."

"Yeah, you, too." Sandra managed to say.

"Nicky, Nicky!" Benji slammed into him for one of his monster hugs.

Sandra pushed the toys off the couch. "Here, come sit. Wanna drink?" She wiped her forehead. "Sorry it's so darn hot in here. Air's broke." Truth was, she didn't need another outrageous bill.

"Got some lemonade?"

Nicky looked cuter than ever, she thought, sitting there holding Ashley's hand. She was almost jealous.

She nodded on her way to the refrigerator. "Yep, even got some vodka to go with it."

"No, no, thanks," Nicky called to her back. "We both gotta work tomorrow."

When she returned with the drinks for them, and the spiked one for her, she found out a few new things. First, this Ashley girl had been around awhile, a full year. Sandra wondered why it took Nicky this long to bring her over. Did Sandra embarrass him?

Second, that Nicky had moved into her apartment. A downtown loft, because "it was larger." *And* that he had moved there before his last visit. Why was he keeping these secrets from her?

Third, and this could turn out a blessing, Ashley was quitting her job next week at Sassy's, because she'd finally gotten her teaching degree. Sandra had heard the tavern was really nice. Not like the Zanesburg Snake Pit.

"Hey! Do they need someone to take your place, Ashley? I can bartend!" Her voice was in a near screech she was so excited by the prospect.

Nicky looked surprised. He knew about her inheritance. "Why would you want to work? And what would you do with Ben?"

She forced her lips to curve upward. "Oh I'm just getting bored, you know. And . . ." she hesitated. "I, uh, I'm sure I can find someone who lives in this development to watch Benji. And it's part-time, right? I can do that."

Benji had let Pepe out and was showing him to Ashley, who didn't seem all that keen about his unique pet. Even after telling her it was de-scented.

"Benji, I think you should put Pepe away and get your jammies on for bed." Sandra looked up at the starburst clock on the wall. "It's almost nine already," she announced, happy to realize.

"But Nicky's here! I can't go to bed!" Ben said, gearing up for a tantrum.

"Oh, I'll be leavin' soon, big guy," Nicky said, picking him up on his shoulders. "If you're good and listen to your mother, I'll come and tuck ya in."

Oh, how Sandra loved that Nick.

After the tucking in, the conversation became all about Benji. "I know it's not any of my business," Nicky began, "but maybe you should start calling him Ben, 'stead of Benji. I mean, it sounds like a dog's name. And once he's in school, the kids could have a field day with that."

Sandra lit a cigarette and shook her head. "Oh, I think I'm going to homeschool him." She blew out smoke. "I've already taught him his ABCs, and how to read 'n' all. And man, you should see what he learns from *Sesame Street.*"

"What?" Nick was half off the couch, leaning into her, looking indignant. Like that grandma at Kmart. "But you don't have a teaching degree. I don't think that's even legal. Why would you *do* that? He's an only child. He needs to be around other kids."

"Goodness sakes, Nicky, cool your jets," she said. "Benji's around kids. He plays with Tyler all the time, and I take him to the playground almost every day."

"Sandra. I believe you need to be accredited to homeschool your child." This from Ashley. *Strike one, girl.*

Shit. She hadn't thought of that. She straightened up her spine. "Not to worry, I'm working on that."

Like hell she was.

She stopped then, to think a second. "Maybe I'll just do it till he's at the age where I don't know much. Then I'll hire a tutor. Ashley, you're a teacher. I can hire you!"

Ashley looked over at Nick, her lips clenched. Well, that had shut her up.

"You can't do that to him! Ben needs to grow up around other kids, like everyone else."

"Well, *my* kid isn't like everyone else!" *If only you knew how true that was.* "Besides, he's *my* kid, not yours. I can do whatever the hell I want."

A few minutes later, they were out the door.

Damn. Now she had another thing to worry about. They were bound to give her trouble about this down the road.

For the umpteenth time, Sandra wished to God she had given that little hospital visit a bit more thought.

20. Dirty Laundry

The first stirrings of the rumor came from Mario. But then, knowing how he felt about her, Charlee could easily shrug it off. Stupid rumors. She knew the kind of man she'd married—the kind that doesn't cheat. She likened Dusty to Billy, who always put Peggy Sue first in his life. Dusty was cut from the same cloth. Both had integrity. Both were loyal.

Yet, she also knew that she and Dusty had been drifting apart. Her husband had become more withdrawn around the same time that Charlee had started enjoying newfound freedom. That freedom was now her lifestyle. It was October 1984 already, which meant her little break from the music business had lasted longer than anticipated. She had gotten used to going out, a lot, with Kat and Diana, and being basically unproductive.

Dusty, on the other hand, was busier than ever. Away from home more than ever. Having established himself as a solid soundman, he was getting phone calls requesting his services. The last one, for a rock-and-roll road summer tour featuring five bands performing at various stadiums across the country. How could he pass it up? As he told her, it would increase his status in the industry and secure future work. At the time, Charlee understood.

But that was over two months ago. She missed him. And she sure didn't need stupid rumors needling her insides, fabrications about her husband with other women. She could ignore the tabloid lies—she'd been a victim of them herself for years—but she found it more difficult to ignore Mario's attempts to rile her up. She couldn't believe he'd told her that a buddy of his in L.A. had seen Dusty at a club one night with some blonde. It was as if Mario had taken it upon himself to dig for dirt. Charlee had nearly laughed in his face. Dusty didn't even like blondes. She knew about his girlfriends before she had come along. Not one a blonde.

Still, the nagging thoughts ate at her. Thank God she had Kat to talk to. Wednesdays were their *Dynasty* nights, so one night during a commercial, Charlee told her what Mario had said. But in a dismissive way. "I think I should stop watching these damn soap operas. They can make you paranoid." Her forced laugh was interrupted by the chiming of the phone.

"Oh hi, honey!" Charlee bounced on her toes at the sound of Dusty's voice. While Crystal and Alexis battled it out on TV, Charlee listened to her husband explain the reason for yet another delay home.

"I picked up a new gig here in L.A.," he told her. "There's this cool band, got a real funky vibe, with a bit of punk sensibility. They're working on their debut album, and want me in the studio. It'll only take a few weeks. Then I'll be home. Promise." He rattled it out fast. As if he knew this news would not go over well.

What could she say? He sounded so excited, she didn't have the heart to yell at him and tell him to get his ass home. Especially just because of some stupid paranoia on her part. "Well, sounds like a good opportunity. I'm happy for you, Dust." She nearly choked on the words, but she got them out.

The thing was, she knew she *should* be happy for him. He would never have to play in a cover band again. He was working with established, creative musicians, getting respect for his work, and traveling the country. She, of all people, knew how exhilarating that could be. And she was his wife. She was *supposed* to be happy for him.

She hung up the phone, told Kat what he said, and burst into tears. Kat wrapped her arms around her. "Ah, come on, hon, don't worry. He said it'll just be a little while longer."

"Yeah, and the longer he's gone the more time he's out there with all the female vultures."

Kat stood up, put her hands on her hips. "Now you just stop that kind of thinking. You've got nothing to worry about, and you know it. Dusty's so devoted to you."

Charlee reached for the end table for a tissue. "Yeah, you're right. I know he loves me," she said, smiling at her friend. "Thanks. It sounds good, reassuring, hearing it from someone else." She rose, blew her runny nose, and clicked off the set. *Dynasty* was over. "Wanna drink?"

Kat's eyes widened in surprise. It had only been a few weeks that Charlee had cut down on her drinking, limiting herself to one, two glasses a night, and only on weekends. Just yesterday Kat had mentioned how impressed she'd been at Charlee's self-control. But it was hard. Charlee had to constantly remind herself why she shouldn't drink a lot. It always started out fun, but then she'd end up depressed by night's end. She'd start thinking too much about too many sad things. Like her wobbly marriage and her missing son. Her baby would be, *was*, four-and-a-half now. Somewhere out there.

"Just one glass of wine. Come on, join me," she urged, pulling Kat's arm toward the kitchen.

Charlee pushed away the other reasons not to. She needed to get back into shape, for one. After the holidays, she wanted to start recording again. And that meant making videos. Which meant looking hot. And thin. Two beauty traits she felt she sorely lacked these days.

But she had two more months yet. One little drink couldn't hurt.

"Honey, I'm home!" Diana burst through the door, saying the same thing she always did every time she walked through the door.

Much as Charlee loved her sister-in-law, the phrase was getting old.

"We're in the kitchen." Charlee called out from behind the open refrigerator door.

"I got the internship!" Diana bounded in, brushing sprinkles of wet drops from her hair.

"Is it snowing?" Kat asked as Charlee handed her a glass of Rosé.

"Not really, just hailing a bit."

"This early in the year? Oh how I hate to see winter come." Kat gave a shiver. "Makes me cold just thinking about it. Ya know, Charlee, I'm gonna pass on that drink. I'm heading home to my fireplace!"

When Kat left, Charlee and Diana stayed in the kitchen, talking. They settled at the island counter as Diana spoke of her new position as veterinary assistant, and plans on, finally, getting her own place. Charlee wondered how things would be without Diana. She not only kept Charlee from feeling alone without Dusty, but also had taught her to be a free-spirit again. A tiny part of Charlee's brain wondered if maybe Dusty was relieved that she no longer relied on him for everything, including her own entertainment. Before Diana had moved in, Charlee knew she had become clingy, needy. So why wouldn't her husband feel relief that they were forming individual lives? That was what mature couples did.

As Diana went on about this and that, Charlee thought about Peggy and Billy's happy marriage. They'd been together for twenty years, not counting those two breakups, and each of them had their own interests, did their own thing. Billy had his radio stations; Peggy, her record label. They both had separate friends, and yet whenever they were together, they only had eyes for each other. That could describe her and Dusty, for the most part. So why did Charlee sense that her husband had drifted emotionally? Their relationship was simply maturing, like most couples who'd been together for a long time. They were going on ten years, married for seven. What they were going through was normal.

For once, can't you just enjoy things, Charlee Sue Campbell? Dusty's crazy about you, she kept telling herself. They'd just grown up, that's all.

Kat called the next morning. "Hey, guess what?"

Charlee wasn't in the mood for guessing, too busy hating herself for having that last, her fourth, glass of wine the night before. Why did she always do that?

"I just got a call from my cousin who lives in West Hollywood. Remember I told you about her? Well, her brother had a ticket to come visit, but now he can't because of work and it's too late to get a refund. So I'm going to take it! I already called Ruby, and she's giving me my vacation pay early, the dear. So I'll be leaving next Tuesday!"

"Wow, that's great, Kat," Charlee said, trying to sound enthusiastic. She held the cordless phone to her ear and made her way slowly down the stairs for coffee. Kat was talking about a week from now. Couldn't this news of hers have waited?

"So now I can get in one more blast of *warmth*, before the dreaded snow. Cool, huh?"

Charlee agreed, and started to say that she'd call her later, but Kat's next sentence stalled her in the middle of the stairway.

"And ya know, Char, if you want, I can pay Dusty a little surprise visit while I'm there. I mean, if you want."

Charlee leaned on the rail, thinking. Kat was suggesting she check up on him, and it sounded devious, just plain wrong. But then, shouldn't Charlee know exactly what her husband, who lately seemed evasive in his calls, was doing in his free time in Los Angeles? It wasn't that she didn't trust her husband. She just didn't trust other women.

And Kat could erase all her doubts. This could be a good opportunity to put Mario and those rumors in their place. Kat would be doing her a huge favor, and it would just be between them. Still, her friend would be spying on her husband, and

Charlee knew that wasn't right. But what could she do? She deserved to be reassured. And better yet, Kat might be able to get him to talk more openly, see where his head was at.

"Charlee, you still there?"

"Uh, yeah. You know, that might not be a bad idea. I can give you his address, and you can just stop in when you get time, see how he's doing n'all. I know in my heart things are fine. But, least it'll put my damn paranoia to rest."

"Yeah, you're right about that. Okay, you got it," Kat's voice chimed.

Five days after Kat left, Charlee still hadn't heard from her. Even more maddening was the fact that Charlee didn't have a number to get in touch with her, increasing Charlee's anxiety. Had Kat discovered something about Dusty she didn't want to tell her? Or had she been having so much fun doing the tourist thing with her cousin that she'd forgotten to even go there?

To make things worse, the night before Kat was due home, Dusty called and told Charlee that he was sorry, but the band needed a couple more weeks to wrap up the album.

"But that'll be close to Christmas," Charlee said, knowing her voice sounded whiny. She forced herself to stay calm. She had learned not to start an argument long distance.

She wanted to ask if he'd seen Kat, but knew she shouldn't, and since he didn't mention it, figured the answer would be no. She suppressed her anger and frustration. She knew how the business went. Once you make a commitment, you were there for the duration. So she couldn't be mad at Dusty. But she *could* be rightly pissed at her friend, who now didn't seem like much of a friend.

How could she leave Charlee hanging like this? Kat *knew* Charlee would be anxious to hear something. How could she ignore her? Leave her to wait until her friend was darn good and ready to contact her.

The day after Dusty's call, Charlee wanted to stay home and wait for Kat to call. Surely, she'd call, or even come over, once she got back to Cleveland. But Peggy called instead, urging Charlee to join her, Billy, Aunt Libby, and Uncle Dave for dinner at Ruby's Place. Since Diana had a date, Charlee had no desire to stay home alone. Besides, that was what answering machines were for. And if Kat didn't call by tomorrow? Well, at least Charlee had her home number. She'd call her there.

At the restaurant, they had all just finished ordering when Ruby came over.

"Hey, guys, what's shakin'?"

Charlee scooted over on her side of the booth. "Hi, Rube, have a seat. It's been too long since we've seen you!"

"Yeah, well, you know this biz. Always something." She squeezed next to Charlee. "And now I gotta find me a new bartender. Kat called this morning and quit. Said she wasn't coming back to Ohio. She's staying in L.A."

A shot of cold rushed up Charlee's spine. "*What?*" She knew her voice was too loud, too high-pitched. She didn't care. "She was supposed to call me all week! I haven't heard a thing from her." She slammed her hand on the table so hard, it came close to spilling all their drinks. "What the hell's goin' on with—"

"Charlee, calm down, what's the matter?" Peggy squinted at her and reached for her daughter's hand. Being unable to tell them of her and Kat's plan, Charlee understood why her reaction seemed odd. And maybe she *was* overreacting. So what if Kat was staying out there? She probably found a hot guy that she was spending all her time with. Hadn't Charlee noticed how self-centered Kat could be? Diana had even mentioned that once. And that would certainly explain why Kat hadn't bothered to call Charlee. It was perfectly logical that, knowing Kat, she'd gotten sidetracked with her own agendas.

Still, she could've made one damn phone call.

"Ruby. Please tell me she left a number where she's staying?"

Ruby scoffed. "Now why would she do that? She was my employee, not my friend."

Charlee sighed, deflated. "Well, I thought she was *my* friend." She ignored the plate of lasagna the server set in front of her. "I just can't understand why she never called me."

This was no longer about checking up on Dusty. Charlee felt genuinely hurt that someone she had grown so fond of, had confided in, had chosen to dismiss her so abruptly. They'd had done so much together that past year. They'd gone on countless shopping trips, taken hikes at the Metro Parks, and anytime Dusty didn't feel like going out to plays, movies, and such, Kat was always available.

But there is always an answer for every action, or inaction, and the following week, Charlee found that out the hard way. In public. In a grocery store. She was in the checkout line when her eyes caught sight of a small photo on the right corner of *National Celebrity* magazine. The headline read, "Is Somebody Doin' Somebody Wrong? The Answer on Page 11." The man in the photo, shirtless, standing next to a woman outside a hotel balcony, looked a lot like Dusty Campbell. Charlee did a quick glance around. The few customers in the store that afternoon were too busy with whiny kids, or caught up in their own thoughts to notice. She yanked the magazine from the rack. Goose bumps bubbled through her body as she tossed the rag on the counter, between the tall package of toilet paper and sack of potatoes. The conveyor belt moved like a slug, tempting her to just grab the magazine and run out the door, leaving her groceries behind. But she forced herself to stay put.

The minute the slowest-cashier-ever completed the transaction, Charlee scooped up the two big bags and rushed to her car. She slid into the driver's seat, pulled out the paper, flipped to the designated page, where the snapshot was larger. And clearer.

Even before reading the short article, she knew the man in the picture was her husband. She couldn't see his bowed face as he leaned against the railing, but she recognized the dark shades he wore. The Ray-Bans she'd gotten him last summer. She recognized the soft curls on his bare chest, and the messy hair spiking every which way, as it always did when he first woke up.

She also recognized the woman in the white halter-top next to him. Her long flaming red hair gleamed in the California sunshine. The she-devil apparently hadn't needed shades as she looked over at Dusty. Her smile wide. *Happy*.

The scream started from her bowels, worked its way through her chest, rushed up her esophagus where it cannon-balled out, loud and primal. The screech lasted a while until a rap on her window made Charlee jump. A woman mouthed through the closed windshield, asking if she was all right. Charlee shook her head through the glass, then, gripping the steering wheel, she started her car, slammed it into gear, and gunned the pedal.

Charlee bit the inside of her lip so hard, she could taste blood. Now she knew why Kat hadn't called her. Now she knew why Dusty wasn't coming home any time soon. In one split horrible second, her life had crashed like a car slamming into a brick building.

She raced home, grateful for the lack of cops on the way. She sped up her drive, stopping just short of the garage door. The tabloid clutched in her hand, Charlee jumped out of her car, fighting the avalanche of tears she knew were on their way. How dare he do this to her, to them? How dare they both?

Pushing open the front door, the first thing she saw was a Christmas tree. Bright, twinkling, cheery.

"Surprise, Charlee!" Diana's head popped out from around the festive spruce. She walked in front of it, and waved her hand out, like one of those models on *Let's Make a Deal*. "So whad'dya think so far?" When she noticed Charlee's expression, she stopped smiling.

"Charlee? You need help with the groceries?"

When she didn't get an answer, Diana put the box of tinsel on the end table and walked over to her. "What's wrong?"

Charlee remained in her place at the door. How could she explain to sweet, innocent Diana, surrounded by all this childlike merriment, how cruel life can be? How cruel people, her own *brother*, can be.

Charlee flung the magazine toward her. "Your brother and our *friend*, has been a bit busy these days."

"What? What are you talking—" Diana looked at the headline, then flipped the pages and stared at the photo. Her mouth opened wider as she read further. "Oh no . . ." She shook her head, then dropped the magazine on the couch. "I don't believe it. Dusty wouldn't do such a thing."

"Oh, but apparently he did." Charlee's tears had escaped. *Damn it*. They didn't deserve her tears. "Every picture tells a story." She stabbed the open page with her index finger. "And there you have it."

"Wow, I really am shocked. Well, not as much as you, I'm sure. What're you going to do?"

Charlee's eyes caught sight of the vase of flowers sent by Dusty the week before. "Well, right now I feel like throwing something. Stand back." She grabbed the pretty blue container, flung it hard as she could, and watched it fly into the fireplace. The flowers scattered, a spray of runaway blossoms. Charlee glanced over at Diana and shrugged. "They were dead anyway."

She didn't know what else to do with her anger. So she screamed again. As loud and hard as she could. "God I hate them! The sons-of-a-bitches!" Then ran up to her room, like when she was a teenager and angry at her mother.

Diana followed behind her. When Charlee fell to her bed, Diana sat down beside her, a gentle hand on her back. "I'm so sorry."

Charlee pounded her fists into her pillow. "Damn them!"

She let Diana comfort her as she sobbed and screamed. What would become of her after this? Her career was at a standstill, thanks to her self-appointed hiatus. And now she'd become tabloid fodder. A sad, pathetic victim of deceit.

And worse, she couldn't even lash out at the two people responsible for this horror because they were some 2,000 miles away. Together.

No, she couldn't do anything about anything.

All she could do was scream.

21. What about Love

Charlee was no mood to celebrate the holidays, even though she was more than glad to see 1984 go. But the next year was bound to bring nothing good, either. How did this happen? She could never have imagined losing Dusty, *and* in such a heartbreaking, and public, way.

How does one go on after being deceived by the only man you ever truly loved?

Before Dusty ruined their lives, Charlee had basked in all the pomp and circumstance that went with Christmas and New Year's. She always looked forward to being with her mother and step-father during that time. Every year, Peggy and Billy had big doings throughout the month of December, which helped Charlee cope with the anniversary of Ray and Jo's deaths when she was eleven. With so much activity and frequent company of family and friends, Charlee rarely thought about that sad event in her young life.

But now she'd have another awful memory. The last thing Charlee wanted now was to be inside her mother's decorated home—which included two live trees from the nearby tree farm—the sprinkled cookies, the happy faces, especially that of Aunt Libby's son, Jack, whose childlike wonder at it all reminded Charlee of what she was missing, without Dylan.

It would all be too much this year. And her mother knew it.

The week before Christmas, Peggy came over and surprised Charlee with a generous gift. A chance for escape. "You know, Uncle Patrick and Aunt Nina are spending the holidays in the Riviera Maya. How'd you like to meet them down there? It'll be Billy and my present to you," Peggy said with misty eyes.

Charlee knew her marital disaster was breaking her mother's heart, too. Peggy and Billy had loved Dusty like a son.

That was when Charlee noticed, for the first time, the streaks of gray highlighting her mother's face. Why had she thought they were bleached strands of platinum? What else had she not noticed lately?

She touched Peggy's arm. "Oh, Mom, I love you. I know you'd rather have me here, but you are so right. I do need to get away. And how great it'll be to see Patrick and Nina again!" She felt an unexpected spurt of excitement.

She also felt a surge of gratitude. Her mother understood that, while her family gave Charlee comfort during the season when she missed her baby the most, now without Dusty with her, Christmas would be absolutely unbearable.

It wasn't as if he hadn't tried to make amends these past few weeks. He just hadn't tried hard enough. It seemed to Charlee that he'd given up all too easily.

But then, whose fault was that?

She had ignored his constant calls those first few days after the story broke. She then refused to see him when he came home on the red-eye, abandoning the recording sessions he had committed to. That action had shocked Charlee because she knew his doing so threatened his burgeoning career, and enrage the band and others involved. It was bound to hurt Dusty's reputation for reliability in an industry where recreational activities, like drugs, alcohol, and women, often got in the way of work. Charlee never dreamed her husband would succumb to any of those calamities. He didn't take drugs, and drank only socially, much less than she did. And women? In their ten years together, she had never once caught him looking at another woman. At least not with sexual interest.

But her Dusty had changed. Still, Charlee had a hard time believing he would do this to them. She did understand that married people sometimes get bored with each other, but she and Dusty had never felt that way. At least she hadn't thought so. Why would he dare risk his marriage for someone who clearly was just a plaything? Someone who'd been his wife's *good friend*?

Why? Because I hadn't paid enough attention to him. And Kat was always around.

Kat, with her glistening strawberry hair, and C-cup breasts, which she was only too proud to display. Kat, who must've had her eye on Charlee's husband the whole time she *pretended* to care about his wife.

And here, Charlee had been busy acting like a teenager, going out too often, leaving her husband to fend for himself. True, Dusty preferred to stay home in the evenings after working all day. But she did not. Yet she knew, she *knew* there were times she should've been with him. Even his own sister had mentioned a few times that maybe Charlee should stay home more often. But Kat . . . *Kat* . . . would always say, "Oh come on, he'll be here when you get home."

Right. Oh, what a fool she had been! Charlee could see everything so clearly now. All those times Kat would be over when Dusty was home, and she'd be wearing her most revealing outfits. Charlee had thought little of it then, accepting that Kat was just one of those girls who liked showing what she had. She enjoyed drawing men's attention. So why had Charlee thought her husband was immune?

She hated them both so much right now. But she hated herself more. For being so damn stupid.

When Charlee told Diana about her trip to Mexico, she assured her sister-in-law that she could continue to stay at the house. "But you have to *promise* me you won't breathe a word to Dusty. I need this time by myself, and I'll never, ever forgive you if you tell him where I am."

A handshake sealed the promise.

The first face Charlee saw when she landed at the Cancun airport was her Uncle Patrick. She dropped her bags and flew into his arms. The last time she'd seen him was in L.A. when she'd been on tour. Which now felt like another life ago.

"Oh God, it's so good to see you!"

"You, too, Shoop," he said, holding her tight, not letting go.

The sound of his special nickname for her prompted a second round of tears. The first being the whole way out in the plane. But at least these were happy tears.

Patrick had labeled her Shoop when she was ten years old and they were dancing in the kitchen to the song, "Shoop, Shoop (It's in his Kiss)" in their stocking feet. But he only called her that when he knew she needed it most.

His wife, Nina, stood behind him, letting them have their moment. Charlee knew her uncle would hold her for as long as she needed, so she was the one to finally break the hug and step back, though still gripping his arms. "Wow, I feel like I've been rescued," she said, letting out a little laugh, feeling silly by her tears. She couldn't explain her feelings any other way. More than anyone, besides Dusty, Patrick made her feel safe, protected.

"You know I'm always here for you." Patrick smacked her cheek, then drew Nina into their fold. "We both are."

Charlee gave Nina a squeeze. "Good to see you, too, Neen. I've missed you both so much."

"Come on, let's get your luggage," Nina said. As they walked toward baggage claim, she added, "You look great."

Charlee smiled back, appreciating the white lie. "You,

too," she said, noticing how, even in a ponytail, Nina's shiny brown hair looked perfect.

As they stood waiting for her bags, Patrick put his arm around his niece. "I'm glad you came."

Charlee leaned her head on his shoulder. "Yeah, so am I." She looked up to meet his eyes. "Thanks for letting me."

He shrugged. "Hey, I figure if you get outta hand, I can always send you packing."

Charlee grinned and faked a sigh. "I'll try to be good, but ya know, I *am* single now. Almost." She immediately regretted bringing it up. Luckily, the moment passed, thanks to the arrival of her luggage.

The exclusive resort was a lavish get-away that only the well-to-do could afford. Charlee didn't know how much money the couple made, but she was glad to see that, between Patrick's photography work at *American Rocker*, and Nina's art gallery, where she sold her oil paintings, they obviously earned enough.

Patrick had booked two large connecting suites for them. The door that separated Charlee from him and Nina, was wide open as they entered, making the space look more like an apartment than a hotel room. After Patrick set Charlee's suitcases in her room, he came over to her and ruffled her hair. "So when 'cha do this?" referring to her short spiky, frosted haircut.

She caught the "why-did-you-mention-it?" look Nina gave him.

Charlee flinched and pulled at the gelled spikes atop her head. "I cut it when my face became newsworthy again, no thanks to my husband and my former slut friend." She grabbed a Salem from her purse. "Thought I'd go for the Annie Lennox look." She grinned and lit the cigarette. "What? Don'cha like it?"

"Oh yeah! Looks great," they both said in unison.

Charlee had to laugh. "Hey, it's already worked couple of times. I sure don't look like Echo now," she added, pulling at her slightly baggy jeans, a result of losing twelve pounds in three weeks. "And this country-western shirt is one of Diana's old hand-me-downs. Not one person on the plane gave me that I-know-who-you-are look. A real blessing these days."

They celebrated Christmas on the beach, and New Year's at a local bistro. Charlee did nothing those weeks but eat, drink, and lay in the sun. By the time Patrick and Nina were ready to leave, Charlee had gained back six of those lost pounds. She had even managed a genuine smile a few times.

She'd also decided to stay. At least until she felt she could deal with her life. She was just getting ready to call her mother to tell her when the phone rang in her hand.

"Mom! I was just going to call you."

"Really? Guess we still have that telepathy thing going. Hey, I've got exciting news for you. A great gig you're gonna love. But you gotta get home right away because it takes place in a couple of weeks."

"A couple of weeks? No way. That's what I was calling you about. I found a beautiful little villa here and just signed a lease to rent it for six months. I figure I can work on songs for a new album. Without distractions." She knew the mention of work would please her mother. Or at least she thought.

"What? No. You can't."

Why did mothers always sound like *mothers*? "Mom. You know I need this time away."

"Look, I'm sorry for the late notice, but this came up suddenly. I didn't know about it until last week and had to jump on it fast. Believe me, you'll want to be a part of this."

Charlee's sigh was audible through the phone lines. Her mother could be so difficult when she set her mind on something. Charlee carried that same trait, which was why this conversation was already doomed. "Mom, I'm not going back right now."

"I understand how you're feeling, but I wish you'd have told me before signing anything. Now listen. I've arranged for you to take part in the 'We Are The World' record that Quincy Jones is producing. Did you hear about it?"

Charlee hadn't a clue what Peggy was talking about. Although there was a *USA Today* paper in the lobby every day, she'd never bothered to read it. She didn't care what was happening in the world. Not even the music world.

When she said as much, her mother responded, "It wasn't in the papers. This is top secret." Then she went on to explain about a recording session involving the biggest names in music to help raise money for African famine relief. "Let me name just a few involved. Michael Jackson, Billy Joel, Bruce Springsteen, Smokey Robinson . . ."

"Smokey, too?"

Charlee's heart sank. She'd last seen the Motown singer at Angela's funeral, and would have been thrilled at the chance to work with him on a record! What lousy timing.

Obviously, her mother had made great effort in giving her this opportunity, too. "Oh, Mom, I'm sorry, really. It sounds great, and any other time I'd—"

"Charlee," Peggy stopped her short. "Just cancel the lease and come back. The recording starts the end of this month."

Charlee couldn't believe her ears. Her mother never, ever, condoned canceling commitments, especially ones involving a signed agreement. To add to her current mindset, Charlee now felt a hefty dose of guilt.

As her mother laid out the details, Charlee weighed the options. Yes, she could call up the nice woman and tell her that something had come up, that Charlee couldn't rent the villa, after all. As she contemplated it, she heard Peggy say the session was taking place in a studio in L.A.

"Los Angeles? Oh, no way! You know Dusty went back there after—"

"After you refused to talk to him." Charlee realized now that this recording wasn't the only "opportunity" her mother had in mind. She recalled their last conversation, on New Year's Day, when Peggy begged her to at least hear what Dusty had to say. "Sometimes things are not as they seem," she had told her.

To which Charlee responded, "Well, they are when you have photographic evidence."

"Charlee, did you ever think that maybe Kat had just gotten there that morning? That they were simply talking on the balcony?"

Charlee had shaken her head at the phone. Her mother, the eternal Pollyanna. "Don't you think I thought of that? But one look at Kat's face in that picture says it all." Then she'd changed the subject.

Now her mother attempted to reason with her again. "Come on, I'll make the plane reservations for you. All you need to do is pack and get a cab to the airport."

"No." She stopped to take a deep breath. "I am not going to L.A. And I certainly can't face my personal idols, who would expect me to bring my A-game. I no longer have an A-game.

"Mom, please. Much as I'd love to do it, I want—I *need*—to stay here. Alone. With my thoughts. I want to figure out what to do with the rest of my life. Without the guy I always thought would be there." She was crying now. "Please don't harp on me."

"Oh, honey, I know. I just think this would be good for you, both personally and professionally. Please give it some real thought, okay? But, so you know, I need to let Quincy know by tomorrow afternoon."

"Mom. I'm not going to change my mind."

Her mother, being her mother, added that if she was so set on staying, that she should be diligent about working on her next album. Peggy proceeded to name the latest female artists enjoying Top Ten hits: Prince's protégé, Sheila E., with "The Glamorous Life," Madonna with "Like a Virgin," and Tina Turner's "What's Love Got to Do With It."

"If Tina can get back on top after that nasty divorce, you surely can, too," Peggy told her.

Divorce? The word made her stomach clench.

Charlee knew this was meant to rile her up, but thinking of those great new songs made her question if she had the ability to compete with those hit records. Did she have one thread of creative thought left inside her aching soul?

When the highly promoted "We Are the World" single was released that March, along with a music video, Charlee felt a stab of regret. Yet she still knew she'd made the right decision. The Riviera was paradise to her. She felt at home in the quaint villa on the secluded beach. She loved basking in the sun's rays, snacking on apples or chips, drinking fancy cocktails, and reading tons of books. She'd forgotten what blissful escapism books could be. And the warm breezes and clear aquamarine water had been the salve she'd needed for her broken heart. The best of all diversions.

She'd even settled into a productive routine. She forced herself out of bed with each sunrise, greeting the sunbeams that streamed through her bedroom window. Then came coffee, followed by a stroll on the beach, notebook in hand. Ready for inspiration to strike.

Most days she'd lounge on the Adirondack chair until the music sounded in her head. When she felt she had enough lyrics for a good song, she'd rush up the hill to her little house, and to the old, but functional, piano that waited for her in the living room like a faithful friend.

Other days, she'd head to the outside café down the street. She loved the townspeople she met at Le Mango.

They were a friendly lot, yet kept a respectful distance. They understood she wasn't there to socialize because they, too, were there to create, or at least be inspired by something along the causeway. The regulars included visual artists, writers and poets, even one playwright. The atmosphere reminded Charlee of Hemingway's *A Moveable Feast*, one of the many books she recently read. His prose gave her the motivation she'd been seeking. Like Papa Hemingway in the 1920s, she lived in an exotic location in which the surrounding beauty itself painted a backdrop for imagination and creativity. In this welcoming seaside café, alongside like-minded souls, Charlee had found a piece of heaven.

By May, she'd composed six songs she thought were pretty good. Although that usually was enough to get her back into the recording studio, she still wasn't ready to come home. In fact, she had grown to love this place so much, she decided to stay indefinitely. Perhaps for the entire year of 1985.

She knew at least one person who wouldn't be happy with this news. While Peggy had plenty of work with other artists on her label, "Echo" was still a major player on Peggy Sue Records. When her mother called to tell Charlee of yet another not-to-be-missed opportunity, this time for Live Aid, an all-star benefit concert for Ethiopia scheduled for that summer, Charlee told her of her latest plans.

First, a pause. Then, a huge sigh. Then, "I don't like how you're handling this, Charlee. You can't hide out forever."

"Yes I can."

Heavier sigh. "You've been gone for nearly six months. You have to come back and get on with your life."

"I *am* getting on with my life. I'm making new friends, and I have enough songs for half an album. I'm being productive, Mother, not just vegetating."

She said this despite the fact that it had been a hot, breezy Mexican day and she had lazed around all morning on the beach. No way would she mention that after her adamant declaration of how *productive* she'd been.

"Dusty called last night."

"What? What did he want?" Since hiding out, Charlee hadn't heard anything from, or about, him.

"He wanted to explain things to me, so I invited him over. Now, I know it's probably none of my business—"

"No, it's not."

"But I, too, wanted to get his side. I figured there's gotta be something he wants you to know and that I could be the messenger. Since he has no idea where you *are*."

Charlee didn't like Peggy's tone. Was she taking his side now?

"And I'd like to keep it that way." Charlee plopped down on the nearby wicker chair. "So what he tell you?"

"Honey, you need to speak to him personally."

"I thought you were acting as messenger."

Another frustrated sigh. "Charlee. You need to get back here and settle this, one way or another. It's not fair to either of you."

"*Mom.* I. Am. Not. *Ready.*"

"Well, damn it, Charlee! You should *get* ready. You need to get in the studio again. Get that album out before no one knows—or cares—who you are anymore. That is, if you still want a career. And even if you don't, you need to, as my father used to say, shit or get off the pot."

Charlee would've laugh at the ludicrous expression if this hadn't been such a serious conversation. One thing she'd discovered while living in this nirvana world, she still wanted to make music. Now it was her turn to sigh. "I'll come home when I finish the other songs. I promise."

Peggy's voice softened. "Honey, don't wait too long. Life is short. Either try and save your marriage, or just get a divorce and be done with it."

Her mother was trying to force her hand. And in her mind, she knew Peggy was right. But in her heart, and despite everything, Charlee did not want a divorce. Then again, Dusty had cheated, so what choice did she have? Talking to him wasn't going to change the facts.

"Give everyone my love," she said. Then she hung up.

The following week, Charlee was once again relishing the beauty surrounding her as the sun beat down on her tanned body. Through dark glasses, she watched the pelicans swarm around, envying their ability for flight. Peggy's words compelled her to review the events of the past few years. She had been no angel in this marriage, either. She'd been so caught up in her grief over Dylan, she hadn't considered her husband's own pain. She had allowed herself to ignore what was going on inside Dusty's head, and chose to focus on exercising her own independence, spending more time with girlfriends than perhaps she should have. Worst of all, she had almost succumbed to Mario's affection. But then, unlike her husband, she *hadn't*.

But it was time to forget about it. If that was possible. It all was a done deal.

Charlee sat up from her chaise lounge chair, grabbed the bottle of lotion, and began stroking her legs.

"Would you like some of that on your back?"

Charlee froze. It wasn't the question that paralyzed her. It wasn't even the fact that this was a private beach where no one came unless invited. It was the voice.

Was she imagining it?

"Yes, it's me."

She wanted to spin around, see Dusty's face again. She had missed him so, in spite of herself. But she willed her body to remain in check. Her hand motionless on her leg.

Until her emotions defied her, and she burst into tears.

"Go away," she said, burying her face with her knees. The tropical smell of coconut oil suddenly nauseated her.

"Sorry, but I'm not going anywhere." He walked around and stood in front of her, hands on hips.

She peeked up at him over her legs. One quick look and her heart sank. He had lost weight. His blue tank shirt hung loose, though his khaki shorts showed he still owned those muscular legs she knew so well. His sun-streaked hair was longer than she remembered, past his shoulders, and curlier, like Robert Plant's. Only thing missing was his trademark hat, her favorite Dusty accessory.

He removed his shades and stared into her eyes. Her soul. *Damn.*

"Damn you!" She pounded the chair, hurting her hand. "Ouch. Damn. Shit." She rubbed her palm as Dusty moved closer—as if by habit—wanting to hold it, make it better. Then he must have remembered, and drew back.

"How'd you find me?" she spit out. It had to have been her mother. She clenched her face. "I can't believe Mom told you!"

Dusty shook his head. "She didn't. She refused to, actually. Even after I begged."

"Oh. Diana! Damn that girl, I'll kill her—"

"It wasn't Diana." Dusty shook his head. "If you must know, it was Patrick."

"Patrick?" she yelled, frightening away a seagull. *How could he, of all people, betray her?*

Dusty held out his hand like a traffic cop. "Now before you make plans to kill him, too, he only did it because he loves you, and he knows we need to clear this up. After I talked to him, he told me to get on a damn plane."

Charlee swiped at her burning face, hot with fury, sprang from the chair, and took off toward the ocean. "Go away!" she yelled, her voice echoing through the gusty wind. "Leave me alone!" She dove into the aqua Caribbean, knowing he'd come after her. And also knowing half of her ached for him to do just that.

The refreshing water had quickly cooled her off, both physically and mentally. She swam, anxiously waiting to feel him grab her. Anytime now he'd come after her, and she'd let him. She'd let him rescue her.

But he didn't.

Finally, she bobbed her head up to look back toward the beach. Dusty was just standing there. As if the sand held him hostage. She dogpaddled in the water, pondering what to do next. Seeing him wait patiently for her to come out of the water, she couldn't stifle a little giggle, despite herself. He knew she had to get out of the water eventually. Where else could she go, but back on land?

Still, she would take her own sweet time.

So she swam. She did the breaststroke, the backstroke, the jellyfish, the butterfly, the sidestroke, then turned onto her back and floated a bit. When she ran out of swimming positions, she flipped over and began gliding toward shore. At the edge of the water, she stood up, brushed away her wet hair, shaking her head in slow motion, like Bo Derek. Then she looked up in the most casual of manners to meet his gaze.

But Dusty wasn't there.

He wasn't by her chair. Wasn't walking along the beach. Wasn't up the hill. She whipped around. No, he wasn't in the water, either.

Well, what'd you expect, stupid girl? You told him to leave you alone!

She stood frozen, barely feeling the waves slapping her feet. She could actually feel her heart sink. She wanted to dive back in the sea and stay underwater, until she drowned.

Instead, she lifted her chin, inhaled a sigh, then walked back to her spot. She grabbed her towel and wrapped it around herself all the while searching for him. No, he really was gone. Her knees gave way then, and she fell into the sand, and let herself have a good cry.

She had blown it. Here, she thought she'd be cute and play hard to get, and in doing so, had ruined any chance they had at communicating. She hadn't even gotten to hear whatever he had come to say.

After some time, Charlee dragged herself up and headed toward her little beach house, her beloved sanctuary. That now looked like a lonely, shallow hut.

She pushed open the door and leaned against the knob to wipe off her sandy feet.

"Don't you lock up the place when you leave? Anybody can just walk right in."

Her head shot up, and she was startled and relieved at the same time. Her heart danced at the sight of him, standing in her little kitchenette. She dropped the towel and started toward him. She longed to run into his arms, feel them around her.

She stopped just in time.

No. She would not give him this. She first needed to hear why he had come. Why it was this important for him to say what he had to, in person. And it had better be good.

"Okay, you win." She walked over to the tiny fridge behind him. "Let's talk."

She reached for the ingredients to make her new favorite drink. It was hard to argue when you had frozen Pina Coladas in hand. She would mix only an adequate amount for two glasses. Just enough to break the ice. She wanted to be clearheaded for whatever came next.

22. Almost Paradise

"So you honestly think I had an affair? With *Kat*?" Dusty asked her. It was the first thing out of his mouth after they'd taken two big slurps of liquid courage.

He sat straight up on the hardwood chair, his arms folded across his chest. Waiting for her response.

Charlee glared at him. Did he take her for an idiot? "You came all the way down here only to deny it? Are you kidding me? The whole fuckin' world saw you two, all cozy there on the balcony."

Dusty shook his head, his lips clenched. "What infuriates me most is that you didn't trust me. I can't believe you fell for that. Remember how we'd talk about that Eagles song, 'Dirty Laundry?' How people love it when you lose. Remember saying how you wouldn't believe anything the tabloids claimed?"

Charlee's mouth dropped. This wasn't about media gossip, and he knew it. She leaned forward, hands flat on the table. "Dusty. She was in your hotel room. Early in the morning."

"Yes. She was." He lit a cigarette. After sucking in a drag, he met her gaze. "Okay, you ready to hear the truth about what happened?"

She wanted to say, *Only if you can prove it was all a lie,* but kept mum.

"I've waited all this time to finally talk to you because I know you. I knew it would take some time for you to cool off and be open to hearing me out. But it's been too long, Char, and now you can't avoid me. So, will you please just listen?"

She sat back against her chair and took another sip of her drink. "Yes. Okay."

Dusty nodded and stamped out the Marlboro in the ceramic ashtray made by one of her new café friends. "Kat pounded on my door at eight that morning, waking me up. I was shocked to see her. I had no idea she was in town. Or why she was there to see me at such an ungodly hour. She said she couldn't sleep. I made some coffee, and she went out on the balcony . . .

"I came out with the cups and set them down on the little table there, and asked what was up. First she hugs me, saying how glad she is to see me. Then she starts yapping about nothing I cared about. When I broke in and asked how you were, she says to me, 'That's what I came to talk to you about. I'm sorry to have to tell you, but Charlee cheated on you. I just think you should know.' Then she told me about Mario."

"What?" Charlee sprang off her chair like she'd been stung by a wasp.

"She said it happened when you two were on tour." His eyes stayed fixed on hers. "That you told her about it yourself."

Oh that bitch! Charlee couldn't believe it. The girl had used her own words in confidence to betray her, end her marriage. But then, of course, she would. Kat had been after Dusty all along.

Charlee felt her face grow hot, despite her will to keep from blushing. The last thing she wanted was to look guilty over something she wasn't guilty of. "Dusty, it never happened."

"No?"

"*No!*" She swung around the table, stood beside him, and placed her hand on his. "Okay, there was one time . . . well, technically, two . . . when Mario made a play for me. And yes, it was when we were on tour. I was lonely out on the road, and he knew it. First time, it was just a quick kiss, but then one night, he kissed me and tried to go further, but I pushed him away. Dusty, I swear. Nothing happened.

"And I *told* Kat exactly that! She lied to seduce *you.*"

To her surprise, Dusty smiled. He gazed at her with an expression that looked a lot like love. "I believe you."

Those words echoed through her body like a harp. "You do?"

He pulled her onto his lap. "It took me a while to figure this whole mess out 'cause I was as incensed about hearing that as I know you were about seeing that picture.

"You see, Sunshine, we were duped. When Kat told me about Mario, I naturally went crazy. I had suspected his interest in you, so when she told me that, I did believe it. At first."

"So you didn't trust me either." She couldn't help use his own assumption against him. "I thought you knew me better."

"Well, I used to. But we've never been right after losing Dylan. You know that. And when I thought about how rocky things had been . . . Yes, I believed it, and I'm sorry. So anyway, Kat began saying all those things a man wants to hear after his heart's been ripped out. Like, how sorry she was, but she just *had to* tell me. And how I deserved better—

"And *that*, my dear, is precisely when that photo was taken. If you look closely at my expression, even with my shades on, you'll see I was kinda dazed. Looking down in disbelief, while the bitch was gazing at me, all lovey."

"Did you kiss her?"

"Yes. I did. I won't lie to you. I went back inside, headed straight for the suite bar. Downed one of those little bottles of Jack Daniels." He shook his head. "Man, don't know how people drink that stuff."

Charlee didn't crack a smile. She needed to hear more. "And?"

"Well, that's when she had me right where she wanted me."

Charlee took in a breath. Did she really want to hear this?

"For about five minutes. She kissed me, and I kissed her back. Then she started getting more aggressive, all the while saying how she'd always wanted me, how we need each other, etcetera, etcetera. But it actually had the opposite effect. Mad as I was at you, I didn't want her. Not even for revenge. I threw her out. Almost bodily."

"Oh, Dusty." She hugged his neck. It felt so good to be on his lap again, like when they were young.

"Charlee, when that photo came out I was devastated. I knew how you'd take it. But you have to remember, I was still angry at you. Still believed about you and Mario. After I cooled down some, I started questioning the whole scenario. When I flew back to talk to you—and couldn't, because you were being so stubborn—I tracked down Mario and confronted him. After a little persuasion"—he smiled a devil's grin—"he told me how he initiated it. Took all the blame. Like a man, I must say. He assured me that you rejected him because you were still in love with me."

Dusty took her chin in his hand and turned her face to meet his gaze. "But then you were gone. And no one would tell me where you were. That was months ago. Then I figured something else out. And got it confirmed just a couple weeks ago. I tracked down the photographer, who admitted Kat paid him a princely sum to conveniently be there in the bushes when the right time came to snap an incriminating photo. She had stepped out onto the balcony that morning on purpose, with that guy there waiting for the perfect shot."

"God, she's relentless!" Charlee started to pound her fist on the table, but this time, Dusty caught her before she made contact. "Don't go hurting that pretty hand again," he said, kissing it.

He slid his fingers through her hair and pulled her head toward him. He kissed her lips so softly, it sent sweet chills through her whole body. "You are still the most beautiful woman on the planet," he whispered in her ear.

"And you"—she slapped his arm playfully—"have a baaaaad, and wooonderful, habit of turning up unannounced," she said, recalling the other time he'd surprised her, in New York.

"And I am *not* sorry for that." He kissed her again, then added, "I've missed the hell out of you, Sunshine."

Then he scooped her up and carried her to bed.

Where they remained for the next two days.

During that time, they discussed how they would do things different this time. Be more patient, kind, and *listen* to one another. As they lay in bed, arms entwined, Dusty admitted his longtime source of pain, "No one ever bothered to ask me how *I* felt about Dylan's kidnapping. Like only a mother could feel how you felt. But the agony seethed through every nerve in my body, just as deep as yours. Yet I felt it was my job as the husband to bury it and concentrate on taking care of you. Still, I resented that my feelings didn't seem a part of the equation."

His words broke her heart. She realized that she had made his pain that much worse because of her lack of response to his emotions. How she hated herself for that.

Her lips quivered as she touched his cheek. "I am so sorry, Dust. I was so selfish."

He grabbed her hand and kissed it. "I wasn't perfect either. We've both learned a lot. We're different people now."

She couldn't agree more. She even felt like a changed person. Stronger somehow. More mentally alert. And more capable of a deeper love.

It all felt like a miracle.

She even surprised herself by telling her husband that she'd be open to the thought of having another baby. But perhaps, she thought, grinning, they'd get a dog first.

On the third day of his surprise visit, Dusty had to say goodbye. He had gotten another recording job, this time for a Cleveland band called Wild Horses. After skipping out on that one job, he'd have to prove himself again as a reliable soundman.

"I'll be right behind you, Cowboy," she said, hugging and kissing him all over his face.

Charlee longed to go with him, but there were too many things she had to do first. She needed a few days to tell her landlord, gather up her things, say goodbye to her pals at Le Mango, and buy a good book for the flight home. Part of her hated to leave this beautiful island, but the excitement over her reunion with Dusty, and anticipation of being home with him again trumped all melancholy.

Living independently for the first time in her life had made Charlee see with renewed perspective. As much as her heart and soul would always ache for the baby she lost, she would no longer let the tragedy control her life, and her relationships. It took almost losing Dusty for her to realize that living life solely to counteract your pain only serves to complicate it. Life was too short to constantly dwell on things beyond one's control.

Something had happened while she'd been away. "I think it has something to do with growing up," she told one friend at the café when she explained why she was leaving.

For the first time, she felt in command of her own destiny. And that felt freeing.

Her heart leapt thinking how lucky she was that Dusty had come for her, and straightened out the whole sordid mess. If it had been left to her, they might have indeed gotten divorced, and ruined their lives. She made a mental note to thank Patrick for being a wise uncle and interfering. And yes, her mom, too, for her persistence.

Now all she had to do was take the dreaded plane ride home. She'd decided on a charter flight to avoid fans, who'd be sure to recognize her now that her bleached blond, spiky hair had grown out and back to its normal look. She hated to fly no matter what, but the smaller private plane guaranteed some solitude.

Turned out, it wasn't a guarantee. At the last minute, Roger, the pilot, decided to let an older couple on board, which meant a stopover in Philadelphia. Charlee thought about offering him more money to just get her home, but then told herself, it wouldn't be that much of a delay. She needn't have worried. After polite introductions, the man and woman chose not to socialize further.

As the plane left the ground, Charlee settled into reading her book, *Wired: The Short Life and Fast Times of John Belushi*. Fans of *Saturday Night Live* were still in shock over the comedian's death two years before. Charlee knew his fascinating, and controversial, life story would help keep her mind occupied through the flight to Pennsylvania. The last hour it would take to Cleveland, she'd be too excited to read.

After an hour, she drifted off to sleep. She'd just started dreaming when she woke in a panic. The plane was shaking erratically. Charlee was seated right behind Roger, and though the shimmying immediately raised her fears, it was the older woman who yelled out, "What's happening? Why is it shaking?"

"Oh don't worry, ma'am," Roger said, "we just hit a pocket of turbulence. Might be a little shaky until we get past this."

Charlee loosened her grip on her seat. Well, she sure wasn't going back to sleep now. She leaned back and reminded herself that people fly every day. She shouldn't let herself get rattled. Shouldn't let a little normal vibration take her mind to any dark places. Not now. She was just hours away from living her new life with her husband. She closed her eyes and thought about Dusty, and the pact they'd made the night before he left.

They'd had dinner on the beach, with a chilled bottle of Cabernet, lit candles all around, and renewed their vows. No clergy needed.

They promised to cherish their love and always put each other first. To trust the other, and communicate their feelings—and never again let other people, or even circumstances beyond their control, fray their bond. This was a lifetime commitment they both were happy to pledge.

Remembering that magical evening made Charlee more anxious than ever to get home, where she belonged. She picked up the book from her lap, hoping it would make time speed ahead. She flipped to the dog-eared page.

Then the plane shook again. Violently.

"Oh my God!" the other female passenger screamed.

This time, the pilot's voice sounded far less calm.

"I'm, uh, I'm afraid it seems we're having some engine trouble. I'm searching for a place to land. Just need to get over this body of water."

Charlee's heart thrashed her chest. She forced herself not to look at the terrified woman next to her. She wanted to have faith in the pilot, but she didn't even know him! Was he capable of getting them through this?

The plane was shaking constantly now. Her fears escalated to the point that she knew she was going to die. All her years of being afraid to fly, and here, she was going to die in a plane crash.

Like her father.

Is this how Frankie London felt his last moments on earth? It had always made her sad to think of the dad she never knew, and now, for the first time, she felt close to him. She was sharing the same terror he must have experienced. She'd always wished she would've known him. The young man her mother had been so in love with. The beloved rock 'n' roll hero, whose death in 1959 at the age of twenty-one had never been forgotten.

Now she, his daughter, was heading toward the same fate. At twenty-seven years old.

Chills bubbled through her skin as she gripped her rocking seat. She'd always thought it odd that Brian Jones, Jimi Hendrix, Janis Joplin, and Jim Morrison all died at age twenty-seven. Now she'd be added to that infamous list. The plane bounced in fits and starts as Charlee watched Roger fight to keep the craft from flipping over.

"We're going to die!" Mrs. Hysterical screamed again.

Her husband, sitting in the co-pilot's seat, turned around and yelled, "Louise, be quiet!" at the same time Charlee shot back, "Yeah, shut the fuck up, will ya?"

"I need you all to stay calm," Roger said. "I've radioed the Miami airport to make clearance. If we can get—"

His voice stopped when the plane took a sudden dip, like an elevator shaft that skipped a floor.

"Hang on, folks. Prepare for landing."

They all bent forward, their heads between their knees, eyes shut tight. Charlee prayed harder than she'd ever done. As the plane fell through the sky, Charlee clung to thoughts of Dusty, his hazel eyes, that sandy hair with the curls on the ends. That cowboy hat. His great love for her . . .

And Dylan! *"No!"* she cried out. She couldn't die! Not without knowing where their little boy was. Not ever seeing him again. She began praying to all those she was on her way to meet. Her father, Jo, Ray, CJ, and Angela. Well, maybe she'd be Dylan's guardian angel.

"No, no," she repeated, her hands on her face. "This can't be happening! I'm not ready!"

Please God, save us. Somehow, someway, get us through this. Let me live.

"Prepare for impact," were the last words Charlee heard before the plane rushed toward the earth.

23. Heaven

The first voice Charlee heard when she woke up was Bryan Adams. He was singing a soft, lyrical song that rang in her ears like an angel serenading her. A smile came to her lips before she tried opening her eyes. "Heaven." The song was one she and Dusty had danced to their last night at the Riviera beach house. They had sung it together, feeling every word, and it really wasn't hard to believe they were in heaven, wrapped in each other's arms. Was that where she was now?

She opened her eyes.

"Hey, my only Sunshine." Dusty was leaning over her and grinning as he caressed her hand.

She looked around the room that smelled of antiseptic and spotted a big radio in the corner, where the music was coming from. "Where . . . where am I?" A stupid question she knew. The familiar faces, all smiling at her, told her that she was the reason they were here. Her eyes moved in a circular motion. To her left, her mother, Billy, Aunt Libby and Uncle Dave. On her right side, Dusty.

"You're okay. Oh, thank God, you're okay." He laid his head down on her belly, his relief evident.

She squinted, trying to remember why she might be here. A car accident? Then she recalled an alarming sense of fear. A sense of free-falling. Had she just dreamed she was plummeting . . . out of the sky? Had that been real?

"Oh, honey, you look so much better today." Peggy's eyes were red, and so wet with tears that Charlee was surprised she could see anything at all.

"Better? Than what? What happened?" Charlee saw their eyes shifted to one another, as if deciding who was going to speak next. Their gaze settled on Dusty.

"Your plane had an emergency landing. It crashed in Key Largo, but you're okay, you're okay," he repeated quickly, trying to assure her, and what sounded like, himself. "The pilot did a great job with the landing. You have a concussion and bruised your ribs. And you have a broken leg, but that's it."

She attempted to sit up. "Ouch. Oh." Yes. She certainly did hurt her ribs. And now she felt the weight, like a brick, on her right leg.

"Careful." Her mother placed a hand on her shoulder. "Don't try to move yet. You've got some healing to do."

"What hospital is this?" She wondered if it was the same one where she'd given birth to Dylan.

"The Cleveland Clinic," Dusty said, still holding her hand. "You spent the first night in the hospital in Key Largo, then once they were sure your injuries weren't life-threatening, we got them to fly you here."

"I got in another plane after *that*?" Charlee tried to smile, but winced instead. "Ow." Even her face hurt. "Well, it's a good thing I don't remember that trip. I don't think I'll ever be able to get on a plane agai— Hey! What about the pilot and that couple? Are they okay?"

The look on Dusty face told her before he spoke. He shook his head slowly. "The pilot's in ICU, but they think he'll make it. The old woman broke her hip and has some internal injuries." He paused before adding, "The old man didn't make it."

"Oh no." Charlee felt like crying. The man had been so nice, and now she felt bad about screaming at the woman. She shook her head. "I don't remember the crash at all."

"And that's a good thing," Billy interjected. He picked up a newspaper on the chair beside him, came over to her bedside. "It's all here in yesterday's *Plain Dealer*."

She grabbed his arm. "Oh, hi, Billy. I didn't even say hello to you." She lifted her head to give her step-dad a kiss on the cheek, but the rush of pain smacked her back down. "Oh, wow, my head hurts, too."

Billy held her shoulder, kissed her forehead. "It will for a while," he said and gave her a big smile. "We're just all so glad you're okay."

She heard music again as he handed her the paper. "Can someone turn the radio off?" It was on low, but Michael Jackson was a bit much for her right now.

"Oh yeah, sure," Libby said, rushing to click off the dial. "We just thought it might help wake you up. You were out of it for quite some time."

"I was?" She grabbed the paper, and saw the date. Friday, May 31st. She tried to think what day she had left to fly home. Wednesday. "I don't remember anything."

"They had you in an induced coma while they fixed you up . . . Got yourself a nice cast, babe," Dusty said. "I was first to sign it." There it was. His Clark Gable grin, making all her confusion and pain disappear. If only for a second.

She started reading the article.

"Plane Crashes in Key Largo, Kills One, Hurts Three, including Rock Singer, Echo"

A charter plane carrying the rock singer, Echo, crashed in Key Largo, Florida, Wednesday, May 29. The pilot, Roger Posner, was forced to make an emergency landing after the Cessna began experiencing engine trouble, authorities say. The accident happened just after 3 p.m. on a beach near the edge of the Everglades National Park.

Echo, whose real name is Charlee Campbell, and who resides here in Northeast Ohio, suffered injuries to her ribs and a fractured leg. She was transferred to the Cleveland Clinic on Thursday evening.

Posner managed to get himself, Campbell, and another woman passenger, Louise Turney, freed before a fire started in the cockpit, which killed Turney's husband, George.

Charlee set the paper down on the bed. Reading the details made the horror painfully real. She remembered now, the paralyzing fear she'd felt as the plane began to descend. She remembered thinking of all her loved ones in heaven. She had prayed for a miracle.

And had gotten it.

Peggy scooped up the paper and threw it on the empty chair, then squeezed Charlee's hand. "I called the paper right away to make sure they wouldn't mention Sherman Falls in the article. You sure don't need a crowd of people around the house when you're trying to get better."

Charlee took her mother's hand and placed it on her cheek. "I love you, Mom. Thank you. You always take care of me."

"What am I, chopped liver?" Dusty feigned a grimace.

Charlee grinned, let go of Peggy, pulled her husband toward her, and gave him a weak squeeze, which was all she could muster. "You know how I love you. *So* much." She looked back at her mother. "We renewed our vows."

Peggy nodded, a glint in her eyes. "I know. He told us."

Charlee reached up to touch her hair. "So how do I look?"

"Beautiful as always," Dusty said, all too quickly.

She patted her head. It felt sticky. "Oh, right, sure I do. Can I see a mirror?"

"You don't believe me?"

She gave her husband a smirk. "Dust, I know how you are. So how bad is it?"

Her husband looked over at her mother, who shrugged her shoulders. "You have some facial lacerations," Peggy said, reaching into her purse for her compact.

Charlee raised her brows. "My, such technical words."

When she saw her image, her mouth fell. She looked like a battered woman. Bruises around her eyes, a swollen cheekbone, puffy face. The dried blood in her hair explained the stickiness. "God, looks like I've been hit by a Mac Truck."

"Honey, you look amazing. You survived a frickin' plane crash, for heaven's sake," Dusty said, taking the compact away.

"Yeah." Charlee nodded slowly. "*Yeah*. Oh my God!" Her soul erupted with a burst of gratefulness. "I survived a frickin' plane crash!" She let out a joyful laugh. "*Wow*. How many people can say *that*?"

"And now that you're conscious," Peggy piped in, "we can get you cleaned up."

The phone jingled next to her.

Dusty picked it up. "Hello? Hey, how's it goin'? Yeah, she's doing great. Wait a sec." He handed Charlee the receiver.

"Who is it?"

"Just take it."

The minute she said hello, she was greeted with a lively voice she knew so well.

"Hey, Shoop! How's our girl?"

"Uncle Patrick! How are you?"

"How am I? How are you? Sorry I can't be there in person. *American Rocker's* got me booked back to back. But one is a photo shoot for an article on The Cars, so that's cool."

"Wow, sure is. Tell Ben I said hello. If he even remembers me." Ben Orr was a Cleveland native and Charlee had met him several times at local gigs.

She asked about Nina, then remembered what she'd wanted to tell him. "Oh, and Patrick? Thank you. *Thank you* for telling Dusty where I was." She squeezed her husband's hand.

Patrick chuckled. "Oh, so you don't hate my guts?" Then his voice grew serious. "You know I want what's best for you. And we all know that's Dusty."

"Yes." She began to tear up. "And I know that, too."

For a millisecond, the thought occurred to her to ask Patrick if he knew the slimy L.A. photographer who had taken that tabloid photo of Dusty and Kat, but then realized she didn't even care. That was all in the past and it deserved to stay there.

The next morning, a young man dressed in nursing scrubs walked into her room. "And how we doing today? I'm Nick and I'll be taking care of you for the next eight hours." He tightened the blood pressure wrap around her arm and pumped. After a minute, he smiled and released her arm. "One twenty-two over eighty. Excellent. Anything I can get you right now, Mrs. Campbell?"

Charlee shook her head. "No, I don't think so." She could tell he knew she was Echo by how he looked at her.

Nick wrote in his chart, then lifted the pitcher by her bedside and poured water into the plastic cup. "I'll get you more when I come back." He handed her the lunch menu, and after she ordered, he said, "I hope you don't mind me asking, but I love your music and wondering if there might be a new album coming out anytime soon?"

She smiled, glad there was still interest out there. She brushed back her straggly hair from her eyes, embarrassed at how she looked. "Actually yes, I've been working on it for a while now. That's why I was in the Riviera, and now it looks like"—she patted her casted leg—"I'll have some down time to wrap it up. Hopefully I can get into the studio soon."

Nick nodded, holding his chart at his side. "Awesome. I recently turned my girlfriend onto your songs. She'd never even heard the MissFits records."

Not exactly what Charlee wanted to hear. Nick noticed her disappointment, and grinned. "She led a sheltered life. And she just turned twenty-one."

Charlee nodded. That explained it. The MissFits broke up before the girl had hit puberty. "You can't be much older than that yourself."

"No, just a few years, but my mom loved you guys. Has every album."

She bowed her head. *His mom*? How could she already be old enough to have someone say *their mom* was a fan?

Through his next two visits, Charlee learned that Nick had been an aspiring musician in his youth. "I was starving to death and frustrated 'bout the gigs I was, or rather wasn't, getting, and decided I better have an alternative plan. So now I'm a frustrated nurse."

Charlee laughed. "And probably a wise decision. The music business can be brutal. And then there's all the media stuff you have to contend with."

She was referring to the gossip on her shaky marriage, but then Nick said, "I know. And I'm really sorry about your baby." He shook his head. "I can't believe that could happen in a hospital. But least it'll never happen again. They've changed security measures since then. So many crazy people out—"

He stopped, catching Charlee's stricken face. "Oh, man, I'm sorry. Wow, that was insensitive. I shouldn't have—"

"Don't be," she said, then looked away. "Nothing anyone can do."

"I'm an idiot," he said, heading toward the door.

"Nick," she called. "Please. Forget it." She forced a smile. "When you come back, can you bring me a Milky Way bar or something?"

His face brightened. "Sure can, Mrs. Campbell."

"Call me Charlee."

Before his shift ended, Nick returned with a bagful of her favorite chocolate bar. They talked some more, and he told her about his upcoming vacation.

"I won't see you before you're released, but I want you

to know that it's been a privilege to care for you. You're the kind that makes my job so enjoyable. Thank you."

Charlee handed him two Milky Ways. "One for your girlfriend. And thank *you*, Nick, for being so nice and fun to talk to." She grabbed the tablet and a pen beside her bed and began writing. "Here. My friend Ruby has a restaurant in Sherman Falls that features an Open Mic night. Used to be called Open Mic Mondays, but now it's on Thursdays, which draws a better crowd. It's great for *frustrated* musicians." She winked. "If you ever get the urge, stop in sometime. And tell her I sent ya."

"Ruby? Ruby from Echo & the MissFits?"

Charlee smiled so wide it almost hurt. "The one and only."

24. The Power of Love

When Charlee returned home a few days later, Diana ran through the foyer to greet her at the front door. Charlee leaned on the crutch and gave her a one-arm hug. During the months she'd been gone, Charlee had kept in touch with her sister-in-law through occasional phone calls, though never discussing too much.

"Ah, Diana, I've missed you!" She smacked her cheek. "And I'm sorry I had to miss your graduation Saturday."

"Well, being in a plane crash is a pretty good excuse, so you're forgiven."

"Oh ya think?" Charlee laughed. "I'm real proud of you, Di. I know how hard you worked for it." She handed Dusty her purse so she could freely hobble to the sofa. "So you're a bona fide veterinary technician now, congratulations!" she said, hugging her again.

"Thanks." Diana said, then turned to Dusty. "Hey, Dust, don't we have a little present for Charlee?" She winked.

"Indeed we do!"

He helped Charlee to the couch, then disappeared. A minute later, he came back carrying a puppy with black and tan markings. And big paws.

Charlee fell in love at first sight. "Aaahhh, where'd you get him?"

Dusty placed the dog in Charlee's lap.

"Well, you know I started working at that Hudson animal clinic," Diana said, plopping down beside her. "Few weeks ago, I came in and here's this little guy just sitting in the cage looking sad. Someone found him outside an empty warehouse, abandoned and starving. Poor thing was in bad shape and almost didn't make it. My boss said he's tough, though," she said, rubbing his paws as Charlee petted his head. "We learned about the plane crash later that same day! So after the shock wore off, I got to thinking how you and he are both survivors, so maybe you belong together. I told Dusty you two are a perfect match, and we took him home."

Charlee recalled her and Dusty talking about having a baby, but maybe a dog, first. She chuckled at the irony. She brought the puppy up to her face. "His fur is so soft." Holding him reminded her of Cassidy, the shaggy sheepdog that Peggy had gotten as a peacemaker when Charlee was a teen and they'd been at odds. Cassidy had been gone six years now, but Charlee would never forget that first pet.

"He's a Shepherd/Rott mix," Diana said. "Very sweet, but also very loyal. He'll be a good protector."

"Yeah, he's gonna be a badass," Dusty added, tapping the dog's head.

"This precious thing? He hardly looks menacing," Charlee said as the puppy started licking her, making her giggle.

Diana suddenly sprang from the couch. "Hey, shouldn't you be lying down?"

"Yeah, okay." Charlee didn't argue. She still felt weaker than she'd like to admit.

Dusty helped put her legs up as she held onto the furry pet. Then he headed to the hall closet where they kept the afghan Peggy had made for her years ago. He returned and tucked the blanket around Charlee and her new best friend.

"What are you gonna name him?" Diana asked, sitting cross-legged on the floor.

Charlee smiled. "Ya know, I was just thinking about that. On the way home, that song, 'Eye of the Tiger' came on. And after you telling me that story, well, since Rocky was a survivor, just like me and this little one, I think that's a perfect name for him."

They all agreed and spent the rest of the evening fawning over the new family member. And basking in gratefulness.

Charlee spent the summer recuperating, and she didn't mind a bit. She had Leona, an older Italian woman Diana met at the animal clinic, to care for Charlee's needs when Dusty and Diana were at work. And she had Rocky to entertain her.

Charlee also took the free time to finish up her album. By August, she had just one more song to write, and a surprise visit from an old friend provided the muse.

One hot afternoon, Leona answered the door and told Charlee she had a visitor. "Says his name is Mario. Shall I let him in?"

"Yes, it's fine," she told her. Although Dusty still held a grudge against him, as she well understood, she, in turn, bore no ill feelings. She and Mario had been friends for years, and their short-lived, and misdirected, attraction was forgotten history.

Charlee had to laugh when Rocky, her "badass" dog, came running right up to Mario wagging his tail as he entered. So much for security.

"Hey, fella," Mario greeted him, before walking over to Charlee, lounging on the couch. He sat down on the end. "Peggy told me you got a dog. He's a beauty."

"Yeah, my big, bad protector," Charlee said, lifting her brows in sarcasm.

"So how are you?"

They caught each other up on their lives before Mario told her the reason for his visit. "I came to say goodbye."

Charlee sat up straight. "Goodbye?"

"I'm moving to Colorado to join a band there. I'm ready for a different atmosphere."

"What did my mom say to that?"

He shrugged. "I don't think she minds. My little CD only did well locally, and, well, I'm sure she prefers my not hanging around here anymore."

"Mario, that's all water under the bridge."

"Maybe in your eyes, but your family isn't so forgiving."

Charlee didn't know what else to say. He wasn't a bad guy. No matter what her family thought.

Mario stood up. "Can I at least kiss you goodbye?"

"Sure," she said, starting to get up.

He jumped up to help her. She had recently gotten her cast off, so she appreciated the assistance. Standing, she turned her face to the side.

He grinned and gave her a peck on the offered cheek.

She followed him to the door, and when he opened it, she put her hand on his arm and smiled. "Other than you putting the moves on me at my most vulnerable time in life, we really did have fun that summer, didn't we?"

"The best." His eyes became watery, which made her blush. "A hell of a tour. I'll never forget it. Thanks for the opportunity."

She nodded. "Enjoy Colorado, Mario. I wish you everything good."

They hugged, then she shut the door, knowing she'd never see him again. His presence unnerved Dusty and she would honor the fact that he preferred they not stay friends.

But she did write about it in her songs. How men and women can be friends, if they can put aside the sexual thing. Charlee recalled her first crush, on CJ, and how that love had morphed into an enduring friendship. It happened all the time. That gave her inspiration, so it became her last song for the album. She titled it, "A Friend Kinda Love." Her favorite line was, *Friendship is a derivative of love, and so, that's special, too.* It was a topic almost everyone could relate to. A guaranteed hit. She hoped.

The joy of finishing up another album, and being reunited with the man she loved was pure heaven for Charlee. Yet, thoughts of Dylan were never far away, and she knew she'd have to learn to live with it. She and Dusty talked occasionally with Tom, the private detective, who continually assured them that the kidnapping would remain an open case, an ongoing investigation. "At this point, we just have to get lucky."

Lucky. She had been lucky most of her life. She knew that. So she counted on that to get her through those days she ached for her son.

That October, Peggy called suggesting a garden party, to celebrate Charlee's full recovery from the plane crash, and also her new album they hoped to get out before the holidays. "I'd like to make it a huge outdoor event! Invite everyone we know," she told Charlee. "I'm thinking the theme could be like Prince's song, '1999,' but call it 'Party Like It's 1985.' I'm thinking since Kid Leo hosted our wedding reception, it'd be fun to bring him back and have him play a mix tape I've made up of all the hits of this year—Huey Lewis, Mellencamp, Springsteen, and your favorites, Tina, and Heart, and then of course, play *your* new songs at the end. Whad'dya say? Can you handle all that activity? I don't want to overwhelm you."

"You kiddin'?" Charlee laughed. "Sounds great. I am *so* ready for a party."

What she didn't tell her mother was that she was also *so* ready to announce her big news. She had found out the day before, and the party would be the perfect place to do it.

She and Dusty couldn't wait to tell their family and friends that they were going to have a baby. An unexpected, and most welcomed, gift from heaven.

Side 2 — The River of Dreams

25. Toy Soldier: 1990

Ten-year-old Ben Jacobs slouched on the metal chair in the guidance counselor's office, waiting to get chewed out again for his "disruptive and unruly" behavior. It was his third time here since school started four months ago.

"Benjamin, step into my office, please."

Mrs. Billings used to be nice to him, but the last two times he was here she acted like he wasn't worth her precious time. Even the way she said his name sounded different. He followed her, hands in pockets, keeping his eyes on the floor. *Here we go again.*

She motioned to the chair. "Sit down." She took a seat behind her desk and leaned forward. "Now. You want to tell me why you cheated off Olivia's paper instead of simply studying for the test?"

She waited for a response.

He gave her a shrug.

"If you shrug one more time, you'll be sitting in the principal's office," she said, gazing at him. "Why'd you do it? You're a bright young man, Benjamin. You should be excelling in math and science, according to your recent IQ tests."

He almost shrugged again, out of habit. "I didn't cheat. Those were my answers."

"Oh, really?" Billings picked up a sheet on her desk and asked him the first story problem on the test.

Nothing was more stupid than story problems. He didn't answer. But he didn't shrug, either.

Then she asked him another question. He wasn't sure if this one was the second one on the test, though it hardly mattered. He was really pissed at himself for getting caught. It wasn't like it'd been his first time. But Olivia Banks, too cute for her own good, saw him lean toward her paper. He'd been so intent on looking at her answers, he didn't see her see him. Next thing he knew, she flipped her page over, stalked to the teacher's desk all annoyed-like, then whispered into Mrs. Sherman's ear. So now here he was. His crush on Olivia gone as swift as an eraser across a chalkboard.

He sat staring at the floor. What else could he do? He didn't know the stupid answer.

Of course, Billings knew that.

"Benjamin."

God, he wished she'd stop calling him by his full name. What his mother called his "Trouble Name." He lifted his head slowly.

"What is going on with you, Benjamin? I told you the last time I didn't want to see you in my office again. Plus, you've been tardy or absent much more than is acceptable." She opened a folder filled with papers he knew had his name written on every one. "I've called your mother. When she arrives, we'll be meeting with Principal Sanders."

So he was going to the principal's office anyway? Whether he shrugged again or not? He crossed his arms and went back to staring at the floor. Adults were such liars. Like his mother. She'd say one thing, then do another. By the time he'd been five, he knew what empty promises were.

Son-of-a-bitch.

"Until then, you will eat here in my office," Billings was saying. "I've sent the aide to get your lunch from your cubbyhole."

In a few days it would be Christmas vacation, but now of course, he'd be grounded the whole time. Wouldn't be allowed to play with Kevin, his first and only buddy since he'd moved here, or ride his bike around the neighborhood.

If life were really fair, his mother would've been grounded too. It was her fault he didn't always get to school on time, and sometimes didn't make it at all. She was the one who was supposed to get him up and off to school. But it all depended on if she'd gone out the night before.

He missed having a sitter. Even the bad ones were at least somebody to watch TV or play games with. But when he turned nine, his mother said he was old enough to take care of himself. Babysitters were expensive.

All through Christmas vacation, Ben ended up staying in his room with his action toys, which wasn't so bad. He had his army men and a real cool Super Powers and Marvel Secret Wars Collection. His favorites, though, were his G.I. Joes. He'd had them the longest and they were like his best friends.

Still, it was fun playing with Kevin, who lived across the hall. When they'd moved to Parma last summer, Ben was so angry. He kept telling his mom how sick he was of moving practically every year, one ugly apartment after another. But it did no good. She said when a lease is up, tenants have to go. But none of the other kids moved as much as he did. He'd been glad they'd stayed at the Shamrock apartments through his whole third, and half of fourth grade, but that came with a price. Some neighbor ratted on them about Pepe' Le Pew and the manager had a conniption and almost threw them out. So his mom got rid of Pepe' and it broke his heart. He'd never forgive her for that one. A few months later, they up and moved again anyway.

So now they lived here on the west side of Cleveland. He and his mother had always lived on the east side, so they might as well have moved to Timbuktu. The worst part was that it was farther for Nick, and he didn't visit like he used to.

So when Nick showed up at their place the day after Christmas, Ben was so happy he almost cried as he ran into his arms and gave him a big hug.

When his mother went to the store that afternoon, Ben told Nick everything that he'd been doing since he last saw him, even about being grounded. Nick wasn't like other adults. He listened real good and never yelled at him. Ben could tell Nick anything. Like how big he was getting, in case Nick hadn't noticed. So big he didn't need a sitter anymore. But then he thought that Nick might take it wrong. "That doesn't mean you," he added right away. "You can come over and watch me anytime. I won't mind. Really." Nick grinned, but his eyes squinted like he was surprised, and not a good kind of surprised.

His mom must have forgotten he was grounded because she let him stay up late that night, even after *Doogie Howser*, which ended at 9:30, his normal bedtime. Nick tucked him in after their game of Hungry Hippos, just like the old days. But Ben couldn't fall asleep. Clutching the new toy soldier Nick had given him, Ben lay there listening to his mom and Nick talk in the living room, though he couldn't hear much of what they were saying because the TV was on. But then his mom got loud.

She started yelling at Nick. Ben heard her say that Nick was not his dad, and nothing she did was his business. That made Ben's stomach get tight. How he wished Nick was his dad! And once again, it made him wonder about his real one. He never thought much about it when he was little, but when he got in first grade, he realized *everyone* had a father but him. Even the kids whose dads only came around on Sundays. So Ben started asking his mom questions, like who was his daddy and where was he and why didn't he come see him? But she'd only get mad and never answer them. He then started asking why he didn't have any brothers or sisters, either. And how come he didn't have grandparents, or aunts and uncles? She got real mad then, and screamed that his dad and her dad were both dead. So he didn't have a dad, or a grandpa, and everyone else was dead, too. That got him bawling like a baby and he never asked her anything again.

Somewhere in the midst of remembering all that, the apartment got quiet, and he got sleepy. He was just drifting off when he heard Nick say, "Well, the boy needs someone. I'll start coming by more often."

Ben smiled into his pillow hearing that. Unlike other adults, Nick was the kind to keep his promises.

After that, Nick did come around more. Sometimes on a school night when his mom was out, and sometimes on Sundays, when they'd play with his toy collection. But then Nick would make him do schoolwork. Like those stupid story problems. He'd say the same things Mrs. Billings said that Ben was too smart not to do well in school.

Things were going good, but then Ben almost ruined it. Nick had picked him up and let him stay at his house overnight because the next day was Martin Luther King Day. Ben didn't have to go to school and Nick was off too, so they went to the zoo.

Ben had two cigarettes and a pack of matches in his coat pocket. He got them from his mom, who always left everything lying around. He had started taking them from her purse during that boring Christmas vacation. His mother usually slept in late, so he'd snatch them and sneak outside the apartment fire escape, and enjoy a morning smoke. The first few times he coughed like crazy, but he got the hang of it, and he was glad. Like his mom would say, smoking calms you down when you're angry about something.

Since he and Nick were having such a good time, Ben forgot the cigs were even there. So when he started running ahead to check out the Bengal tigers, the matches fell out, then one of the cigarettes.

Suddenly Nick was behind him, grabbing his collar and holding the crumpled Tareyton up to his face. "What's this?"

Ben wanted to lie, like he usually did, and say it wasn't his, but he couldn't lie to Nick. So he just stood there in the freezing wind, hugging his coat around him.

"I asked you a question."

"I got it from my mom's purse, but you can see I didn't smoke it!" Ben tugged on Nick's parka. "Don't hate me, Nick, please don't hate me."

"Come over here." Nick pulled him against the lavatory building. "Listen, I can never hate you. You're my bud. But I'm a nurse, remember? I know how bad these things are for you. How long you been smoking?"

Ben shrugged, but came clean. "Since Christmas."

Nick looked kind of relieved. "Well, good. Easier to quit before it becomes a habit."

Nick emptied Ben's pockets and told him if he ever touched another cigarette he would know and Ben would be in the biggest trouble of his young, short life.

And Ben believed him.

On Ben's eleventh birthday that March, Nick came over with Ashley, carrying a huge present. Ben had no clue what it could be. The package was so big and heavy, Ben set it down to open it. When he did, his eyes nearly popped out of his head.

He tore at the paper, then read the description on the brown box. *Acoustic Guitar with Natural Gloss Finish.*

Nick sat on the floor beside him and helped him open it. Ben pulled out the biggest guitar he had ever seen. "I also got you your first five lessons at Marvin's Music Shop," Nick said, grinning.

He looked as excited as Ben felt.

Ben stroked the smooth, shiny instrument and strummed the strings while Nick continued to talk. "Marvin's is right next to Tommy Edward's Record Shop," he said. "You can even walk there, if need be."

Ben knew Nick said this because of his mom's habit of forgetting to take him places. Like school.

"You just gotta promise me two things," Nick pointed his finger. "You have to keep your grades up, and you have to practice every day. Even if it's only ten, fifteen minutes. It's the only way you're gonna learn how to play." Nick stuck out his hand. "Deal?"

Ben extended his over the guitar. "Deal!"

They shook on it, but even if they hadn't, Ben knew he'd be spending all his time with this totally awesome birthday present.

When his mom went into the kitchen, Nick whispered in Ben's ear, "This should keep your hands busy now. Instead of those cancer sticks." He winked.

Ben nodded, but felt embarrassed that Nick had brought it up. He couldn't care less about cigarettes now. Wow. A guitar! How many times had he watched MTV and played air guitar with his favorite bands. He loved watching the guitar guys in Rush, Dire Straits, ZZ Top, Guns 'N Roses, and Van Halen. He was also a big fan of Pat Benatar's guitarist, Neil Giraldo, after learning that he had lived in Parma once, too, which was really cool. Ben always thought that playing a real guitar was just one of his crazy daydreams.

He looked up at Nick. "But I'm left-handed," he said, clutching the Gibson against him.

"What?" Nick leaned forward. "Don't you know how many genius guitar players are left-handed?"

Ben shook his head.

"I'll give you just two names from a long list," Nick said. "Paul McCartney and Jimi Hendrix."

Ben's mouth fell open. "Really?"

"Really. And if you start getting good, I can bring you

along to Ruby's, where I play sometimes on Open Mic Night. Maybe they'll even let you play."

"Really?" he repeated. He couldn't believe this was happening. "That'd be way cool!"

"But hey, that won't be for a while." He squeezed Ben's shoulder lightly. "Like I said, ya gotta practice every day so you can *really* play."

Ben barely heard him. He was too excited. He had never felt so happy in his entire life. He moved the guitar out of the way and hugged Nick real tight. "Ah man, thanks a lot! I love my guitar!"

Just saying "my guitar" gave him goose bumps. His mom came out of the kitchen just then, carrying a cake with eleven candles lit. They all sang "Happy Birthday," and everyone looked so happy. Even his mom.

That right there gave Ben hope that from now on, things were going to be a whole lot better.

26. Coming Out of the Dark

Charlee and Dusty never imagined they'd find themselves in a Chuck E. Cheese pizza place. But their lives were much different now that they had their little girl. Charlee had always heard how parenthood changes your life, but then she'd been robbed of that experience. That was, until May 29, 1986—ironically, the anniversary of her horrible plane crash—when she gave birth to their daughter.

"That's what I call kismet," Peggy had said that day she held her new grandchild in her arms. "You were meant to survive, Charlee, so you can have this little one."

No disagreement there. Charlee indeed felt God had finally decided to make up for the devastating loss of Dylan. After years of fighting off the idea of having another baby, Charlee had found the cure to her and Dusty's heartache. Although their son would always remain in their heart—and they would always hold onto that faint, stubborn, kernel of hope—they both knew the chances of finding him diminished with each passing year. That March, Dylan Thomas Campbell had turned eleven. Like every year before, Charlee prayed that he was still having birthdays. Somewhere in the world.

Charlee and Dusty named their baby girl Tammi Sue. Her first name to honor Tammi Terrell, the Motown singer Charlee had met at Hitsville when she was thirteen, and for a year after, wore a cap just like Tammi used to wear. (In fact, Charlee still had it.) The Sue, of course, was tradition. Both Peggy Sue and Charlee Sue felt it was right that this beloved baby share their middle name.

"I swear this place is louder than a rock concert." Dusty yelled into her ear as they stood with a watchful eye on their five-year-old bouncing up and down in the ball pit with her kindergarten classmates.

Charlee glanced at her watch. "Well, I think we've done our time. Let's scoop her out of there and go see Ruby. I told her we'd be there by five."

The Indian summer day had turned chilly, so after they dropped Tammi off at the sitter's next door, Charlee ran home and grabbed her faux fur-lined jean jacket.

Tonight Ruby was celebrating her birthday at her restaurant. As her longtime best friend, Charlee was glad they were the first to arrive. She scooted into their waiting booth, wondering how they'd gotten this old! They related to the TV show *Thirtysomething* that, to their dismay, had been cancelled last season.

"I find it hard to believe Ruby's a thirty-four-year-old woman," Charlee said, shaking her head as she opened the menu.

Dusty smiled and kissed her cheek. "Uh, honey, I hate to inform you, but you're right behind her."

She playfully slapped his arm. "Heeey, you don't have to *inform* anyone." She laughed, though a part of her did worry about aging out of her career. Many of the newcomers were twenty-somethings; Whitney Houston, Mariah Carey, Janet Jackson, Paula Abdul. And that girl group that Ruby was obsessed over, Wilson Phillips. All female. All younger than Charlee. Even Peggy Sue had started putting younger people on her label.

Charlee knew it was all about the business, yet she felt like she had let her mother down. Her last album hadn't done all that well, although to be fair, there were factors involved. Charlee had planned to go on tour right after the album's release that Christmas, but the minute she found out she was pregnant, she cancelled the tour. No way was she going to risk her baby's health by going out on the road. She knew first-hand how grueling that could be. And a growing belly would prevent her from wearing the sexy outfits she was known for on stage, or allow her to make the vigorous moves she always did.

To add to it, getting airtime on MTV was more difficult than it had been in the past. Gone were the days the station execs were open to most any artist with a video. They now were airing more metal, hip-hop, and a new sound out of Seattle called grunge. In contrast, Echo's songs didn't fit. She felt lucky when she'd secured a return spot on *American Bandstand*—how she loved Dick Clark!—but even that appearance didn't hike up sales as much as she'd hoped.

She knew she couldn't blame her age. Madonna, just a year younger, was enjoying hit after hit and was now considered the pop music queen. And the elder Tina Turner was still riding high after resurrecting her career.

Charlee feared her glory days were over. Yet, a part of her was okay with that. Right now, she had other priorities. Wonderful, blissful priorities. She devoted herself to loving her husband and being a mother to their beautiful, spunky daughter.

She wiggled off her coat, just as Ruby ran over to greet them, looking like an '80s flashdancer in a shimmering sequin top hanging over one shoulder, silver leggings, her black Jheri curls clipped on one side with a big red satin bow.

"You look amazing," Charlee said, giving her a big hug.

Ruby plopped down beside them. "Ah, thanks. I'm so glad you're here. Nick's starting Open Mic early. It's gonna be great. Wait'll you hear this kid he's bringing to play. I saw him at this coffeehouse in Kent last month. Man, he will blow your mind."

"Well before that starts, we need to share a birthday drink with you." Charlee waved over the server. "We'd like a pitcher of Singapore Slings, please. Your boss hasn't had one in some time." She grinned at Ruby. "Remember when we drank those on the MissFits European tour? We thought we were so cool!"

Ruby laughed. "Ah, man, I'd forgotten about that!" She put an arm around Charlee and squeezed. "But don't you start getting all sentimental on me, girl. This night is for the present. And for partying!"

By seven o'clock, the place was jammed with friends, family, and music fans. Charlee and Dusty shared their booth with Peggy and Billy, and Libby and Dave, who'd brought their sixteen-year-old son, Jack. Soon Nick, the host of the Thursday night event, arrived with a young boy following behind. Both carried guitar cases and began setting up on the stage.

Charlee was excited to see Nick again. He had been her favorite nurse in the hospital, but once she'd been released, she didn't see him again for a couple of years, when Nick had finally gotten around to checking out Ruby's Open Mic Night. Since then, she saw him and his wife, Ashley, only occasionally. As new parents, she and Dusty preferred staying home, only going out on special nights, like this one.

While the others chatted away, Charlee's eyes were drawn to the stage where Nick was helping the boy plug in his amp, getting ready for his big debut. She recalled that the last time she'd seen Nick, he'd mentioned how he and Ashley had been trying to help some kid out. Something about his having no father, and something about a mother who was "unfocused." That was the word he'd used, and she remembered thinking at the time it sounded odd. What did he mean by that? Charlee knew, of course, that there were some mothers who didn't focus their time and energy on their children, but she could never understand it.

Dusty interrupted her thoughts. "That's no kid," he said. "He's a mere baby."

Ruby laughed. "I know! I meant to ask Nick that night how old he was, but after seeing him play, I forgot all about it."

Now Nick and the boy walked over to their table. "How's it goin', people?" Nick put a casual arm around his buddy. "This here is Ben." He introduced everyone at the table, leaving Charlee for last. "And, Ben, that lovely lady there?" he said, pointing to her, the arm still resting on the boy's shoulder, "is Echo. Remember I told you about her?"

The boy's eyes widened. He hadn't said a word yet, but now he started talking as if someone let air out of a balloon. "Wow, Echo. It's so nice to meet you." He extended his hand, and began to pump it up and down. "Wow, really. Nick had me listen to all your records. I really like your guitar playing. I really like your '70s stuff. The MissFits were awesome. That's so cool you got to tour Europe and everything. It's amazing what you got to do and all." He finally let go of her hand.

Charlee laughed. Flattered by his enthusiasm, but a tad disappointed that he hadn't mentioned her latest "stuff." But then, the kid probably listened to acts like Milli Vanilli and New Kids on the Block. Despite his Van Halen T-shirt.

Later, when he got up on stage, Ben proved Charlee's assumption wrong. The kid started out with Springsteen's "Glory Days," then played Dire Straits "Sultans of Swing," followed by impressive renditions of Stevie Ray Vaughn's "Look at Little Sister," and "Pride and Joy."

The entire place clapped and cheered and didn't stop until he was done.

"I can't believe it," Charlee yelled over the music to anyone who could hear. "He's too young to be that good."

The kid got a standing ovation. When he jumped off stage, Charlee ran up to him and in her excitement, gave him a quick hug. "Wow, Ben, that was great." She let go, but her hands remained on his shoulders. "I'm very impressed. Come with me, I'll buy you a Coke." She wanted a few minutes with him away from the others.

Guiding him with her arm, she led him through the crowd of people, all slapping his back and giving him high-fives. When they reached the bar, Ben said, "I prefer 7-Up, if that's okay."

"After that performance you can have anything you like. Well, except alcohol," she added with a smile.

The boy nodded politely. "I know. Thank you, Echo."

"Call me Charlee. Two 7-Ups," she told the bartender, feeling funny drinking alcohol in front of the boy. When the bartender set the glasses down, Charlee led the way to a quieter corner.

"So, can I ask how old you are?"

"Eleven." He gave her a smirk, half proud of this and half daring her to argue the point. He was rather short for that age.

"Eleven? Wow, you're so talented already! You know, my so—" She almost said *my son would be ... is ... your age.* But she stopped just in time. The old familiar pain pinched her chest. She took a big sip of her drink and mentally wiped away the thought, like so many times before.

Ben sipped, too, looking over at the other musicians getting ready to play.

"Gosh, you must have been playing since you were what, six?"

He grinned, proud-like. "Nah, just started earlier this year."

"You're kidding me?"

"Yeah, I mean no. Nick gave me the guitar and I started practicing every day. I love it. Had some trouble mastering 'Sultans of Swing,' but I really like it so I worked on it all summer and finally got it down."

Charlee's mouth fell open. He talked like he was twice his age. "Well, you nailed it for sure. You know, I didn't even start playing till I was thirteen. But once you're hooked, that's it."

He looked straight at her and his face lit up. "Yeah, I know! That's just how I feel! It's all I wanna do."

"Well, then, you should meet my mom." Charlee grinned, and with a gentle tug on his arm, they headed toward the table.

Nick and Ashley came over just as Peggy started talking to Ben about his music. "Hey, little buddy, time for you to hit it. You have school tomorrow. I gotta stay, but Ashley'll take you home."

Ben's face fell. He'd been having the time of his life, Charlee could tell. She felt bad for him. His face had changed from a confident young guitarist to a sad little boy. It now occurred to her that his mother, the "unfocused one" hadn't come. What could possibly be more important than her son's big debut?

Of all people, the boy's mother should've been here.

That night, as she nuzzled up to Dusty in bed, her head on his bare chest, Charlee couldn't stop thinking about Ben.

"That kid was amazing, wasn't he?" she asked Dusty. "It's almost uncanny how good he is at his age. He told me he just started playing some eight months ago."

Dusty rubbed her arm. "Yeah, and wait'll your mom gets a hold of him. He's bound to go places. A little prodigy."

"That's for sure. I can just hear Ruby now telling customers how she knew him when, and that his public debut was at *her* bar."

"Right. I bet she's already got him booked till he's out of high school."

"Oh, I have no doubt." Charlee laughed, then kissed Dusty's cheek. "Such a fun night, wasn't it?"

"Sure was, Sunshine," he said, caressing her breasts.

When she started talking more about Ben, Dusty shut her up with a deep, longing kiss on the lips. "I love you," he whispered in her ear, rolling on top of her, his hands holding himself up so he could gaze over her. He lifted his eyebrows up and down, giving her his I-want-you-now smirk. Which made her giggle.

"Oooooh, Dust, we need more night's out like this," she said, pulling him down, proceeding to make mad, happy, love to this man who still thrilled her after so many years.

Afterward, as they lay in each other's arms, she brought up Ben again. "Don't you think it's weird that his mother wasn't there tonight?"

Dusty frowned at her. "Now look, you can't start worrying about every kid you see, wanting to save all the children in the world. The kid looked pretty well adjusted to me." He kissed her forehead as if to put a period on the statement.

"I suppose. Guess it's just the mother in me."

"Yeah, I know." Dusty threw her a crooked grin, then patted her thigh. "Come on, let's get some sleep."

But Charlee didn't sleep much at all that night. Seeing a boy the same age as Dylan made her wonder what their son would look like by now. Did he like music, too, like her whole family? Was he going to school, and where? *Where*? Where the hell *was* he? And *who* was raising him? She truly believed deep in her soul that whoever had taken him was desperate for a child and that the person, despite the fact she had *stolen* him, would not hurt him. Charlee constantly comforted herself with that thought. That whoever she was, the woman was taking care of him.

Charlee prayed every day, with all of her heart, that she was at least right about that.

27. Out Of Touch

Sandra loved working at the Lion's Den. She'd run out of money over a year ago, having spent every last dime her daddy had left her. So she'd made it her 1992 resolution to get a job. She couldn't get unemployment benefits because she hadn't worked in God-knew-how-long, and Nicky made her feel guilty about taking the welfare she'd been living on.

"You can't keep taking advantage of the government that way, Sandra," he'd told her. "You're perfectly capable of working."

Somewhere along the way, her relationship with Nick had changed. It'd been better when he'd just been her neighbor, a college kid who came by and played with Benji and babysat. Now that he was a big shot at the Cleveland Clinic and had started telling her what she should and shouldn't do, like he was her father or something. And yet, she kind of liked that part. At least he cared. He came over regularly now, and she did what he told her to because she was afraid if she didn't, he'd get disgusted and not come around anymore. She'd seen that look of disgust on his face a few times, and she never wanted to see it again. She wanted Nicky to respect her.

She wanted her boy to respect her, too, but lately he wanted little to do with her, which hurt like hell. She understood that he was on his way to becoming a testy teenager—she'd been one herself, so she was acquainted with the signs—but being on the other side of those rolling eyes and heavy sighs and slamming doors, made her feel like the most hated woman on the planet.

She figured if she got a job and showed Benji that she was responsible, and had interests other than drinking, that he'd like her again. She wanted him to look up to her, like he'd done when he was a little tyke. Back then, it didn't matter what she did or did not do, she was the queen of Benji's world.

But that was then and this is now, and ever since Nicky gave him that damn guitar last year, she'd been replaced. At first she didn't mind because it kept the boy busy. He didn't seem so needy, and best of all, it gave him something to do when she went out and had to leave him alone. Made her feel less guilty. But then, Benji had started hanging out with older musician kids at the coffee shop down the street, and that fall, Nicky had taken him to that fancy supper club, Ruby's. When she called it that, Ben corrected her by saying it wasn't a *supper club*, just a nice restaurant. "Whatever," she'd said, using his favorite word.

That was about the time Benji had started getting all high and mighty and complaining about *everything*. First, it was about all the moving they'd done since he was little. Said it screwed him up socially.

Where does a twelve-year-old get that from? Older kids, musicians—that's where. The kind who thinks they're better than everyone else.

In truth, they'd only moved five times since they'd left that little town in P.A. The last two had to be subsidized apartments because of their financial situation.

She couldn't believe when the snarly kid started on her about the welfare benefits. He must have overheard Nicky harping on her about that and was now using it against her. "I hate using these stupid welfare coupons at school," became his new mantra.

"They ain't welfare coupons," she told him. "They're complimentary lunch tickets and without them, buddy, you wouldn't be able to eat."

"So guess I won't eat 'cause I'm not going to look like some stupid poor kid," he'd yelled, then stomped to his room, slamming the door behind him.

The next week, the shrill ringing of phone startled her from a sound sleep. She let the machine pick up, but she could hear the message from the couch she'd fallen asleep on.

"Mrs. Jacobs, this is Principal Daley. Please call me as soon as possible. It's not an emergency, but we'd like to speak with you about Ben. I'll be here until 4:30 today."

Her heart started pounding, like every time the schools called. She still worried about the birth certificate thing. When she'd enrolled Ben in first grade, they'd asked for the document that no way she could produce. So she told them that her apartment back in P.A had caught fire and she'd lost everything, and that was why they'd moved to Cleveland. Fresh start and all. They bought it and said to bring it in when she got the copy. Lucky for her, they must have forgotten about it. After that, only one other school asked for it, but ended up accepting his report cards from the previous school. Sandra hoped her luck would hold out.

When she returned the call, they told her that Ben hadn't been using the lunch tickets. A teacher caught him balling them up and throwing them in the trash. When Sandra confronted him, Ben repeated his rant about not wanting to look poor. "And I do eat. I take the stuff off the plates other kids don't want."

She almost said that made him look just as poor, but clamped her mouth shut. Everything she said to him these days was useless.

So when Casey, owner of the Lion's Den, fired the young and dumb barkeep, Sandra begged him to let her have Rachel's job. It had taken quite a bit of charm on her part because Casey had seen her get loaded way too many times. But she promised him she'd never drink on the job and threw in the part about her kid having trouble in school because they had no money. That sealed the deal. Casey, like everyone who ever met the boy, had a soft spot for Benji.

Sandra surprised herself at how good she was at bartending. She got so that she knew all the regulars, not by their names, but by their drinks. Which was more important. She loved hearing all those country songs on the jukebox, which played a lot of Garth Brooks, George Strait, and that hunk Alan Jackson. And of course, Reba. If only her daddy could see her now, he'd be wearing a big ol' smile. Sandra grew up when "country western" music was twangy and downright depressing. She always gave him shit for listening to that crap. Well, lo and behold, the tables had turned. But only because today's country music was more her style— upbeat and toe-tapping. Even the sad ones were good. She'd dance along to all of them on the jukebox as she worked, her latest favorite being "Achy, Breaky Heart."

That jukebox, which was always playing, helped her move fast so she could handle a full bar by herself and keep up so that no one had to wait long for a drink. Something that cute little Rachel couldn't do if her skinny ass depended on it.

By that summer, Sandra was working nights fulltime and wasn't home much, but she knew Ben didn't care. By now, he'd learned to cook for himself when he got hungry and lived for that guitar he'd named Layla, and had started to play out more and more.

Whenever she thought about that, it made her sad. Her little boy didn't need her anymore. He didn't miss her a bit when days would go by and they wouldn't see or talk to one another. He was usually asleep when she got home, or at his buddy's place across the hall. Colin had a guitar, or a *bass,* as they called it—like she should know the difference. The two were inseparable, practicing all the time and dreaming up crazy notions about being rock stars.

God help the neighborhood.

She was grateful, though, that Colin's dad, Roy, kept an eye on them so she didn't worry much about them getting into trouble. It was just too bad she and Roy never hooked up. How nice that would be for all of them. He was real cute for a guy pushing forty. She had five years on him, but feared he thought she was even older. When his wife died last year—cancer—she tried getting him to go out. Suggesting he meet her at the Den sometime. But Ben told her he wasn't the drinking type.

She often felt bad that she hadn't done such a hot job being Ben's mama. And sometimes she even felt bad that she'd robbed Benji of his true family. Especially when Sandra saw Echo on MTV, or heard her songs on the radio. That was when the flush of guilt would hit her, like a scorching rush of fire, and she'd flick off the dials as fast as her fingers could get there.

Other times, she felt redeemed. Like the day she saw that story in *National Celebrity* about Echo's husband with that hot chick on the hotel balcony. Sandra told herself then and there that she'd done the right thing, taking the poor child away from that rock star, despite not knowing at the time it was Echo's kid.

Yes. God knew that Benji was better off with Sandra than that fancy, rich singer. She might not have that couple's money, and all those swanky things, but at least the kid didn't have to deal with his friends knowing his daddy was out screwing some bimbo miles away from his mama.

Sandra had given Benji a simpler life. *And* out of the eyes of those media scoundrels. Sometimes she was tempted to tell him that. Let him know how fortunate he was. Make him understand what she'd saved him from. But, boy, would that open up a can of sardines.

Besides, all had turned out well. Echo had another kid, so now the pressure was off both of them.

As she stocked the beer cooler getting ready for a busy Friday night, she told herself that, while it may be true Sandra Jacobs would never be crowned Mother of the Year, Benjamin was turning out pretty darn good, overall. No, he wasn't a great student, but then, she wouldn't want any kid of hers being a candy ass. What he *was* good at was playing that guitar. He had picked up that thing and held it against him like it had been an extra arm or something he'd been missing all along. Of course, that made perfect sense. He had it in his genes, with his grandpa being Frankie London and all. And then his real mother had kept up the musical tradition. Sometimes it killed Sandra keeping that knowledge to herself.

She could slap herself for not thinking of getting him that guitar. Now if her boy got famous like his biological family, she, the woman who had raised him through thick and thin, would get no credit at all.

She stepped around the bar to hit the jukebox and play some Tanya Tucker. "Walking Shoes" was a tune she could sure relate to. But now she had a good guy, due here anytime. She was getting all worked up already, thinking about him walking through that door.

Jerry was a hoot. She'd met him on a Friday night, August 21st, she'd never forget, and it was love at first beer. He liked having a good time, same as her. When business was slow, he'd come up behind the bar, grab hold of her and pull her out on the dance floor and twirl her around and around. He made her laugh like no one, not even her papa, had ever done before.

She may be losing Benji to hormones and that guitar, but now she had new boyfriend. And hope for the future. She vowed that she would do, and be, everything Jerry wanted, so he would stick around. If she could pull that off, then he was bound to ask her to be his wife. And the sooner the better since she wasn't getting any younger.

He was the one. She just knew it.

28. Smells like Teen Spirit

Ben wasn't at all mad that Sandra—how he referred to her in public, though she'd have a shit-fit if she knew—had forgotten to pick him up from school that Friday. Now that he was in seventh grade, taking a school bus was lame, and so was getting picked up by your mom. He preferred walking home, although Sandra promised to pick him up whenever the weather was bad. Today, it had started snowing, but not by much. So now he could make a detour.

Ever since Ben discovered the Nirvana album, *Nevermind,* he'd been obsessed with the group. He'd heard their next album was coming out in December, so he'd stop into Tommy Edwards Records to see if it was in.

Soon as he opened the door, Denny grabbed him by the shirtsleeve. "Hey, man, guess what we just got in?"

"*Yes!*" Ben pumped his fist. "Freakin' awesome!"

Denny was cool. He was a senior and had been working part-time at the record store since he turned sixteen. He'd taken a liking to Ben when he started coming in last year. He'd even sold him his old Fender Strat. Ben had been complaining that, though he liked the Gibson acoustic Nick had given him, he needed an electric guitar to play what he really wanted. So when Denny's mom got him a new Fender, he offered to sell Ben his old one for 100 bucks. After telling Sandra about it, she just up and gave Ben the money, which shocked him no end. Ever since getting that new boyfriend, Sandra was like a different person. Well, sort of.

Ben slyly gazed around to make sure no girls were in the store then shook off the flakes of snow in his hair. He hated how it got all curly when it rained or snowed. Made him look like a dirty blond Al Yankovich. He followed Denny to the new records section.

"Check it out." Denny shoved the CD into his chest. "*Incesticiiiide.* Cool title, huh? I like the first and last track best. See what you think."

Denny went behind the counter, retrieved another copy. "I'll play it now. Like for the sixth time." He laughed. "Hartman's not in today," he added, referring to the day manager who no one liked. George Hartman was like a hundred years old and still thought Frank Sinatra and Dean Martin were hip.

Ben hung around for the entire album then borrowed money from Denny to buy it. "I'll pay you back next time. My mom's getting laid regular now, so she's suddenly gotten generous." Then he waved goodbye and walked out the door, the store bell jingling behind him.

The snow had thickened and was coming down steady, but Ben was too happy to care. He'd eat something, then spend the rest of the night trying to nail down Kurt Cobain's guitar riffs.

When he got home, Sandra was sleeping on the couch. At five in the afternoon. He shook her awake. "Mom, get up, I'll make us some mac 'n' cheese."

She grumbled, then her eyes slowly opened. "Oh, hi, honey, when you get home?" Then she took a good look at him and sprang up. "Ah shit, I forgot to get you, again, didn't I? You're soakin wet."

"It's cool, no sweat. I hung at the record store a bit. Got Nirvana's new CD." He waved the package in the air.

Sandra pulled herself off the couch. "Well, first, get that wet jacket off and hang it up. I'll make dinner. The least I can do after . . ." She put an arm around him, "I'm sorry I fucked up today." Her hand shot to her mouth. "I mean, *messed*—"

Ben shook his head, combing a hand through his wet hair. "Like I never heard *that* word before." He ducked from under her arm and headed to his room.

He couldn't see the reasoning in Sandra trying to correct her language around him. Why bother now? He'd heard them all by the time he was six. It was only when he went to school and started using them that he learned, after trips to the corner, that "foul language" was taboo. Least in certain circles.

But he knew Sandra was trying to be a better mother lately. He also knew she didn't have a clue what that meant. Sandra wasn't bad when she wasn't drinking, but alcohol wiped out any good sense she had left at her age.

He did love his mother. Weren't you supposed to? But she just didn't seem right sometimes. She never talked much about her life before he was born, but Ben had overheard conversations through the years. She'd bring dudes home from the bar and her amplified voice would jolt him from a dead sleep. That was when he learned things. Like about Sandra's mother leaving her dad for some doctor when she was little, and she never saw her again. That had to screw you up. Sandra may not be the best mom in the world, but Ben couldn't imagine growing up with no mother at all. He remembered seeing a documentary or something, probably on MTV, about Madonna not having a mother growing up and how it messed with her head. But obviously she overcame it. Madonna was now the most famous chick on the planet. Ben didn't like her or her music, too girly for him. But you got to respect someone like that.

Sandra, well, she made her own problems, every last one of them. All his life he heard how she was going to get him a nice daddy, but then she'd go out and get hammered and who the hell wants someone like that? When he'd get the nerve to tell her so, and demand she quit drinking, she'd smack him across the face, and call him names like snot-ass kid, lil' bastard, or ingrate, which he had to look up in the dictionary. Sometimes the words hurt him worse than the slap, even though he knew they were just alcohol words.

Closing his bedroom door, Ben pulled the CD out of his jacket pocket and laid it on top of his Boombox. He yanked off the wet coat, threw it onto the floor, and fell on his bed. He lay there, hands folded on the back of his head and thought about his life.

When he was younger, he didn't mind Sandra when she got drunk, or nursing a hangover, because he didn't know any better. But in the last few years, it sickened him. The whole scenario was getting old, like her, and he'd just tune her out, or disappear to his room or to Colin's. At least his friend had a dad who drank nothing but Pepsi.

Ben's life mission was to be good enough on guitar to get some recognition and moneymaking gigs. Then he could quit school and make cool records like Nirvana, or maybe go out on his own like Clapton, or Prince. How cool it would be to spend all his time on tour, and have all the money he could want and get all those hot chicks, like the ones he saw on MTV.

Colin kept talking about putting a band together, but Ben didn't have the heart to tell him he had a long way to go before he'd be ready. Playing guitar came easy to Ben, but it took most people a lot longer to catch on. Danny, his guitar teacher, and people at the gigs always praised Ben up and down. At first he thought they were just being kind. But he came to understand that he really did have a gift, like he'd read that some people have. They called it a gift from God, but Ben wasn't sure he believed in an all-knowing, all-powerful God. It sounded too *Wizard of Oz*-ish to him. Still, wherever his passion and ability came from, he was grateful. It was the only thing that made him feel truly alive.

And he believed with all his heart, way deep in his soul, that he was going to be a rock star someday.

He couldn't tell anyone, of course, because who would believe him?

He had a bunch of songs he could play, but now he started writing some of his own, which he found more fun than he'd thought it would be. Time for the next step.

He was going to talk to that record label lady again. Echo's mom. He hadn't seen her since he first played Ruby's last year, but she'd seemed interested in his talent. She had even given him her card, told him to speak to his "parents" about maybe making a record with her company sometime in the future. But he lost the card. And besides, he didn't think he wanted to do that because frankly, the woman was kind of old, and, well, a chick, which dampened his enthusiasm. In his mind, he envisioned being on one of those cool labels with a bunch of guys in the studio who knew how to make his music sound the right way. No offense against Echo or the other artists on Peggy Sue Records, but none of them were into hard rock, punk, heavy metal, or grunge, the kind of music he loved.

Ben also worried that his buddies would laugh if he made a record on a woman's label. But then he read that article on the history of Peggy Sue's Records in the November issue of *American Rocker*. He hadn't realized how much he didn't know about them. He learned some fascinating stuff about Frankie London. He'd heard of him, naturally, and remembered times when his mom played his Greatest Hits album. But to Ben, he was just one of those rock stars who died in a plane crash. He'd read the list once in another music magazine and it was sadly long. Cool dudes like Buddy Holly, Ritchie Valens, Otis Redding, Rick Nelson, the guys in Lynyrd Skynyrd, and just two years ago, the great Stevie Ray Vaughan.

Ben didn't like to think that if he became a rocker, he too, would have to ride in airplanes all the time. But then, unlike her old man, Echo had *survived* a plane crash, so at least there was that possibility.

He also hadn't known about the kidnapped baby. That was some crazy shit. He felt sad reading how the family would never get over it, and it gave him chills when he realized that it happened around the same time he had been born. Which meant the kid would be his same age now, if he was still alive. In the article, Echo and Peggy Sue said they would never give up hope and believed the kid was still out there somewhere, but Ben kind of doubted it. Anyone crazy enough to steal a baby . . . well, the odds weren't good.

So now that he realized how well respected Peggy Sue Records was in the industry, he decided it might be a good place for him to start. Especially since the studio was right in his hometown.

He jumped off the bed and ran to the kitchen wall phone to call Nick. "Can you take me to Ruby's next week? It'll be off for Christmas vacation."

Nick and Ashley picked him up the following Thursday, and Ben was secretly glad that Sandra had to work and couldn't come. God knows what she'd do, though he had a pretty good idea. After a few drinks, she'd most likely start dancing around, acting crazy. And she'd be calling him "Benji" all the time. Man, he'd never be able to show his face there after that.

Ben walked into Ruby's feeling excited and confident. His hair was combed back so he would look older—he'd learned that from Leonardo DiCaprio from *Growing Pains*—and he wore the new Lee jeans Sandra had bought him for cleaning the house every Saturday. And a Doors

T-shirt, since much of Ruby's crowd was into that. When he pulled it out of his bottom drawer, Sandra got all giddy about it. He never wore it because he'd overheard Sandra tell someone that she'd gotten it off some guy who came into the bar selling old band T-shirts, two for $5. Seems nothing at all embarrassed her.

He did like some Doors' tunes, though, especially "The End," but when it came to the old stuff, he preferred the blues. The chord progressions and guitar licks those old black guys did were insane.

As they started setting up, Ben hoped that Peggy Sue and Echo would remember him. He knew they'd be here because Nick told Ruby he was bringing him and asked her to spread the word. After his debut last year, he had played one other time, but Ben didn't count that because it had been a dead night, not even Peggy Sue or Echo were there.

He knew he was good by now. In the past year, he'd played coffeehouses, a couple of dive bars, and one Mic Night in Lakewood. Ben hoped to get some real—as in paying—gigs from this night. Not to mention a chance to sway Peggy Sue so he could make his first record.

"Gonna be great tonight," Nick said, pulling out his guitar. "They'll be all sorts of folks in for the holidays, so guaranteed a full house."

"Hey, Ben, great to see you again." Ruby shook his hand, like he was somebody. "We were wondering what happened to you." She bumped Nick's shoulder with her fist. "Nick did real good keeping you away."

"Ah, come on, Rube, the kid's been in school, ya know." He tilted his head toward Ben. "And last summer was a wash considering he was grounded most of the time."

"All summer?" Ruby threw her head back in mock disbelief. "You don't look like a problem child. Well, you just keep playing that guitar. That'll keep you outta trouble."

Ben smiled, nodded. "Yeah, I know," was all he could muster.

By show time, the place was filled to capacity. Several people came up to him saying they remembered him from the year before. "Wow, Nick," he whispered just before they started, "I can't believe how many people remember me."

Nick poked him in the ribs. "You kiddin'? They ask about you all the time, but I wanted to make sure you were ready for the big time." His eyes moved across the packed room. "And this, my friend, is the big time." He nodded toward the table where Peggy Sue sat with her daughter and their husbands. It was as if Nick had been reading Ben's mind.

He knew he'd have to make a good impression, so he had practiced every day on songs he was certain would get him noticed by Peggy Sue.

He started out with a Michael Stanley Band song, "Let's Get the Show on the Road" to get the crowd going—everyone in Cleveland was a MSB fan—with Nick on vocals. Then he did a song by a national pop/rock group on Peggy Sue Records.

Now it was time to pull out the big guns. He approached the microphone. "This next tune is for all of you who lived back in the '70s," he said, sparking laughter from the mostly baby boomer audience. Then he ripped into "National Guard Guards Who?" the song Echo wrote with her friend, CJ, about the Kent State Shootings. He'd read about that in the *American Rocker* article and got his teacher, Danny, to help him learn it.

And then . . . "This last song is an oldie, but goodie." Again, a roar of laughter. Ben stepped back and began playing Frankie London's "Wishing, Dreaming, Hoping." Toward the end, he snuck a glance over at Peggy Sue and Echo. Both had their eyes locked on him, and it looked like they were crying, but he couldn't tell for sure.

But they *were* smiling. And that was good. Real good.

29. Wishing on a Star

The four of them didn't say a word the whole time Ben was playing. Only when Dusty squeezed Charlee's leg at one point did she avert her eyes from the stage, but only for a second. Charlee felt dazed hearing this boy play the song that she and CJ had written so long ago. She hardly ever listened to her old stuff anymore, because of 20/20 hindsight. A lot of those songs could've been better, but the MissFits had been urged by their first label to get the product out fast, the quality of the music being secondary. Most times when Charlee heard their singles on the radio, she switched the station.

Except when she heard "National Guard Guards Who?" That one really was good, and held a special spot in her heart because she wrote it with her dearly missed friend. As Ben played the familiar song, Charlee closed her eyes, wishing with all her heart that CJ were still among them. She would always miss him, his zany sense of humor, and how he used to walk around with that big purple pick in that bushy head of hair of his. *How he would've loved seeing this kid do our special song.*

Charlee opened her eyes, now moist with nostalgia, to watch how Ben handled the last chorus, its most notable riff. When he pulled it off, she shot out of her seat and clapped, with others following her lead. She was not only impressed, but relieved. She would have been so sad for Ben had he screwed that up.

Peggy, sitting across from her, leaned over, yelling over the applause, "I am not letting that kid leave tonight without him promising me to do a record."

Billy heard her and added, "Well, you better catch him before someone else—"

He stopped mid-sentence when Ben started playing Frankie London's song, "Wishing, Dreaming, Hoping." Billy's eyes raised as he looked at Peggy. He grabbed her hand and kissed it. In turn, Dusty pulled his Charlee closer, rubbing his hand along the back of her neck, then massaged her shoulder as they listened. Both men knew what Frankie and his music meant to their wives.

The minute Ben finished, the crowd gave the boy another standing ovation, and Peggy Sue began to walk toward Ben just as he jumped off the stage.

Peggy squeezed past two young girls heading in the same direction. "Ben," she called out so he would stop in front of her. "Do you remember me?"

The boy looked more diminutive and shy than he had just a moment ago on that stage. "Yes, I do. Nice to see you again, Mrs. Lawrence."

Peggy gave a little laugh at him using her maiden name, which she only used for business. This distinguished her company from her personal life, which came in handy when someone called the office. If they asked for Peggy Dalton, her secretary knew it was a friend or family member.

"You have time to join us, Ben?" she asked, worried that Nick might whisk the kid out of there, like he had the last time.

Ben's face brightened, his shyness suddenly dissolved. "Sure." He followed her, ignoring the girls Peggy had beaten to the punch.

Like a true pro, the boy came to the table and extended his hand to Billy, then Dusty, nodding appreciatively as they praised his performance. When he got to Charlee, his eyes widened. "Hi, Echo. I mean, Charlee."

Charlee stood and gave him a quick hug. "You were great." Then she pointed her finger at him. "7-Up, right?"

He grinned. "Wow, you remembered."

How could she forget? The night Charlee had met this boy was engraved in her memory bank. She often thought about him because he represented her son, in a way. The son she didn't have. Ben's presence got her wondering what kind of kid Dylan was growing up to be. If, in fact . . . The familiar dark thoughts came rushing back. She forced them away.

Then she heard her mother invite Ben to her annual Christmas party coming up the following Saturday night.

"We would love to meet your mother," Peggy was saying. "Nick and Ashley came last year and really enjoyed it, maybe you can all come together. You'll get to meet more people in the music industry."

Boy, she's pulling out all the stops. Charlee grinned. Yet she had mixed feelings. It was one thing to have the kid coming into the studio to record, but by inviting him to the big holiday gathering made him part of their circle. She didn't need this constant reminder of the boy she'd lost.

But looking at Ben now talking to Billy and Peggy, sipping on his pop, Charlee couldn't help but be fond of him. Especially after he'd played those songs. Of all the ones he could've picked to play that night, Ben had managed to choose the two songs that meant the most to her.

She warned herself not to get too involved. Though that might be next to impossible.

Peggy knew everyone looked forward to her and Billy's annual Christmas party. So she always began preparations weeks in advance. What to serve, who to invite—she added new names each year to keep the gathering fresh—and who would play. She'd choose the latest bands on her label and set them up in the great room of their roomy Victorian home. They were particularly excited about this year because it marked the gala's twentieth anniversary. It was fashioned after Aunt Jo and Uncle Ray's yearly tradition that had ended with their unexpected deaths. Then a few years later, in their honor, Peggy and Billy resumed the holiday get-together, and as Peggy Sue Records expanded, so did the party. Peggy began including her staff and their significant others, as well as important business associates. Then came Billy's own list of radio personalities and executives from his radio stations, along with their family and personal friends, and the festive gathering had turned into a large catered affair.

This year, the only ones missing would be Patrick and Nina, who were talking babies, and had decided to take a two-week holiday cruise before becoming stay-at-home parents.

At eight p.m., Nick and Ashley arrived with Ben and his mother. As hostess, Peggy greeted them at the door in her glittering green sequined dress, her blonde hair swept in an old-fashioned updo. Upon introductions, she hoped her surprise didn't show on her face. Hadn't Nick told Ben's mother this was a formal affair? The petite woman wore a Christmas sweater with a big jolly face of Santa front and center, that stopped short at her round waist. The black leggings were stretched to capacity over a potbelly. Black well-worn flats completed the ensemble.

Perhaps more startling was her makeup. It looked hastily applied, with too much of everything; thick foundation with dark red blush, black eyeliner and dark blue eye shadow that overtook her aquamarine eyes, her best asset. Her patchy frosted hair was chopped like Liza Minnelli's in the movie, *Arthur*, but spiked up with too much gel.

Peggy suspected this woman had been pretty once, but the years had not been her friend.

When Sandra smiled at her and extended her hand, Peggy chastised herself for the harsh critique. After all, who knew this woman's story? Peggy returned the smile, and grabbed her slightly trembling hand.

"Welcome to our home, Sandra." A rush of artic cold rushed up her spine from Sandra's icy fingers. "Come into the living room by the fireplace and warm up. Would you like an eggnog? My husband makes the best."

The woman's eyes widened. "Sure would, thank you." She touched her son's shoulder. "And Ben here can have one, too, seeing how's it's a special night," she added, beaming with the look of a teacher giving her student a prize.

Peggy opened her mouth to ask, *Isn't he only twelve?* But she knew he was, so she clamped her mouth shut. She didn't feel right about giving the boy alcohol, yet she didn't know how to say it without sounding critical.

As the four began to mingle, Peggy rushed into the kitchen and caught Billy's arm. "She wants Ben to have an eggnog."

Billy was making the drinks and placing them on the waiter's tray. "Who does?"

"Ben's *mother.*" Peggy leaned into her husband and touched his shoulder. "I don't think we should do that. Can you make him a separate one, without the rum?"

"Well, I don't know. He *is* going to be in the music business," he teased, then wrapped an arm around her waist. "Whatever you want, my love," he said and kissed her cheek.

"Thanks, dear." She winked at him.

When she grabbed the eggnogs, she made sure to memorize which one was the virgin cocktail. She found Sandra sitting with Ashley, who was pointing out various people well known in the Cleveland music scene.

"Here you go." Peggy handed Sandra her drink, and gazed around. "Where'd Ben go?"

Ashley nodded toward the great room. "Where the music is."

That gave Peggy a surge of excitement. The boy had exactly the kind passion needed to go where she was anxious to lead him.

She spent the next half hour chatting with Sandra. She liked getting to know the families of the artists she acquired on her label, and her party was perfect for that. The more they talked, the more Peggy felt ashamed for her rather callous first impression. The woman may not know how to dress for a party, but she could keep a conversation going. She talked about Ben, of course, and how long she'd known Nick, and told funny stories about some of the regulars at the bar where she worked. Peggy had a hard time keeping up with it all. She talked fast, and in fragments, jumping from one thing to another. It was a bit unnerving how on edge the woman seemed. Peggy wondered if Sandra felt intimidated with so many famous people in the house, but why be nervous talking to her? Peggy was hardly a celebrity.

"I knew my boy had talent soon as he got that guitar," Sandra said, stopping to take a big swallow from her glass. "He practices all the time. I mean, *all the time*. I hardly see him out of that room. But I know it's good for him. Keeps him out of trouble. He's got a lot of energy, that kid."

Peggy smiled, thinking, *And so do you.* But she was happy to hear how devoted Ben was to music, and it verified her suspicion that the woman was aware of Peggy's interest in him. As Sandra continued on, Peggy could see the love this mother had for her son, which surprised her. Sandra didn't look like the doting mother-type. More the type who let a twelve-year-old drink liquor.

This woman, who snatched another eggnog as the waiter passed by, was a swirling maze of contradictions. Yet, by the time Billy grabbed Peggy and pulled her onto their makeshift dance floor, she decided that she liked Ben's mother. And after the dance, she'd discuss her plans with Sandra about Ben's musical career.

30. Broken Promise Land

He had a wife. That son-of-a-bitchin' Jerry had a wife! Every time Sandra thought about it, her chest tightened so hard she could barely breathe.

How could she not have figured it out? For a whole damn year? Of course, it all made sense now. How they'd always go to *her* apartment for sex. And when she'd asked for his number one day, he said he didn't have a phone. "Got so mad at those damn solicitors calling at all hours, I ripped it off the wall one night and never felt the need to replace it." Then for good measure, he'd added, "Besides, I know where I can find my girl," and gave her one of his big bear hugs that always made her weak. After that, she never gave it a thought. Not even when he'd made some lame excuse why he couldn't accompany her last Christmas to Peggy Sue's big party.

She made the discovery of his marital status by accident, or on purpose, however one might look at it. She had been so anxious for August 21st to come around so she could tell people they've "been together a year now," which was longer than she'd ever had a boyfriend. And by now, he had to be ready for more of a commitment. She couldn't figure what was taking him so long to propose.

The first few months they dated, it was all good times; laughing and drinking and screwing. But he never told her he loved her and that started jacking her up but good. Even Bob had said the magical words after just one month, and would repeat it every time they were in bed. So she tried getting it out of Jerry. Tried a couple of times. They'd have sex and she'd curl up under his strapping arm and hint at it by remarking how good they were together and how she'd never met a man like him, and so on and so on.

Nothing. He'd just rub her chest and they'd either fall asleep or start up again.

So now it was time to force the issue. She was tired of his excuses as to why he never took her to his place. His story for that was that he'd lost his house to his first wife four years prior, and had to live with his mother until he could redeem his losses. "And the woman's a pack rat, worse than you can imagine."

When she poked his ribs and said, "Well, I'm sure your bedroom has enough room for two," he said, "Now, darlin', I can't bring a nice woman like you to a place like that. Just be patient. I'll be gettin' my own place real soon."

That was six months ago.

She did know that he lived near the local Kmart—she'd gotten that much out of him one night he'd drunk too much Johnny Walker Red—but he never told her his street. And the more she thought about that—and other signs pointing to those big red flags flapping in front of her blind eyes— the more the hairs on her neck started bristling and she started growing anxious.

So on Friday, she talked the Den's daytime bartender, Cindy, into borrowing her car, saying her Nova was giving her trouble and she had to go to the doctor. "Female trouble," she'd said. And that part was no lie.

That afternoon, Sandra sat in her decoy, a shit-gray Ford Escort, at the far end of the parking lot where Jerry worked at the factory plant. She knew he got out at 3:30, so all she had to do was wait, then follow his truck. Jerry always went home to clean up before he came to the Den.

The best scenario would be that Sandra would finally get to meet his mother.

The worst scenario was exactly what happened.

When Jerry pulled into the drive of a nice ranch home on Chester Street, Sandra pulled alongside the curb two doors down. Enough for her to watch, and him not to notice. As she sat in Cindy's air-conditioned car—a bonus since the Nova's air was on the fritz—her heart pounded with anticipation, even though she wasn't sure what to anticipate.

She sat there staring at the modest beige house with brown shutters, and nicely mowed yard, and waited. About an hour later, her patient surveillance was rewarded, if you can call it that. She saw the front door open and a woman, clearly not Jerry's old, half-crippled mother, walked out. Sandra wasted no time. She bolted out of the car like it was on fire, afraid she'd miss her opportunity. She slammed the door and sprinted down the concrete driveway. "Excuse me, ma'am, 'scuse me," she called out.

When the surprised woman turned to face her, Sandra got a good look at her competition. She was around the same age as Sandra, but that's where the similarity stopped. This one had shoulder-length black hair that obviously had been hot-ironed so that it practically glimmered in the sun's rays. Her well-powdered face smoothed any lines that might be there, and her brown eyes were dabbed with bronze eye shadow, making her look queen-like.

One thing Sandra had going for her was her body, for once in her life. She might be on the porky side, but this woman was robust. A cow. She had to outweigh Sandra by thirty pounds, easy. The polka-dot dress with black patent leather belt around her waist didn't help her cause any.

Still, this lady seemed way too fancy for Jerry. So once Sandra had her attention, she came right out and asked. "Are you Jerry Feldman's wife?"

When Cake Face replied, "Yes. Can I help you?" Sandra felt a hot rush of blood run through her like a lit match to turpentine. She moved slightly, just enough to block the woman from getting in the car.

"Well now, how interestin' since he's been banging *me* for a year. Never once mentioned—"

Sandra had lots more to say, but Mrs. Jerry started screeching. *"What?* Why you Skank," and swung her black patent leather purse—to complete her outfit, natch—at Sandra's face. From there it was balls to the wall, as her bar crowd liked to say.

Sandra grabbed her arm and turned it, forcing her down to the ground as a jet-stream of cuss words flung with every punch, kick, and slap.

They started having it out right there on the Feldman's pretty manicured lawn. Their catfight brought out the neighbors, who probably rarely got to see two middle-aged fat broads beating up on each other, an unexpected outdoor show. For free.

Somewhere in the midst of it all, Jerry, hair wet from his after-work shower, dashed out of his house of lies. He tried breaking it up by lifting both of them up, one in each arm, but that only put him in direct line of fire. So in the end, they all looked like they'd been in a wrestling match.

When the police car came roaring up the drive and two cops got out, that put a kibosh on the whole drama.

Sandra came out of it with a black eye and bruises over her arms and legs, but she'd gotten in a few good ones, too, though not enough, from what Sandra could see as they sat in the back of the cruiser. After giving their information, they each were handed a ticket for domestic disturbance, which added insult to injury. Once the paper work and lectures were done, Sandra got into her borrowed car. She drove past the scene of the crime slowly, enjoying Mrs. Jerry squawking at Sandra's former lover, and him, trying to yank her into the house as she wiggled away, yelling, "Don't touch me, you bastard!"

That gave Sandra her one and only smile of the day.

By the time she got home, reality had set in, and she let loose in her apartment. She screamed and swore and threw a living room ashtray. She banged pots and pans and threw up. Then she fell on her bed, exhausted and let herself have a good cry. How she wished she had some of Jerry's stuff at her place just so she could throw it all out on the lawn like other women get to do.

No, Sandra Jacobs, the loser, didn't even have the satisfaction in doing that.

Lucky for her, Ben hadn't been home during that fiasco. In fact, he'd been hardly home all summer, busy as he was playing gigs, hanging out with his buddies, and working on his songs. That spring, he'd made a four-song EP, which he explained to Sandra meant "extended play." A couple of them got airplay on college radio, so the kid was pumped. And Sandra, proud mama that she was, had talked her boss into putting it on the jukebox so she could play it to all her customers. And as she did, she bragged about her Benji being signed to Peggy Sue Records, with his first genuine album coming up around Christmastime.

It was exciting, sure, but having her boy in that family circle really screwed with her head. Sometimes she had nightmares that the Peggy Sue Camp, as she referred to them, would figure out Ben was Dylan. She'd wake up shaking and heart pounding, but glad it was a dream. She constantly had to tell herself that no way would they recognize a thirteen-year-old kid after not seeing him since he was two days old. No way in hell.

What also bothered her was that here was a kid that had more going on than she did. Everybody loved him to pieces, and she missed having Ben all too herself. First Nicky, then Ashley, who called herself his "big sister," which was hogwash. Sandra didn't like it, but what could she do? If she said something, Nick would get mad at her. Ben also had his best buddy, Colin, and his dad, who treated him, but not her, like family.

Family.

What were the odds of Ben getting involved with Charlee and Dusty, and Peggy Sue—his real fucking family? Of all the coincidences in the world. Sandra would never forget that Christmas party last year. She tried getting out of going after Jerry backed out, but Nick threw a fit saying she had to get more involved in her kid's life, and what a big opportunity it was. Oh, she knew it was big! Bigger than Nick or anyone could ever imagine! The whole time she was at that house, she was paranoid. Like if they looked close enough, they might recognize some features. His dark eyes, like Charlee's. His wavy dark blond hair, like Dusty's. And that nose. A few years ago, she watched the movie, *The Frankie London Story*, and at the end, they showed footage of the real Frankie. And there it was, that prominent, distinguished-like nose.

Those eggnogs had helped her relax, and she enjoyed chatting it up with Peggy. For all her money and prestige in the music business, Peggy was real kind. And so pretty! Sandra knew she must be in her fifties by now but you couldn't tell. Sandra started feeling bad, even sad, about taking away her grandkid. But then, Charlee came over and wasn't all that friendly to her. Just a polite hello before asking Peggy to join her in the music room—they actually called it that—then left with a half-ass nod. She acted too big for her britches, if you asked Sandra, which got her back to thinking how glad she was for saving Ben from the likes of her. Her and her swanky friends, who she had busily flitted from one to another all night.

Sandra began flitting around, too, after eggnog number three. She met all kinds of local TV and radio personalities that night. Sandra introduced herself to Wilma Smith, who'd been on the news for eons. And Brian & Joe, the funny guys on that morning radio show. And Paula Balish, Sandra's favorite from the classic rock station, WNCX. Sandra liked her voice, and after hearing country music all the time at the

Den, she enjoyed calling into Paula's nighttime show on those lonely nights she didn't work. She'd never forget how thrilled she was when Paula said to her, "Oh I know you, Sandra," because of all the times she'd called in with requests.

She tried flirting with the debonair mystery writer, Les Roberts, the most famous author in Cleveland, but then his girlfriend came back from wherever she was and put a possessive arm through his, flashing Sandra that 'he's mine' look.

She then moved on to that "music room," to be with Ben, Nick, and Ashley. There she met other celebrities, like members of the Raspberries. She nearly fainted meeting their drummer, Jim Bonfanti, who she had a mad crush on when she'd been young. She met Jerry Shirley, too, a real Englishman! He'd been the drummer for Humble Pie, and was now living in Cleveland.

So all in all, it had turned out to be a real memorable night. And best of all, Sandra had kept it together. She had been proud of herself for stopping her drinks at number four. She did it for Ben's sake. She didn't want to embarrass her son.

And he was still her son. No matter what happened down the road, Benji would always be hers.

31. Hold On My Heart

Charlee loved her morning jogs through the quiet streets of Sherman Falls. She had started the sport last spring to give herself time alone, and the activity had become as necessary to her as eating, sleeping, breathing. She'd run through the spring's rain, the summer's heat, and now the fall's chill. October was her favorite month of all. Not only did the brilliant fall colors brighten her senses, but the brisk air gave her a jolt of energy that lasted all day.

Every morning, she'd rise at five, splash her face with water, rake a comb through her hair, throw on her sweats and sneakers, and leave the house before Dusty and Tammi woke. In the forty-five minutes she allowed herself, Charlee would plan her day, think about people she needed to call, ponder ways to solve the world's problems.

And she would think about Ben. Despite her efforts to remain neutral, Charlee couldn't squelch her maternal feelings now that he was a part of their world. Being an artist on Peggy Sue Records meant he was now performing often throughout the town to get his name out there. And, well, Charlee had to be there to cheer him on. Especially since his own mother obviously lacked interest.

Since having her daughter, Charlee felt a strong urge to mother everything, from stray kittens—they now had two, who, luckily, got along with Rocky—to the children in Tammi's second-grade class, who Charlee saw each day when she picked her up from school. She gave regularly to children's organizations, and ached to save every kid she read about with bad home lives. The more she got to know Ben, the more she suspected he fit into that category.

Dusty often had to remind her not to get too involved, and several times he'd kept her from actually calling Sandra to ask her, in a nice way, why she didn't come to most of the functions they invited her to. Peggy always encouraged musicians' families to be present at their events, but Sandra hadn't even attended the EP release party Peggy hosted for Ben back in the spring. Charlee learned, too, that Sandra's no-shows extended to school functions as well. When Ben mentioned that his mother hadn't "been able to" attend his seventh-grade end-of-school concert, Dusty had to practically hold Charlee hostage from the phone for days to prevent her from making that call.

What Ruby told her yesterday disturbed her even more. And after telling Dusty about it last night, her husband reminded her, again, not to get involved.

"But we're already involved," she'd said, as they sat in the recording studio.

She had gone with him as he worked on the mix for Ben's CD, called, simply, *Meet Ben Jacobs*. As soon as Dusty sat next to her to take a break, Charlee let him in on the latest about Ben's mother. "Wait'll you hear this one. Remember that clam bake Ruby and Rob were going to over the weekend?"

Dusty was leaning back in the swivel chair smoking a cigarette. He nodded, only half-listening. But she knew she'd get his attention soon enough.

"Well, one of the guests was a Parma policeman and he began telling them this story about breaking up a catfight that took place out on a woman's lawn last August. At one point, the cop's wife turns to Ruby and says, oh by the way, they'd learned that the other woman involved is the mother of that kid who plays sometimes at your restaurant."

That got Dusty's head to turn. "Really? A catfight? Boy, that Sandra sure is something, isn't she?" She saw a grin start to form, but he quickly changed it to a frown. "Sweetheart, I agree she's not exactly Mother Theresa, but a catfight is hardly something you can go to children's services about. I know this bothers you, but Ben's thirteen. It's not like he's five." He snuffed the Camel out and reached for her hand.

Charlee yanked it away. "You don't get it, Dust! That right there shows she's got a tendency toward violent behavior. Who knows what she does in the confines of her home!"

Dusty repeated his mantra on the drive home. "I feel for the kid, too, honey, but he doesn't act, or look, like he's being abused."

"Well, looks can be deceiving," she countered, thinking of Kat, but not daring to bring up *that* ancient history.

They'd come home, relieved the sitter and Dusty proceeded to take her mind off of it, if only temporarily, by making passionate love to her. The best of all distractions.

But now as her feet pounded the pavement and the sun rose up the hill of the little town's business district, she was determined to convince Dusty that teenage boys needed stability in their lives, and that they could give it. Somehow she'd make her husband understand that their intervention might just save this kid's life. Or at the very least, his future.

Peggy Sue had never been more excited, and nervous, about launching a new artist. But Ben was special, in many ways. For one, there was his age. How rare for a boy just entering his teens to play guitar like he did. That had been the easy part—helping him hone the instrument. He picked up new chords like they were born in him. She also was pleased to discover his knack for songwriting, another bonus.

But his voice, in the midst of changing, presented a unique challenge. His singing constantly wavered, and after some frustration, Peggy decided to turn an obstacle into an asset. She brought in one of her best singers to help control his tone, then enlisted the aid of a songwriter on her roster who could shift some of the melodies of his songs to best suit his changing voice.

Although she'd seen Ben many times in the past year, it wasn't until he began working in the recording studio that Peggy noticed his mannerisms. They reminded her of Frankie. Ben played his guitar nearly down by his knees, with one foot forward, one behind, just like Frankie used to do. Ben's nose had the same shape as Frankie's, too. He didn't resemble Sandra at all, so those features must have come from the father's side. Whoever he was. Neither Sandra nor Ben ever mentioned a dad.

What endeared Ben to Peggy most had been when he played "Wishing, Dreaming, Hoping" that night at Ruby's. Hearing that song again had brought so many suppressed emotions to the surface. There were still times Peggy Sue could not believe Frankie London had been gone all her adult life. And she still missed him. Billy was her true soul mate, she knew that, but first loves, especially in her case, stayed with you forever. Their incomplete love story would always be in constant rotation, like a vinyl record in continuous spin. As much a part of her as her own beating heart. She'd learned to live with it, of course. And as the decades passed, thoughts of Frankie had stayed in the recesses of her mind. But Ben, with his youth, that prominent nose, and his stance as he played guitar, brought Frankie's memory back, as if he'd never left the earth. Funny how life was sometimes.

Once, Peggy even got a crazy thought and asked Ben when his birthday was. "March 27th," he'd said. She remembered how she'd sighed. Well, it *was* a crazy thought. Luckily she never told Charlee about that. Her daughter didn't need to get all worked up over a false hope. Again.

The CD had taken some time to complete. They rearranged

several songs. They changed the photo cover twice. They added more to his bio in the liner notes so listeners would feel they knew him better. That took a bit of creativity because what do you say about a boy who'd only lived a mere thirteen and a half years? Billy was the one who included the story of how Ben started playing, and how, when he wasn't in school, he'd be with "his first love, Layla," to underscore the boy's dedication to his music. They ended up with enough to fill the first two pages of the little booklet that slid inside the CD, along with the lyrics to his songs. The latest trend was to exclude song lyrics in the packet, but Peggy knew teenagers. They loved singing along, and it helped sell more records when listeners understood a song's meaning.

With Dusty at the mixing boards, the final product had everyone pumped. Peggy, Billy, and all the session musicians who played on it, all agreed that there were at least three songs that could be hits. Ben's style was a unique combination of Stevie Ray Vaughn and Kurt Cobain, and this new release was so good, they believed there might be a Grammy in his future. That would be a first for Peggy Sue Records, since Charlee had missed out on that one in 1982.

Peggy's biggest concern was not the boy's talent, or if the CD would generate hits. As special as it was, his age could also be a problem. And so could his mother. Turning Ben into a mega-rock star at his age could have disastrous results. Peggy had read plenty about what happened to childhood stars. The drugs, alcohol, depression . . . she worried about the risk. Especially when Ben's mother, according to Nick, already had an alcohol problem, and seemed a bit unstable. So Peggy decided to hold off the release. She wanted more time to groom Ben, help get him ready emotionally for what would surely come.

Nick had never been as concerned about Sandra as he was now. It had started when that married guy broke her heart, and she hadn't bounced back, like she usually did. Then she got fired from the Den for not showing up for work one time too many. So she'd lost out on all that money she would have made during the Christmas holiday. And she didn't seem to care.

What troubled him most was the effect it was having on Ben. Through the long cold winter, Nick worked hard to keep Ben busy with more gigs, both for money and to keep his mind off things, but the kid's performance was becoming more lackluster each time, which wasn't good for someone ready to launch a new CD. He didn't know what else he could do for him. All he knew was something had to be done.

By April, he suggested to Sandra, gently, that she see a good psychologist he knew at the Cleveland Clinic. She responded by throwing an ashtray at him, and told him to get out of her apartment. The next day, he talked to someone who worked at children's services about having Ben stay with him for a bit. If Sandra wouldn't let him help her, he had to help her son.

Ben had been disappointed when Peggy had pushed back his CD release until "probably April." First it was going to come out in November, and he'd told practically his whole school. Then he had to explain to everyone that there had been delays with "packaging," and announced the spring release, after Peggy explained how springtime was a good time to launch new music. He tried to be patient, but it was hard because it was the only thing he had to look forward to. School sucked, living with Sandra sucked—he was starting to think she was half-crazy—and even playing out didn't give him the exhilaration it used to. Peggy had hired Nick as his manager, which was great at first, but now he was on him about everything, from putting on a more energetic show, to making him wear stupid striped shirts or ones with collars. Ben liked wearing his band T-shirts and holey jeans. That was the style nowadays, didn't Nick understand that? Ben didn't want to look like freakin' Neil Diamond. As time grew closer to the release, Nick became more business than fun these days. So that sucked, too.

Then April came and Peggy decided to push it back even further, until summer "sometime." His fury over that was short-lived, though, because a week after that news, he had other things on his mind.

His musical hero was dead.

Ben had stopped in at Tommy Edwards Record Store that Friday, like he usually did after school. Denny stood behind the counter, looking dazed, staring at the glass that displayed all the new CDs.

Ben walked over to him. "Hey," he said, then bent his head down, too, to get his attention to get him to look at him. "Hellooo?"

When Denny looked up, Ben thought someone must have died. "You okay?"

Denny shook his head. "Ah, man. Ben, I got some serious bad news."

Ben remembered the chill that shot up his spine. Whoever died had to be someone he knew, too.

When Denny told him about Kurt Cobain, Ben ran out the door before anyone could see him cry. He didn't stop running until he hit his street corner. He slowed his pace, then once he reached the apartment building, sat down on the step of the entrance, not wanting to go further. No way did he want to deal with Sandra right now. She was bound to be home because she didn't have a job, and she never went out anymore because she didn't have a job. And since last summer, she didn't have a boyfriend to take her out, and she couldn't find another one because she didn't go out. It was like that book he'd read last year, a real Catch-22.

Ben used to feel sorry for her when life threw her punches, as she'd say, but now her presence made him nervous. He never knew what he'd come home to. Some days she'd act normal, sitting on the couch watching TV. Other days, he'd walk in and she'd be ranting about whatever came to her head. She'd go off about things he knew she didn't really give a shit about. Like since when did she care about his "pigsty" room? Or his dirty clothes piled in the corner by his bed? "You're old enough to do your own damn laundry," she'd yell, then add things like, "You're not a high-and-mighty rock star yet, buddy, so ya better learn to take care of yourself. I'm not here to cater to your damn needs."

But the days she'd spend in her room, all quiet, were even more unnerving. Sometimes, he'd hear her sobbing behind her closed door. The first time it happened, he knocked and asked if there was something she needed, or that he could do for her, and she'd scream, "Get the fuck away." So he never bothered anymore, just let her have her little cries.

Now it was his turn to cry, and he needed to get to his room, hopefully bypass her on the way. But there was no hurry; it was nice and quiet right where he sat. Kids were either in their after-school programs, or inside watching TV, with their sane moms in the kitchen, getting dinner ready. Or whatever real families did.

He sat there staring at his dull surroundings. Cleveland had yet to see spring. The grass was still brown, the trees still bare, and for the first time, he noticed the gray, doom-like atmosphere in which he lived. All the cars in the parking lot were at least ten years old. All the people who lived here, even the ones who worked, didn't have much money and that's why they lived here—on the poor side of town. Like the Johnny Rivers song.

Since meeting the people in Peggy Sue's crowd, Ben realized how much better other people have it. Successful people drove cool-looking cars, all spanking new. They wore clothes that told you right away they didn't shop at those discount stores. And they wore shiny jewelry, both the women *and* the guys. Fancy rings and watches that sparkled in the dim lighting of the clubs and restaurants Ben had started playing in.

And most had backyard swimming pools. Not the kind that sat on top of someone's grass, but real YMCA type in-ground pools that were bigger than this whole apartment building. Maybe that was why Nick wanted him to dress nicer, now that he thought of it. He wanted Ben to be accepted, to look like he was one of them.

That was what he didn't understand about Kurt Cobain. The dude had it made. How could someone as rich and famous as *Kurt Cobain* want to kill himself? He had the world by the balls. People idolized him; he was this huge rock star. Everywhere the guy played, he got tons of money and attention. He had practically invented grunge, and that was historic.

But the longer Ben sat there thinking about it, he began to get it. If other things in life weren't going right, all the money in the world couldn't change it. He knew people got depressed for all kinds of reasons, and then they'd take drugs. He'd seen Sandra get down-in-the-dumps lots of times, since he was a kid. And he'd seen her medicine cabinet. All those pill bottles. He knew when she took them, because she'd act so different. When he was eleven, curiosity got the best of him, and after struggling with that darn cap, he got one of the bottles opened and took two—the recommended dosage—of the white capsules labeled 'Xanax,' just to see what it felt like. He ended up sleeping that entire Saturday. His clueless mother thought he had the flu. He felt like shit for two days afterward and that ended his curiosity.

Knowing how depressing depression can be, Ben could

kind of see now how someone like Kurt could feel there was no way out, even if he was a rock star. Maybe it didn't matter how rich and famous you are. If you're not happy inside, you can feel just as lost as if you were a nobody, sitting on a stoop of a drab apartment building with sorry looking people all around you.

And the sorriest was his mother. Ben stood up now. The kiddies had started coming out to play for their after-dinner romps, so he was forced to go inside. When he entered, she wasn't around, her bedroom door closed. It was going to be one of those nights. He tiptoed into his room, hoping she wouldn't hear him and come out.

He plopped on the bed, still thinking about Kurt Cobain, but also about those rich people he knew. They had problems, too, but they were all so tight. There was a lot of love in that Peggy Sue camp. Maybe because they all had someone to share their lives. Peggy had Billy. Charlee had Dusty. Nick had Ashley. Ruby had Rob. Libby had Dave, and their son, Jack, who had become a friend of his, too, even though he was a lot older, nineteen. He smiled to himself. Yes, he had some cool friends. And all those classy people he knew really cared about him.

He sat up now, feeling an urge to look in on his mother. He knew she needed him. She seemed so lonely lately. Maybe if he'd be nicer, they could be close again, like when he was little.

He went down the hallway to her room and knocked. "Mom? Hey, I'm gonna make something to eat. Can you join me? I got bad news today and I want to talk to you about it." He held his breath, gearing up for a possible "Fuck off" response.

Then he heard her bed squeak. "Oh, Benji. I didn't hear you come in." Her voice grew closer. "You know, I am kind of hungry."

When the door opened, Ben saw a woman who looked ten years older, with puffy eyes and dark circles and a forced happy smile, still wearing her pajamas at six in the afternoon.

He took her hand. "Come on, Mom, I'll make us one of my famous pizzas," he said, leading her into the kitchen. "Remember we bought the stuff for it the other day? We'll cook and we'll talk."

He threw her one his charming smiles. And for the first time in a long time, she smiled back.

32. Runaway Train

Sandra planned to leave her gift to Ben on Mother's Day. That Saturday, she began preparing by cleaning the house and doing Ben's laundry. At four o'clock, she ate some SpaghettiOs to coat her stomach a bit. When the wall clock read seven p.m., she took a shower, sprayed her favorite *Navy* cologne all over her body, then got dressed. She would wear her best black jeans and the new frilly top—blue to match her eyes—that she'd bought for the occasion.

As she dried her hair, she swore out loud for chopping at it last week when she was feeling sorry for herself. It reminded her of that '70s commercial, where the girl says, "Why did I cut my hair? I look like a squirrel." Well, at least when she got done with the curling iron, it would look halfway decent.

Once in the kitchen, she clinked ice into the tall Budweiser glass she'd lifted from the Den, carried the fifth of Jack Daniels and 2-liter bottle of Coke to the dinette table, set them down, and proceeded to mix her first drink. Her mission had begun.

Earlier that morning, she had told Ben that she didn't feel good, and that he should stay at Nick's that night after playing his downtown gig. "Don't want you catching whatever I'm getting," she'd said. He was only too happy to comply.

She surprised herself with her calm demeanor. She wasn't even scared. More like relieved. She was so sick of this shit. For once in her god-awful stinkin' life, she was going to do the right thing. She wanted to do right by that kid. That thought alone felt good.

She mixed the cocktail (3/4 JD, splash of Coke) stirred it with her finger, took a good swig, then walked into the living room to her father's old roll-top desk, the only thing of his she managed to keep through the years. She bent down, pulled out the bottom drawer, and grabbed the pink stationary and a pen. Then she reached further back for the pill bottle she'd been hiding. She returned to the table and arranged everything, just so.

Taking another guzzle, she imagined all the drama that would ensue tomorrow once things got going. Not that she thought the first part would be good. She knew Ben would be sad because, despite everything, she knew he loved his mama. Or, who he thought was his mama. She didn't want him to be upset, but when she thought of the reunion, she was excited for him. She knew he really liked those people, and now her baby would have a full-fledged normal-ass family. He deserved that, with all that she'd put him through. Besides, she had nothing going on. Never really did. The last six months had been the real kicker. She would never get over the shock of discovering that the one man she thought would make her dreams come true was just another lying *married* scoundrel. The son-of-a-bitch.

Drinking had always been her answer to pain. But after Jerry, she needed more than that. She couldn't believe how easy it was to convince doctors to give her the pills. She went first to the one she'd been to before, and got a prescription for Prozac. From there, she took a bus to two others in different towns and both gave her Percocet. Just last week, she talked to yet another doctor, saying how her anxiety had reached its peak since she'd found out her son had autism—she'd read about the new affliction somewhere and it just kind of popped into her head—and how hard it was trying to handle everything as a widowed mother with limited income. It had worked like a charm. This guy prescribed Paxil, some new drug they'd come up with. Although out of all of them, she preferred the Percocet. They gave her the best happy boost.

So at least she had that one talent. An uncanny flair for convincing people—who were supposed to be smarter than her with fancy degrees—that she was this unfortunate soul who'd just had a string of bad luck. Being a single mom had only helped the cause. Everyone knew how hard that was.

Especially when you don't have a job to keep your mind off things. She couldn't believe when Casey cut her loose. She was damn good at that job, better than any of those young, dumb ones on the payroll. So what if she got there late sometimes? She always offered to stay later to make up for it. And whenever she called in sick, she really *was* sick. Casey didn't need to know about the nights she passed out from the pills and booze. The one time he asked her if she was on drugs, she'd told him, "No! I don't touch pot or coke!" And that much was true. When he still fired her a week later, right before the holidays, she'd been so pissed she'd grabbed four of the top-shelf liquor bottles and smashed them on the floor. Then before he could call the cops, she hightailed it out of there, walking the whole three miles home because, like Jerry, the ol' Nova had crapped out on her, too.

Thinking about that day made her weepy. Working gave her a purpose and she'd really missed it. She missed her little boy, too, who wasn't so little anymore, and no longer needed her. That was when she'd decided it was time. That, and the fact her conscience had finally gotten the best of her.

She polished off the first drink, then opened the prescription bottle and let all the pretty-colored pills, blues, greens, and yellows, spill out onto the table. She'd been saving a bunch from each bottle for a special occasion. She giggled now, thinking how good the combination was bound to make her feel. She'd go out on a high note for sure.

Closing her eyes she circled her finger above the swarm of colors and picked one. Blue. How about that? Her favorite color. She grabbed it, poured drink number two, and gulped it down. Time to get writing before her penmanship got all wiggly. Benji had to be able to understand every word. And even though she'd rehearsed it all in her mind for days, she wondered if she'd remember to mention everything.

Sandra lit her last remaining cigarette, pulled out a stack of paper from the Hallmark box—who knew how many pages she'd need?—and snatched up the pen. The drink and pills in front of her were distracting, so she pushed them away toward the middle of the table. She needed to concentrate on her words.

Okay . . .

My dearest little Benjamin.
I have done a very terrible thing.

She took a long drag. Shit. This was harder than she thought. There was so much she wanted to tell him. Maybe she'd just write it all out, then go over it and tweak it. She had all night. Well, at least until everything took effect.

Okay. Again.

Please don't hate me for what I'm going to tell you. Please remember how much I love you. I didn't mean to hurt anyone. I just wanted a baby I could call my own. And you were the best little boy I could have ever hoped . . .

Shit, the tears were starting already. She swiped them away and rose from her dinette chair to grab the box of tissues in the bathroom. Might as well pee while she was there. When she came out, she saw how dark it was getting and went to close all the curtains, clicked on the lamp in the living room, then the kitchen light. She sat back down and pursed her lips.

Her head was spinning with a maze of mental pictures from the past. She had to stop them. She had to focus. She smashed out the burning cigarette in the ashtray, picked up the pen again, and forced her brain to concentrate.

Her plan was twofold. She was giving her son the best gift of all. His true identity. She was also giving back what she had taken from innocent people. This was the most important thing she'd ever do in her lousy life. This would be her legacy. How she explained everything was essential. She wanted them all to understand she wasn't an evil person.

Although Sandra didn't care much for Charlee, the woman hadn't deserved getting her baby stolen. And while it was possible that Charlee, having another kid now, might be over the loss, Ben deserved to be with a better rank of people. So she was really doing this for him. He'd be happier with his own flesh and blood. Plus, it would be nice for Peggy Sue, who had been so good to Ben, helping him out with his career and all. The thought of doing this nice thing for her, giving back her grandson, got her pen moving again.

I'm sorry you have to find me like this but there was no other choice. Now before you call 911, you need to know something. Like I said, honey, I did this horrible thing.

No, she already said that. She scratched out that last sentence. Took a swig of her drink. Started again.

Okay, here it is. I kidnapped you when you were born. Yes. I really did. At Holy Cross Hospital right here in Cleveland, not in PA, like where I'd said you were born. I know you know by now that Charlee-Echo's baby was stolen fourteen years ago and, and, well, oh shit, Benji, honey. YOU are that baby. But believe me, I didn't know you were that famous baby. Really I didn't. I just picked out a name in the baby announcements in the paper cuz I needed one so bad, and I didn't know what else to do. I wanted a boy and there you were, Baby Boy Campbell. It seemed like fate. How did I know it was Echo's? I didn't know her real name.

Sandra picked up her drink and downed it. *Oh god, how's he gonna take this?* Writing it all out made it sound so awful. Maybe if she'd done this in those first few days, she'd have given him back. It *was* a god-awful thing she'd done. She'd really screwed up people's lives.

Gazing over at the pills, she reached for a yellow one. Was this the Paxil or the Percocet? And why did they all start with the letter P? Oh right, for Pain. And Party. She giggled. She liked when she made herself laugh. The Pain started sliding out of her body, to make way for the Party. She grabbed a green one, too, and downed them together with the last of her drink. She picked up the JD bottle and poured all the way to the top of the glass. No Coke required.

Well, damn, she better get going and finish this while her mind was still working. She'd already run out of space on the first page. She turned it over, started again.

And oh, your birthday is really March 20th. I'm sorry but you can understand why I had to change it—your birthday was broadcast all over the news pracally every year. I know, I know, sweetie, I'm so, so sorry. This news is gonna freak you out but isn't it wonderful that you are that world-famous baby? That's probly why your so good at guitar. You got the best dam bloodline! And tis time you know it. I'm giving you back honey cuz you deserve to be with them. It's my Mothers Day gift to you!!!

She added a little smiley face.

This was going to be great. She was going to redeem herself. Ever since she'd decided to reveal her sin, she knew this was her only option. Once it got out, she'd be taken to jail and never again see the light of day. Worst of all, Benji would hate her forever and never come visit her. This way, he may hate her at first, but she'd be able to tell her side, make him understand her way of thinking. Besides, doing it on Mother's Day ensured that he would think of *her* every year, not so much of Charlee. After all, *she* was the one who raised him, and look how good he turned out. She had to at least get credit for that.

Uh-oh, she was feeling swirly now. She should've written this earlier. She took a sip and wrote faster.

Ok, my little benji getting sleepy now but remember how much I love you. Please please please understand I didn't mean to hurt anyone. I didn't. I just wanted to be a mama so bad. And you were, are, the perfect little boy. OH AND HIDE THIS NOTE!!!!! DON'T LET THEM GET IT! This is YOURS to keep forever.

I love you baby. Don't forget that! You will always be my lill Benji no mattter what.

Your loooooving Mama

Ok, that's it. She set the pen down, didn't want to think anymore. She polished off her glass, then filled it up again. She grabbed as many pills as her hand could hold and swallowed several at a time with her delicious Jack. The glass was empty before she got all the pills down, so she had to stop for a refill before getting the rest in.

There. She slammed the glass down on the table, and smiled to herself. *That oughta do it!*

She knew it would, because despite all her drinking through the years, and the last few months of popping pills, she was a lightweight. It never took her much to get wasted. Plus, she was down to a hundred and ten pounds, so she was even more of a lightweight. She giggled at the irony. *Now* she was skinny, looking fine in her jeans. For all the good it did.

The table jiggled a bit when she leaned on it to help herself up, knocking the Coke bottle down. She stood it back up, and snickered at the emerging fizz. *It's like how it'll be tomorrow, everything rising to the top.* She was sorry she'd have to miss it.

She staggered down the hall, the note clenched tight in her hand. God, she hoped her baby could make sense of her letter.

When she opened his bedroom door, she banged her head, but it didn't hurt much. She leaned on the knob and gazed around the room she'd been barred from since he'd turned fourteen. *When did he replace the Guns N' Roses poster with one of Hendrix?* By God, the kid was finally getting it. Her generation still had the best damn music! She smiled seeing the pile of folded socks, T-shirts, and underwear on top of his dresser. *Since when did the kid get so neat?* But then she noticed his half-made bed. Well, okay, he *was* a normal teenager.

She fell backward on his rumpled bedspread, and as she did, let out a yell. Something was jabbing her back. She reached behind and pulled out a green spiral notebook. What was this? She placed her crumpled letter next to her, picked up the book, and opened to the first page. It looked like song lyrics, every sentence on its own line. She tried reading it, squinting as hard as she could, but the words were like blurry ants.

She tossed the book by her note, feeling so sleepy. But so good. This wasn't bad at all. She'd never felt so wonderful in her whole life. She thought about her daddy. *I'm coming, Daddy!* She spoke out loud, but the words didn't sound right. Still, she knew he'd make it out. The thought of seeing him again made her happy.

She lay there and tugged at her short bangs, trying to pull them down to cover her large forehead, then patted the top of her hair, hoping it wasn't sticking up. She attempted to fold her hands, prayer-like over her stomach, but her fingers wouldn't cooperate, so she just let them go. She hoped she looked okay. She wanted Benji to remember how nice his mama looked.

Her body felt like rubber now. Like that cartoon character. Gumby, was it? She tried to giggle again, but her mouth was too lazy. She turned her head to the side to make sure the note was still there. She patted it with the back of her hand. Yes. Good.

She had lied when she wrote in the note about being sorry she'd taken him. That boy had made her whole rotten life worth living. All the partying she'd done, all those men she'd had, none of them made her feel important like her Benji had.

No, she could not be sorry for taking him. Never. Never. Never.

But it was good that she'd put that in the letter. Let them think it.

She was swirling now, spinning round and round. She was dancing in her head. Part of her wanted to get up and dance for real, but she couldn't move. She was so, so tired. But she was feeling beautiful. So light, like she was being lifted on a fluffy cloud.

And then there was nothing.

33. Under the Bridge

When Nick dropped him off Sunday morning, Ben was anxious to show Sandra what he had done. Since he decided to be nicer to her, he had spent the other night writing a song for her as a Mother's Day gift. It was probably the hardest one he'd ever written because he wanted to say only nice things about her being a mother. There were a few, but a lot of other stuff kept getting in the way. He'd worked on it for hours, and in the end, he kind of lied, made up a few lines that weren't really true. Like how she had always been there when he needed her. But she'd buy it because he knew Sandra believed that to be true. One thing he'd learned about his mother through his growing up, she believed what she wanted to believe.

Careful not to bang his guitar case against the rail, he raced up the steps to the second floor apartment. At the door, he set the case down to retrieve his key from his front pocket. It was only around ten o'clock, so Sandra would still be asleep. When he got inside, he placed the guitar on the couch, and his eyes caught sight of the kitchen table. What a mess! Anger welled up inside him. Sandra obviously had her own little party last night. Which means she'd be hung-over all day. And crabby as hell.

Damn! She couldn't give it a break even for Mother's Day? She would probably sleep 'til noon now, ruining his whole plan. He was going to make her a nice breakfast, then get out his notebook and play his song to her on his guitar. It was going to be so special! But even if he did that later, he'd have to clean all the shit off the table first. The Coke had hardly been touched, but she'd left only a mere mouthful of the Jack Daniels. What the hell? She had to be bombed! He put the Coke in the fridge, grabbed the liquor bottle, spilled out the little that was left, and threw it into the trash. He put the empty Bud glass in the sink and went to dump the ashtray. Only one cigarette butt? She must have run out. Normally, the metal dish—the one she'd bought that time they'd spent the weekend at Geneva-on-the-Lake—would be covered with smashed up stumps from the night before. Then he saw the crumpled cigarette pack on one of the chairs. Yes, that explained it.

When he got done cleaning off the table, he realized he was starving. Fuck her! He'd make breakfast anyway, but just for himself. But when he went to grab the eggs, the container was empty. He flipped opened the breadbox, slammed it shut. He couldn't even have a friggin' piece of toast!

"That's it," he said. He'd had it. She'd gotten worse and worse these last few months and he was putting a stop to it now. So what if he woke her up? Why let her sleep in when she did nothing around the house anymore? He did everything. Cooked, cleaned, and lately, kissed her ass. And she didn't appreciate any of it.

He stomped to her bedroom and flew open the door. "Mom, get up. Now!" he yelled, then noticed she wasn't in her bed. "Where the hell are you?" he yelled through the hallway. Then he saw his door half open. He always kept it closed when he was gone. He'd been meaning to get one of those doorknobs that you can lock. Ah, man, she'd been snooping! That was all he needed, for her to find his *Playboys* in his bottom drawer, or the stash of Trojans he was saving, for whenever. She'd go crazy. Although Sandra could do anything she wanted, *he* always had to be her perfect little boy, her pure little "Benji." Right. Well, those days were gone.

He pushed open the door. There she was! Why had she fallen asleep here? Too drunk to make it to her own room, he supposed.

"Mom, get up. You're in my room!"

She was really passed out. He walked over to shake her. When he touched her, his arm shot back. She was really cold. And she didn't look right. He gazed around the room. Something smelled funny.

"Mom? Come on," he said louder, backing away. His body started shaking.

But Sandra didn't move. Her chest didn't move. She wasn't breathing! Goose bumps scuttled across his skin like a prickly team of bugs crawling over him. His heart raced and no way could he slow it down.

"*MOM*!"

Then he saw a pink wrinkled slip of paper next to the pillow with his name scribbled at the top in large letters. *BEN, PLEASE READ NOW — BEFORE 911!!!!!*

"Aw, shit, Sandra, you didn't. *SHIIIT*!"

He remembered the pills he'd seen in the bathroom cabinet and ran to check it. Not a bottle in there. He ran back to his room and stared at the note, not wanting to pick it up. His mind flashed to the article he'd read about Kurt Cobain leaving a suicide note.

He knew what this was.

His hands were trembling so bad when he picked it up, he had to take it to his desk and sit down to read it. Wait. Shouldn't he call the cops first? Or Nick? But she'd told him to *READ NOW*. Good son that he was, he obeyed.

He flattened out the note, steadied himself by placing his elbows on the desk. His heart pounding, he fought the onset of tears. He blinked several times, and began to read.

My dearest little Benjamin. I have done a very terrible thing . . .

I'm sorry you have to find me like this but . . .

He had started reading fast, now he slowed down.

I kidnapped you.

He squinted. Read that again. What? He lifted the note, gripping it with both hands as he read on. He felt so lightheaded he thought he would faint. The kidnapping part was bad enough, but then he got to the part where she said he was Echo's baby.

"Oh my God!" he yelled. *He* was that baby he'd read about in *American Rocker?* Charlee's baby? He stopped for a minute. It couldn't be possible. He remembered feeling bad reading about that baby, and wondering what had happened to him. He'd been reading about himself?

That's probly why your so good at guitar. You got the best dam bloodline!

"Oh My God, my Gooooddd!" He stood up, trying to jolt himself out of this crazy dream.

He turned the paper over.

I didn't mean to hurt anyone . . . I just wanted to be a mama so bad.

"Are you fuckin' kidding me?" he screamed at Sandra, lying there, not saying a word.

He rubbed his forehead, a futile effort to stop the throbbing. He finished Sandra's last words, where she said how much she loved him. He tried to think, think clearly, but thoughts and images jumbled around in his brain like an animated action flick, his head pounding to the intense rhythm of his heart.

He had to call Nick.

He threw the note down and raced to the kitchen phone and dialed. "Nick, Nick, you gotta come right away. My mom. She, she, killed herself. I don't know what to do." He started bawling. "Please hurry . . . And there's something else, too. Unbelievable."

"Okay, buddy, okay. Hang tough. Don't do anything. I'll be right over," Nick said.

Relieved, Ben fell to the floor, sobbing in his hands. *This can't be happening.* Wiping his eyes with his sleeve, he caught sight of the pill bottle on the floor, under the kitchen table. He reached over and picked it up.

They would want this, whoever *they* were. He set it on the table. Then remembered. *Hide this note! s*he had written. *This is YOURS. Don't let them get it.*

He ran to his room, scooped it up off the desk, folded it into small squares, and tucked it inside his right boot. He did not look over at Sandra. He did not want to see her that way again. He ran out of the room.

Back in the kitchen, he pulled out a chair and sat, trying to keep his heart from exploding out of his chest.

He rocked back and forth, telling himself over and over that help was on its way.

34. Found Out About You

Nick bolted through the door, not bothering to knock, shaking Ben out of his daze. Nick grabbed his shoulders. "You okay?"

Ben nodded and pointed. "She's in there."

"Okay, stay here. I called them. The rescue squad'll be here soon. I'll be right back."

Ben knew Nick would want to check in on her, like maybe there was hope. Ben started to say, *Don't bother*, but Nick was a nurse and had to see for himself. The distant roar of the sirens began to turn this nightmare into reality. He couldn't sit there alone. He followed Nick down the hallway, but stopped short at the doorway. Nick knelt over his mother, checking.

Ben waited a moment before trying to get his attention. "Nick?"

Nick's face lifted. Ben saw that his friend was crying, and maybe he shouldn't have shocked, but he was. Nick and his mom had battled it out a lot over the years, and at times Ben thought the guy didn't care much for her. Apparently he'd been wrong.

"She left a note, Nick, but you can't tell anyone. She wanted me to keep it. I'm afraid they'll take it away, like for evidence or something." He recalled TV shows where the cops took away suicide notes and never gave them back.

Nick guided him out of the room, back to the kitchen. "Where is it?"

"In my boot."

Ben wanted to show it to him right then because Nick always knew what to do and was anxious to see his response to his big news. Nick may be crying over Sandra now, but wait till he heard what she had done.

Ben bent down to get the note, but the pounding at the door interrupted, and Nick rushed to greet the people who would take Ben's mother away. Forever.

The quiet room turned loud as a team of medical people, along with two policemen, came storming in. Ben watched the guys in white coats with serious looks carry their bags down the hall. Nick took one of the cops, the tall, big one, aside, whispered something. Then the cop came over to Ben and asked him questions. Like, when did he find her and what happened? Now he was even more scared. He stared at the ape-man's badge. Did they think *he* had something to do with this? "I wasn't home. I was at his house." He pointed at Nick. "All night."

That was when Ben began to wonder how long Sandra had this all planned out. How did he not see any signs? All he could remember was that she had acted pretty normal the last few days. He shook off a chill. "I just got home," he added, though the "just" was a lie. He must've been here a pretty long while by now. Too long.

"Sir, can I talk to you again in private?"

Nick was going to get him out of here, Ben could tell.

More whispering, then Nick came back. "I'm going to take you my house, okay?"

Ben nodded. Thank God for Nick.

At Nick's house, Ashley made them all chicken soup, even though it was May and even though Ben wasn't hungry. He tried getting a few spoonfuls down to be polite, but then quit. No point. He wondered when Nick would ask to see the note, but Ashley was there the whole time and this was between the two of them. Tomorrow was another day.

It was still light out when Nick suggested he try and get some sleep, and Ben didn't argue. He wanted to be alone, in the room they'd been calling "Ben's room" for years.

He hoped he could stay here for good. Where else could he go? He couldn't live with Colin and his dad, and no way could he ever go near that apartment again. He made a mental note to send Nick to get Layla and his clothes and stuff.

Ben said goodnight, went upstairs to the room, closed the door, and sat on the edge of the familiar bed. His head didn't hurt anymore, he just felt numb. Exhausted. He pulled off his left boot, then the right, and the note fell out. He stared at it, lying there on the floor. He'd have to read it again. This time more carefully. Memorize every word.

He leaned against the headboard, unfolded it. He still couldn't believe this was true. How the hell did she get away with it? He searched his mind for hints in his past that might have given him a clue. He struggled to recall every detail he'd read about the kidnapping, tried to retrieve his earliest childhood memory. All that came to him was a birthday party, his third? Whatever it was, he was real little, and Nick had been there.

In all his good memories, Nick had been there. In the bad ones, Sandra had been there. He remembered a couple of times when he was little, she spanked him and he got so mad, he screamed that she couldn't be his real mother because real mothers didn't hit their kids. He bet that must have given her a jolt.

But she had never slipped. He knew that much. If she had, anyone in their right mind would've called the cops. Even that nice Bob guy would have, despite being the only one who seemed to genuinely care about her. But probably not Jerry. He'd have kept quiet, for his own married cheating good. Ben had met him only once and could've told Sandra that he was an asshole, but she wouldn't have listened anyway.

He wanted to hate her right now, and part of him did, but he couldn't keep from being sad she had done this. He rubbed his face with the back of his hand. Even now she still kept breaking his heart.

How could you? he whispered, shaking the paper in his hand. She had taken away his whole friggin' childhood! His very identity! He wasn't "Ben Jacobs" at all. He was Dylan Campbell and he had a famous family. A family he really liked.

That part should've excited him, but it just made him sadder. He had missed out on so much. All his life, he wasn't the person he thought he was. He imagined the kind of childhood he could've had, if not for Sandra. All this time, he could've been living with that nice, *normal* family. All this time, he could've been a happy kid, belonging to totally cool people. People with money and nice things, and nice friends, too. He could've gone to nicer schools . . .

He had so much to think about, he wanted to go over it all, but his eyes were too heavy, and swimming with tears. He allowed them to shut.

"I hate to wake him," Ashley said as they sat with their morning coffee. After Nick had called Ben's school.

Nick looked at his watch. "Well, it's only ten-fifteen. Let's give him some time to himself."

"Maybe he doesn't want time to himself."

He rubbed his face. "Yeah. Maybe you're right." He rose from the chair and went upstairs.

When he got to the bedroom door, he stopped. This was going to be one hell of a day for this kid. First, the cops wanted to question him more—"police procedure" the sergeant had said. Then they'd have to discuss all those terrible details. A fourteen-year-old kid shouldn't have to make decisions involving funerals and burials and such. Yet, he was Sandra's only living relative. That much Nick knew. He wondered if she'd left any kind of instructions. He hadn't a clue if she had any special wishes. Or insurance. Probably not. Hopefully, she'd made it easy on the boy and that note Ben mentioned would give them some guidance. But knowing Sandra as he had, it probably was a mushy note to Ben. Nothing with any real details they needed now.

Nick leaned against the wall. How'd he ever get mixed up in all this? In a way, he wished he had never met Sandra. She'd been a tough person to have around. Always some sort of drama. And yet, she could be funny sometimes. One time he told her she should be a stand-up comedian, and she stopped, gave him a weird look and said she didn't want to be famous. The comment threw him because Sandra lived for attention. But then, she was always saying off-the-wall things, even when she wasn't drinking. Still, he had grown fond of her.

But right now, he was enraged at her for doing this to Ben. Nick knew she had been miserable for a long time so the suicide didn't really surprise him, but to let her own son find her like that? What the hell was she thinking? Ben would have that memory the rest of his life. And that baffled Nick, too, because he knew that Sandra loved that kid more than anything—more than life itself.

Boy, that letter had better explain a lot.

He put his ear to the door hoping to hear some kind of stirring. It worried him to think what must be going through that kid's mind. He took a breath and knocked lightly. "Hey, buddy, you awake?" Whether Ben was sleeping or not, Nick was going in.

He opened the door. "Ben?"

Ben was sitting up in bed, staring at the wall.

"I'm sorry for barging in, buddy. I just, well, wanted to see how you were doing." He walked over and sat down next to him. "Wanna talk?"

Ben looked over at him. His eyes were puffy and their redness bold against his ashen face. Nick's heart hurt.

"Close the door. Please," Ben said. "I gotta tell you something. You ain't gonna believe it."

He wasn't sure if it was Ben's expression or his words, but something made Nick edgy. He rose, shut the door, then sat down beside him.

Ben lifted his pillow, pulled out a wrinkled pink slip of paper. "Here. You might as well read it for yourself." He handed it over.

Nick squeezed his arm, and gently took the letter.

He started reading, and when he got to the part about Sandra being the one who kidnapped Charlee's baby, and that *Ben* was that baby, blood rushed to his head and his mouth fell open. This was mindboggling! He shook his head over and over through the rest of the note.

When he finished, he looked at Ben, trying to come up with some kind of comfort words. There weren't any. "God, buddy, I am so, so sorry. This is unreal."

"Yeah, tell me about it."

Nick had never been more shocked about anything in his life. Nothing he could say, or do, could make this "all better." That was for sure. What to do now?

"I don't wanna tell them yet, you know, anyone. Not right away," Ben said, taking the letter back. "I think I need more time to, like, grasp it all."

Nick put his arm around him. "I know. I'm having a hard time myself. God, I've known you both all these years and never in a million—"

"Yeah, who would've thought Sandra could pull off something like that?" Ben grinned a bit, a feigned attempt to lighten the reality, Nick knew.

He grinned back, squeezed Ben's shoulder. "We both know she wasn't, well, quite right in some ways, but no matter what, don't ever forget she loved you like crazy."

"Yeah, like crazy." Ben threw Nick another half-hearted grin. "Oh, thank God I have you," he said, giving Nick a hug. Then he drew back and asked, "What's going to happen now?"

Nick didn't know how to answer that. He wanted to tell him that they couldn't keep this a secret for long. Technically, it was police matter. And of course Dusty and Charlee deserved to know as soon as possible. He wanted to say a lot of things right then, but now was not the time. "Come on, you need to eat something."

The shock that day warranted a quiet day. Nick and Ashley let Ben take the lead. "Can we just watch TV and movies all day?" So that was what they did. Nick did call the sergeant as requested, but he did so in another room where Ben didn't have to hear any more about the matter. At least not today. There would be enough drama in the coming week.

The next day began at the police station, where Ben was asked a few more questions. One of them was if he'd found any kind of suicide note. Nick was glad he'd been allowed in the room with him, and now watched Ben carefully. The kid just shook his head and said, no, he hadn't seen any. Nick noticed a slight blush on his face, but apparently the officer bought his lie.

Then the man told them that they had all they needed. "Unless the autopsy reveals anything unusual, our business is done."

Afterward, Nick took Ben to Marvin's Music Shop at the boy's request. The store had a backroom where customers could try out new guitars and amps, and the place was nearly empty on a Monday afternoon. "You be okay till I get back?"

Ben was already picking up a shiny gold Stratocaster. He looked at Nick and managed a grin. "Take your time."

Nick squeezed his shoulder, then walked to the counter and whispered to Joe, the manager, who they knew well. "His mother died over the weekend and he needs somewhere to be while I make arrangements. Can you let him just hang here for an hour or so?"

Joe nodded. "Wow, sure. He can stay all day if he wants."

That was what Nick wanted to hear. Who knew how long things were going to take? He went home to get Ashley and the two spent the next hour searching Sandra's apartment before Nick found what they were looking for. Documents. A manila envelope stuffed in a closed sneakers' box at the top shelf of her bedroom closet.

"Okay, let's see what this is," he said to Ashley, grabbing her hand.

They sat together on the animal print bedspread and Nick pulled the papers out of the wrinkled package. They found a will, dated 1988. "Oh, I think I know when she did this," he said. "She'd gotten drunk one night and lashed out at Ben for something. He was just eight then, and told me about it the next day. She had started screaming and cussing, then pushed him so hard he fell backward onto the glass coffee table and the glass shattered underneath him. Other than a few cuts on his arm, he was fine, but it scared the wits out of them both. She quit drinking after that, for a time." He lifted the paper. "I bet that's when she did this, when her mind was clear enough to do something right."

After reading that Sandra had willed all her "worldly possessions" to Benjamin Jacobs, Ashley pointed toward the bottom of the paper. "Look. It says if she dies before Ben's eighteen, you're to be his guardian."

Nick looked over at her. "Looks like she never planned on ever revealing what she did. Wonder what changed her mind?"

"Probably plain old guilt," Ashley said. "How long can you live with something like that? Especially after she'd met the family and saw how they were helping him with his career." She paused and repeated. "Yep. Guilt."

Then she frowned, touched his arm. "Nick, don't be beating yourself up now. There was no way you could've ever imagined she had kidnapped him. You didn't even know she'd lived in Cleveland before you met her."

He nodded. "I know. But my mind keeps going back to reading about the abduction, and hearing it on the news. And then I'd see Sandra at her apartment with this new baby, born around the same time. It never occurred to—"

"Of course it wouldn't." Ashley stood up. "Now stop. Please, honey. It's all futile."

"Yeah, you're right. But how's this going to affect Ben? If *I* have a hard time understanding, accepting, it all, I can't imagine how he'll be able to deal with it. To find out that you aren't who you thought you were? *And* that you come from this famous family? A family he's known for years? It's so crazy."

"Ben's the toughest kid I know. He'll be okay," she said, pulling him off the bed. "Just think how bombarded with love he'll be once the family finds out. Speaking of which, they have to know. You have to convince Ben we need to tell Charlee and Dusty soon as possible."

Nick wrapped her into his chest. "There you go, being right again." He grabbed the envelope and they left on their mission.

After picking up Ben at the music store, Nick could tell the boy wasn't in the mood to talk.

He ate two bites of Ashley's stir-fry dinner, and set the fork down. "You guys mind if I just go to my room?"

Nick's heart bled seeing the forlorn look on Ben's face. Grieving would take time, and Nick needed to give it to him. "Whatever you want, bud."

Ben pulled out the chair and gave him a weak smile. "I started to jot down some lyrics to a new song at Marvin's, thought I'd go finish it."

"Wow, that's great." Nick's face brightened. This was a good sign. Writing and music had always helped Ben through difficult times.

Later that night, Nick quietly dialed Charlee and Dusty's number. He had to tell them about Sandra's death. The rest, he decided, could come later.

Twice he called, and twice, the line was busy. By then, it was nearly eleven o'clock. No use calling this late. He'd wait and try again in the morning.

35. The Power of the Dream

Since talking to Ruby on the phone last night, Charlee hadn't been this excited since giving birth to Tammi. The idea had come when she'd decided to rearrange her cedar chest Monday afternoon to make room for all of Tammi's drawings. The seven-year-old had decided she was going to be an artist/singer/ballerina when she grew up, so besides saving all the toe shoes and tutus, Charlee wanted to keep all her artwork, too.

Sunday had been Charlee's best Mother's Day ever. It'd started with breakfast in bed, with Dusty's help, of course. After Charlee devoured the French toast and bacon, her daughter presented her with a decorated hand-made card with big bright flowers all across the top. Inside, carefully written words on how she was the *Best Mommy in the World.*

The sentiment had made her cry tears filled with love and joy. From the moment of the girl's birth, Charlee had become a more grateful person. Even for that plane crash! The trauma of almost dying had made her realize the precious gift of life. And so, had opened her heart to having another baby. While she would always ache for Dylan, she had still ached to experience motherhood. That plane crash and her little girl had given her this precious new life. A life that had never been happier.

When Charlee placed the cherished card into the chest, she'd come across memorabilia from the Echo & the MissFits's 1973 European tour. She sat on the carpeted floor and went through it all. The posters, the UK record album, the concert bills from England, Germany, Japan, Paris . . . all those cities they had played in. The keepsakes brought more tears to Charlee's eyes. That had been such a special time in her life. How lucky they'd been to see places some people never did in a lifetime.

Charlee gazed at the photographs of the four happy, excited, young faces. She was glad she'd stayed close to Ruby all these years, but now Charlee wondered how the others were doing. Even Johnnie, who had caused so much trouble with the band.

It seemed that time had blotted up all the dark spots like a dishrag, and Charlee felt a strong urge to be reunited with the other girls. Funny how life had taken them all to other places, without much thought on staying connected.

That was how Charlee had gotten the brainstorm for a MissFits reunion. All the older bands were doing that. Reforming and taking advantage of baby boomers' mood for nostalgia.

Dusty had come in the room just then, after dropping Tammi off at school, and she'd told him her plans.

"Sounds great, but get back together with Johnnie? I thought you hated that girl?"

Charlee smiled as she put everything back in its place. "Yeah, I hated the fact she'd gotten together with CJ. And I hated the way she dressed. And I thought her playing sucked."

Dusty pulled her off the floor, laughing. "Well, then, getting back together makes perfect sense."

She laughed, too. "I know, I know. Guess it does sound crazy, but we were so young . . . and it *was* a good band."

"True."

"I think it'd be really fun. And if Johnnie's playing still sucks, we can try and get who replaced her, remember Carolyn? Though to be honest, Johnnie was more popular with the fans."

"Ah, yes, I do recall." Dusty grinned. "Those low-cut blouses, the skintight jeans."

Charlee had thrown him a mock jealous look, then she ran downstairs to call Ruby, who had been too busy at the restaurant to talk just then.

It was almost ten that night when Ruby finally got back to her. Her first reaction to Charlee's idea was not a big surprise.

"What you've been smokin' there, girl?"

But then Charlee refreshed her memory on how good the band was, and the great times they did have together. She also added that she was more than willing to let bygones be bygones when it came to Johnnie.

"My, oh my, we sure have grown up, haven't we?" Ruby said with a chuckle.

They'd talked about it for more than an hour, and by the time they'd hung up, they had made arrangements to hunt down their lost band members.

Tuesday was Charlee's turn to drop Tammi off at school, and afterward, she got her nails done, then went grocery shopping before arriving home around noon. Grabbing a couple of bags on her way in, she plopped them on the kitchen counter. She looked over by the sink and saw Dusty. Just standing there. His facial expression made her heart leap with concern.

"Dust? Something wrong?"

"I just got a call from Nick."

She put her purse down alongside the bags. "Nick?"

"Ben's mom committed suicide Saturday night."

"Oh my God. Poor Ben! Wait, Saturday? And they just found her?"

"No, no. Nick kept Ben at his house Sunday to help him through the shock, then he tried calling you last night."

"Oh hell! I was on the phone with Ruby!" She rushed to the kitchen phone, adrenalin already pumping. "I gotta call him back." She had to make sure Ben was all right.

"No need. He's coming over here."

"Oh, okay. I'll call mom. She'll want to know—"

"Wait." Dusty grabbed her arm. "Nick told me to make sure we don't talk to anyone yet. He said he needs to talk to us first about something. Said it was important. And he's bringing Ben."

"Wow. I wonder what that's about?" She touched Dusty's arm. "Maybe Ben wants to live with us. That would be okay with you, right?"

"Of course. You know I love that kid, too."

Yes, she did. Charlee shook her head in disbelief. "Jeez, I know his mom had her problems, but how could she do that? And leave that poor boy an orphan?" Charlee knew she should feel bad about Sandra, but she had never gotten to really know her. She was more concerned about Ben. He didn't deserve this. Yet she had to keep in mind that people who did such things weren't thinking right.

When the doorbell rang, Dusty opened it with Charlee right behind him. After heartfelt hugs, Dusty broke the silence. "Come on in. It's nice outside, let's sit out on the patio."

Charlee tried acting normal for Ben's sake. She served the men coffee and retrieved a 7-Up from the back of the fridge. It had been there since the last time Ben had been over.

As she handed out the beverages, she noticed how nice Ben was dressed, like for a school recital. Blue-striped shirt, beige khakis, shined-up black shoes. Several times she tried giving him a sweet, comforting smile, but he wouldn't look at her. Or Dusty. His eyes stayed locked on the swimming pool. Was he thinking of the good times they'd all had here last summer? The time they talked excitedly about Ben's debut record? Was he wondering if they'd let him live here? Charlee couldn't tell what he was thinking.

They sat in a circle around the unlit fire table as Nick gave a run-through of the details about Sandra, which included plans for a short, private service later that week, adding that Sandra already had a plot next to her father at a nearby cemetery. The whole conversation felt awkward and Charlee was anxious for Nick to get to the part he'd come to say.

To lighten things up a bit, Charlee told them about the MissFits reunion. "Once we contact the other girls, we'll get the wheels moving on when and where. My mom is even going to compile a 'best of' album, to get people excited about it." She looked over at Ben. Even that news didn't turn his head. Something else was very wrong. She stopped talking, hoping Nick would take the lead.

He took a sip of his coffee then, looked up, and sighed. "Man, even though Ben and I have discussed how to tell you this news of ours, I don't quite know how to start. It's pretty shocking, but it's also—"

Just then, Ben stood up. "I want to tell them."

Nick looked surprised. "Uh, are you sure?"

For the first time since they'd arrived, Ben forced himself to look at Charlee and Dusty, his real parents.

Ben nodded at Nick. "I need to be the one to tell them."

He stood up. He didn't know why, but standing seemed appropriate.

He couldn't believe all the emotions surging through him, all strung together, entwined like a tight rope. Sadness, and anger, over Sandra. Yet happy to know he was part of this great family he liked so much. But confused, too. What would it be like being someone else? Once it was out, he would no longer be who he was. All these sensations made him feel dazed, lightheaded. But he had to keep it together. Be a man about it.

He swallowed hard, fighting the urge to let Nick take over. No. He wanted to see their facial expressions, wanted them to be looking at him when he told them he was their long-lost son.

Ben looked over at Nick, who nodded in support.

"My mom, er, Sandra, left me a note." His lips started to quiver. He took a deep breath. *Come on, you can do it.* "And in it she said something really, *really* unbelievable. I mean, I still can't—"

Ben stopped, inhaled another breath. He saw Dusty lean forward in his chair. Charlee sat up straighter, hands clasped. Their eyes wide. He knew they were anxious for him to get to it already, but he didn't want to just blurt it out. He combed his fingers through his hair, then pushed his hands deep into his pockets.

"My name's not really Ben."

Confusion spanned their faces.

"Sandra . . . she . . . uh, she stole me. When I was a baby."

Charlee was the first to rise off her chair, her hands clasping her open mouth, as if waiting for his next words to confirm what she already imagined to be true.

"She's the one who took me." He paused, then continued with a shaky breath. "I'm Dylan. Your son."

The screams and "oh my Gods" attacked his senses. An overwhelming shot of bliss gushed through his body, and he started sobbing as Charlee and Dusty wrapped themselves around him so tight he could hardly breathe.

"My baby! Our baby!" Charlee gave Dusty a quick but forceful kiss, before going back to kissing Ben's cheeks. "Thank God! Thank God, you're okay! I can't believe it's *you!*"

Ben smiled wide through the mass of tears and squeezes. It was like he was back in the womb. Warm. Safe. Secure. Wrapped in love. *Happy.*

Charlee was crying so hard, his nice shirt—the one he'd picked himself for this occasion—was sopping wet by the time they let him go. And when they did, he saw that Dusty, and even Nick, everyone was crying. He knew right then, that even if he did become a huge rock star someday, there would never, ever be a more special moment in his life than this.

He was home.

36. I'll Remember

Peggy Sue got the call as she and Billy were mixing up a healthy salad for dinner. In their fifties now, they had agreed to begin a strict regimen of diet and exercise.

"Mom, Mom, you gotta come over. Now. I have the best news in the world! Is Billy there?"

"Uh, yes. We were just sitting down to eat."

"Put me on speakerphone."

Peggy pushed the button. "Okay. What is it?"

"I don't want to tell you over the phone. You and Billy have to get over here."

"Can it wait till we eat?"

"No, put it away. I have food here, but believe me, you won't want to eat once you get here."

Peggy looked at Billy and shrugged. "No hint?"

"No hint. Oh hell, but there is bad news first. You see, Sandra, Ben's mo—" She stopped for a second, then continued. "Well, this is awkward, because it really is terrible, despite— Anyway, she took a bunch of pills and a mass amount of alcohol last Saturday. Because she couldn't take the guilt anymore. Over what she had done."

What had that woman done now? "Oh jeez, is she okay?"

The sigh was audible. "No."

"Oh, no. How is Ben?"

"He's okay. But don't feel too bad for her, Mom. Because she was a horrible person."

"Charlee, stop. That's not nice, the woman had problems, but—"

"No, you don't understand. Just come over, please. I don't want to say any more."

When they hung up, Peggy turned to Billy, confusion etching her face. "Let's go. That's the craziest call I've ever gotten. What could be so good about Sandra committing suicide? And why does she want us over immediately?"

"Beats me," Billy said, putting the salad in the fridge.

Peggy shook her head. "Guess we'll know when we get there."

When they got there, Charlee hugged her tight and led her to the back, where Peggy saw Dusty, Nick and Ben, engaged in conversation. She was surprised. Ben didn't seem as upset as she'd expected for a boy who'd just lost his mother. She walked over to him. "Hello, Ben, I'm so sorry about your mother. If there's any—"

"Mom?" Charlee interrupted. "He's not really Ben."

"What? What are you talking about?"

Charlee reached for her hand. "Ben wasn't Sandra's son at all. *She* was the one who stole him! This is Dylan, Mom. *Our* Dylan!"

Peggy's knees buckled underneath her. Thankfully, Billy was there to keep her from hitting the patio floor.

They decided to keep the secret among themselves until after Sandra's funeral—attended by only those her "son" wanted there. They needed time to absorb it all, before the police and media got involved. They also wanted a chance to share their news privately with friends.

But most of all, Charlee and Dusty needed time to tell their little girl that she had a big brother. "Wow, what a birthday present!" was her first reaction. With all the shock and excitement of the past week, Charlee had nearly forgotten that Tammi's eighth birthday was just two weeks away.

In her delight, the girl didn't even ask many questions, though Charlee knew they'd have to explain it all to her, somehow, before she saw it on the news.

In the meantime, Charlee had a spare bedroom to get ready. They'd decided that Ben would stay with Nick and Ashley until after the services, then he would live with her, Dusty, and Tammi.

Their baby, though no longer a baby, but a fine young man, was coming home to stay.

The Sunday before they announced it to the world, Charlee and Dusty, along with Peggy and Billy, hosted a small dinner party at the Campbells' home. They invited only a select few; Nick and Ashley, Ruby and Rob, Libby and Dave, and their son, Jack. An ecstatic Patrick and Nina hopped on the first plane to join them, as did Diana, who'd been living for years in Chicago with her boyfriend, a veterinarian, of course. Their newfound son had invited his trusted friends as well. His best friend, Colin, Denny from the record store, and his guitar teacher, Danny. They also welcomed Tom Reeves, who'd be holding a press conference the next day.

Now that they knew the truth, they all admitted a twinge of guilt for not figuring it out themselves. How could they not have noticed several of the boy's characteristics that seemed so obvious now? Peggy Sue, especially, was upset with herself. She had recognized those Frankie London traits, yet had dismissed it all too quickly. As the group talked about it that night, they came to the conclusion that after so many years, there was no conceivable way anyone could have figured it out.

Later that night, Ben clinked his glass of 7-Up, and called out for everyone's attention.

Standing on their patio deck box, he addressed them all, said he had a request.

"I just want to say a few things." He paused, looked over at his parents. "I know I'll always think of Sandra as my mother," he began, looking at Charlee, hoping she understood. "I can't erase those years, no matter how I would try. I'll always remember everything. And despite what she did, all the pain she caused—for all of us—she did raise me and I know she loved me.

"But that life is over now. Ben died with Sandra. My real mother and father named me Dylan Thomas Campbell, and that's who I want to be from this day forward." He smiled at Charlee and Dusty. "I realize it's gonna be weird at first, getting everyone to call me Dylan, but it's gonna be all over the news tomorrow, and once everyone knows, well, I think it'll be easier to call me by my given name. And that's what I want."

The press conference that Monday afternoon was short and to the point. Tom, surrounded by authorities who had worked on the case, produced a copy of Sandra's confessional suicide note as proof that, after fourteen years, and thousands of tips that went nowhere, the kidnapping of Echo's infant son had been solved. Case closed.

"The family would appreciate if everyone, the media especially, will respect their privacy at this time," Tom said, then walked out of the room filled with reporters.

Echo and her family did not attend.

37. Rock and Roll Dreams Come Through

That summer, Charlee and Ruby stayed busy putting the MissFits back together for a one-time only reunion.

After several phone calls to old friends, they tracked Sherry down in L.A. They were thrilled to learn that she was still drumming, but as a session musician. They also got lucky because Sherry had kept in touch with Johnnie, who was married and living in Columbus, Ohio.

Although Johnnie admitted she hadn't picked up a bass in years, her husband's brother, Phil, was a bass player in a local band and promised he could help her "get back in the groove."

"This is such a great idea," she told Charlee. "It'll be so fun being together again."

Johnnie's enthusiasm boosted Charlee's as well. "Yes, it will," she agreed. "I can hardly believe it's been almost twenty years. So much has changed."

Johnnie's voice grew soft. "You got that right. And, Charlee? I read about your son. I'm so happy you got him back."

"Thanks, it's all been so unreal."

"I bet." Then Johnnie's voice rose again. "Gee, I can't wait to kick ass again on stage! I'll make damn sure to practice like hell, don't wanna embarrass myself." She laughed, then added, "I know I could've been better back then, but I promise, Charlee, I will not disappoint you this time."

They only had three months to get it all together, but somehow Charlee believed her.

This time, there would be no drama or ego involved. They had all grown up. And it seemed, like her, Johnnie had mellowed, and the problems of their past were no longer valid.

Echo & the MissFits had made plans to spend the month of August practicing together at Charlee's house. Billy booked the event and worked on radio promotions, and Peggy Sue put together a "Greatest Hits" compilation of all their songs.

The concert, scheduled for September 3rd at the Cleveland Stadium, was going to be historic. In more ways than one.

The concert sold out, thanks to all their efforts. Charlee knew that some of the ticket buyers weren't MissFits fans at all, but curiosity seekers. While the media did, for the most part, leave the Campbells alone, the tabloids and TV celebrity shows, still managed to cite "sources close to the couple" with a myriad of tales on how they were all doing after the "tragic story with the happy ending."

Still, Charlee knew that most of the crowd that would be there, were fans who grew up with their songs, and couldn't wait to hear them play live again. What those fans didn't know was they were in for a special surprise.

When the big night arrived, the backstage was filled with flowers from well-wishers, along with people running around everywhere, taking great effort in making sure everything went smoothly.

By the time the lights dimmed, the energy level in the large outdoor stadium was at its peak, the audience hyped up with anticipation.

Echo & the MissFits bounded out on stage to a loud roar of applause. They opened with their first hit, "Shine It On," then played "Not Your Daisy May," before cranking out "Too Much to Dream Last Night," the song by the '60s group, Electric Prunes, that they had always included in their set.

Then Charlee addressed the audience. "Thank you, thank you," she said into the mike. "You don't know what this means to all of us. We're having a great time up here, how about you?"

The crowd yelled and clapped.

They played four more of their most recognized songs, then Charlee waved her hand to the band. Her signal for them to stop.

Charlee turned and nodded to someone behind the stage curtain. Then she spoke to the crowd. "As you know, our little boy was taken from us fourteen years ago, and we have finally been reunited with him." She had to stop and wait for the roar of cheers to die down so she could continue. "Of course, he's not a baby anymore, but a wildly gifted guitarist who inherited his amazing skill from his famous grandfather, the late, great Frankie London. And okay, maybe a bit from me and his father, too." She grinned and the crowd roared again.

"So at this time, I'd like you all to meet him."

The fans were up on their feet cheering, clapping, screaming with delight.

Charlee had to practically scream herself to get in her next words. "And I know he's ready to meet you all, too!"

Just then, her son came running out on stage with Dusty and little Tammi behind him. Charlee, her face beaming with happiness, pride, and tears, took his hand and yelled into the mike.

"Ladies and gentlemen, I am more than pleased to introduce you to this talented boy. Please give a very warm, *official,* Cleveland homecoming to our son, Dylan Thomas Campbell!"

The noise was deafening as Dylan approached the mike. "Thank you, Mom," he yelled over the din. "And I thank all of you guys out there for such a great welcome! It is so good to be, *truly,* home."

Now the crowd grew quiet, anticipating what else he would say.

It wasn't much. Didn't have to be.

Dusty walked up now, and handed Dylan his new gold Fender Stratocaster.

Dylan turned to address the band. "So whad'dya say, my fellow MissFits? Let's rock this place!'

And they did.

Also by **Deanna R. Adams** and **Soul Mate Publishing**:

PEGGY SUE GOT PREGNANT

Set in the era between Buddy Holly and Joan Jett, this rock 'n' romance suspense novel tells the story of an ill-fated love affair between a Southern boy and Midwestern girl, and a long-held secret that threatens the legacy of a beloved music icon and future of his rock star daughter. After one reckless night with the boy she loves, sixteen-year-old Peggy Sue Lawrence's life changes forever. It is 1957. "Nice" girls don't have sex before marriage, and if they do and it leads to pregnancy, they are whisked out of town. In Peggy Sue's case, she's put on a bus in Hereford, Texas, headed for Cleveland, knowing she'll probably never see Frankie London again. She gives birth to a daughter, Charlee, and hands the baby over to an aunt and uncle, who adopt her with the agreement that the truth never be revealed. But it's too late. Someone knows. And that person will haunt Peggy Sue for years. When a teenaged Charlee forms an all-girl rock band, and gets international press, Peggy Sue is confronted with the realization that keeping secrets is sometimes worse than the secret itself.

Available now from Amazon: <u>http://tinyurl.com/l5pm4qj</u>

DEANNA R. ADAMS is a writer, speaker, instructor, award-winning essayist, and author of three nonfiction books. Her debut novel, ***Peggy Sue Got Pregnant: A Rock 'n' Roll Love Story***, was released in June 2013. Deanna's first book, ***Rock 'n' Roll and the Cleveland Connection*** (Kent State University Press, 2002), was a finalist for the Ohioana Award, and the ARSC Award (Association for Recorded Sound Collections) for excellence in research. Other books include ***Confessions of a Not-So-Good Catholic Girl***, and ***Cleveland's Rock and Roll Roots***. Deanna is also founder and director of several annual writers' conferences and retreats. See her website at www.deannaadams.com

CPSIA information can be obtained at www.ICGtesting.com
Printed in the USA
BVOW09s0651091014

369944BV00003B/5/P

9 781619 355989